NO TURNING BACK

Four friends: Alex is failing as a father; Ian keeps dangerous secrets; Jenn wants adventure, and Mitch wants Jenn. They are all just scraping by, finding comfort in each other and the hope that things will get better. But as their twenties fade in the rear-view mirror, none of them are turning out to be who — or where — they hoped. In a time when CEOs steal millions while their employees watch savings dwindle, these four are tired of the honest approach. They're going to stop waiting and start taking. They have a failsafe, victimless plan that will change their lives for ever. What could possibly go wrong . . .

Books by Marcus Sakey
Published by The House of Ulverscroft:

THE BLADE ITSELF

MARCUS SAKEY

NO TURNING BACK

Complete and Unabridged

CHARNWOOD
Leicester

First published in Great Britain in 2010 by
Corgi
Transworld Publishers, London

First Charnwood Edition
published 2011
by arrangement with
Transworld Publishers
A Random House Group Company, London

British Library CIP Data

Sakey, Marcus.
   No turning back.
   1. Suspense fiction.
   2. Large type books.
   I. Title II. Sakey, Marcus. Amateurs.
   813.6–dc22

   ISBN 978–1–4448–0728–8

Published by
F. A. Thorpe (Publishing)
Anstey, Leicestershire

Set by Words & Graphics Ltd.
Anstey, Leicestershire
Printed and bound in Great Britain by
T. J. International Ltd., Padstow, Cornwall

This book is printed on acid-free paper

For Sean and Michael and Joe,
who always help me fix it when it's broken

PART 1

The Players

'There was something seriously wrong with the world for which neither God nor His absence could be blamed.'

— Ian McEwan, *Amsterdam*

Later, Jenn Lacie would spend a lot of time trying to pin-point the exact moment.

There was a time before, she was sure of that. When she was free and young and, on a good day, maybe even breezy. Looking back was like looking at the cover of a travel brochure for a tropical getaway, some island destination featuring a smiling girl in a sundress and a straw hat, standing calf-deep in azure water. The kind of place she used to peddle but had never been.

And of course, there was the time after.

So it stood to reason that there had to be a moment when the one became the other. When blue skies bruised, the water turned cold, and the undertow took her.

Had it been when they first met Johnny Love, that night in the bar?

Maybe. Though it felt more like when she'd opened the door at four a.m., bleary in a white T-shirt and faded cotton bottoms. She'd known it was Alex before she looked through the peephole. But the tiny glass lens hadn't let her see his eyes, the mad energy in them. If she hadn't opened the door, would everything be different?

Sometimes, feeling harder on herself, she decided, no, the moment came after the four of them did things that could never be taken back. Not just when they decided; not even when she

3

felt the pistol, the oily heaviness of it making something below her belly squirm, a strange but not entirely uncomfortable feeling. Like any birth, maybe her new life had come through blood and pain. Only it hadn't been an infant's cry that marked the moment. It had been a crack so loud it made her ears hum, a wet, spattering cough, and the man shuddering and staring as his eyes zeroed out.

But late at night, the sheets a sweaty tangle, her mind turning relentless carnival loops, she wondered if all of that was nonsense. Maybe there hadn't been a moment. Maybe that was just a lie she told herself to get through the day, the way some took Xanax and some drank scotch and some watched hour after numbing hour of sitcoms.

Maybe the problem hadn't come from outside. Hadn't been a single decision, a place where they could have gone left instead of right.

Maybe the road the four of them walked never had any forks to begin with.

4

1

Ian was aware of the cliché. That's what made it OK. It was one thing to be the trader wearing a suit that belied your debt, sitting in the company men's room at almost eight at night, blasting coke from the hinge of your thumb, and believing you were Gordon Gekko. It was another to see it for the sordid little scene it was. As long as you knew that, you were still running the show.

Screw it, he thought, then bent forward and snorted hard.

It was good stuff, coating the inside of his skull with ice, a moment of brain freeze that released slow and sweet into a glorious warmth. He poured a bump for his other nostril — had to be democratic — and blew that one too. Then he leaned against the toilet tank, the porcelain cool and hard and kind of pleasant through the starched cotton of his oxford.

There we go. There it is.

His toe wanted to tap, but he fought the urge, glanced at his watch instead: 7:58 in the p.m. Almost there. He'd worked here for years, noticed it only subliminally at first. The kind of pattern the human brain catches a bit at a time. Part of him wanted to count the seconds down, but that would have been cheating.

When the air conditioning shut off at 8:00 exactly, a sudden absence of sound that had

5

measured the whole of his day, he smiled.

Silly, he knew. But if eighty percent of his waking life was going to be spent sitting in a gray corporate office — which, by the way, he didn't remember voting on, thanks very much — he'd seize his little triumphs where he could. He arrived most days before six, in time to hear the fans turn on, and worked the same day over and over in a blur of predatory action, the headset so much a part of his body that he sometimes forgot to take it off when he stood up from his desk, got jerked back by the cord. Maneuver after maneuver, each the one that might get him out from under, might return him to wunderkind status, the guy who had cracked Hudson-Pollom Biolabs and made a quick half-mil instead of the also-ran everyone was starting to suspect he might be. Lunch at his desk, stolen in bites. A bathroom break midmorning and midafternoon, two quick white blurs to keep his energy kicking. Staying after the phones went quiet to read the blogs, make his plans for tomorrow, and try, in an amiable, distracted way, to figure out how to make up what he'd lost.

And finally, the retreat here, to his porcelain palace, to blow a good-night kiss to work and start the evening properly.

He pinched his nostrils, then rattled the toilet-paper dispenser like he'd been using the john. There was no one in the bathroom, but habits were important for the day he didn't hear his boss come in. He flushed, stepped out, washed his hands, then checked himself in the mirror. Nose clean, tie straight. Ready for the world.

He smiled, made guns of his fists and shot the mirror, an intentionally cheesy joke meant only for himself — it seemed like most of his jokes were — and then headed for the door.

It was Thursday night, and his friends would be waiting. Alex behind the bar in a bleach-worn shirt, the cuffs spotted with old stains. Jenn sipping a vodka martini, never a cosmo, not since *Sex and the City*. Mitch rocking his stool on two legs, trying not to get caught looking sidelong at Jenn. The Thursday Night Crew. Thinking of them made him smile again. Funny how their unlikely foursome had remained friends when all the folks he'd grown up with, the ones who signed yearbooks and made pledges of eternity, had all fallen quietly away. Moved to New York or the suburbs, gotten married and had children. That might be sad if he let it.

But why would he? He was young, secretly high, and his friends were waiting.

★　★　★

When Mitch climbed on the bus, there was only one seat open, next to a black guy wearing a puffy Looney Tunes jacket and loose jeans, his leg thrown across the open seat. Mitch walked over, stood looking down at the guy. 'Excuse me.'

For a long moment, the man ignored him. Then, drawing the gesture out slow, he swiveled his head to look up at Mitch. His eyes pitched half open, a toothpick stuck to wet lips. Nothing in his expression at all. After a moment of staring, he turned back to the window. He didn't move his leg.

Asshole, Mitch thought and moved back a couple of rows, stood gripping the hand bar, swaying with the motion of the bus. His heels felt like someone was cranking wood screws into them, and the steady ache in his back that began around noon had stretched up to his shoulders and neck. Occupational hazard of spending all day standing up, smiling on cue as he opened and closed the heavy glass doors of the Continental Hotel.

It's only a couple of minutes. Not worth making a thing over.

He shifted from the edge of one foot to the edge of the other. The bus was warm, humid with body odor, and he was afraid some of it came from him. Nothing to do about it, just a day's worth of sun beating down on his jacket and tie, but he wished he could have showered.

After all, tonight was the night. He'd made up his mind that he was going to take the plunge with Jenn. If the right moment came up at least, when the guys weren't there. And probably best to get a couple of drinks in to unwind from the day. Be loose. Loose was good. Like, 'There's this new sake lounge we could check out, you know, laugh at the yuppies.' Or was that too casual? He didn't want her to say it sounded great, why didn't they invite the others. Maybe more like, 'It'd be really nice to get a chance to talk, just us.' Though he didn't want to put her on the spot.

He ran lines until his stop, but couldn't find

8

the right one. Maybe he'd wing it.

Rossi's was one of those identity-crisis places, a bar-slash-restaurant that drew families for dinner but an after-work crowd for drinks. Perched on a stretch of Lincoln that fell between more fashionable areas, the place had become their haunt in the last few years mostly because with Alex there, they could drink cheap. Funny, really; in a city filled with terrific bars, they chose to meet every week at a half-assed restaurant that they'd otherwise never have noticed.

After the heat of the bus, walking into the air-conditioning felt wonderful. Mitch nodded at the hostess, moved past the dining room, with its rich smell of bolognese and carbonara, and into the bar. The postwork crowd was thinning but not gone, men in business casual, women laughing, glasses filled with pink and green and pale yellow, specialty martinis made with syrups and liqueurs. He moved through them, looking toward their customary seats.

Dammit. Other than Alex pulling drinks, he was the first one there. He should have showered.

★ ★ ★

'That prick,' Alex was saying as she walked up. 'He should be, I don't know. Drawn and quartered.'

'Who should?' Jenn smiled at him, careful not to hold it too long, then hugged Ian, the blades of his shoulders sharp through his shirt, then Mitch, still in his uniform, the jacket with the

9

hotel logo slung over the back of his chair.

'Tasty,' Alex said, 'right on time, as usual.' He smiled back at her, his eyes warm. Normally she wouldn't have liked the nickname, Tasty-sort-of-rhymes-with-Lacie, but he had a way of saying it that sounded warm instead of dirty. 'Hot date?'

'Kickboxing class. Who should be drawn and quartered?'

'That Cayne guy.'

'Who?'

'James Cayne. He was the CEO of Bear Stearns,' Ian said. 'It's a securities firm, the one the Fed just bailed out. They've had a lot of trouble lately. The whole subprime mortgage collapse? Started with their hedge funds.'

'Apparently,' Alex said, 'while the company was tanking, he was playing in a bridge tournament. Guy's company is responsible for half of America losing their houses, he's playing cards.'

'It's a little more complicated than that.' Ian gave that sharp-edged grin. 'There were market forces in play.'

'Hi, Jenn,' Mitch said.

'He should be killed,' Alex said again, pouring a martini from a stainless steel shaker and setting it in front of her. He stabbed three olives with a toothpick shaped like a sword and balanced it across the top. 'Line him and that Enron guy, Ken Lay, and the rest of them up against a wall and shoot them.'

'Ken Lay is already dead. Heart attack.'

'OK, well, everybody else from Enron.'

Jenn said, 'Bad day?' then laughed when all

10

three of them nodded. 'OK. Next round is on me.'

Her mother found it strange, the way her closest friends were guys. She was always asking unsubtle questions about which one Jenn was dating. Hoping it would be Ian, whom she'd never met but had come to believe must be a nice boy, a judgment that had a lot to do with the fact that he worked as a trader.

Jenn had always gotten along fine with women. But her friends, especially as she'd gotten older, they tended to be guys. It wasn't that she was a tomboy or the perennial little sister or one of those women who talked sex all the time to keep the boys nearby. Somehow, though, as her twenties had slipped into her early thirties, it had gotten harder to have real girlfriends. The married ones retreated into couplehood. The single ones looked over her shoulder every time the door opened, checking the men at the bar, scoping shoes and ring fingers. Wondering if the guy walking in was the one for them, the one who would let them jettison this tedious phase, the single apartment and Christmas with the parents and the fear that they would end up owning cats. Ever hopeful that a cute stranger would spill coffee on them and have just the right line to follow it up. Romantic Comedy Syndrome.

Which was fine, and she wished them luck. They just made for lousy friends, whereas the boys kept things easy. Which was how she ended up here every week, all four of them at the end of the bar. She, Alex, Ian, and Mitch, the Thursday

11

Night Drinking Club. 'Which game tonight?'

'Tonight,' Ian said, 'is clearly a Ready-Go night.'

'Why?'

'I'm feeling hypothetical.'

'I feel that way all the time,' she said. 'OK. In the spirit of the evening: If you had half a million dollars. Ready, go.'

'Only half?' Ian cocked his eyebrow.

'I'd buy a house,' Alex said. 'Nothing fancy, just something with a spare bedroom for Cassie. I think she'd stay with me more often if she had a room of her own. In Lincoln Park so she could walk to the shops, the lake.'

'Somebody hasn't looked at real-estate prices in a while,' Ian said.

'What?'

'A house in Lincoln Park for a half million?'

'No?' Alex looked genuinely wounded, as though the neighborhood pricing was all that was holding him back. 'Huh. All right, a condo. Whatever. How about you?'

'I'd quit the firm. Work from home. Day trade. I could turn that into ten million in no time.'

Alex snorted. 'You'd be broke in a week.'

Ian smiled that thin smile again. 'Jenn?'

She sipped at her martini, pulled off an olive, chewed it slowly. 'Travel.'

'Where would you go?' Mitch leaned forward.

'Everywhere. All the places I book trips for other people. Paris. St Petersburg. The islands. I'd like to spend a while in the islands. A little cabin on the beach, someplace with screens for walls, where you could hear the ocean day and night. Drink coconut drinks. Live in a bathing suit.' It was strange hearing the words come out of her mouth, like this was a long-held fantasy. Truth was, she hadn't known what she was going to say until she'd started.

'Sounds nice,' Mitch said.

'Sounds boring,' Ian said. 'I'd be out of my head in a week.'

'Then you're not invited. Alex, Mitch, you guys want to come to the islands with me?'

'And leave all this?' Alex laughed and picked up a cloth, started buffing the bar. His sleeves were rolled to his elbows, and the muscles of his forearms were knotted ropes. 'At this rate, in just twenty short years, I'll be full manager. At which point if one of you wanted to shoot me, I'd thank you for the favor.'

'Why don't you quit?' Mitch said.

'Why don't you?'

'I — well, I mean, it's a job, right?'

Alex nodded slowly. 'Yes. It's a job, all right.' He glanced down the line, where a plump, tanned guy stood with finger crooked, a gaudy ring flashing on one finger. 'Speaking of.' He dropped the cloth and started away.

For a moment, silence fell. Then Ian raised his glass said, 'Fuck work.'

Laughing, they clinked glasses. Jenn leaned into the bar, feeling good, a little bit of that old energy swirling around, the kind she missed, the sense that the evening could go anywhere, that there were adventures yet to be had. Ian asked the next Ready-Go question: What was something they would never, ever, do? Ready, go — and she settled in, let the night flow.

13

Mitch wasn't drunk. Tipsy, OK, but not drunk. He'd had a couple of shots with Alex before the others arrived, and three or four beers since, a fair bit for two hours, but it had been a long day.

No, he wasn't drunk, so that wasn't why he was pissed off. Or it was only part of it. The real reason was that he'd finally caught his moment, and then the asshole had come over.

It was the guy Alex had gone to see. Mitch didn't recognize him but guessed he was some sort of a bigwig, because Alex had nodded a lot and then disappeared into the back room and hadn't returned. Which was perfect, because a few minutes later, Ian excused himself. The guy was famous for long bathroom breaks — they had a running joke that he must be restocking the toilet rolls — and so it had been just him and Jenn.

They had made small talk for a couple of minutes, Mitch still polishing lines in his head. When the conversation dropped off, he'd finished his beer and leaned forward. Now or never.

'So, I was thinking.' He wanted to meet her eyes but couldn't, stared at his empty beer glass instead. Spun it on the edge. 'You know, it might be fun sometime — '

'Hello, beautiful.' The voice that smooth tone of someone used to getting what he wanted. 'How come I've never seen you in here before?'

Mitch had looked up to find the guy standing between him and Jenn, right between them, giving Mitch his back like he wasn't even there. A shiny silk shirt and sharp cologne.

Jenn said, 'Maybe because you haven't been here before?' She turned slightly on her chair, legs crossed at the knee and then recrossed at the ankle, a tangle of dark jeans and soft leather boots.

'No, couldn't be that. Must be I've been in the office most of the time,' the guy said. 'I own the joint.'

'Yeah?' She said it with a slight challenge, but Mitch couldn't help but notice that her arms weren't folded.

'That's right. This one, a couple others. Keeps me busy. But if I'd known you were out here, I wouldn't have worked so hard.' The guy held out a hand. 'John Loverin. People call me Johnny Love.'

She laughed. 'You kidding me?'

'I know,' he said and laughed too, the smug bastard. 'What do they call you?'

Don't say Tasty. Please don't say Tasty.

'Jenn,' she said. 'And this is my friend Mitch.'

'Oh, yeah?' The guy turned at the waist, gave a quick nod, then turned his back again. 'Nice to meet you, Jenn.'

Mitch cleared his throat, said, 'Listen — '

'Let me get you a drink. On the house.'

'Well — '

'Hey.' The guy nodded to the bartender who was covering Alex. 'Get the lady a — what is that, a martini? Get her a Grey Goose martini, would you? And a Glenlivet for me. Double.'

Unbelievable. Mitch leaned back on his stool, tried to catch Jenn's eye. Ian would be back

15

before long, and then Alex, and then it would be too late. He'd have to wait for next week. But damned if Jenn wasn't smiling. He thought it was her amused smile, like she was enjoying the show, but he couldn't be sure.

'Hope I'm not being too forward. I'm a little jet-lagged still.'

'Yeah?'

'Just got back from Cancun,' Johnny said. 'Why I'm so tan. I like to go down there every couple of months, relax. You ever been?'

She shook her head, took an olive off the toothpick, a move Mitch always found hypnotic, the way she slid the toothpick into her mouth, lips tightening as she gripped the olive and drew it off. The way her cheekbones flared as she chewed, carefully, like she wanted to squeeze out every drop of flavor.

'I gotta tell you, it's beautiful. Paradise.'

'Isn't Cancun pretty much due south of here?'

'About.'

'So how are you jet-lagged?'

He laughed at that. 'You got me.' Took a sip of his drink. 'Flying can wear you out, though. And the airports, shoes off, belt off, arms out, stand, spin, hula dance. But I got this place down there, right on the beach, private, makes it worth the trouble.'

'You own a house there?'

'Sure do. You should come down sometime. Check it out.'

'Right. How about tomorrow? We could get married in the surf.'

'Hey,' he said, 'no need to bust my balls. I've

16

got two bedrooms. You could just relax, see if you like it.'

All right. Enough. Mitch leaned forward and put his hand on the guy's shoulder. He didn't push, not exactly, but the booze made it maybe harder than he'd meant.

Johnny Love turned, set his drink down. He stared at Mitch. 'Something you want?'

'Yeah.' He felt the blood in his forehead, anger plus a little liquid courage, and decided to go with it. 'I'd like you to leave us alone.'

'Hey — ' Jenn started.

'It's OK,' Johnny said over his shoulder, like he was protecting her. He straightened, ran his tongue against the inside of his lip. 'You got a problem?'

'I just told you.'

Johnny stared, his eyes flicking up and down. Very slowly, he smiled, then gestured to Mitch's blazer, the pocket emblazoned with the hotel logo. 'Nice outfit.'

'You too.' *Asshole.*

The man's eyes narrowed. He stared for a moment, then held up his left hand, flicked his thumb against his pinkie ring. Dice, a five and a two. 'You see this? Platinum, ninety-five percent pure. Two and a half in flawless stones.'

'So?'

'These shoes are handmade in London. This shirt cost four hundred dollars.'

'So?'

'So fuck you.' Johnny laughed. 'Tell you what. I own a Laundromat over on Halsted. Why don't you come work for me? Least you wouldn't have

17

to dress like a monkey.'

'Listen — '

'No, you listen. The lady and I are having a conversation. Why don't you mind your own business?'

Mitch glared. His hands were shaking with adrenaline, and he could hear his pulse. He slid off the stool, stood as tall as he could.

'What?' The guy smiled, showing bright white teeth. 'You going to do something, busboy?'

'Johnny.' Jenn stood, put a hand on the man's shoulder. 'This is my friend. Come on.'

'Jesus, I don't need — ' Mitch started.

'Don't take that tone with her.' The man leaned forward, eyes menacing.

'Everything OK?' Alex had reappeared behind the bar, his eyes panning back and forth, concerned. 'This guy is a friend of mine, boss.'

'Mitch didn't mean anything,' Jenn said, from behind. 'You just got off on the wrong foot.'

The wrong foot? What the hell? Why was she talking that way, coming on like he'd been an asshole? Trying to *save* him? He didn't need that. He'd been trying to save *her* from this sleaze.

'Really, Johnny, he's a good guy,' Alex said. 'Good customer, too. Here every Thursday night. We all are.'

The man stood straight, his eyes locked on Mitch's. The moment held for a long time. Then the guy nodded, said, 'All right. You both vouch for him, I'll let him be.' He turned to Alex. 'But it's Mr Loverin.'

'Sure. Sorry, Mr Loverin.' Alex spread his hands.

18

Loverin turned to Jenn. 'I apologize about this. You deserve better. Tell you what, why don't you come back sometime, I'll treat you to dinner, just you and me. Chef'll make up something special. What do you say?'

She hesitated, then put on a smile. 'That sounds nice.' Mitch knew her well enough to know the smile was fake, but still.

The man nodded, then said to Alex, 'Her tab's on me.' He snorted, then, jerking a thumb contemptuously over his shoulder, said, 'His too.' Mitch started to argue, but Alex caught his eye, gave him a warning look, then said, 'That's nice of you, Mr Loverin. Thanks.'

The man turned and walked away. Mitch watched him go, the guy actually strutting. There was silence for a moment, then Alex said, 'What the hell?'

'What?' Mitch shrugged. 'He came over, started being an asshole.'

'You were kind of rude,' Jenn said. 'He was cheesy, but you started it.'

'*I* started it?' He couldn't keep the incredulity out of his voice. 'What are you talking about?' Mitch shook his head. 'I'd like to go get him, tell him to meet me outside.'

'No, man. You don't do that.' Alex took Mitch's glass, held it under the tap. 'I know he looks silly, but he's serious.'

'What do you mean, 'serious'?'

'I mean serious. Like, made-his-money-selling-drugs serious. He used to run crack back in the eighties. In a big way.'

'Really?' Jenn said, a lilt in her voice.

19

'Really. He doesn't do it anymore, but he's still got connections. I been working here a long time, I've seen some shit.'

'What kind of shit?'

'Italian guys coming in carrying briefcases, walking out empty-handed. That kind of shit. He's not somebody to mess with.'

'How come you never told us about him?'

'I don't see him much. He owns a couple of places, leaves running them to the managers. He still comes in, but sits in his office, people coming to talk to him. Shady people.'

'Whatever,' Mitch said. 'I'm not scared. He's a punk.' He drained half his fresh beer in one go, the remnants of adrenaline and shame making his hands shake. 'I'd still like to take him outside.'

Alex chuckled.

'What?'

'Nothing.'

'No. What does that mean?'

'Just that' — Alex shrugged — 'I mean, come on, man. You're not exactly a street fighter.'

'You don't think I can take care of myself?'

'I don't mean anything.' Alex exchanged a look with Jenn. 'Just relax, OK? Let it go.'

Mitch stared at him, then at Jenn, her eyes locked on her glass. Was this what they thought of him? He wanted to yell, to throw his beer and storm off to find that scumbag ex-drug dealer. Bad enough to have a scene like that in front of Jenn. But then for Alex to basically call him a wimp? His forehead was hot, and he had a sick feeling in his gut, one he hated, the same one that he got every time he held the door for some

20

rich asshole who didn't even bother to acknowledge he existed.

'Hey,' Ian said, pulling out his seat, eyes bright and smile toothy. 'What'd I miss?'

★ ★ ★

The night ended much earlier than Ian had in mind. The combination of a handful of drinks and the maintenance trip to the bathroom had him wide-awake, ready to roll. The place was more restaurant than bar, and it shut down at eleven; they'd hung out while Alex finished his closing duties, but the scene with the owner had apparently soured everybody's mood. Instead of their usual retreat to a back table to bullshit until one or two, Jenn had looked at her watch and suggested they wrap early. Mitch, even quieter than usual as he sat drinking with grim determination, had nodded, and then suddenly they were outside. Alex and Jenn lived in the same direction and split a cab north.

'You'll make sure he gets home?' Alex said, one hand against the roof of the car.

'I don't need a babysitter.' Mitch ran the words together. Ian ignored him, said, 'Sure,' to Alex, then kissed Jenn on the cheek, closed the door, and thumped the trunk. He felt good, lucky. Maybe after he dropped Mitch off, he'd hop in his car, spin down to the game.

'Greasy little cheeseball.' Mitch wobbled across the street.

'Sounds like a character. Sorry I missed him.' He held up an arm for a cab that blew right past.

21

'He really own the place?'

'Whatever.' Mitch rubbed at his forehead. 'So he has a lot of money. So what? That mean he gets to treat people that way?'

'I wonder how much he has.' Ian waved again, and this time a cab glided to a stop beside them. They climbed in, and he gave the driver Mitch's address. 'He was a drug dealer, huh?'

'I don't get it. How does money give you a-a-a permission slip to be a douche bag?'

'Makes sense that he would have restaurants.' Ian ran his tongue over his gums, enjoying the faint numbness. 'Cash businesses. The Laundromat, too. He probably bought into them quietly, has people run them, just watches his money grow. You almost have to admire him.'

'Or hate him.'

'Half of admiration *is* hatred, man.'

'And Alex! What was that? What'd he mean about me not being able to take care of myself?' Mitch straightened. 'I can handle myself. Everybody thinks I can't, but I can. Just like the people at the hotel. The guests. They give a tip, five measly bucks, treat you like they bought you. Like you're a slave.' He hiccupped. 'Yes, massa. I hold the door for you. Or worse, like you're invisible. Not a doorman, a door *mat*.'

Ian turned to him. 'You ever gamble?'

'What?'

'You know, blackjack, roulette.'

'Nuh-uh.'

'You ought to. There's nothing like winning.' Ian smiled. 'Or really, even before that. It's the moment between when you set your chips on the table and the ball stops, the card drops. It's a crazy rush. This one time,' he said, 'I'm at the boats, playing blackjack, and I get two nines. So I split them. You know what that means? You put down more money and play them like separate hands. So I get the next card, and it's a nine. So I split again. Next card? A nine. Can you believe it? Split again. It was incredible. I could have gone on all night, the dealer just putting down nines and me putting down chips.'

For a moment, Mitch was quiet. Then he said, 'Even the game, the question game.'

'Huh?'

'Your question game. The one Jenn asked, what would you do with half a million dollars.'

'What about it?'

'Nobody asked me. Alex wants a house for his daughter, you want to quit your job, Jenn wants to travel. But nobody asked me.'

'So what would you do with it?'

Mitch opened his mouth, closed it. Held his hands out, then said, 'That's not the point. The point is that nobody asked me. Like I'm invisible.'

'Well, I'm asking now. What would you do?'

'I don't know,' Mitch said. 'I'm tired. And drunk.' He paused. 'So what happened?'

'When?'

'With the nines.'

'Oh. Dealer had a three and an eight, drew a ten. Twenty-one.'

'So you lost all of them?'

'Yeah, but that's not the important thing.' Ian wanted a bump or another drink, could feel the

23

liquidity of his buzz fading — and the problems teeming behind it ready to jump him if he let them. 'What's important is that there was that moment, see, where I could have won them all. And every time he put down a nine, that moment stretched, got bigger. And the payday with it.'

'But you lost.'

'Right, but — '

'So there wasn't a payday. You just lost four times bigger.'

Ian laughed. 'Yeah, well.' He looked out the window, watched the closed shops and open bars, the people on the sidewalks. No place like Chicago in the summer, every window open, laughter and music spilling onto the streets. He liked the feeling of riding past it, a pane of glass between him and the rest of the world, but all of it right there, close enough to touch if he wanted to reach out. He glanced at the cabbie. A lot of them were Middle Eastern, too strict, but this was a black dude, middle-aged, wearing a Kangol. Hell, what was the worst that would happen? Ian reached into his pocket, took out the amber vial. Without letting himself think too much, he shook a little pile onto the back of his hand and snorted quick, like he had the sniffles. The driver glanced in the rear-view mirror, and Ian held his gaze until the guy looked away.

Mitch said, 'Was that — '

'Yeah.' Ian turned to look at him, gave a shrug and a sideways smile.

'You do a lot of it?'

'Every now and then. You want some?'

Mitch shook his head.

'You sure? Cheer you up.'

'No,' he said, and leaned his head against the window, closed his eyes. 'No, it won't.'

'How about coming gambling with me?'

'Jesus, no. Indiana?'

'Not the riverboats. I know a private game. We can be there in twenty minutes.'

Mitch shook his head. 'I'm going home.'

'Come on, man. Don't be like that,' Ian said.

Silence.

'You know, you can't win if you don't bet.'

'Can't lose, either.'

★ ★ ★

Jenn turned on the faucet, let the water run. It took forever to warm up in Alex's place. She straightened and looked at herself in the mirror, finger-combed her hair behind her ears. She'd always wanted a pixie cut, something short and sexy, but never quite had the guts.

When the water was hot, she cupped her hands under the faucet and splashed it on her face. Alex only had bar soap, not the facial scrub she liked, but one of the rules of their whatever-this-was was that they wouldn't leave things at each other's places. He said that it was because he didn't want his daughter to notice it when she came over, start asking questions, but she suspected it was more that he wanted to be perfectly clear that they weren't dating.

She found him in the kitchen, still naked, rummaging in the fridge. He had a great body:

25

gym-built muscles that were iron-hard but not flashy or ridiculous, black tribal tattoos around his biceps, nice legs, just enough chest hair. 'Beer?' he asked.

'Sure.'

He came out with a couple of Sierra Nevadas, popped the tops, and passed her one. She leaned against the counter, the Formica cool against her bare skin. He opened the drawer, took out his reserve cigarettes, lit up. 'Weird scene tonight.'

She nodded. 'That guy's a trip.'

'He's an asshole.'

'Well, yeah. Didn't take much to spot that.'

'What really happened?'

She ticked a fingernail against the label, peeling the edge up. 'I think he was about to ask me out.'

'Johnny?'

'Mitch.'

He took a long pull of beer. 'You know, if he ever does, I don't want to stand between — '

She shook her head. 'I've caught him looking, but I don't think it's anything serious.' The post-sex glow was fading and leaving in its place a familiar sadness. 'Is he dangerous? Your boss?'

'Nah. I mean, he knows people. But he's kind of a blowhard. One of those guys who used to be scary and isn't anymore, not unless you provoke him. I just said that stuff to keep Mitch from doing anything stupid.' He shrugged. 'I love the guy, but he's not Holyfield. His idea of a good punch is left chin to right fist, you know?'

Men and their alpha politics. The feeling in her chest grew worse, coupled with a hint of panic that she'd been getting lately. Like she was in the wrong place. 'Do you ever feel,' she hesitated, 'like you missed something?'

'I miss my daughter.' He took another hit off his cigarette, then threw it in the sink half-smoked. 'All the time I'm not with her.'

'That's sweet, but not what I mean. I'm talking about something abstract. Like' — she took a sip of beer — 'it used to be that when I went out on a Saturday night, I'd have this lightness inside, this openness. The night could go anywhere. I could meet somebody incredible, or dance in a fountain, or have a conversation that would blow my mind. Have something really *amazing* happen, an adventure. Something that mattered. Life felt . . . imminent. You ever feel that?'

He nodded, said nothing.

'I don't get that much anymore. Now I just go out, I come home, I go to work and book trips to places I've never been, probably won't ever go. There's no meaning to any of it. Those days are gone, and nothing that amazing happened, and now I'm out of time. All there is left to do is wait to turn into my mother.'

'Would that be so bad?'

'Have you met my mother?'

He laughed. Dropped his empty beer in the trash and opened the fridge for another. 'You know, when I was twenty, I had it all figured out. Finish college, go to law school, get a job in the city. Then Trish got pregnant.' He paused. 'I wanted her to have an abortion. But she said she couldn't live with herself. So I did the' — he

27

made air quotes — 'right thing. Quit school, married her, started bartending. Told myself I could take classes on the weekends.'

'But you didn't.'

He shook his head. 'But it was OK, because Cassie was born. Best thing I've ever done. Only thing, really. The moment I saw her, all red and wrinkly and screaming . . . I don't know. That angsty feeling you were talking about, it went away. Just went away.'

'You still see your ex?'

'Trish? Every time I pick Cassie up. She's remarried, a guy who works in the Loop, does something corporate. He's OK.'

'What about her?'

'She' — he hesitated — 'She doesn't think much of me these days.'

They fell silent. Jenn could hear the hum of the over-head lights. Alex was staring at his beer bottle. They'd been sleeping together on the sly for more than a year, a secret in a group that supposedly didn't have any, and yet this was the most intimate conversation they'd had. All the games the four of them played, the way they kept the world at bay with them, it wasn't just the world that was excluded, she realized. They'd also held themselves in reserve from one another.

All she'd wanted from life was adventure, something that mattered, that was exciting and maybe a little bit dangerous and had rewards to match. And yet here she stood, naked in the kitchen of a guy she knew well and yet not at all. A fuck-buddy. She wasn't taking risks or reaching for anything. She was just killing time.

'You know what?' Jenn finished her beer. 'I think I'm going to go.'

Alex looked up, surprised. 'Yeah?'

'I've got things to do in the morning. You know.' She dropped her bottle in the trash, went to the bedroom. Stuffed her panties and bra in her purse, pulled on her jeans and shirt, then sat on the edge of the bed to wrestle with her boots. The covers were still tangled from sex, and she had a flash of Alex beneath her, arching upward as she rode him, her knees astride his hips, sweat running between her breasts, her head thrown back. For a moment she hesitated, but that feeling was still there, frustration and faint panic and, yeah, a little bit of self-loathing, too. She finished zipping her boots.

At the door, she went with a hug and a kiss on the cheek. 'Have fun with Cassie tomorrow.'

'Thanks. The four of us still on for breakfast on Saturday?'

'Sure,' she said, 'whatever.'

'Hey.' He stood framed in the doorway, still naked. 'You OK?'

'I'm fine.' Then she turned and went down the stairs to hail a cab.

2

The health club was swank, one of those places yuppies paid big money to not use. Not the good doctor, though. Bennett had been watching for a while now, and apart from one very interesting weakness, the doc was about as exciting as oatmeal. Up in the morning, coffee with the wife — through the windows she looked like she'd once been pretty — then the gym. Thirty on the treadmill, thirty in the pool, a massage, a shower, and off he went.

Bennett liked people who kept a routine. Sure as a poker tell, it meant they had some part of their lives where they varied, went a little crazy. Everybody needed something to hold back the press of days. Dieters binged, teetotalers threw down punch at the Christmas party, faithful husbands got blown by flirty sales associates on business trips. Screwing up was wired into the DNA.

And thank God for it. Man had to make a living.

He walked in the front door of the gym, offered his pass to the pretty boy behind the counter, who said, 'Your guest membership expires tomorrow. What do you say — ready to make a better you? Should I get the enrollment forms ready?'

'I'll think about it,' Bennett said, then headed for the pool.

Four lanes, half-Olympic length, under bright fluorescent lighting. A fat woman in a bathing cap did a slow breaststroke, her expression painfully earnest. Beside her, the doc cut through the water with a nice clean crawl, four strokes to a breath, flip-turns at the end of the lane. He wore goggles and a Speedo, and managed three laps to every one of the woman's. Bennett stood behind the glass and watched, chlorine in his nostrils.

After ten minutes, the doc pulled himself out of the water. He stood on the edge and stretched, then headed for the exit. The lady's eyes tracked his retreating back, something like hunger in them. Bennett held the door open.

'Thanks,' the doc said.

'No trouble.'

Bennett stood for a few more minutes, watching the woman swim. There was something about her that touched him. She had to know that she was never going to change, that next year, and the year after, she would still be here, still be fat, still be swimming her clumsy breaststroke before showering and going home alone. And yet here she was, water weights on, plugging away. Human drama, right in front of him. Broke the heart.

He walked down the hall to the massage rooms. A hatchet-faced girl with big hands was heading for a closed door.

'Excuse me,' Bennett said.

'Yes?'

'I know this is odd, but I work with the doctor. There's been an incident at the lab. I need to

31

speak to him right now. It's urgent.'

She hesitated, then said, 'Well, I suppose I — '

'Thanks,' he said, one hand on the door handle. She stood there for a moment, and he said, 'Sorry, but as I'm sure you know, our work is sensitive.'

'Umm . . . '

'I appreciate it.' Then he stepped into the room and shut the door behind him.

The doc lay on his belly on the massage table, a towel across his ass. Candles glowed from a Zen stone arrangement in the corner, and soft music came from somewhere. Swank.

'Cindi,' the doc said to the floor. 'Afraid you've got your work cut out for you. My shoulder's killing me. I think I pulled something.'

'That's one way to put it,' Bennett said.

The man's head whipped around, and he planted his hands on the table, came partway up, then hesitated, seeming to realize he was naked under the towel. 'What — '

'Easy, Doc.' Bennett strolled around the edge of the table. 'Don't want to aggravate that shoulder.'

'You filling in for Cindi?' His eyes narrow, but no fear in them. The kind of guy who saw the whole world as the help.

'Let's talk about who you are.'

'Who *I* am? I'm sorry, I don't understand — '

'You're a senior chemist at K&S Laboratories. You guys have a couple of steady contracts supplying medium-sized pharmaceutical companies with organofluorine compounds. Word is

32

you're likely to be running the place in a couple of years. Some folks might say it's because you married the boss's daughter, but I don't credit that. Best I can tell, you're a talented scientist.'

The man's face went through a series of expressions, his eyebrows raising, then lowering, nostrils flaring, mouth falling slightly open. He looked like he'd been trying to tell a joke but at the last second forgot the punchline.

'You also have a bit of a naughty streak, don't you?' Bennett squatted to lower himself eye to eye.

The guy began to push himself up, saying, 'I don't know who you are or what —— '

Bennett broke his nose.

'Unnuhhuh!' The man's eyes went wide with shock, hands flying to cup his face, propping himself on his elbows.

'Hurts, right? They say that in a fight, you should strike with an open hand, aiming the heel of your palm into your opponent's nose. Disorienting as hell, the world spins, the pain slows them down. Plus, if you keep your hand at the right angle, a lot of times your fingers will go into their eyes. Why I went with a closed fist that time.'

Blood was flowing between the man's fingers — another benefit to a good nose punch, it looked dramatic — and the fear was in him now, that arrogant assumption of control gone. He scrambled backward on the table, the towel slipping off to reveal his bare white ass.

'Sit still, Doc.' Bennett stood and took the Smith from behind his back.

The man froze halfway up, flaccid penis

33

dangling, looking for all the world like he was about to take it doggy-style.

'Good boy.' Bennett reached into his pocket with his left hand, pulled out a handful of pages. He tossed the folded stack on the massage table. 'Take a look.'

For a moment, the man just stared, that prey gaze they all got when you put the screws to them. Then he reached out with a trembling hand and unfolded the papers. First a gasp, then a low moan that dragged on as he moved from photograph to photograph.

'Walking the wild side, huh? Obviously, black-and-white can't really demonstrate the full-color glory of the originals. But I think you get the point.'

The man's hands were shaking and his face had gone pale. 'Where did you . . . ?'

'You're too smart to ask things you already know the answer to. I'm sure you haven't forgotten your little adventure. So why don't you use that big brain of yours and come up with a better question? There's really only one.'

The doctor stared at him, then at the pictures. Slowly he eased himself to a seated position, one hand on his nose, the other covering himself. Helpless to stop his whole world slipping away. Bennett had found that a flair for the dramatic was useful in his line of work. The man wouldn't have been nearly so cowed sitting behind his desk, wearing a cashmere sweater and tailored slacks. There was a moment of silence, and then, staring at his feet, the man said, 'How much do you want?'

'Right neighborhood, wrong address.'

'Huh?'

'Don't want money.'

'Then what?'

'Nothing that will take much time or effort. Just want you to cook me up a little something.' Bennett pulled another piece of paper from his pocket and held it out. Did it purposefully, wondering which hand the guy would use to take it. After a second, the doctor let go of his nose to grab the paper. Better to let blood run down his face from a broken nose than to expose his cock. Bennett chuckled. 'Now, you know what that is?'

The man focused on the page, his eyes growing wide.

'I'll take that as a yes. You make that for me, you got my word, I'll delete the originals. They aren't really my taste anyway. Though if you like, I'll be happy to send you copies first, give you a little souvenir.'

'I . . . you know what this is?'

Bennett sighed, then leaned in and flicked the man's broken nose with his middle finger. The guy yelped, dropped the page.

'You think I'd be asking if I didn't?'

'I don't know how to make it.'

'You're a smart guy. I'm sure you'll figure it out. And you have one heck of a chemistry set at your disposal. A lab like yours, deals with pharmaceutical companies, you probably have most of what you need in stock, right?'

Looking like it hurt, the man nodded.

'Good. You've got three days.'

'Three days, that's not enough — '

'There you go again.' Bennett tapped the Smith against the table. 'Talking without thinking.'

The man swallowed, said nothing.

'Better. Now' — Bennett stood — 'I've got your cell number. I'll be in touch. I were you, I'd get to work.' He slid the gun back into his belt, started for the door. 'By the way, I think the lovely you were swimming beside might have a crush on you. Just between us, eh, brother?' He winked, then stepped out, leaving the man naked and bleeding.

An excellent performance. Hitting the right tone was key. He strolled down the hall, feeling good. He was almost to the stairs when the masseuse stopped him.

'Everything OK?'

'Right as rain,' he said. 'But you know what, hon? I've got a feeling the doctor's going to skip his massage.'

3

His ex-wife's house was only a forty-minute drive if traffic was good, but it was so far out of his world Alex sometimes felt like he needed a space suit.

It wasn't the house itself, which was typical suburban: two stories of aluminum siding and painted shutters on a broad green corner bounded by neat sidewalks. Not one of the McMansions with four garages and a swimming pool and enough space for an extended Korean family. And it wasn't the suburbs that bothered him. He'd grown up in them — in Michigan, not here, but the thing about suburbs was that they were the same everywhere — and so the strip malls and wide-laned roads and chain restaurants were familiar in a nostalgic sort of way.

It was something else. The mothers pushing strollers and chatting. The kids racing on bicycles, legs pumping as they leaned on the handlebars. The quiet, tree-shaded streets. Everything seemed settled here. Proper. The predictable result of a series of calculated decisions.

He thought of Jenn the night before, standing in his kitchen, pale and naked and unselfconscious. Holding her beer bottle by the neck and saying that all she'd wanted was to get swept up in an adventure. Beautiful, with her bright skin and small nipples and the faint marks of his fingers bruising her slender biceps. The kind of woman men could obsess over. And he cared about her, he really did. But as he'd looked at her, nothing in him had stirred the same way it did looking at the broad porch and well-kept lawn of his ex-wife's house.

Whatever. It was a shiny blue morning, he wasn't working until six, and he had a date with his favorite ten-year-old. He unfolded himself from his car — the Taurus was solid and cheap, but a little small for six-two — and went up the walk whistling.

The whistle died when Trish met him at the door. She wore jeans and a fitted T-shirt. Her hair was in a pony-tail and her face was closed. 'You're late.'

'Traffic.'

She nodded, stepped inside. Turned and yelled over her shoulder. 'Cassie!' She looked back at him. 'You want some coffee?'

He shook his head and thought he saw relief in her eyes. Alex put his hands in his pockets, ran his tongue around the inside of his mouth. Glanced at the foyer, the floor spotless, mirrors on the wall, a small end table with keys and a stack of mail. He rocked from one foot to the other.

'Listen, Alex — '

'I know,' he said. 'I'm late with my check. We had a screw-up at the bar, everybody's pay was held. It should be hitting the bank today. I'll put it in the mail tomorrow.'

'And what about last month?'

'I told you. The IRS, they — '

38

'You always have an excuse.'

'It's not an excuse,' he said quietly, 'if it's true.'

'Last month wasn't the first time. More like the tenth.'

'Trish, what do you want from me? I'm working double shifts. I live in a dump. I'm not spending money on hookers and blow. If the lawyer your father paid for hadn't gotten the child support set so ridiculously high, maybe I could make some progress.'

His ex shook her head. 'We were very generous.'

'You're generous about letting me see her. But I owe you half my paycheck. How am I supposed to live?'

'She's your daughter. This is a way of showing that you'll always be there for her.'

'Hey.' His voice rough. 'I will *always* be there for her.'

She looked downward as she spun her new wedding ring. 'I know you love her. I do. And she loves you. But it can't go on like this.' She sighed. 'Listen. There's something — '

Behind him, Cassie rumbled down the steps like an avalanche. 'Hi, Daddy!' She came straight into his arms with a hug. He scooped her up and squeezed her tight. Over her shoulder, Trish opened her mouth, closed it, then looked away. Alex was content to let her. Whatever she had been about to say, it hadn't sounded good.

Cassie was all happy chatter as they drove out of the neighborhood: the Rollerblades his ex-wife's husband had bought her, a reality show on MTV, how her soccer team was going to the play-offs, and could he make the game?

'I'll try, sweetie.' He stopped at a red light. 'Where do you want to eat?'

They settled on TGI Friday's, the corner booth. A perky teenager seated them, plunked down plastic tumblers of water. Eighties pop drifted through deep-fried air. While Cassie studied her menu, he studied her, amazed, as always, at her sheer physicality: her tan forearms and bright eyes and the way she twisted a curl of hair as she concentrated. She wore a tank top with lacy straps, and her ears were pierced. That was new, and he didn't love it.

They ordered, an elaborate salad for her, hold the cheese, dressing on the side, and a cheeseburger for him, rare. 'Want a milk shake?'

She shook her head. 'I'm on a diet.'

'A diet?'

'Yup.' She seemed proud of it, and he didn't push, didn't tell her that she was perfect just the way she was, bright and beautiful and softly rounded with the remnants of baby fat. He just ordered a chocolate malt of his own, and two straws.

The server left, and they looked at each other. 'So.'

'So,' she said and smiled.

'How's tricks, Trix? Tell me everything.'

She giggled and started in, and he leaned back, content to listen. Sometimes she was solemn and asked him questions about his life that seemed like they'd been prompted by a discussion he hadn't been privy to. But today she was her normal self, bubbly and concerned only

40

with the everyday things that made up a ten-year-old life. Their food came, and he pushed the milk shake forward just enough that she could reach it.

'We're going to Hilton Head next month.'

'Yeah?'

'Scott is taking us.' She always made a point of referring to Trish's new husband by his first name, at least around him. Maybe at home she called him Daddy too, but never in front of Alex. 'We have a hotel right on the beach. With a pool, too. And there's dancing at night, Mom says.'

'Sounds like fun.' His burger was bitter and burned.

'Maybe you could come too.'

'I wish I could.'

'I bet Mom and Scott wouldn't mind.'

He was positive that wasn't true, and even more positive he couldn't afford the hotel. 'I've got to work, kiddo. It's not summer for me.'

She wrinkled her nose. 'It's never summer for you.'

'Too true.' He put a hand over his heart. 'Oh, to be ten again.'

'Grown-ups always say that.'

'We do?'

She nodded. 'I think you forget how much it sucks to be a kid.'

'Sometimes it sucks to be an adult, too.' Thinking of Trish looking down, that hesitation, like she was about to say something he really didn't want to hear.

'You don't have homework.'

'We don't have summer vacation, either.'

41

'But you can drive. And live in the city. You can do anything you want.'

'Not anything.'

'Most anything. I can't wait to grow up.'

He felt the wince but didn't show it. 'Don't be in too much of a hurry.'

She stabbed a tomato with her fork, eyed it dubiously, then took a small bite. 'So, I was thinking,' she said, chewing. 'I got all A's and B's last year.'

'Uh-oh.'

'And you always say I'm very mature for my age.'

'Who said that? I said that? I don't remember saying that.'

'Yes, you did. You say it all the time.' She set her fork down and pulled his milk shake toward her. 'So I was thinking that I should be able to have a cellphone.'

He raised his eyebrows.

'Actually, an iPhone.'

'Specific.'

'They're the best. You can play music on them and instant message and I could call you whenever I want.'

'You can call me whenever you want now.'

'Yeah, but if I had one, I could call you when I'm not home.' She drained an inch of the chocolate malt, then looked at him expectantly. 'All my friends have them.'

'I don't know, kiddo.'

'Come on, *please?* I'll be really careful with it.'

His stomach felt off, and he put down his burger. The previous night's conversation with

Jenn came into his mind again, how he'd had a whole different plan than being thirty-two and living paycheck to paycheck. 'What does your mother say?'

'She said to ask you.'

Bravo, he thought. *Thanks, Trish. Much appreciated.*

'I think you're a little young.'

'But, Dad — '

'Sorry, Cass. Ten is too young.' He chewed a cold french fry.

She started to pout, then paused, then took another sip on the milk shake. 'Is it because you're broke?'

'What?'

'Mom said that you barely make enough to afford your fleabag apartment.'

'She said that to you?'

'Well, no.' Cassie shrugged. 'I overheard her on the phone.' She looked at him openly, too young to realize the effect of her words, that the last, worst thing she could ever give him was pity.

He stared, wanting to tell her the truth, tell her all the things he'd given up for her already, and all the things he would again. But kids didn't need to know about child support and rent and gas at four bucks a gallon. Otherwise they stopped being kids. 'Your mother was joking.'

'Yeah?' She didn't sound convinced.

'I'm made of money. You know, fleabag apartments aren't cheap. You have to pay extra for the fleas.'

'Dad.'

'Plus flea food.'

'Dad.'

'And flea grooming. Fleas are very particular about their grooming.'

She giggled, and the solemn expression fell from her face. It was something.

★ ★ ★

Ring.

  Ring.

  Ring.

  'John Loverin.'

  'Johnny Love, Johnny Love. You know who this is?'

  'Sure, kid, I know. How the hell are you?'

  'Depends on whether you have my money.'

  'You don't trust me?'

  'I look like a Democrat?'

  'Ain't it the way. Since you bring it up, the price you're asking. I'm thinking an even two instead.'

  'Hmm. Let me consider that. I don't want to say anything rash.' A pause. 'Nope, I had it off the bat: Blow it out your ass.'

  'Hey — '

  'Hey my ten-inch cock. You know you can turn it around for double what I'm charging. So let's not play.'

  'All right, all right. Can't blame a guy for trying.'

  'You have a buyer lined up?'

  'Yeah.'

  'Not someone you want to disappoint, I'm guessing.'

'Not so much, no. So I can count on you, right, kid?'

'Anybody tell you that whole 'kid' thing is kind of annoying?'

'Most people are too smart to take that tone.'

'You find someone else who can get you this, you can tell me to walk. Till then, I take any tone I like. Another thing. Tuesday. It's not going to be me.'

'What do you mean?'

'It won't be me comes in to see you. I'm sending someone.'

'Are you shitting me?'

'Nope.'

'Who?'

'Crooch.'

A laugh. 'Jesus. Anything to avoid a little dirty work yourself, huh? You must really have that pasty-faced loser twisted around your finger. What did you catch him doing?'

'Everybody sins, Johnny. I'm just there to see it. So we OK? You're fine with Crooch?'

'Kid, so long as he brought what you're selling, I'd be fine if it was Big Bird squeezed his feathery butt through my door.'

'Glad to hear it. Let's keep everything simple. A nice, clean deal.'

'You deliver, I deliver.'

'Fair enough. Have a happy fucking weekend.'

★ ★ ★

After Alex dropped Cassie off, as he was battling traffic eastward and holding off the mood as best he could, his cellphone rang. He checked the screen. Trish. No way he wanted to talk to her now. Instead he leaned back in the seat and sucked deep on the emotions that had been waiting for him, a cocktail he drank often: two parts rage to one part aching frustration, flavored with a dash of self-pity. Damn her for talking about him that way in front of Cassie. And damn her for her snide attacks about the child support. Sure, over the years he'd missed a couple of payments. But he was doing the best he could.

Still, he couldn't find it in him to hate her. He knew her too well. She wasn't cruel; she was just practical in a relentless sort of way. All about the end result. They'd split up in part because she didn't want to be married to a bartender. She was young, had her looks and her brains, and though Cassie limited the dating options, for a certain type of guy — the kind who had worked harder than he meant to for fifteen years, then looked up and realized his life was empty — a kid was actually a bonus. Insta-family, just add wedding ring and mortgage payments.

Of course, now there wasn't much room for an ex-husband. Especially one who still tended bar.

The joyless irony of it all was that he had to go to work even now. Right now, in fact. He stewed for the rest of the commute, then swallowed his cocktail like a man and went inside.

At this hour, Rossi's had that hollowed-out look, like a house where the owners were on vacation. The hostess stand was empty, and servers were rolling napkins in the dining room. He walked past to the bar. His kingdom. Jesus.

The thought made him wonder if he remembered how to tie a noose. An early shift
bartender was setting out bottles. He nodded at
Alex, said, 'Johnny wants you.'

'What for?'

'Didn't say. Just wanted you to come back to
his office when you got in.'

'He's here? At three o'clock?'

'Will wonders never, right?'

Alex nodded, reached around the tap for a
glass, filled it with Diet Coke, then went to the
back room. He paused to check the kegs — he'd
been easing a few better beers into rotation, a
couple of taps of Lagunitas and Victory, good
American draft beers to add to the usual crap
that people drank — then noticed that the back
door to the alley was unlocked yet again. The
kitchen staff went out back to smoke and never
locked it. He threw the bolt, went to the office
door, and stepped inside.

Johnny Love sat behind the desk, facing away.
He whirled at the sound of the door opening.
'What the fuck?'

'Ahh — ' Alex hesitated. 'You wanted to see
me?'

'Don't you knock?' He straightened in the
chair, positioning his body to hide something
behind him.

Alex fought the urge to point out that this was
more often his office than Johnny's, that he and
the restaurant managers used it day in, day out,
instead of the occasional drop-by. Instead, he
said, 'Sorry, Mr Loverin. My mistake.'

Johnny turned back around and did something

47

with his hands. Alex couldn't see what he was doing, but heard a creak, and then a dull metal clank. Johnny was putting something in the safe. Alex waited, rocking from one foot to the other, until his boss swiveled back around and slowly raised one foot and then the other to set them on top of the desk. Said nothing. Marking his territory as clear as if he'd pissed on the desk.

Alex repeated, 'You wanted to see me?'

Johnny stared. It was a look that Alex supposed had once been scary, back in the days when the guy was actually a player, carried a gun. He said, 'How'd you like to earn a little extra money?'

'Doing what?'

'Simple thing. I've got a meeting this Tuesday night, I'd like you to join.'

'What kind of meeting?'

'What do you care?'

'I just mean, what's this about?' There had been talk that Johnny was buying into another restaurant. If it was true, he might be looking for somebody to manage the place. The step up in salary might make the difference Alex needed.

'What it is, what you need to know, it's just a little side deal I've got going on. A guy I know who likes to pretend he's tough. I want you to stand around, wear a shirt shows off those muscles.'

'You want me to be a bodyguard?'

'Nothing like that. It's a, what do you call it, a pageant. You're there to make things look a certain way. You're set dressing.' Johnny nodded at that, pleased with the description.

48

'Set dressing.'

'Yeah. You stand with your arms folded. Don't say anything. Just look mean.'

'Umm.' Alex hesitated. 'I'm not sure — '

'Two hundred bucks. Should only take ten minutes or so.'

Alarm bells started chiming in Alex's head. A meeting in the back office, him pretending to be muscle? He remembered the things he'd told the others, Italians coming in with briefcases and leaving empty-handed. Whatever this was, it wasn't about a new restaurant. 'You know, Mr Loverin, that's not really what I'm about.'

'What do you mean, it's not what you're about?'

'I mean, whatever this is — I just — well, I'm really not into that kind of thing.'

Johnny took his feet from the desk, sat up straight. 'What kind of thing?' His voice thin and his eyes narrow.

Shit. 'That came out wrong. I just mean, if it's OK with you, I'd as soon stick to my regular job.'

'Your regular job.'

'Yeah.'

'You work for me, right? So your regular job, it's doing what I tell you, isn't it?'

All right. First Trish, now this. Enough. 'When some drunk gets rough in the bar, I handle it. But this is something else. I've been here a while, and I've heard some things, and whatever this is, I don't want any part of it.'

For a long moment, Johnny said nothing. Then he ran his tongue slowly over his lips. 'That's a pretty big speech, kid.'

'I don't mean any disrespect.'

'A pretty big fucking speech indeed, coming from an assistant fucking manager. You've heard some things? Good for fucking you.' He cracked his thumbs. 'There's a recession, you know that? Every day I get people in here looking for work. Plenty of people who could do your job. You ever think of that?'

'Mr Loverin — '

'You had your say. Now it's my turn. You do this very simple thing I'm asking or you find yourself another job. But you better not even *try* to tell people you worked here. Because when they call — and they will — I'll tell them that I fired you for stealing from the register. I'll tell them you're an ungrateful little punk been ripping me off for years.'

'That's not true.'

'I said it, so it's true. Get me?'

How the hell had they ended up here? One minute he was coming in to cover a shift, now he was in danger of losing his job? Part of him wanted to stand up and tell Johnny Love to screw himself.

But then he remembered his bank account, maybe two hundred bucks in it. He thought of Trish, and the way she'd started in on him about the child support from the moment he saw her. He could find another job, but Johnny was right; if he tried to go to another bar, the owner would call. Sure, he'd be able to find something eventually, probably something better. But how long would it take? And what would Trish say when he told her he'd been fired?

What would she say to Cassie?

Then Johnny smiled. 'Anyway, you've got this all wrong. It's no big deal. Just a show, kid. No need to get your stockings twisted.'

Alex felt another cocktail of emotions coming on. Two parts sickness in his stomach, one part pissed-off, with a twist of what-choice-do-I-have? 'Mr Loverin, I need this job. But — '

'Good. Tuesday. And you know what? Let's call it three hundred.' He reached for the phone, dialed, rocked the chair back on two legs. 'Mort! How the hell are you.' Johnny laughed, then looked up at Alex as if surprised to see him still standing there, and jerked his head toward the door.

4

He wasn't going.

Mitch lay on his back, one arm behind his head. The night had been cool enough to leave the bedroom windows open, and the breeze blew the curtains in flips and swirls, morning sunlight blinking as they parted. The room went from dark to bright to dark.

He could imagine the scene this Thursday night. Them asking where he'd been, why he'd missed brunch. Just shrugging, saying something came up. Playing it cool, like Jack Nicholson. Aloof. In control.

Of course, Jenn would be there. Probably wearing a sundress.

He stared at the ceiling. Sundress. Jack Nicholson. Sundress.

Mitch kicked the covers off and rolled out of bed. Maybe he'd be late.

He showered, NPR in the background. The subprime housing crunch, the Dow plummeting, the Bush administration pushing for war with Iran because the two wars they already had were going so well. He shaved carefully, then killed the water and dried himself with the same towel as always, even though there were two hanging in the bathroom. Two because that's what grown-ups had, just in case someday there were two people showering.

He put on a pair of jeans and a T-shirt. Made

52

coffee. Sipped it slowly. The clock read 10:37. If he left now, he'd be right on time. He poured a second cup, picked up a novel.

It was funny. When the four of them had started hanging out, they'd all had other people they thought of as their 'real' friends. But time kept passing, and those people got married or moved away or just got lazy in that late-twenties way, never leaving the house, always saying they'd love to get together but never doing it. And so Thursday nights went from optional to mandatory, and before long, they started adding more occasions. Dinners at Ian's condo in the sky. Cubs games in the summer. And lately, Saturday brunch.

That seemed to be the way with life. The things you were now, today, were the things you really were. Maybe you used to play guitar; maybe in the future you'd take up bowling. But what you did *now*, the people you saw, the books you read, the dreams that woke you, they were the real you. Not some construct of what you wanted to be or once were.

At 11:02, he stopped pretending to read and went for a cab.

Though named like a convenience store, Kuma's Corner was a cross between a heavy-metal bar and a café, with tasteful lighting and tattooed waitstaff, eggs Benedict and burgers named after bands. Mitch had timed it right, strolling out on the small patio to find the three of them already there. Jenn flashed white teeth, motioned to the empty chair beside her. No sundress, but a strappy shirt that showed off her shoulders.

He sat, smiled, then saw Ian. 'Whoa!' The

53

guy's left eye was swollen nearly shut, thick flesh ringed in bright purple and dark black. 'Jesus,' Mitch said. 'What happened to you?'

'He won't tell us,' Jenn said. 'But I think it was a woman.'

'I did tell you. I tripped. I was out late, came home buzzed, caught my foot on the mat.'

'And hit the doorknob with your eyeball?'

'Yeah.' Ian reached for his beer, drained half in a pull. 'Nice shot, huh? Doorknob, one; Ian, zero. But I've got plans for revenge.' He smiled. 'Anyway. You're missing a hell of a story. Alex is beginning a life of crime.'

'It's not funny, man.' Alex had dark circles of his own.

'Hold on. Let me order.'

'I did it for you,' Jenn said. 'Chilaquiles, right?'

Mitch looked over and smiled, suddenly ten feet tall and lighter than air and very glad he'd come. 'Yeah. Thanks.' He held the look a moment, then turned to Alex. 'So?'

'His boss is using him as muscle,' Ian said. 'He's gonna get medieval on some tough guys.'

'Would you quit it? This is serious. My boss is — '

'An asshole?'

'Well, yeah. Yesterday he was fiddling with the safe when I walked into his office, and he freaked like I caught him jerking off.' Alex shook his head. 'I calm him down, very polite, use his last name and everything. And he says he wants me to come to a meeting. Like, an after-hours kind of meeting. A side deal, he wants me to be his bodyguard.'

'No shit?'

'No shit. And I say no, still very polite. He says I don't do this, I'm fired, and he'll tell everybody I've been stealing.'

'Hmm.' Mitch could picture it, the skeezy guy condescending and threatening at once, big tough Alex having to stand there and take it. The thought almost made him smile. *Payback's a bitch*. Then he saw the look in his friend's eyes and immediately felt bad for feeling good.

'You got that far before,' Ian said. 'So? Are you going to do it?'

'He signs the checks, right? But then — ' Alex stopped at the arrival of a ferret-faced blonde balancing plates down the length of a tattooed arm. Ian ordered another beer. After she walked away, Alex said, 'But then it got worse.' He pushed his plate forward and leaned on his elbows. 'I got to wondering what Johnny was doing in the safe, right? I mean, he was so concerned with it.'

Mitch cut into his breakfast, scooping up corn tortillas and salsa verde and pulled chicken.

'So after he took off, I went back into the office, and I opened the safe.'

'I'm surprised 'Johnny Love' gave you the combination,' Jenn said.

'He didn't. A couple of months ago he was after some information in there, something about a real-estate deal. Manager wasn't working, didn't want to come in, so he called and gave me the combo. It's Johnny's birthday. He makes a point of showing up every year on his birthday to see who remembers.'

Jenn gave a sharp, high laugh. 'This guy gets better and better.'

'Worse and worse.' Alex's features went dark in a way that reminded Mitch of his fluttering curtains, blinding sunlight to deep gloom. 'You know what was there?' He paused, then looked over his shoulder. Pitched his voice low. 'Cash. A lot of it. Like, stacks of hundred-dollar bills.'

Mitch stopped chewing. Next to him, Jenn leaned forward the barest amount, more an intake of breath than a calculated motion. For a second, the crowded patio seemed to fall silent, and he could hear the rustling of leaves above them, the sound of traffic on Belmont.

'Nice.' Ian picked up his water glass and held it against his bad eye, the ice cubes tinkling. 'You had me going.'

Jenn looked around the table, at Ian, at Alex, at Mitch, at Alex again, back at Ian again. 'Is he kidding?'

'Of course he's kidding.'

'I'm not.' Alex said it simple and quiet and firm. 'I wish I were.'

'You're serious?' Mitch set his fork down.

Alex nodded. 'On my mother.'

The silence fell again.

'What did you do?'

'I packed my pockets and snuck out the back. Brunch is on me.' Alex stabbed at his eggs. 'What do you think? I locked up, went back to the bar, and quietly shit myself.'

'You didn't touch it?'

'No.'

'Come on.' Ian set down the water glass. No

56

less puffy, his bad eye was now just slick with condensation. 'Not even a little?'

'No.'

'How much was there?' Mitch asked.

'I don't know,' Alex said around a mouthful. 'A lot. Thing is, I got to thinking. What if it's got something to do with the meeting? I had figured, you know, he was having trouble with his vegetable suppliers, wanted me there so he could look like the old tough Johnny Love. But there had to be a couple hundred grand. What if he's going back into the drug business? Meeting with Colombians?'

'Or Outfit guys,' Mitch said. 'Or undercover cops.'

'Jesus. If he got busted and I was there . . .'

'You have to find a new job.' Jenn's voice was sharper than normal.

'Ya think?'

'You're missing the worst part,' Ian said. 'Insult to the injury. The money.'

Alex's jaw fell open, then he gave a sound that wasn't much like a laugh. 'Three hundred bucks. I'm a bodyguard at a six-figure drug deal, and the cheap bastard is offering me three hundred bucks.' He made the sound again.

'You know what you should do?' Ian held a beat. 'Clean out that safe before you quit.'

'Tempting,' Alex said. 'But I think even Johnny Love could figure that one out.'

'Well, all you need to do,' Mitch said, 'is not quit. Do it on a night you aren't working, and don't quit.'

'Right. Right.' Ian nodded, cracked his

57

knuckles. 'Keep a straight face.'

'Better yet,' Jenn said, 'we should take it.'

'Yes!' Ian gave her gun fingers. 'That's it. In fact, do it on a night you *are* working. You stand at the bar all night, meanwhile, we're emptying the safe.'

'We could cut through the roof with a torch,' Jenn said, 'and then rappel from a helicopter.'

'Or tunnel in from the building across the street,' Mitch said, getting in the spirit.

'Meanwhile, I distract Johnny,' Jenn said. 'I'll wear one of those Bond-girl dresses from the Connery years. The short, mod ones that the villains' girlfriends had. I've always wanted to.'

'I love it when a plan comes together,' Ian said, and raised his glass. 'To screwing Johnny Love.'

'Screwing Johnny Love.' They clinked. Mitch leaned back in his chair, glad he'd come. A flawless blue sky and good friends. A sudden scrap of music began, Brandon Flowers urging *smi-ile like you mean it*, from the cellphone beside Alex's napkin. He picked it up, shook his head, then hit a button to silence the notes.

'Work?'

'My ex.'

It seemed like maybe a look passed between Jenn and Alex, but it was just a flickering thing. Mitch dug into his neglected breakfast.

Ian said, 'You guys know what the Prisoner's Dilemma is?'

Alex groaned. 'Not again.'

'What?'

'Let me guess. It's another game.'

'Funny you should say that,' Ian deadpanned. 'In fact, yes.'

'You do anything besides play games?'

'So,' Ian said, 'two criminals are arrested. The cops know they did it, but they don't have enough evidence. So they put them in separate cells and offer each a deal. If one rats on the other, he goes free. His partner, though, gets ten years. If they both keep quiet, the cops can only hit them with something minor, say, six months. But if both of them betray the other, bam, the cops can nail both, and they each get five years.'

There was something elegant in the situation. Mitch could see the whole game, almost see the equation behind it. He'd always been decent at math. 'They both stay quiet.'

'You'd think, right? But the thing is, they can't talk to each other. If one trusts the other and is betrayed, he gets *twice* the sentence he would have if they both ratted.'

'How well do they know each other?' Jenn asked.

'Not the point.'

'Sure it is. If they're good friends, then they'll trust that the other guy will do the right thing.'

'Ahh, but that's a big assumption. I mean, imagine you make that leap, and find out your buddy screwed you? He walks free, you get ten *years*. That's such a huge consequence that it becomes less important what you can gain, and more important what you could lose. Which means it's not about trust.'

'What is it about, then?'

'Iteration. If you play only once, the best thing

59

to do is to betray before you're betrayed. Even if the other guy is a friend. Because he's thinking the same thing.'

Jenn shook her head. 'Did your mother not hug you or something?'

Ian gave her the finger. 'But see, if you're going to be playing again and again, then you keep the faith. Because six months in prison beats the consequences of mutual betrayal. So over time, the best result is to play square. But only over time.'

'Where do you *get* this shit?' Alex asked.

'Game theory, baby. So how about tomorrow night?'

'For what?'

'Screwing Johnny Love.'

'Yeah, fine,' Alex said. 'I can't believe I have to find a new job. And you know what? Johnny is enough of a dick, he probably *will* tell everybody I stole from him.'

'He won't know it was you.'

'No, I mean from the registers . . . ' Alex paused. Set his glass down, turned with a bemused expression. 'Are you serious?'

Ian gave a shrug that was more eyebrows than shoulders. 'Why not?'

'Because it's stealing?'

'So what? You said this guy made his money selling drugs. You know how many people probably died because of that?'

'So?'

'Robbing a drug dealer, that doesn't seem wrong to me. Plus, there's no way we would get caught,' Ian said. 'I mean, who would ever suspect us? None of us with a record, none of us ever having done anything like this, and you with an alibi. Big payoff for low risk. Betray and win.'

'This isn't one of your games.'

'Everything is a game. This one is the Prisoner's Dilemma. If you're only playing once, your best bet is to screw the other guy. Because you know he will screw you.' He leaned forward. 'Look at us. The four of us are all nice people, employed, call our mothers, do the things we're supposed to, right? But guys like Johnny don't play that way. He just takes what he wants, and since we're playing nice, he wins. Same with Ken Lay and James Cayne and all the others, the criminals in the expensive suits. You were the one who said they should be lined up and shot, right?'

'I didn't mean I'd be pulling the trigger.'

'But why not? This guy is blackmailing you. He's breaking the rules and he's winning, and the question is, are you just going to take it? Or are you going to beat him at his own game?'

The mood around the table had changed. There was a strange tension, the joke running further than anyone had intended. Something Mitch had read that morning came into his mind. 'You know what Raymond Chandler said?'

'No, Mitch,' Alex humoring him, 'what did Raymond Chandler say?'

'He said there's no clean way to make a hundred million bucks.'

'There you go,' Ian said. 'There you go.'

Alex looked around the table, his expression incredulous. 'You serious?'

Not really, Mitch thought. It did sound doable, and the money, well, that would change his life. But was he actually serious? Not when it came down to it.

Which is maybe why you stand holding a door for people who don't know you exist, the voice in his head whispered.

'We're not robbing my boss.'

Ian shrugged, leaned back. 'Your loss.' He put on that smile, his caustic armor.

There didn't seem to be much to say to follow that, and they picked at their breakfasts. Mitch could almost hear the thoughts, read them like they were printed on everyone's cheeks. He was a good watcher. People mistook not wanting to be the center of attention for not paying attention. Ian was easy, the narrow hunger on his face, the way he held himself straight. Alex had the tense stillness and wide eyes of a courtroom defendant, and Mitch could see him thinking of his daughter and whatever white-picket house she lived in. Jenn had a furtive glow to her. She looked, frankly, turned on.

The scrape of silverware was loud. Finally, Alex looked at Ian, said, 'You are making me wonder, though.'

'Yeah?'

'How'd you get that black eye again?'

5

It was amazing, Bennett thought, how much of the world looked really boring. The office park where K&S Laboratories was located, for example. A series of two-story shoeboxes centered around what had to be the lamest fountain he'd ever seen, water rolling in a piss trickle down an angled slab. How people got up every day and commuted an hour in traffic just to work in a place like this, he'd never understand.

Of course, on the inside, the lab probably looked more exciting. According to the research he'd done, about twenty percent of pharmaceuticals used some form of fluorine, which acted as a stabilizer, improving efficiency by delaying absorption. It was pretty nasty stuff; as a subcontractor developing compounds for drug companies, K&S probably had clean rooms, positive airflow suits, three kinds of safety precautions. Maybe on the inside it looked like something out of a Bruckheimer flick.

Bennett still liked his office better. With one hand on the wheel of the Benz, he dialed his cell. 'Doc. You know who this is?'

'Y-Yes.'

'Good. You do what I asked?'

'I . . . I . . . '

'Easy. Take a breath.' He waited for a beat, then said, 'Better?'

The man's voice came through hollow and miserable. 'I made what you wanted.'

'Good. I knew you were a smart guy. Now, you haven't told anyone about our chat, have you?'

'No.'

'Your wife, the police?'

'No.'

'You're not lying to me? Because those pictures' — he sucked air through his teeth — 'I mean, that kind of thing, you wouldn't want *anyone* to see that.'

'I haven't. I swear.' The voice was quick and panicky.

'Then relax, brother. This will all be over soon. Here's how it's going to go.' Bennett gave him an address. 'Let's see you there in twenty minutes.' He hung up before the guy could respond, then slouched in his seat and watched the front door.

Two minutes later, the doctor hurried out, one hand pulling keys from his pocket. The other held a duffel bag in fingers clenched bloodless. Bennett let the doc get in his Town Car and spin out of the lot. Didn't follow, just waited and watched. No squad cars followed, no unmarkeds roared to life.

When the clock on his dashboard said that ten minutes had passed, he dialed the phone again. 'Where you at, Doc?'

'I'm on the way. You said — '

'Changed my mind. Why don't we meet at your office in' — he pretended he was looking at a watch — 'five.'

'But I'm ten minutes — '

'Drive fast.' Bennett hung up.

64

It took more like seven, but when the Town Car hit the lot, the tires were squealing and the engine was roaring. Again, no sign of anybody following.

Bennett let the doctor park, then slid out of his car and started over. He had that hyperalertness that always came with a deal, the feeling he could see in seven directions at once, breathe jet fuel instead of air. He knocked on the passenger-side window and enjoyed seeing the man jump.

After the guy collected himself enough to unlock the door, Bennett slid in. 'Hey, Doc. How was your day?'

The man just looked at him. His nose had gauze packed in the nostrils and tape across the bridge. His fingers gripped and released the steering wheel.

'Rough one, huh?' Bennett smiled. 'We're almost done.'

The man nodded, started to reach for the bag.

'Not so fast. Let's get out of here.'

'Where?'

'Take a ride. First, though, do me a quick favor.' Bennett jerked his head. 'Hike up that shirt, would you?'

'My shirt?'

'Yeah. I hear swimming is good exercise. Want to check out your muscle definition.'

'Listen, I did what you wanted, but this is getting ridiculous.' The man trying to take control back.

Bennett smiled, shrugged. 'OK. Well, nice seeing you.' He reached for the door handle.

65

'No! Wait.' The man grimaced, then untucked his shirt and pulled it up to show his bare skin. 'I told you, I didn't go to the police.'

'Can't be too careful.' Bennett gestured at the road. 'Let's go.'

It was after seven o'clock, and traffic was just beginning to thin. Bennett directed the doctor one street at a time, having him get on and off the highway, make sudden turns. He watched the mirrors. No one.

God, he loved predictable people.

'OK. You know how to get to O'Hare from here?' Bennett leaned forward, turned on the radio. Scanned the dial — crap, crap, car commercial, crap, the Beatles. He put a foot on the dash, lowered his window, and reclined the seat a notch.

As they neared the airport, the doctor said, 'About those pictures. I never did anything like that before. It was . . . I don't even know why I did. I was just . . . curious. Wasn't thinking. I swear to *God*, though, I've never done anything like that before. I'm begging you.'

'You do what I wanted?'

'Yes.'

'And didn't fool around? Try to make something a little different, figure I won't be able to tell?'

'No, I swear.'

'Long-term parking.'

'Huh?'

'Head for long-term parking.'

The man nodded. 'I love my wife. My daughter. More than anything.'

66

Bennett cocked an eyebrow.

'I know. I *know*. It was stupid. I just. It's a weakness. A compulsion. It's not my fault, something I would choose.'

'Go up to the top level.'

'If I have to pay for what I did, that's fine. I just don't want anyone to know.'

'Park over there, in the empty part.'

The doctor pulled in, killed the engine. 'I'm sorry. I'm so very sorry.'

'I believe you, Doc. And if you did what I wanted, everything will be fine. You've got my word. So' — Bennett jerked his thumb toward the backseat — 'I'm going to ask one last time. Did you get clever with me? Admit it now, I'll give you an opportunity to make good. But if it turns out that you messed with me . . . '

The man was shell-shocked, eyes red and nose swollen. 'I made what you asked for.'

'Then your worries are over.'

Even with one window down, the shot was deafening in the closed confines of the car. The bullet took him right in the temple, passed straight through, and shattered the driver's-side glass, spattering the car door with gore. Bennett didn't waste time looking around, just wiped the gun off, wrapped the man's dead hand around it, then dropped both to the seat. The gun bounced and slid to the floorboards. Bennett set three photos in the doctor's lap, then wiped off the radio dial, took the duffel from the back, and started for the terminal. Kept an easy pace, just a businessman on his way to a flight. He opened his cellphone, dialed.

'Yello?'

'Crooch. It's me. We're on. Be ready Tuesday night.'

'Yeah, listen, about this. I don't know, man. I'm having second thoughts.'

'What's not to know? It's simple.'

'If it's so simple, why don't you do it?'

'Ahh, Croochy, you're looking at it the wrong way.'

'How's that?'

'You're missing the opportunity. This is a painless way for you to settle up with me. Just run an errand, drop off one bag, pick up another. That's it. And in return, think of the weight off your shoulders. Do right Tuesday night, come Wednesday morning, your worries are over.'

'And we'll be square? Clean?'

'Absolutely, brother.' Bennett smiled. 'You got my word.'

6

Coming off a double, bone freaking tired, the first thing Alex noticed when he came home was that the light on his answering machine was blinking again.

Not much sleep the last couple nights, and that filled with dreams of Cassie handing him stacks of hundred-dollar bills, of strange dark rivers and the sound of waterfalls, of flying that turned to falling. All he wanted was a big vodka, a shower if he could summon the will, and bed, where if he was lucky the pillows might still smell like Jenn.

He walked to the machine, almost hit Play, picked up the phone instead. Pressed the Caller ID button, then the back arrow.

Trish.

Alex stomped into the kitchen. Glass, ice, vodka. He took a long sip, felt the muscles in his back unclench. Took another, then refilled the glass, tucked the bottle back next to the frozen pizzas.

Over the past few days, she'd left a couple of messages. He'd checked them just to make sure Cassie hadn't been hurt, but hadn't otherwise responded. They'd all been terse little things, and the tone had scared him.

The street light outside his front window brought a globe of tree limbs into brilliant relief, the leaves bright green near the light, then fading to brown and gray and finally black as they moved outside the circle. He had this theory that life was kind of like that. A circle of now that could be seen clearly, and then a past and future fading out, growing disconnected. When he thought back to earlier versions of himself, he could remember things, moments, some of them crystal clear. Birthdays in the backyard. Shooting hoops in his driveway, the smell of tangled forsythia bushes that backed the hoop, the warmth of the sun, the clean ease of stretching for a rebound. But it felt so far away that it wasn't even just like it hadn't happened to him, it was like it had happened to someone that a friend had told him about. Two degrees removed.

The foursome was a perfect example. He, Jenn, Ian, and Mitch had started as a lark, a random evening that had been a surprising amount of fun. That evening led to another, and another. And after a while, he'd realized that the friends you saw every week were your best friends, and that the people you were in the habit of considering your best friends actually belonged to a past life.

We're all living in our own globe of light. Seeing just so far and thinking that's all there is. The vodka shivered through his chest. He took another gulp and pressed Play.

'Alex, it's me.' A pause. 'Are you there? Pick up.' A sigh. 'I know you're dodging my calls . . . ' Her voice was more trickling out than sounding pissed, and that hit him, put him in mind of old conversations, late at night, her head on the

70

pillow next to his. There had been times when they made sense, the two of them.

'OK.' Her voice firmer, her get-things-done tone. 'I have something to tell you. I was going to when you picked Cassie up, but she interrupted . . . ' She paused again. 'Damn it, Alex, why are you making me do it this way? Can't we be grown-ups for once?'

Standing in the dark of the apartment he lived in alone, Alex felt something tangle sticky fingers in his stomach. He leaned over the desk, head right above the answering machine, like he could talk to her through it, convince her not to say whatever she was about to.

'If this is the way we have to do it, fine. Scott got offered a job. It's a big promotion, he'll be leading his team, and . . . well. It's in Phoenix.'

The spectral fingers clenched tighter.

'He's going to take it. It's too good an opportunity. We're still working out the details, but it looks like we'll be moving there.' She cleared her throat. 'That's not true. It doesn't look like it. We're moving, the three of us.'

Alex clenched the edge of the desk so hard the wood bit into his skin.

'I know it's far, but it's not like you won't see Cassie anymore. We'll figure something out. You can come anytime you want, and maybe part of the summer she can stay with you. Thanksgiving. Something.'

No, he thought and was surprised to realize he'd spoken aloud.

'I know that's not what you want to hear,' she said, like she'd heard him. 'And I'm sorry. But I'

71

— she paused — 'I spoke to my father's lawyer, and he said that because you've been having trouble with the child support, we're in the clear. Not that I want to get legal, but he said that if it came to that, given the money you've missed, and because Scott and I are married and providing a home to Cassie . . . ' She stopped. 'I hate this. You knew I wanted to talk to you. But you've been doing that thing you do, sticking your head in the sand hoping that will keep things from happening. Just like still working at that stupid bar, all these years later.' She hesitated, spoke with a gentler tone. 'Anyway. We'll be heading out in a couple of weeks. They need Scott right away, and he doesn't want to be away from us. Of course, you can see Cassie before then, a couple of times maybe.' There was a long pause, and she said, 'I'm sorry. Call if you want to talk. I'm sorry.'

Then the fumbling sound of her hanging up, and the machine beeped.

Alex stared. The fingers in his gut had tightened into a fist. His hands were shaking. Phoenix. Phoenix! They couldn't do that. Take his baby girl and move halfway across the country, they couldn't. Yeah, OK, he'd missed a couple of payments, been late on some others. But he wasn't a deadbeat. He'd been working his ass off, hadn't made one forward step in his own life because half of what he made went to Cassie. That lawyer of Trish's — not hers, her father's. Alex remembered the lawyer, a bland man with glasses and a shirt so white it shone, working the system so the child support was staggeringly high, telling him he was lucky that Trish still cared, that she was being so generous with custody, that —

He grabbed the answering machine in both hands and yanked, feeling the tension and then the delicious snap of the cords as he hurled it at the wall. It flew like a discus, hard and straight, and cracked a jagged hole in his drywall before falling to the ground, the cover breaking off. He wanted to go over and jump on it, stomp on the thing until it was just parts, until he ground the parts into his carpet. He stood flexing and opening his fists, a man alone in the dark of a lousy apartment.

This couldn't be happening. It just couldn't.

Leaving the vodka glass sweating on his desk, he opened the door and stepped outside.

★ ★ ★

Jenn was on a motorcycle, not a Harley, but one of those low Japanese numbers, what her brother had called a crotch rocket. Leaning into it, the pulse of the thing thrumming in warm vibrations through her body. Zooming on an open road, so fast the striped line turned solid as she raced toward an indigo horizon. There was a pounding sound, a thumping, maybe something from the bike, but she just leaned harder, went faster, the wind streaking her hair behind. The thumping came again, and she fought it, cranked the throttle harder —

And woke up curled sideways in her bed, a pillow squeezed between her thighs. Blinked at

73

the green light of the clock: 4:11. The pounding came again, a real sound. The door. Someone was at the door.

It was enough to make her sit up straight, the sheet slipping from her shoulders. The hammering came again, loud and insistent. She sat frozen for a moment, an animal reaction, part of her wanting to bolt and scurry.

Relax. She swung her legs off the side of the bed, reached underneath for the Louisville Slugger. The heft of it made her feel better. She padded barefoot out of the bedroom, her thoughts straightening as she moved, and by the time she looked out the peephole, she already knew who it was. Jenn lowered the bat, then unlocked the dead bolt and opened the door half-way.

Alex loomed in the hallway, seeming bigger than normal. The yellow lighting gave his skin a sallow tone, but his eyes were furiously alive, bright and wide and bloodshot. He stared at her. She was suddenly conscious of how she looked, worn cotton pajamas and a baseball bat, hair tangled with sleep.

'Let's do it,' he said.

She crossed her arms over her breasts. 'That's romantic.'

'Not that.' He took a step forward. 'The money.'

'What?'

'Let's screw Johnny Love.'

She rubbed at her eyes. Thoughts quick with adrenaline moments before now seemed sluggish. 'It's four in the morning.'

'They're taking Cassie.'

'Who is?'

'My ex and her new husband.'

'Alex — '

'Can I come in? Just to talk.'

She stared at him, thinking of the evening she'd already endured. The blind date that was nice enough but smelled like an aquarium; three hours of talk that got smaller by the minute. She thought of her bed, a cocoon of warm blankets, and the dream of the motorcycle, flying fast over smooth blacktop. Imagined spending the remainder of the night fighting yawns while Alex babbled about another woman.

'Please?'

She sighed, leaned the bat in the corner. 'Come on. I'll make coffee.'

The kitchen lights seemed particularly brilliant with night pressing against the windows. She gestured to a stool, pulled filters from a drawer, poured coffee from the bag in the freezer.

'Trish called tonight. Her new husband got a job in Phoenix. They're moving there, and taking Cassie.'

'Can they do that?' She held the pot under the faucet.

'Apparently. I've missed some child support payments, and I guess that gives them the right.' He paced behind her, stalking the cage of her kitchen. 'I miss a couple of bills, and they take my girl from me.'

She set the pot on the base and flicked the machine on. It gurgled and hissed. 'You want a drink, something else?'

He shook his head. 'I've been drinking all night. Since I got the message. Can you believe that? She left it on my answering machine. I'd just got home from working a double' — he made a sound in his throat, blew air through his nostrils — 'Anyway, I've been trying to figure how to stop her. Thinking all kinds of crazy things.' His motion fast, hands running across his shaven head. 'Like going over right now, grabbing Cassie, taking off.'

'Alex, no — '

'I know. I *know*. But she's my daughter. All I've got. Anyway, I figured a better way. The child support. All I have to do is pay, and they can't do this. Her husband wants to move, let him, and Trish too. Cassie can move in with me.'

'Does it work that way?'

'What?'

'Can you just pay the late child support and then — '

'Of course. That's the only thing they've got. I pay that, she can't just move away.'

Jenn gave a non-committal sort of nod. That didn't sound right, didn't make a lot of sense, but she didn't see any point in saying so. She wasn't a lawyer, it wasn't her business, and she didn't particularly like talking about his wife. Ex.

'So all we have to do is get the money — '

'Alex.' She spoke firmly.

'What?'

'Sit down.'

He opened his mouth, then closed it, and moved to perch on the stool. 'Sorry. I must sound crazy.'

'Little bit.'

'I'm just . . . I love that girl, Jenn. I love her more than anything. They can't take her from me.' His expression so earnest it had sharp edges.

'One step at a time. How much money are we talking?'

'I don't know. Enough. If they added everything over the years, too much. Her lawyer is slick, probably got it figured to the penny with interest.' He laid his hands on the counter, palms down, fingers spread. 'More than I can come up with, even borrowing. Unless.'

'Unless you rob your boss.' She said it as flatly as possible.

'I've been thinking ever since Ian suggested it. Because he's right, you know? Johnny *is* a bad guy. He's exactly what's wrong with the world. He breaks the rules — the ones that are really supposed to matter — and gets away with it. And people like you and me, we end up drinking in his bar. Calling him Mr Loverin.'

'Think about what you're saying. You're talking about robbing a drug dealer.'

'Ex-drug dealer. He's not a tough guy now. A middleman, maybe, but so what?'

'What if you get caught?'

'We won't.'

'It's still stealing.'

'So what?'

'You're not making any sense, Alex.'

'Come on,' he said, and leaned across the counter. 'I know you were thinking about it. I could tell. You were excited.'

She shrugged. 'It was a game. Thinking about it was fun.'

'It was more than that. Remember what you said? How you'd been looking for adventure? Well, here's your chance.' He wore his cowboy smile. That smile was probably the reason she'd first decided to sleep with him. She'd cloaked it in rationality: They were friends, consenting adults, and there was nothing wrong with finding a little pleasure in each other. But truth was, it had been the smile. That and his wrists, which were at once thick and graceful, like a gymnast's.

The coffeemaker hissed. She took a couple of mugs from the cabinet, poured carefully, surprised to realize that she was a little turned on. Not in a wanting-to-do-it kind of way. Something subtler. She'd read a novel once where a lonely woman took off her panties and drove a convertible too fast through the desert, wearing a sundress and no underwear and chasing the sensation of being alive. It was that kind of feeling.

'Think about it. We do this one thing, a real-life adventure. We all get not rich, but ahead. A chance to do the things we said we wanted to. You could go on that trip, spend a month in the islands. Maybe we'll go together.'

'Maybe I'll go alone.'

He smiled again, said, 'Everybody wins. I get what I need to keep my daughter. Ian gets his money, Mitch gets his revenge, and you, you get — '

'I look like a windup toy?'

'Huh?'

She blew steam off her coffee, then sipped at it. 'You want to rob your boss, rob your boss. Why come here at four in the morning and try to manipulate me?'

'I'm not trying to manipulate — '

'Don't.' She set the mug down, brushed her hair back behind her ears. 'Don't.'

'All right.' He ran his tongue around the inside of his lip, making the skin bulge. 'I need you.'

'We're not doing this.' She straightened.

'No,' he said. 'Not like that. I mean I need you to pull it off. If I try it alone, Johnny's going to figure it was someone who works for him. But if all four of us do it . . . '

'Why four?'

'One keeping watch, two to do the robbery, and me on duty, looking perfectly above board. But you're the key. I know Ian is up for it. I think he's got some sort of money trouble. That shiner, things he's said. But Mitch.'

'You think he'll do it if I do.'

'I know he will.'

'Even if you're right, and I don't know that you are, and even if I'd be willing to exploit that, which I'm not, why should I?'

'Because it's an adventure. Because you don't want to turn into your mother. Because you're too hungry for life to pass up something this easy. Because you could help me keep my little girl. Because Johnny Love is a drug-dealing asshole. But that's all secondary. You want to know the two best reasons?'

'Sure.'

'I figured out the perfect way. A way that no

one, *no one*, will ever guess it was us.'

'What's the other reason?'

'Because you want to.' He smiled at her, and she felt something in her stomach roll as she realized he wasn't wrong.

7

Something was up.

Mitch couldn't put his finger on it. On the surface, everything seemed OK. Ian deciding to host an impromptu dinner had been a surprise, but not a startling one. His building was a trip; thirty stories of gray brick and wrought-iron perched at the bend in the river and surrounded by skyscrapers. Through the floor-to-ceiling windows, the city gleamed close and bright, the skeletal frame of the unfinished Trump Tower near enough to chuck a beer bottle at.

When Mitch had arrived, it was Jenn who opened the door, looking dynamite, pale arms glowing through the gauzy black sleeves of her shirt thing. He'd held up a bottle of red the guy at the liquor store had said was decent, then given her a hug, trying not to linger over the smell of her hair.

'Just in time,' she'd said. 'Ian's about to kebab Alex.'

As if in response, a jovial yell echoed down the hall. 'Mitch, thank God. Would the two of you get this asshole out of my kitchen?'

Alex wandered out, smiled, shook his hand. 'I swear, he's an old woman. Just needs an apron.'

They poured the wine and moved to the living room, chatting in front of the windows, That was when the feeling first hit. It reminded him of the way his parents had acted in the months before they told Mitch they were getting divorced. A sort of forced cheer. Alex talked more than usual, laughed a little too hard at a joke Mitch had heard at work. Jenn nursed her wine and stared out the window. He was just about to ask what was going on when Ian announced that dinner was ready.

He may have been touchy about his kitchen, but the dude could *cook*. They started with a warm spinach salad with some sort of cured meat fried crispy, followed by a risotto with gorgonzola and then blackened swordfish. But Mitch noticed that while everyone else attacked the food, Ian mostly pushed his around the plate, restless to the verge of twitching. How much coke was the guy doing? Mitch had tried it once, years ago, liked it OK, but he couldn't imagine being wired to want the feeling all the time, like drinking ten espressos while socking yourself in the mouth.

Still, the food was great and the wine was flowing, a second bottle empty by the time they finished. Alex pushed his plate back, slapped his stomach. 'Damn. I guess all that stainless steel in your kitchen makes a difference.'

'It's not the hardware. I'm just that good.'

'Modest, too.'

'How's your eye?' Jenn asked.

'I'm starting to like it.' The swelling hadn't lessened, and now shades of yellow and sickly green crept around the purple rim of the bruise. 'Makes me look tough, don't you think?'

She snorted. 'Boys.'

They fell silent, one of those moments. Alex

opened a new bottle and refilled their glasses, holding by the bottom and twisting professionally when he was done.

'I've got one,' Ian said.

'One what?'

'Ready-Go question. What would you do with fifty grand?'

'Foul. We did that the other night.'

'That was five hundred. This is different. Go.'

Alex spoke slowly and deliberately. 'I'd make up the child support I owe so my ex-wife couldn't take my daughter from me.'

'Your — what?' Mitch glanced back and forth. 'Your ex is trying to take Cassie?'

'Yeah. To Arizona.'

'Can she do that?'

'Sure,' Ian said. 'She's the mother, providing a home, and with missed child support payments . . .'

'What about you?' Alex's voice was hard. 'What would you do?'

Ian gave one of his cryptic smiles. 'Oh, just pay some bills.'

'I bet. The late fees look like a bitch.' Alex tapped his forefinger below his eye.

'I told you, I tripped. Jenn?'

'I'd start by quitting my job. Take some time to figure out what I want to do with my life.'

'What's wrong with your life?' Mitch felt like he was on a cellphone with bad reception, his questions coming a second too late, the rhythm all wrong. There were undercurrents of meaning that he didn't understand, agendas he wasn't privy to.

'How about you, Mitch? What would you do?'

'What is this? What are you talking about?'

Ian cracked his knuckles one at a time. Alex kept his eyes steady, a challenge.

Fifty thousand. Did that mean something? Why would they be talking about —

'Are you *kidding* me?' His voice came out higher than he meant. 'Fifty thousand. You saw a couple hundred in the safe. That's what this is about, isn't it? That split four ways. You're talking about robbing the bar.'

Alex shook his head. 'Not the bar. Johnny.'

'What's the difference?'

'You know the difference.'

'You're joking, right?' He looked from one to the other.

'No,' Jenn said. 'No, we're not.'

'I figured out a way to do it,' Alex said. 'It's safe.'

Mitch had a gentle buzz softening the edges of things, making him a little slower than he'd like. 'You've been planning this? The three of you?'

'We weren't keeping it from you. I just talked to Jenn last night. Ian this morning.'

'If you talked to her last night and him this morning, how exactly is that not keeping it from me?'

Alex leaned forward. 'Listen, before you react, will you hear me out?'

Mitch stared, flushing from the wine and the old junior-high feeling of being an outsider, of everybody looking and pointing. He leaned back, set his napkin on the plate. Finally, he nodded.

'It was really your idea.'

84

'*My* idea?'

'You got me thinking the right way. I talked about quitting and taking the money, and you said it would be better to do it while I was working, so it wasn't obvious.'

'I was kidding.'

'Still, you were right. But just being there isn't enough. There has to be absolutely no way it can come back on us. If I'm at the bar, I'm a suspect like everybody else.'

Mitch rocked his chair back. Finally said, 'OK. Against my better judgment.'

'We don't do it any old night I'm working. We do it Tuesday. The night Johnny is doing his deal. The night I'm working as his bodyguard,' Alex said. 'In other words, don't just rob Johnny Love. Rob him while I'm protecting him. *And rob me, too.*'

'I get it. If we tie you up right next to him — '

'Maybe even hit you,' Ian interjected.

'Then it looks like outside people, thieves, heard about the deal.'

'You're warm.'

Mitch paused, then got it. 'Better. It looks to Johnny like the guys he was dealing with decided to rip him off. And the same in reverse.'

'Those books you read are paying off,' Alex said. 'Exactly. The timing is tight, but it's worth it.'

'Except for one thing.'

'What's that?'

'We're not criminals.'

The big man's smile widened a notch. 'Exactly.'

'Huh?'

Ian said, 'That's just it. We're not criminals. We're normal people. No one, not the cops, not Johnny, *no one* would look at us. It's like if four people robbed a liquor store down the street. Would you start by checking to see if a trader, a travel agent, a doorman, and a bartender were involved?'

'And you know the best thing?' Alex leaned back. 'You'll like this part. Two days later we show up calm as anything, like normal. Just four folks who meet on Thursdays.'

Despite himself, Mitch laughed. 'Only the drinks are on Johnny.'

'For a long time.'

They fell silent. An almost physical tension hung over the table. From the speakers, a voice serenaded that nothing mattered when they were dancing, whether in Paris or in Lansing. Lights flickered on in a room in the opposite building. 'How would we — how do we — '

'Simple. You and Ian come in the back. I'll make sure it's unlocked. The kitchen staff leaves it that way all the time anyway. You wear masks, come in hard and fast, guns out — '

'*Guns?*'

'And cow us both. Ian, you're right — it would look better if you hit me. I'll make a move to stop you, one of you club me. Tie us up, take the money, head out the back. Jenn will be waiting in the car. Poof.'

'And you?'

'Eventually someone will come and untie us. Johnny will be pissed, but he won't call the cops.

He won't want them digging around. And since there's nothing to connect us, it doesn't really matter how he goes about getting his revenge.'

'And life just goes on.'

'Easy as breathing.' Alex sipped his wine. 'See any flaws?'

'Not offhand.'

'Me either.' Alex said. 'It's not the kind of thing any of us would normally do, but that's part of what's so brilliant about it.'

'And you're serious.'

'Yeah.'

'So what, you want me to say right now, sure, let's rob your boss?'

'I know it's scary. But the meeting is the day after tomorrow, and we go then or not at all. And I can't do it alone. So, yeah, right now, all of us. In or out.' Alex paused, then said, 'Ian?'

'In.'

'Jenn?'

She smiled slightly, the skin around her eyes crinkling. 'Me too.'

'*Really?*'

'Yeah,' she said. 'He who risks nothing has nothing, right?'

'How about it, Mitch?' Alex spoke gently. 'Want to screw Johnny Love?'

He looked around the table, at Ian's fingers piano-tapping on the table, Jenn with the corner of her lip drawn in, Alex waiting. Then he said, quietly, 'No.'

Alex seemed surprised. Smug fucker. No wonder there had been a weirdness to the air all night. They'd all been waiting to run through the formality of roping in good old Mitch. 'No,' he said again. 'This is stupid.'

'Why?'

'Because . . . *because*, man. What do you mean, why? This isn't one of our games.'

'Treat it like one.'

He shook his head. 'I'm not doing it, and I'm not going to sit here and let you try and convince me.' He said the words without thinking, and they fell heavy. There was a moment of silence, and then really only one thing to do. He stood slowly, pushing his chair back as the others watched. The music kept playing, the carefree notes weirdly incongruous to the situation.

Alex said, 'OK. I understand.'

'Good.'

'Can you do us one favor?'

'What?'

'Just keep quiet about it, OK?'

'You're doing it anyway?'

The three of them looked at one another, and one by one, nodded. That feeling of being an outsider bit deeper. All along he'd thought they were a team. Now the others were going ahead without him. The thought was almost enough to make him sit back down, but his pride burned. 'Fine.'

Alex looked at Jenn. 'We're going to need you inside.'

She nodded. 'What about the car?'

'We'll leave it out back, doors unlocked, keys in. Whoever gets in first drives. It's riskier, and we won't have a lookout, but that's the way it is.'

Mitch stared, unbelieving. They were so calm,

so matter-of-fact. The plan sounded good, but what plan didn't? To actually do it, go in waving guns? Not only that, but for Jenn to be right in the thick of it . . .

They're playing you, said a voice in his head. *Alex is, at least. He's counting on your feelings for her.*

So what? asked another voice. *She'll still be there.*

He opened his mouth, realized he had nothing to say. Just stood, palms sweating, watching his friends walk away from him.

'We'll need masks,' Jenn said. 'And gloves.'

'Yeah.' Alex paused, looked up at him. 'Look, Mitch, don't take it the wrong way, but maybe it would be better if you didn't hear this.'

It was all messed up. Somehow the whole world had turned upside down.

And suppose they pulled it off? Would the four of them ever go back to being what they had been? He'd have drawn a line, stepped away. He could see it, a slow-motion tease of the future. For a while they would still get together on Thursday nights. But the brunches, the dinners, the hanging out, one occasion at a time they would 'forget' to invite him. He'd never be able to get with Jenn, tell her how he felt, not after this. Once again Alex would look like the hero, tall and muscular and decisive.

He thought back to that pudgy asshole laughing at him. Holding up his ring, talking about how much his shirt cost. One more person certain he could put Mitch in his place.

'It's OK.' Jenn gave him a shallow smile. 'Really.'

He stared at her. Had a weird feeling he'd only gotten once or twice in his life, the sense that he was facing a clear fork in the road. Go left, go right, either way, never stand here again. Either enroll in community college or else take the job his uncle had lined up for him as a doorman; good money in tips, just something to do for a little while. Watch ten years pass in a blink.

'We'll need clothes,' he said. 'Not our own. We should get them at a thrift store, so they're used. And shoes too.'

'Mitch?' Alex raised an eyebrow.

'Different sizes than we wear. Double up socks, or jam our feet into them. Also used. That way they'll have different wear patterns.'

'Wear patterns?'

'The marks on the bottom. If we leave footprints, they won't match our shoes either in size or marking.'

Jenn was staring at him, something happening to her smile. Depth and warmth filling in what had been a façade. Depth and warmth and maybe, just maybe, a little bit of admiration.

He pulled out his chair and sat back down.

'You sure about this?' Alex spoke quietly. 'If you're in, you're in. No backing out.'

'Fuck you.' Saying it, he felt cool, strong. He stared the bigger man down. Alex leaned back, raised his hands.

'OK,' Ian said. 'What else?' He had the same sparkle in his eyes as when he'd talked about playing blackjack, splitting nines all night.

'A lot of little details,' Alex said. 'And one big one. We need guns.'

'No other way?' Jenn asked. 'What about knives?'

'No. The point is to scare him silly and act fast. He's not going to be scared of a couple of guys with steak knives. Not for the kind of money we're talking.' He paused. 'What about those replicas that shoot pellets? They look real. There's even a law they need to have a big orange tip because cops were shooting kids. We could buy a couple, paint the front part . . . ' Alex trailed off.

'What about a gun fair? They still have those in the South, don't they?' Jenn looked around. 'We could take a road trip.'

The discussion was so ludicrous that Mitch almost laughed. All that tough talk, all for nothing. Some criminals they were. Now that they came to the hard facts, it was obvious that they couldn't handle it. He relaxed, knowing the whole thing was about to be scrapped.

Then Ian spoke quietly.

'I can take care of the guns.'

8

Yeah baby yeah. It was on.

Ian had that magic tingle, the edge-of-life feeling, when for a second he could almost see past the world and into the machinery that ran it: the man behind the curtain, the gears that powered the watch, the silicone that made the model. Perfect how things had worked out. Just when life was getting a little too serious, wham, out of nowhere, this impossible opportunity. With a simple night's work, he'd be even. More than.

'Here is fine,' he said to the cabbie and passed a twenty forward.

'Here' was a Milwaukee Avenue corner too far south to be fashionable, a bleak stretch of shops with Spanish signs in the window offering financing no matter the credit. Tucked between a Popeye's Chicken and a payday loan place was a depressingly well lit bar. Half a dozen patrons sat in silence, ogling the back wall, where six-packs and fifths were available for purchase at liquor store prices. None of them even turned when Ian stepped in.

He glanced at the bartender, nodded, then walked through the back door and into a narrow vestibule. A security camera pointed from the corner, and he gave a two-fingered salute. For a moment, nothing happened. Then a buzz sounded from the steel-reinforced door in front of him, and he opened it and stepped through.

The room on the other side was done up with a simple elegance designed to seem luxurious and yet not so comfortable it invited lingering. No seating, a humidor but no ashtray, a side bar with glasses but no ice.

'Ian.' The girl behind the desk managed to make it sound like three syllables, a slow purr. She uncrossed and recrossed million-dollar legs. 'Back so soon?'

'Business this time.' He winked at her. 'The big man in?'

'Let me check.' She picked up a headset, held it to her ear, then pressed a button. 'Ian Verdon is here to see Mr Katz.' After a moment, she said, 'No problem.' She cut the connection, then hit Ian with her hundred-watt smile. 'Go ahead.'

'Thanks, D.'

'Want me to pull some chips for when you come down?'

'Nah. Not today.' He started for the stairs, readying his pitch. Katz would resist at first. He'd remind Ian of his debt, maybe play the tough guy to save face. But in the end, he'd go for it. Why wouldn't he? A simple business proposition.

There was another door with another security camera at the top of the stairs, and again he waited. This time, when it opened, it wasn't a swimsuit model on the other side, but a neckless black man, wings of muscles straining from shoulders to skull.

'Terry. How you doing?'

'My man Ian.' The man smiled, held a hand

93

up, and Ian clasped it, slid the fingers to lock, then pulled away with a snap. 'How's it goin', dog?'

'Life is beautiful. You?'

'Can't complain, baby. Can't complain.' Terry gestured him forward.

The room at the top of the stairs was everything the one below was not. Leather couches flanked a glass coffee table with an open bottle of Gran Duque and a marble ashtray. The air was rich with the smell of good tobacco. Four flat-screens mounted side by side showed horse races and a baseball game. He could curl up and spend the rest of his life here.

The man in the center of the far couch had thinning hair and a newspaper in his lap, a faded Navy anchor on one thick forearm and watery dark eyes. 'Ian.'

'Mr Katz. Thank you for seeing me.' Ian set his briefcase down, then sat and crossed his legs. 'Any surprises this morning?' He hooked a thumb at the televisions.

'One or two,' Katz said. 'You.'

His palms went slippery, but he held himself still. *Show respect, but not fear.* 'I've fallen behind.'

'It's out of hand.'

'I know. I appreciate your patience.'

Katz nodded. 'How's the eye?'

'It'll heal.'

'You understand my position.'

'Of course. You were doing what you had to.'

'I like you, Ian. You're a good customer. But you play recklessly. You bet too much, and at the wrong time. Normally, someone gets as deep as you, it would not be just an eye.'

'That's what I'm here about.'

'Good. Good.' Katz picked up his cigar and took a long puff, then blew expert rings. 'A man should pay his debts.'

'I agree.'

'The case is for me?'

'What?' Ian looked at it, then back up. 'No, I'm sorry. You misunderstood.' Katz's eyes narrowed, and Ian spoke quickly. 'I mean, I will pay you. That's what I'm here about. But I don't have the money yet.'

'No?'

'Not yet. But I'm going to get it.'

'When?'

'Very soon. The day after tomorrow.'

'How much?'

'All of it.'

Katz nodded warily.

'The thing is, I need a favor first. It's a small thing. In order to get your money, I need something from you.'

'You want me to loan you more money for gambling, no? Hoping to win back what you owe?'

'No. No, sir. I know better than that.'

'A lot of foolish people think they can.' Katz rolled his cigar between his fingers. 'So, then, this favor.'

'I have a way to get the money. But I need' — Ian paused — 'I need weapons.'

'I don't understand.'

'Guns. Two or three of them. I can return

them with the money,' he said, feeling foolish the moment the words were out of his mouth. The blast he'd taken before he arrived was wearing thin, his invulnerability fading. He hurried on, tongue thick in his mouth. 'I mean, if you want them. They won't have been used. Fired, I mean. But I need them to get the money from someone.'

Katz stared at him, the old Jew's face expressionless. He never played cards in any game Ian had heard of, but he had a hell of a poker face. Katz leaned forward and set his cigar in the ashtray.

Suddenly, Ian felt something behind him, a force like a moving brick wall. An arm shot around his neck, and he just had time to say, 'Terry, Jesus — ' before he was yanked upward, the muscles tightening around his neck, his air cut off as he was dragged backward halfway off the couch. His hands flew to the bodyguard's unwavering arm. His legs kicked as he fought for breath, eyes bugging.

Katz rose from the other couch. Normally a study in slowness, now the man moved in a blur. His hands went to Ian's shirt, fingers sliding inside the fabric. He yanked open the oxford, buttons flying to bounce on the glass table.

Ian tried to speak, couldn't get a word out, not a breath. Spots shimmered in the corners of his eyes. Katz moved to Ian's belt, fingers deftly undoing it, then tearing the catch of his pants and zipper. His trousers slid down his legs. Katz took hold of his underwear and jerked it down. Without any squeamishness or hesitation, he reached out to cup Ian's testicles, his fingers dry and cool as he lifted them, felt behind.

After a moment, he stepped back. 'Who sent you?'

The arm around his neck loosened a notch, and Ian gasped, sucking air into his lungs. He coughed, the shudders razors in his throat. 'Wh-what?'

'Who sent you? Not the police. Who?'

'No one! No one sent me. I swear to God.' His body was shaking. His hands fought for purchase against the slab of granite encircling his neck. 'What is this? Terry, let me go, what are you — '

'You come to me asking for guns. Why?'

'I need them to get your money. That's all, that's the only reason.'

Katz stared at him. He turned, picked up his cigar, sucked in, the cherry glowing bright red. When he replied, his words were smoke. 'You think I'm a fool.'

'No! Jesus, no.' Ian felt a flushing warmth in his belly, realized he was about to piss himself, barely shut it down. What had happened, how was he in this position, hanging half-naked from the arm of a bodyguard? 'I just need the guns to get what I owe you.'

'How?'

'There's a guy I know. He has a lot of money, cash, in a safe.' He knew he shouldn't say anything about the job, but the look on the old man's face . . . 'I'm going to get it from him.'

'You're going to rob him.'

'Yes.'

'You.' Katz snorted. 'A degenerate, a drug

97

addict in a suit. Who will be frightened of you?'

'It's . . . I won't be alone. My friends and I, we have a plan. I'll get your money, all of it. I swear.'

Katz stepped forward. 'These friends. Do they have the money you need?'

Ian stared. For a second, he almost lied, anything to get free, get out of here. But where would that lead? 'No.'

'But they'll help you.'

'Yes.'

'You know how much you owe?' Katz put one finger to his temple, tapped it. 'More than thirty thousand dollars. You know what I do to people who owe that kind of money and cannot pay?'

'Yes.'

Katz laughed. 'No. You think you do, but you don't.' He stepped forward. Put his right hand close to Ian's chest. The heat from the cigar a hairsbreadth away felt nice for a fraction of a second, then quickly began to burn. He wanted to struggle, but any motion might push his bare flesh against that glowing ember. He felt tears in his eyes.

'Mr Katz, sir, I will pay you every cent I owe. I swear I will. I *swear*.' He locked his eyes forward, the heat against his chest a living thing, so close, like it wanted to burrow into him.

'You have good friends,' Katz said, 'to help you this way.' He moved his hand, the cigar tracing a burning line down Ian's belly. 'Especially since you're not such a good friend. You know why? Because your friends, now they are part of your debt. You are not the only one who owes now.'

'No, I . . .'

'Shh.' Katz slid his hand down farther. The glowing ember of the cigar was a half-inch from his balls. Ian whimpered and squirmed.

'You know what happens now?'

'Please. Please. No.'

Katz smiled. 'No?'

'Please.'

'If I give you what you ask, what then?'

'I'll get the money. I'll bring it straight here. I swear to God.'

'You'll run.'

'I won't.'

'If you do, your friends . . . '

'I understand.'

'And if you get caught with these guns?'

'I will never say your name. No matter what.'

The man put his left hand against Ian's cheek. Slapped it softly twice, like a favorite uncle. 'Good. That's good.' Then his right hand shot forward. The searing tip of the cigar bit into a testicle.

The pain was shocking, unbearable in its suddenness. A terrible smell of scorched hair rose. Ian screamed and jerked, helpless as the ember burned deeper.

Then the cigar was gone, and Katz turned away. 'He is OK now, I think.'

The arm around his neck vanished, and Ian collapsed onto the couch. His hands went immediately to his crotch. He stared downward. The burn was the size of a quarter, the skin peeled and furious with ash and blood. He wanted to break down and cry, to call for his mother, to just vanish.

'Terrence. Three pistols for our friend. Make sure they're clean.'

Ian gasped for breath, his hands shaking. 'Mr Katz, I swear — '

'Enough swearing. We understand each other now. Right?'

'Y-Yes.'

'Good.' The man ground the cigar in the ashtray. 'My money. All of it. By Wednesday. Or' — he shrugged — 'for you and your friends.'

Katz bent, picked up Ian's briefcase. He popped the latches, then Terry set something metal inside. Katz shut the case and held it out.

With trembling hands, Ian reached for the handle. He rose slowly. His pants were pooled at his feet, and he bent to haul them upward. The motion sent fireworks of pain up his spine.

'Now. Go.'

Ian left.

The stairs were a blur, nothing but a hint of color. He held his pants closed with one hand, the case in the other. At the base of the stairs, the woman behind the desk said something that he didn't hear. He pushed past her to the vestibule and the bar. No one glanced up as he half staggered, half ran out the door into bright summer sunlight.

On the sidewalk, he looked in all directions, wild-eyed. A Hispanic couple stared.

Jesus, Jesus, Jesus. Get control!

He set down the case. The catch to his pants was broken, but his belt was still in the loops. He fastened it with fumbling hands. Pulled his shirt closed and tucked it in raggedly. Ian took a step, then the world went spinny. He grasped at the metal rim of a trash can and leaned over, acid in his throat, his mouth a desert. He fought for breath, struggling to keep from vomiting, shirt torn open, pain twisting through his belly.

No one seemed to notice.

9

There was enough space between the oncoming traffic and the double-parked cab to drive an eighteen-wheeler, but the jerk in the Lexus laid on his horn anyway, creeping past at two miles per. Why was it, Jenn wondered, that the people with the nicest cars were the worst drivers? Was it that they fetishized them and were afraid of any little ding? Or were they people who didn't feel all that safe to begin with, and figured an expensive car protected them somehow?

Whatever. She hadn't owned a car in years, and liked it fine.

She crossed mid-block, heading east. In high school, she and her friends used to come here, Clark and Belmont, to visit the head shops and thrift stores, play at being punks in the Alley. Back then Mohawks didn't draw a second glance, and most everyone had a biker jacket. Now it was expensive boutiques, the old army surplus rebuilt into a multistory chrome thing that belonged on the cover of *Architectural Digest*. Nice enough, but she missed the grimy feel the area used to have. Not truly dangerous, but fit for a little wild-side walking.

Speaking of . . .

The thought ambushed her again. Ever since Alex had showed up at her door, full of arguments and plans, every so often the reality of what they were doing would yank the world out from under her. She'd be going through her day, talking on the phone, helping a couple plan their honeymoon, sunlight through the front windows, everything normal, and then — *wham!* — all of a sudden she'd remember that tomorrow night she was going to be wearing a mask and holding a gun.

And each time it happened, a delicious shiver ran up her spine.

It was scary, sure. But in that good way. Sometimes she didn't want a guy to be gentle, to touch her softly and whisper in her ear. Sometimes she wanted him to shove her face-first on the mattress and slide into her hard, to have one hand yanking her hips back and the other twisted in her hair, to do it rough and fierce and primal, without all the gloss. To drive the bed across the floor and knock the books off the shelves. Maybe not the most feminist desire, but there it was.

The thrift shop was hipster heaven, complete with retro furniture, silly gifts — who actually wanted a Jesus action figure? — and punked-out counter staff, each posing harder than the last. She checked her purse with a girl sporting a twice-pierced lip, got a laminated picture of Chuck Norris in return, and moved to the racks of clothes.

After the dinner party, Alex had asked if she wanted to come up, and she'd almost said yes. The whole adventure had her charged, and while he was a good lover to begin with, under the circumstances, it would have been something else entirely. But in the end, she'd mumbled an excuse about needing sleep. It wasn't that she didn't want him; she did, on one or two levels. But it just didn't feel right anymore. It was like she'd been sleepwalking the last years. Now that she'd been slapped awake, she didn't intend to let that feeling go.

Jenn picked through the racks, looking for simple, dark clothing, unremarkable, settling on faded jeans and a couple of work shirts, the stitching worn. The shoe selection was limited, but it was easier buying footwear that purposefully wasn't supposed to fit.

Mitch had surprised her that night, coming up with good ideas, practical points they hadn't thought of. Not only that, but he'd pushed back against Alex, told him to fuck off. She wasn't one of those women turned on by chest beating, but it was good to see him stand up for himself.

Of course, he's doing this for you.

Not true, she argued with herself. Well, maybe a little bit true, but it wasn't like she had asked him to, had batted her eyes or put on a simpering voice. She'd even told him it was all right if he didn't want to go along, and she'd meant it.

Still.

Well, OK, so what? Certainly was a contrast to what she'd grown accustomed to, the emotional distance so many men cultivated. Alex was a good guy, but he'd gone out of his way to make sure they stayed a secret. It was kind of nice to have someone not just *wanting* her, but also doing something for her. Risking himself. Another feminist paradox — the last thing she

104

was after was a man who didn't respect her strength, but what woman didn't secretly relish knowing a guy would stand up if called on?

Enough. First things first. Once they were done with Johnny Love, once life had settled into a new version of normal, there would be plenty of time to think about Alex and Mitch. Or not. Meanwhile, she had to find a place that sold ski masks in the middle of summer.

The tingle hit again. She smiled.

★　★　★

The YMCA speakers were playing dance crap, but Alex had headphones on the Hold Steady singing how some nights the painkillers made the pain even worse. He leaned back on the bench, hands behind to catch the bar. He pressed it firm and smooth off the cradle and started his third set, the grip rough against his hands, timing each move to his breath, down slow, up smooth, no wavering or wobbling. The first ten were easy, the second ten a strain. He thought of the phone call from Trish, of her new husband moving to Arizona. And what was he supposed to do? Hang out here in a shitty apartment? Move to the desert, trailing after his ex-wife and her new husband like a puppy? Give up his daughter?

No. Lift. Goddamn. Lower. Way. Lift.

Working out calmed him, burned off the stress. He was in the mood to hit it hard, tear all his muscles and wake up with that good, deep ache, but tomorrow night was too important to be slow or hurting. He limited himself to another half hour, then showered and walked home through summer streets.

'Alex.'

The voice came from the darkness behind him, and he spun, the gym bag slipping from his shoulder. Squinted. 'Mitch?'

The man stepped away from the tree he'd been leaning against. 'We need to talk.'

'Jesus, you scared me.' He bent for the bag. 'Come on up.'

'No.' There was something unfamiliar in his tone. 'I'm not staying. You and me, we have to clear something up. I know what you've been doing.'

'Huh?'

'With Jenn.'

Shit. He thought they'd been careful, had kept it from everyone. Not that it mattered, exactly, but it had just seemed simpler to not make an issue of it. Jenn might fool herself, but he could see the size of the torch Mitch carried. The kid went all fifth-grade anytime she blinked.

Still, why bring it up now? Unless . . . double shit. If Mitch knew about him and Jenn, he might back out of tomorrow night. If he did, the others might too. The whole thing could fall apart. 'Listen — '

'No, you listen. I know you think you're the big man, our fearless leader, but that's bullshit. And I'm tired of you treating me like I don't exist.'

'What are you — '

'Using her to get me involved. You knew that I wouldn't let her go in there with just Ian to

106

protect her, and you used that.'

'Mitch — '

'Admit it.'

Alex sighed. 'Yeah.'

'That ends now. All of it. Trying to tell me what's what, that there's no changing my mind, that everything runs the way you want. Johnny Love may be your boss, but you aren't mine, or hers.' Mitch stepped closer, his face hollowed out by the streetlight above. 'You think you're such hot shit? You're a bartender, Alex. A bartender who can't pay child support.'

Confusion was turning to anger. 'Watch it.'

'Or what? You'll kick my ass? This isn't middle school. I'm smarter than you. And you need me tomorrow, and afterward.'

'Look, ease up. I didn't mean any harm. I just needed your help, man.'

'Yeah, well, I'm tired of being ignored, *man*. Tired of you thinking you're better than all of us. I'm going tomorrow night. But I'm not doing it for you, and I'm not doing it because you manipulated me. I'm doing it for me. And yeah, because I'm worried about Jenn. Something you ought to be as well.'

'I am.'

'Bullshit. You're only thinking of yourself.'

'I'm doing this for my daughter.'

'She's not my daughter.'

Alex took a deep breath. He had the strongest urge to tell Mitch where to cram the tough-guy act. But he couldn't risk it. Everything depended on tomorrow night. 'Is that it?'

'One more thing. You ever try to play me like

that again, you ever lie to me, and we're through. At very least.'

'What does that even mean?'

'It means that if you want to be my friend, start acting like one. Or I'll start acting like we're not.' With that, Mitch turned and walked away, a quick, nervous step.

Alex watched him go. Part of him wanted to run after the guy, apologize, remind him that they were buddies, that he was sorry if he'd been a dick. Another part wanted to tell Mitch about the noises Jenn made just before she came, the way she mashed her eyes shut and made soft, quick moans that barely left her throat. See how the guy liked that.

Get through this first. Then we'll see what's left to say.

Alex shouldered his bag, turned, and walked up the steps to his empty apartment.

★   ★   ★

The condo was cold, the AC cranked all the way. Ian sat on the couch in just a pair of briefs, a bag of frozen peas between his legs. The flat-screen was on HBO, some monster movie, a screaming heroine running down a long dark hallway. With the volume muted, it seemed almost existentially horrifying, the way her lips opened soundlessly as she stumbled and fell before getting up to stagger forward again.

Ian leaned forward, picked up the mirror, held it to his nose, sucked in a long rail of white, and then another in the same nostril. His left had

started bleeding earlier, and he had a Kleenex twisted into it, the end hanging out like a tail. He wiped the bitter coke residue on gums gone numb, then set the mirror on the coffee table. Beside it, three pistols lay in a neat line, the metal gleaming dull.

Outside the windows, the city burned.

10

'Jesus. You look amazing.'

Jenn smiled, gave a little curtsy, one thin arm holding the edge of her skirt. 'Like a Bond girl?'

'Like all of them,' Mitch said. 'Rolled into one.' The words came unplanned, and he had a sudden fear that they were the wrong ones. But her smile widened.

'Let's get to it,' Alex said from behind her. 'I have to be at work soon.'

Mitch followed them into the living room. Ian's condo was spotless as ever, something out of a magazine, except for the table in the center of the room, where masks and gloves were piled alongside a brown paper bag.

'Mitch,' Ian said. He wore baggy black jeans, a bowling shirt, and brown work boots. 'Thanks for suggesting the outfits. I look like an idiot.'

'You do not,' Jenn said. 'You should wear real-people clothes more often.'

'Suits are real-people clothes.' Ian gestured at the table. 'Yours are there. You can change in the bedroom.'

'Hold on,' Alex said. 'Let's see the rest of it.'

Ian walked to the table, picked up the bag, and held it out. For a moment, everyone stood still. Then Jenn stepped forward, reached in, and pulled out a chrome revolver. She looked hypnotized, the gun in her palm, fingers not quite wrapping around the grip.

'It's heavy,' she said.

Mitch stared at her. The dress she wore was designed at the intersection of elegance and sensuality, something he imagined a two-thousand-dollar-a-night call girl might wear, strappy to show off bare shoulders and cut to mid-thigh. With the gun in her hand and the intense look on her face, she was the single sexiest thing he'd ever seen.

'It's loaded,' Ian said. 'So be careful.'

'Where did you get them?'

'A guy I know.' Ian looked away.

'What kind of guy?'

'Does it matter?'

'OK,' Alex said. 'Jenn bought gloves and masks for all three of you. We went over everything the other night. No need to do it again, right?'

'Actually, I was thinking,' Ian said. 'The timing. Why don't we just go into the office and be waiting when Johnny comes in?'

'No,' Mitch and Alex said in unison. They looked at each other, a little smile playing on Alex's lips. He nodded a *go-ahead* gesture.

'No. Johnny might go into the office alone. You and I have to come in when he and Alex are both there. That's the whole point. Plus, if we're waiting, the safe will be locked.'

'So? We know the combo.'

'But how would we? It will get Johnny wondering. We can't afford that.'

Jenn said, 'How do we know that Johnny won't wait for these guys, whoever they are, to come in the front door of the restaurant, and then all of

111

you head back together?'

Alex shook his head. 'Not his style. Remember, he wants to be the big man. He'll wait back there. A king on his throne, granting an audience.'

'You sure?'

'Trust me.'

'If you're wrong — '

'If Alex is wrong, we won't do it,' Mitch said. 'The point is that there isn't much risk. None of us are going to be stupid about it. Right?'

Ian's eyes darted back and forth. 'Wait a second. We have to do this.'

'Why?'

Ian wiped at his nose with one shaking hand. 'Well. Yeah, you're right.'

Shit. Of course. Mitch stared at him, said, 'You OK?'

'What? Sure. I'm just, you know, excited.'

'Look, we do this right, it's simple,' Alex said. 'No danger to anybody.'

'Easy for you to say.'

'What?'

'Well, you're not the one robbing the place, are you?'

'I'm in this just as much as you.'

'Sure. We're carrying pistols, you're filling pitchers.'

'Fuck you, man.' Alex stared hard and level. Mitch made himself stare back. It felt good.

'Guys,' Jenn said. 'Stop. We're in this together.'

Alex turned. Mitch blew a breath. 'Yeah. Of course.'

'I better go.' The bartender bent, pulled his

112

jacket from the arm of a chair. 'I'll see you soon.' He walked to the door, pulled it open, then stopped, turned back. 'Good luck.'

Mitch started to say something sharp, then caught himself. Why was he coming on so hard? They were friends, the best he had. It was just the stress of the thing. 'You too, buddy.'

Alex smiled, nodded, then stepped out. The door swung closed behind him. For a moment, they stood in silence. Then Jenn closed her fingers around the grip of the pistol, extended her arm, and sighted down the barrel at the city.

'Bang,' she whispered.

★ ★ ★

The rental was a four-door Chevy that smelled new. It was also a bright metallic orange. 'Subtle,' Mitch said.

Ian shrugged. 'What they had.'

'I like it,' Jenn said. She opened the passenger door and slid in, tucking her skirt beneath her legs. Ian started the car and pulled out of his parking garage, fingers tapping a manic beat on the steering wheel. Nerves, she supposed. She knew she had them. Last night, laying in bed, she'd been socked with a tidal wave of fear. Miles from the pleasant shivers she'd been riding, this was pure, animal panic. She'd grabbed at the phone on the bedside table, started to punch numbers, to call the others and cancel.

It took all her will to hang up the phone, get out of bed, and walk into the bathroom to splash water on her face. And when she did, the woman in the mirror looked unfamiliar. She had the same cheeks, the same eyes and lips, but there was something different. She looked tired. Beat down. Someone who had never seized the chances life offered.

That won't be me. I won't let it.

So she'd forced herself back to bed and spent the rest of the night staring at the ceiling. And in the morning, the face in the mirror was just a face. But the nervousness remained.

In silence, they drove north, battling the after-work migration from the Loop to the neighborhoods. With traffic, it took almost half an hour to make it to the restaurant. Ian pulled to a stop and put on the blinkers. He was piano wire and static electricity.

Jenn sat with her purse in her lap. Her heart pounded fast and hard. She felt awake, slapped by life.

'It's not too late,' Mitch said from the back. For a moment, she wanted to collapse, to thank him. To climb gingerly back down the steps of the high dive and tell herself it didn't matter.

Instead, she reached for the door handle. Stepped out, heels clicking on the concrete. Mitch got out as well. His expression was complicated, concern and fear and something else. 'I'll be OK,' she said.

'Anything happens, anything at all . . . just be careful, OK?'

His concern touched her. He and Ian had the riskiest part of the plan, and yet here he was, worried about her. She stepped forward and kissed his cheek. He smelled like aftershave. She felt his arms tense, and then his hands slid around her back, fingers warm on her skin. For a moment they held it, then she moved back, not sure if she was embarrassed or not. 'For luck.'

He nodded, said nothing.

You're a Bond girl. You're a heartbreaker with a pistol in your purse. She forced a smile, then turned and walked toward the door.

★   ★   ★

Ian had tried to hold off. He wasn't an idiot. He knew he was doing too much of the stuff. But about twenty minutes before the others came over, he gave in and chopped up four lines. Just a little pick-me-up to sharpen his edge. When this was done, he'd ease off. Maybe quit entirely.

'When do you think they'll get here?' Mitch sounded nervous.

'Probably after dark?'

'They're meeting inside. What does it matter if it's dark?'

'I don't know. Isn't that when criminals do things?' Ian leaned forward, clicked on the stereo, then spun through his iPod. 'You in the mood for anything?'

'Am I in the mood for anything?'

'Music.'

Mitch stared at him, shook his head. 'Jesus.'

Neutral Milk Hotel it was, then. A little bit discordant with a lotta genius running through. Ian didn't have the first idea what the singer was talking about, but he liked it anyway, liked the

115

way it wove against his thoughts.

'How much did you do?'

'Huh?'

'How much cocaine, Ian?'

'You want some?'

'No.'

'Then mind your own business.' He tapped his fingers against the wheel, sang along, '*The only girl I ever loved, was born with roses in her eyes, but then they buried her alive . . .*' The light turned green, and he went right. They were swinging in wide blocks, circling the place every couple of minutes. 'Anyway, relax, would you? This is going to be easy.'

'Easy. Sure.'

'I'll bet you ten grand it goes fine.'

'I don't have ten grand.'

Ian smiled. 'You don't have it *yet*.'

★ ★ ★

Alex threw himself into work. Most bars, Tuesday night was quiet, but the restaurant did enough business that they got plenty of overflow, yuppie happy hour, Internet daters who started with a drink before deciding if the other was cute enough to buy dinner. He filled the ice bins and wiped the back bar, replaced a couple of bottles that were running low.

'Hey, stranger.' Jenn flowed into a chair. She looked better than good.

'You want a drink?'

'I probably shouldn't.'

'One won't kill you.' He reached for a shaker,

poured vodka, splashed vermouth.

She looked around, then leaned on her hand. Whispered, 'Is he here?'

'Talk normal. Yeah, he's in the back.'

'He say anything?'

'He fired a cook, then said that it was getting harder and harder to find good wetbacks.'

'What a peach.'

Alex shook her drink hard. Too many people thought you were just supposed to mix it, but the whole point of a martini was to shake till the ice cracked into tiny slivers. After a minute, he poured it into a glass, skewered a couple of olives, set them on top. 'Are you all right?'

'Of course,' she said, and smiled. She reached into her purse, pulled out a cellphone. 'So I programmed the message for the boys in advance. One line. It took, like, five minutes. Is it just me, or is texting the stupidest form of human communication ever invented?'

'I think that's MySpace.' He poured himself a shot of vodka, clinked glasses with her, tapped his against the bar, and then threw it back. A group of twentysomethings in shiny shirts came in, talking loudly, and he went to serve them. As he poured their drinks and made their change, he could barely hear the noise of the bar over the contrary thoughts jumbling in his mind, skidding and colliding like cars out of control.

He wanted to call the night off. He wanted the night to go forward, but for it to be over. He wanted to be twenty again, he and Trish and Cassie still together, a family, the future open and bright. He wanted to pull Jenn off the stool and take her in the back and yank the straps of that dress off her shoulders. He wanted a cigarette.

None of that matters. Only Cassie matters. This is just one more thing you have to do for her.

'Goddamn. There is such a thing as angels.' The voice pulled him from his trance. Johnny Love looked Mafia chic in an orange shirt with a paisley silk tie, his hair slicked back. He leaned on the bar next to Jenn like he owned the world.

'Johnny,' she said and smiled. 'Nice to see you again.'

'You too, sweetheart. Here for that dinner?'

'Not tonight. I just came to see Alex, have a drink.'

'You know, you're breaking my heart.'

'You look like a big boy.' She brushed her hair behind her shoulder. 'You can take it.'

Johnny laughed, gestured to her glass. 'You're empty.'

'That's OK — '

'Nonsense. Can't let a woman like you go thirsty.' He turned to Alex. 'Make her another, huh? Grey Goose, on me. Then let's go back to my office.'

The muscles of Alex's shoulders locked tight, and something soft traced the inside of his thighs. He fought the urge to look at Jenn. 'Sure.'

Johnny said, 'Forgive me, gorgeous, I got work to do. But stick around. Maybe we can have a drink together later.'

Alex picked up the shaker, his fingers numb on the metal. He didn't hear the rest of what

Johnny said to Jenn, didn't hear her responses. He focused on the cocktails. Hers was easy, but his — one part shit-scared, two parts resolved, a twist of a prayer, knock it hard and bang it back — that one was tough.

He set the martini down, then followed Johnny to the back room. At the door, he risked a glance over his shoulder. Their eyes locked as she reached for the cellphone.

Point of no return.

★ ★ ★

He knew it was probably nothing, but Mitch couldn't help but think of the way Jenn had kissed him. They hugged all the time, and she threw in a cheek kiss often enough. Just a friendly gesture. But this time, something had felt different. When he'd put his arms around her, he hadn't been hugging her like a friend. And she hadn't seemed to mind. Had, in fact, seemed to lean into it a little bit.

And that wasn't all. Ever since that night at Ian's, when he'd spoken up, took control, he'd felt strange in a good sort of way. Like something inside him was breaking loose. Standing up to Alex, the thing with Jenn, it was part of the same process. All of it tied to this thing they were doing, this crazy chance. Four normal people who had never won deciding to storm the casino. Could life really be that simple?

The phone in his pocket vibrated and he jumped like he'd been stung. He pulled it out and keyed the button to read the text.

The philosophical mood vanished like smoke. Jesus Christ. They were really doing this. He stared at the screen, blinking.

'What?' Ian looked over with wide eyes. 'What is it?'

Mitch could hear his pulse rage in his ears, feel his face begin to flush. This was going to go wrong. He knew it, felt it.

'Are we going?'

It had been a game until this second, but playtime was over. His lungs felt like they had a leak.

'Mitch?'

'Yes,' he said. 'We're going.'

Ian spun the car in a U-turn. A guy in a pickup heading the opposite way laid on his horn. Ian gave him the finger.

'Easy.'

'I'm easy.'

Mitch took a deep breath, then another. *Get it together. She's depending on you. They all are.*

He opened the glovebox, took out a pair of driving gloves. His fingers were sticky, and he had to fight to get them on. He set the mask in his lap, the black cotton staring up at him like a Halloween ghoul. Outside the windows, twilight was giving way to purple dusk, about as dark as the city ever really got. A group of teenagers hung on a corner, chatting and laughing, and for a stabbing second he envied them.

Envying teenagers? Now you know you're scared.

120

The thought made him smile inside, just for a second, but it helped.

They passed the restaurant. At the corner, they turned left, then left again into a narrow alley behind the building. Ian drove thirty yards to nose the car up to a rusting steel Dumpster, then killed the engine. The music died with it, leaving only the sounds of their breathing.

'Is this really happening?' Ian's face was pale.

Mitch rubbed at his temples with gloved fingers. Huffed a breath in, one out. Then he straightened, passed a mask and gloves to Ian. 'Here.'

'Are we — '

'It's too late now.' Mitch looked over. 'Just keep it together.' He opened the door and stepped out. The alley smelled faintly of rotten milk. The summer air was humid. He rapped on the trunk, waited as Ian fumbled for the release.

The brown paper bag holding the two remaining pistols looked harmless. Mundane. He glanced over his shoulder. Nothing. Latin music played faintly, tinny like it was coming through a cheap radio. He unrolled the top of the bag and took out one of the guns, a black automatic. He started to tuck it behind his belt, then froze. Pulled it back out, staring down at the unfamiliar metal in his hand.

And flipped the safety off.

As Mitch closed the trunk, through the rear window he saw Ian hold his hand to his nose. He wasn't — goddamn it, he was. He yanked the driver's-side door open. 'Give me that.'

'What? No — '

Mitch snatched the amber vial from his friend's hands. He wound up and threw it overhand down the length of the alley. It landed with a soft plink.

'What the fuck?'

'You're a moron, you know that?'

'Jesus, relax.' Ian stared up at him, one eye still swollen half-shut. 'I needed to be on my game.'

'You're stoned out of your gourd already.'

'I'm not. I just had a moment of panic, that's all.' He stepped out of the car. 'Give me my gun.'

'Leave the keys.'

'What?'

'The keys. Leave them in the ignition. Remember?'

'Right.' Ian bent back to insert them, then closed his door. They stared at each other, the ticking of the engine mingling with the distant music and the muffled sound of laughter. Mitch felt like he had stepped behind the world, like the world was a stage set and he'd wandered into the wings.

Does that make it the beginning of something? Or the end?

'Listen to me,' he said, and got in close to Ian's face. Anger gave him strength, and the strength felt good. He tapped into it again, the new-and-improved Mitch. 'You get your shit together right now. We're depending on you, Ian. All of us.'

The man stared back at him, something flickering in his eyes. Finally, he nodded. 'I'm sorry. You're right.'

This is crazy. What are you doing? Just get

*back in the car. If you don't go in, he won't, and
if he doesn't, nothing happens.*

Right, a different voice in his head replied.
Nothing happens. Is that what you want?

'Put your mask on,' he said and handed Ian
the second pistol.

★ ★ ★

'All right, kid.' Johnny Love unlocked the door to
the office. 'Now, like I said, this is going to be
child's play.' He flipped off the overheads, then
turned on a green banker's lamp. Dropping the
keys on the desk, he surveyed the room, then
adjusted the visitor's chair to its lowest point and
raised his to the highest. 'You got a shirt on
under that one?'

'What?' Alex touched his white oxford. 'Yeah.'

'Good. Take off the button-down. You're
supposed to look like muscle, not a parking
attendant.'

His hands tingled and his arms felt heavy, like
he'd ripped a serious set at the gym. He started
to undo the buttons, then remembered the part
he had to play. 'Mr Loverin, listen, you know
I — '

'Enough. I told you, this is nothing. You're a
showpiece.' Johnny sat, cracked his knuckles.

*A showpiece. We'll show you something,
asshole.* Alex undid the rest of the buttons,
pulled the shirt off, wadded it up, and tossed it
in the drawer of the file cabinet.

'Good. Those tats are good. You look tough.'
His back was to Alex as he spun the dials of the

123

safe. 'Now, tonight is business. What kind of business, you don't need to know. Point is, the guy coming in isn't going to try anything.' The safe swung open. He hauled out a heavy black duffel bag and set it beside the desk.

'So what — I mean, what do I —

'Jesus, kid, ain't you ever seen a movie?' Johnny sighed. 'He gets here, you open the door. You don't need to say anything. In fact, don't. You're mute. Just look mean. I'll say, you know, it's OK, he's a friend. Then you come around back here and stand behind me. We'll talk a little bit, do a little business. You stand there and think about something else. When we're done, I'll give you a couple of hundreds, you can take that daughter of yours out, buy her something nice.'

'What if he — '

'Just do what I tell you, OK?'

Alex shrugged. 'All right.'

'Attaboy.' Johnny put his feet up on the desk. 'So, what do you think? The Cubs got it this year?'

11

They moved down the alley side by side. Adrenaline throbbed in Mitch's blood; fear, yeah, but excitement, too, and something almost like hilarity. This afternoon he'd stood around in a monogrammed jacket saying yessir, thank you, sir, and now here he was about to steal a couple hundred thousand dollars.

The door was metal, scarred with rust and years. A sign below the address read DELIVERIES ONLY. Mitch reached for the handle, palms wet inside the gloves.

It was unlocked, just like Alex had promised. Inside, fluorescents lit the room surgically bright. Steel wire shelves held kegs and hoses, boxes of supplies. There were two doors, one a swinging wood thing that would lead into the bar proper, the other a cheap hollow-core. The latter should be the door to the office.

His shoes were two sizes too big, and the extra socks he wore to compensate made the heat worse. Ian already had his mask on, and Mitch pulled his from his pocket, slid it over his head. The cotton was warm and itchy against his skin. He took a careful step toward the office, then another. He could hear a voice through it, faint, saying, 'Bullshit. They aren't never going to make it happen so long as they play in Wrigley. No incentive, you know? Stadium sells out whether they win or not —'

Johnny Love. What an asshole.

Mitch pulled his gun from behind his back. Holding it made him feel better. Power seemed to flow from it like a totem. He put a hand on the knob.

For a second, he could almost hear Jenn's voice: *He who risks nothing, has nothing, right?*

Time to test that theory.

★ ★ ★

The door flew open hard, banged against the wall. Even knowing it was coming, it startled Alex, and he spun to see two men in dark clothes and masks, both with guns out and up.

'Don't either of you fucking move!' Mitch's voice, but not. He sounded like he did this all the time, his voice firm but not so loud it would bring people from the other room.

'What the — ' Johnny said.

'Shut the fuck up, fat man.' Mitch locked the gun on Johnny.

Ian moved to the other side, closer to Alex. Their eyes met.

Here goes nothing. Alex cocked his hand back, stepped forward, leveling a hook. Ian saw him coming, moved in, right hand flying back and then forward in a blur, the gun butt coming at his face — shit, the gun —

White stars burst behind his eyes. His head jerked sideways, and he felt his brain bounce in his skull. Everything went slippy. Sick agony raced through his body. He staggered, tried to get a hand out to catch himself on the edge of

126

the file cabinet, missed. He felt air against him, and then he hit the floor. Primal instinct pulled him fetal, hands up to his face. Through a haze, he heard Johnny say something, then Mitch again, saying, 'I told you not to move.'

* * *

Jenn walked down the block, blood singing in her veins. It was happening, it was really happening. She tried to picture it, Mitch and Ian in ski masks, Johnny on the floor, all that money. It was hard to force herself to walk slow and natural, even put a little sway in her hips. There were people on the street, and it was important not to do anything that might seem strange.

She rounded the corner, then glanced at her watch: 9:41. If the boys had gone in as soon as they got the text message, and assuming there wasn't any problem — which there wouldn't be, couldn't be — they'd be back out in a few minutes. All she had to do was get the car started and be waiting for them. Her purse felt heavy, the weight of the pistol in it, and knowing it was there heightened the thrill.

The rental car was parked in shadows, and she couldn't see inside. It was possible that they had lost their nerve, that they were waiting for her. And if they were? Would she tell them to go inside? Or would she do as Mitch had, and try to let them off the hook?

She didn't know. But it didn't matter. Ten feet from the car she could see that it was empty. She walked to the driver's side, her body alive and raw.

Something crunched behind her. She looked over her shoulder. A car was pulling into the alley.

Her thoughts scattered like marbles. There was a split second when she could have ducked out of sight, but then the headlights were on her, dazzling. Her mouth went dry and she had a childish urge to turn and sprint. The car was big, and rattled as it pulled in behind the rental.

Shit. Behind the rental. They were blocked in.

Be cool. You have to be cool. Who was it? The cops? An employee? The guys Johnny was meeting with?

It didn't matter. Moment of decision — get in the rental and ignore whoever it was, or make a stand? What would she do if she had nothing to hide?

She turned and stepped forward, one hand shielding her eyes, the other up in a half-greeting. The car was a beat-up whale of a Cadillac. The door opened, a figure stepping out, leaving the engine running and the headlights in her eyes. A man, medium build. Alone. She swallowed, said, 'Hey, you're parking me in.'

The figure stepped to one side, and she got a better look at him. A pasty guy, thin, with black hair gelled into a pompadour. He wore an expensive-looking motorcycle jacket and had a hand tucked in his back pocket. He stared at her for a moment, eyes trailing up and down her body. A new fear joined the ones she already had, that fear no woman ever got too far from, especially alone in a dark alley, wearing a dress.

'What are you doing back here?'

His tone scared her a little, but she forced herself to cock her head, said, '*Excuse* me?'

'Dressed pretty nice to be hanging out by the Dumpster.'

The humidity in the air seemed to be clinging to her. Something about the guy reminded her of biting into metal.

'I'm waiting for my boyfriend,' she said.

'Your boyfriend.' The man shuffled forward, glanced in the rental car. 'He work here?'

'Yes.' She stepped back, nothing too obvious, but not wanting him closer. Who was this guy? Not a cop. He could honestly be looking for a place to park. But he'd left the Cadillac running. Besides, wouldn't a normal person just have apologized, moved his car?

Unless he was hitting on her. A ridiculous possibility in a dark alley, but you never knew with guys.

'What's his name?'

'Whose?'

'Your boyfriend.'

She thought about saying Alex, or Johnny, or making one up. But then she remembered what she would do under normal circumstances. 'None of your business.' She put a hand on one hip. 'Look, how about you move your car so I can get out?'

'I thought you were waiting for your boyfriend.'

'I mean, maybe you could park somewhere else?'

'I got a better idea,' he said, and stepped forward.

★ ★ ★

'I told you not to move,' Mitch said, and leveled the gun right at Johnny's head. His heart was slamming against his ribs. Alex was on the ground, moaning, blood between his fingers. How hard had Ian clocked him?

There wasn't time to worry about it. 'Put your hands on the desk. Do it now.'

Johnny stared at him. 'Do you know what you're doing, kid?'

Very consciously, Mitch slid a thumb up and cocked the hammer back. Johnny's eyes went wide, and for a moment, Mitch had a terrible urge to pull the trigger, to feel the thing kick against his hand. 'Now.'

Slowly, Johnny raised his hands and put them on the pressed-wood desk. 'All we have is the money from today. Take it and get out of here.'

'Tape him.'

Ian didn't move, just stood over Alex, staring down.

'Hey! Tape him.'

'What? Right.' Ian slid the gun into his waistband, pulled a flattened half roll of duct tape from his back pocket.

'You move, you make any trouble for my friend, and I'll shoot you right now. You get me?'

'You're making a mistake, kid. You know who I am?'

'Yeah. You're the guy getting fucked.' He was

130

every bad guy in every movie ever made, and it felt great. He stepped sideways to keep a clear shot as Ian moved around the desk.

'Put your hands together.' Ian pulled an edge of tape up, then began wrapping it around Johnny's wrists.

'Make it tight.' Mitch waited till Ian had four or five loops around Johnny's hands, then let his eyes dart around the office. A small space, maybe eight by ten, with a cheap desk, a couple of chairs, some filing cabinets. A swimsuit calendar on the wall, a Budweiser mirror. There was a big black duffel bag beside the desk.

'Kid, you're about to be in shit you have no idea how deep. Walk out of here now and we'll just forget this happened.'

'When you're done with his hands, get his mouth.'

Ian nodded, wrapped the tape another half-dozen times, then ripped it. 'Sit back and shut up.'

Think, think, think. You cannot afford to miss anything. The safe was on the wall, closed. The money had better be in that bag, or else it was going to get complicated. He'd check in a minute. Alex moaned, said, 'My eye, you fuck!' Mitch ignored him, stepped forward, yanked the phone cord out of the wall. Johnny was glaring as Ian wrapped loops of tape around his head. He wasn't a threat anymore. Mitch uncocked the gun, carefully, then slid it behind his back. He took the tape from his own pocket, kneeled by Alex.

'Put your hands out.'

131

'Oh, Christ.'

'*Put your hands out.*' He tugged at them, wishing he could ask Alex if he was OK, whisper some comfort, knowing he couldn't do any such thing. Alex resisted at first, then gave in. His face was a mess, a gash pouring blood into his eye. Mitch winced, then forced himself to tape Alex up, hands and feet, then tore a six-inch strip and covered his mouth, hating himself for it, not seeing any choice.

When he rose, he saw that Ian had Johnny secured. So far so good. He strode over to the side of the desk, picked up the bag. It was heavy. He unzipped it, stared inside.

So this was what winning looked like.

Johnny started bucking, making noise against the tape. Mitch grabbed him by the shoulders, shoved him out of the chair. He landed heavy, the chair skittering away to hit the back wall.

'First, we're not here for today's take. Second, don't disrespect the Cubs.' Mitch leaned over him. The guy glared at him from the ground.

Remember last week, asshole? When you told me how much your shirt cost? He smiled, then pulled his leg back and kicked Johnny in the gut, hard. Air blew out his nostrils, and his face went red.

It felt great.

★   ★   ★

'I got a better idea,' the man in the leather jacket said as he stepped forward. 'How about you tell me what you're *really* doing here?'

Jenn's pulse ran frantic. This wasn't just some random creep. Not under these circumstances, not with that hair, that car. And especially not the way he was acting. There was only one explanation that made sense. This was the drug dealer Johnny was buying from.

Which changed everything. Their plan had been based on the idea that Mitch and Ian would be able to get in and out quickly enough that the dealer wouldn't have arrived. That's why she'd sat inside to let them know the exact moment Johnny went to the office. Add to that the fact that they hadn't guessed he would come to the back, and it had seemed an acceptable risk.

Less acceptable now, though. 'What do you mean?'

'Are you with Johnny?' He took a step forward, and she retreated. She bumped the edge of the Dumpster, the metal cool and greasy against her bare arm. Shit.

She could dash for the mouth of the alley. But heels were hardly running shoes. Besides, she'd be abandoning the guys. Getting away wasn't enough. Somehow she had to get him out of here.

How, though? She had the gun in her purse, but he was so close . . .

'Come on. What's going on?' His breath was faintly sour.

And then it came to her. A way to make any man move, random creep or hardened drug dealer.

'If you don't leave right now,' she said, 'I'll scream rape.'

He stiffened. 'Why would you do that?'

She took a deep inhale, opened her mouth. Stared him straight in the eye, watched him calculate how long and loud she could scream, how many people might be around to hear it. It was dark but not late, and Lincoln had plenty of traffic, plus the apartments nearby . . .

'OK.' He put his hands up. 'OK.' He took a step backward. 'Easy.'

'Keep going.' She moved away from the Dumpster, the purse in her hands.

'There's no need to get crazy.'

'Just move your car and leave me alone.'

He grimaced, and glanced over his shoulder. Checked his watch. 'Let me make a phone call.'

'*Now.*'

The man sighed. 'You win.' He took another step back.

He had just pulled out his keys when the back door to the restaurant swung open.

★   ★   ★

Ian was fighting the urge to bounce on his toes, to howl at the moon. They'd done it, they'd really done it. Johnny Love was on the floor, taped and gasping from Mitch's kick. The duffel bag was on the desk, more than enough in it, even split four ways, to cover what he owed Katz. He was back on top. 'We good?'

'Yeah.' Mitch stepped back from Johnny, looked around the office. Took keys from the desk, then hoisted the duffel bag to his shoulder. 'Let's go.'

Ian led the way back out of the office, the gun still in his hand. He liked it. Maybe when this was all over, he'd get one of his own. It felt good.

The back room was just as they'd left it, too bright and packed with crap. Mitch closed the door to the office, then stopped to fiddle with the key ring. He tried a handful until one turned.

'That's cold, man.'

'Just being thorough,' Mitch said. 'Nice work.'

'You too.' They stood in masks, grinning at each other like kids.

'All right. Let's get out of here.' Ian pushed open the back door and stepped out.

Into the glare of headlights. What the —

'Fuck!' A man's voice.

Everything slowed into crystalline cocaine clarity. Ian saw Mitch freeze behind him, one hand still on the door, the bag over his shoulder. The orange rental car parked twenty feet away. Beside it, two figures, one of them Jenn, her hands going to her mouth. The other a guy, in silhouette. He was moving, keys falling from his hand as it swept behind his back, holy shit, coming back with a gun. Ian stared, his mouth open, as the man slid into a target shooter's pose, feet apart.

Then the thought hit. *You have a gun too.*

He started to raise his pistol.

'Don't.' The man's voice was high, unsteady. 'You,' he said over his shoulder. 'Lady. Don't move.'

You can do this. This guy has three targets. He's nervous. He's not ready. You are.

'You two! Drop your guns!' The man in the

leather jacket swung jerkily from person to person.

All you have to do is wait for him to turn again.

'Oh God,' Jenn said.

It was coming down fast, but he was faster, he could feel it. Just like playing cards, there came a moment when someone's bluff looked so good that you wanted to fold. The mark of a real player was the strength to see past that fear.

The man said to Jenn, 'Move over by them.'

His attention on her.

Mitch yelled, 'Ian, don't — '

He let his body take over, lowering to a crouch as he brought his pistol up. The man swung back to him. Ian stared down the barrel, finger moving for the trigger.

★　★　★

Jesus but his head hurt.

Alex's temples pounded and throbbed. His vision was blurry, one eye closed, sweat and blood on his face. Through his good eye he saw Mitch's and Ian's feet walk past, saw the door close. There was the sound of keys.

Why had Ian hit him that *hard*? All they needed was to show Johnny that he was clean, not lose an eye in the process.

Relax. You're in pain, not thinking straight. The worst that happened is maybe he cracked a bone in your cheek. You're probably fine. He forced his breathing to slow.

Near him, Johnny wriggled, trying to worm his

136

way to a sitting position. Alex thought he ought to do the same, but even the idea of moving was enough to send fresh agony sheeting through him.

It's over. At least it's over. Other than the hit to your head, everything went fine. The pain will fade. What you did here will change your life. Cassie won't move. You'll have enough money to figure out what you want to do. Quit bartending, maybe go back to school.

It's over.

Then, muffled by the walls, he heard yelling, and a gunshot.

PART II

The Rules Change

*'There's no need for red-hot pokers.
Hell is other people.'*

— Jean-Paul Sartre, *No Exit*

12

Someone was kicking the door. Alex watched through a haze as it bowed and buckled. *They're doing it wrong. You don't kick the middle. You kick the side.* Hadn't they ever watched a cop show?

Shock. This must be clinical shock. That's why the pain felt farther away, why he hadn't panicked at the yelling, at the —

Gunshot.

Jesus!

There had been a gunshot. How long ago? Time seemed strange and elastic. Maybe thirty seconds? He strained to hear, listening for voices. As if on cue, another shot rang out.

What was happening? Who was shooting?

Oh God. Who had been shot?

The thought made him blink and focus, which brought the pain throbbing back. He had to get out of here. See if his friends needed help.

Johnny had made it to his knees. He was trying to shout something, his voice coming out vowels behind the tape. The person on the other side of the door kicked again, and a boot broke through the hollowcore door in a shower of splinters. Someone swore, and then the foot was pulled back and a hand replaced it, fumbling for the knob. A moment later the door swung open, and a figure, someone he knew, who? The other bartender. Chip. His name was Chip. Why had it been hard to get the guy's name? They'd worked together for years.

'Oh my God,' Chip said. He stood wild eyed, frozen. Johnny made incomprehensible sounds, held up his arms. Chip got it, hurried to him, started pulling the duct tape. 'Are you OK?'

Johnny coughed as his mouth was freed, gulped a breath. His face was slapped-red where the skin had been peeled. 'What does it look like, you asshole? Do my hands.'

Chip started to unwrap them, then Johnny said, 'Scissors. In the drawer.' A moment later he was free. He took the hand Chip offered, stood up. 'Call the police.'

'What about him?'

'I'll take care of him. Go!'

Chip turned and sprinted out.

Johnny groaned, stretched. He knelt beside Alex, pulled the tape from his mouth. 'You all right, kid?'

No, I'm fucking not, there was someone shooting out where my friends are. But he couldn't say that, couldn't give any hint of concern. 'My eye.'

'It'll be OK. We'll get it checked out. Hold still.' Johnny leaned over, put the scissors against the bonds holding Alex's wrists. He started to cut, then stopped. Rocked back on his heels.

'What?'

Johnny held the scissors up, stared at them. 'We need to talk.'

The shock wasn't thick enough to block the sudden fear. Had he slipped up? 'What? Cut me free.'

'In a minute.' His boss glanced sideways, then reached over to push the door closed. 'We don't have a lot of time, so listen up.'

Alex moaned, and Johnny leaned forward and tapped his cheek. It felt like a blow from the wrong end of a claw hammer. 'Jesus!'

'I said listen. You'll be OK. It doesn't look that bad. But in a minute there are going to be a bunch of cops here, and I'm gonna need you to stand up.'

'Stand up?'

'Kid, you're loyal, but you ain't too bright. We're going to get you taken care of. I'll cover the medical bill. But you need to do something. The cops are going to ask a lot of questions. I don't know what happened out there, but right this second, it doesn't matter. What matters is that we tell the same story.'

'Johnny, my head really hurts.' He tried to speak calmly, but his body was slicked with sweat, and his voice came out hoarse. He had to get free, had to find out what was going on. Were his friends OK? Had one of them . . .

'Here's what you tell the cops — exactly what happened, that two guys came in with guns and robbed us. But don't mention the meeting or the duffel bag. Other than that, tell them anything they want to know. They ask if you wear pantyhose, you tell the truth. But not about those two things. You got it?'

Alex took a deep breath. The world was wobbling and pulsing. 'You want me to lie to the cops.'

'You do this, I'll get you taken care of, cover

143

the bills, and pay you for the trouble. A lot more than a couple hundred.'

He could hear sirens now, rising and falling. 'I —'

'You tell them anything else, then I'll be forced to say you were in on it. That daughter of yours? Next time you see her, you'll be wearing a jumpsuit. Get me?'

Everything seemed to be moving at a weird speed, jerky fast, awkward slow, like a projector eating a film-strip. Someone had been shot outside, maybe more than one person. One of his friends could be hurt, dying. Johnny leaned in, the scissors in his hand, inches from Alex's good eye. He could see light play off the edge of them.

'I understand.' He forced himself to stay calm. Raised his hands. 'Cut me out.'

Johnny nodded. 'That's good.' He worked the edge of the blade beneath the tape.

Footsteps, loud, and then Chip was pushing open the door. 'The police are on their way. Are you two OK?'

'We're fine,' Johnny said. 'Alex needs an ambulance, though.'

'What happened?'

'We got robbed.'

'By who?'

'Fuck if I know, kid. But I'm going to find out. You can bet on that.'

The world was narrowing to a pinhole. Alex decided to let it.

★ ★ ★

144

Frozen in the doorway, ears ringing from the crack of gunfire, Mitch stared. Trying to put the pieces together.

They had left the office. Gone out the back. A second car had been there, a man standing near it. He had pulled a pistol. Ian had aimed at the guy, his intentions glowing like a billboard. Mitch had yelled for him to stop. The drug dealer had drawn a bead, fast. There had been a blast of light and sound from over by the cars.

Ian must be hit.

Mitch looked down. His friend seemed fine. He wasn't screaming or clutching his chest. He was just aiming his pistol and tugging the trigger. Nothing was happening. The safety still on. The shot hadn't come from him, and hadn't hit him. So who —

Mitch turned to the alley. The man was on the ground, one hand clapped to his shoulder, face twisted in pain. Jenn stared like a zombie, the revolver she'd used to shoot him still in her shaking hand.

No. Oh, no. He slipped the duffel bag and launched himself forward, ran a handful of paces. The man on the ground was moving. Mitch got to him, kicked at a dark metal object on the ground, the man's pistol, knocked it skittering across the broken concrete.

The guy gasped, one hand flopped up at a weird angle, the other pressed to his shoulder. Blood pulsed through his clenched fingers. His teeth were tight, and breath whistled through them.

'I' — Jenn's eyes were sick porcelain — 'I didn't. He's — '

'Hey,' Mitch said. He moved over to Jenn, put hands on her shoulders. 'Hey.'

She stared at him. 'I didn't know what to do. He was going to — '

'It's fine,' he lied. 'Everything is fine. Come on. Let me have this.' Gently, he eased the revolver from her hand.

'I — oh God.' She stood over the man she had shot. Ian came up beside her, the three of them staring down. *Like kids on a playground,* Mitch thought, *only it's not a twisted ankle or a skinned knee, and no one can yell timeout. This game keeps going, like it or not.*

'What do we do?' Ian's voice was thin.

'We have to take him to a hospital,' she said. 'It's just his shoulder. He'll be OK. Right?'

So if this is a game, what are the rules? Mitch stared, let his friends talk around him. *There has to be more than what you're thinking. There has to be.*

'And tell them what?'

'We don't have to tell them anything. Just drop him outside.'

He barely heard the others. *Don't lie to yourself. It's too late to lie. Lies won't save you.*

'He'll tell them about us.'

'He doesn't know anything.'

This is the way it is. You know what you have to do. There's only one option.

Ian said, 'He saw your face.'

'But so what? I've never been arrested — '

'It's not just the cops.'

'So what do we do?'

'I don't know.' Ian's voice hysterical. 'Christ, I don't know.'

'Why didn't you put your gun down?'

'This is *my* fault? I didn't shoot him.'

'I had to!'

This is the game. These are the stakes.

Do it.

The man was staring at them, his pupils wide but alert. Staring at the two men in masks, and at the woman standing between. Staring like he was memorizing her face.

Or like he already had.

Mitch raised the revolver, looked down the barrel, and pulled the trigger.

13

A small space, vibrating, bright. On his back. Sirens. Movement around him. Cool pressure on his eye. Words. 'Male, approximately thirty, blunt trauma to the head and eye, probable concussion . . . '

'Am I . . . where?'

'You're in an ambulance. Lay still.' The figure touching his cheek, his nose, sliding something into his nostrils. 'What's your name?'

'Alex.'

'Alex what?'

'Alex Kern.'

'Do you know what year it is, Alex?'

'Ummm.' For a moment he wasn't sure. '2008?'

'Good. And who's the president?'

'Fucking George Bush.'

The technician snorted. 'I'm going to put an IV in. It may pinch for a second.' There was a brief sting in his right elbow.

'Am I — '

'You're going to be all right. The blow tore your skin, but your eye looks OK.'

'What about — who got shot?'

'I don't know about that. Lay still and try to be calm.'

Calm, Alex thought. *Right. Calm.* He took a deep breath, held it, then let it out slow, wondering what the fuck had happened.

'What the fuck happened?' Jenn sounded like she'd been awake for a week. Mitch didn't answer. He just leaned back into her couch. His hand tingled, felt very . . . present. Like the kick of the gun had left an imprint.

'Mitch. Are you — '

'Yeah,' he said. He felt at once powerful and weak, strong and shaky. 'Yeah.'

It was his first time in her apartment, and it looked different than he'd imagined. He'd pictured frilly things and too many pillows. Clay-colored walls. The standard midtwenties Pottery Barn space. Instead it was tastefully minimal, with less furniture than he had expected. The walls were painted airy colors, and the windows had soft, sheer curtains that flowed with the breeze.

The last half an hour had been the strangest of his life. Like a Lynch film, everything mixed up and weird. Panic and exaltation coiling through his belly. It had all happened so fast. One minute they were walking out of the restaurant, he and Ian, the job done and a new life about to begin. Cut to him standing over a man, Jenn's pistol in his hand, only one option, one freaking option, and he'd stared at the guy, first at his eyes, then, when he knew he was going to actually do it, at his chest, staring till he was looking at a pattern instead of a person, and then he'd pulled the —

Stop.

Fast-forward.

— to the sirens tearing the night, drawing

149

closer. There had been a sense of causality, as if by twitching his finger he'd set the world in motion. Hundred-proof power. King of the world.

Not knowing what else to do, he'd rolled with it.

He'd ordered Ian into the rental, then he and Jenn had climbed into the drug dealer's Eldorado. Originally he'd only planned to move it out of the way, but the sirens were closing in fast, and so he'd spun north, the engine old but still boasting Cadillac power, and he'd had the strongest urge to jam on the gas, open it up. It had taken an effort of will to drive at a steady five above.

Thoughts and images sliding across him like rain on a window:

The good firmness of the trigger.

Her voice asking, 'Where are we going?'

An explosion of light and a sound that hurt. The deeper darkness of the shadows that fell after.

'Your place,' he'd answered. 'It's closest.'

Expecting her to argue, but she'd said nothing. The drive was blurry in his memory. The whole time he'd been steering, braking, stopping, he'd been conscious of two things —

Jesus, you shot him, you really fucking shot —

Stop. Fast-forward.

— and Jenn beside him. He could smell her, not perfume, her, the gentle smell of sweat and hair, of girl. Once he'd caught her looking at him, but her eyes slid away before he could read them.

150

And now here they were, sitting in her tasteful apartment, waiting for the smoke to clear. Wondering if they'd like the view when it did. Mitch coughed, straightened on the couch. 'Are you both OK?'

Ian and Jenn looked at each other, then at him.

'I mean, neither of you were hurt.'

'No.'

'Uh-uh.'

'Good. That's good.'

'What about Alex?' Jenn was in the opposite chair, her knees three inches apart. He had an adolescent urge to look up her skirt.

'Of course he's OK.' Ian was pacing. 'Why wouldn't he be?'

'You hit him pretty hard,' Mitch said.

'I didn't mean to.' He paused, made a strangled laugh. 'It was my first pistol whipping.'

'What?' Jenn straightened. 'You hit him with the *gun*?'

'It was in my hand.'

'What about your other hand?'

'I — look, I just did what we talked about. Mitch was there. Right?'

'Yeah,' he said. 'I was there.'

Another silence, then Jenn said, 'What do we do?'

A fair question. He decided to think about it, and was surprised to realize that he could. That in fact, he felt sharp. 'OK. Let's go through this. That guy.' He had a flash of the man's face, buried it. 'He must have been the drug dealer Johnny was meeting with. Damn. I really figured

151

we'd have time before he arrived. He must have known Johnny — what?' Realizing Jenn was staring at him.

'What are you doing?'

'Trying to get my head around this.'

'Get your *head* around it? Get your head around *what*, that you, that we . . . '

'Yes,' he said.

'Can we look on the bright side?' Ian's eyebrows high. 'The cash?'

Funny. Mitch had forgotten about the money. He straightened, pulled the bag to his lap. Opened the zipper. What he saw inside, less real than raising the gun and pulling the — *stop, bury it* — was bundles. He reached in, took out a handful, packs of hundreds and twenties.

'Wow.' Ian sounded reverent. 'How much?'

'I don't know.'

'I'm saying, count, man.'

'No.'

'OK, let me.'

'No.' He stuffed the money back in the bag. 'We're not talking about the money now. We have to think first.'

'About what?'

He looked up, met Ian's gaze, held it. 'About how to get away with this.'

'Get away with it?' Jenn made a squeaky sort of sound. 'How?'

'One step at a time.' Mitch's thoughts came clear and clean and logical. Like a machine, a big industrial machine that stamped out part after perfect part. 'First. In the restaurant. We were wearing masks and gloves. Ian, you didn't take your gloves off, did you? Get sweaty, wipe your hands?'

'No.'

'You're sure?'

'Of course.'

'I might have touched something,' Jenn said quietly.

'Touched what?'

'I don't know. Something.'

'In the alley?'

She nodded.

'That's OK. It's an alley. Hundreds of people go through it.' His body felt like it was getting low-grade electrical shocks. He stood, cracked his knuckles. Pulled the pistol from his waistband and dropped it on the table. It hit loud and heavy. 'This was the only gun we fired, right? So that's lucky.'

'Why?'

'It's a revolver. Revolvers don't leave casings.' He saw Jenn's expression, said, 'The part that comes off a bullet.' He took two steps forward, spun, took two back, feeling muscles in his legs. Stopped, looked at Ian. 'What were you *thinking*, man? Pulling out your gun like some freaking gangster?'

'I was — '

'You didn't even have the safety off.'

'Yeah, well, I'm not the one who shot him.'

'No. You're just the one who left us no choice.' He glared at his friend, feeling the anger run through him, remembering the guy doing coke in the goddamn car. Ian tried to meet his gaze, then looked away, at the window, his feet.

153

Shuffled them. Looked up again, something in his eyes.

Something like fear.

Strange. Mitch couldn't remember anyone being scared of him before. 'OK. That doesn't matter now. These guns, the guy you got them from, who was it?'

'Just a guy I know. He runs a private casino. Some other stuff.'

'What kind of stuff?'

'I don't really know. Prostitutes, I think.'

'Can the guns be traced to him?'

'I don't think so.'

'Why not?'

'Because he would have worried about us getting caught. He'd have given me ones that couldn't be traced.'

'OK,' Mitch said again. It felt good to say, to mark off little increments of thought, like ticking off items on a list. 'You're right. And we didn't leave any fingerprints, and the bullets can't tie to us. So, then.'

Jenn stared at him. Hanging, he realized, on his next words.

'So then we're OK.'

'OK? You killed — '

'We. We killed.' He closed his eyes, rubbed at them with his forefinger and thumb. 'But he was a bad guy, a drug dealer. And he saw you.' He moved to her, dropped to a squat beside the chair, took her hands in his, not thinking about any of it, just doing. 'Jenn, he saw your face.'

She said nothing. Something was happening behind her eyes, though he couldn't have said

154

what. He kept speaking, talking fast, wanting to make everything better. 'But now we're safe. Things didn't go exactly how we planned, but we got the money and got out, and didn't leave anything that would lead to us.'

'But we — '

'Yes,' he cut her off, his patience snapping. 'Yeah, we did. Which is just one of the reasons I didn't want to do this in the first place, remember? You wanted your big adventure? Well, now you've got it.'

'That's not fair.'

'What's fair got to do with it? It happened, damn it. Do you get me? It happened. It's real. Do you understand?'

Jenn's eyes were wide. She nodded yes in a way that meant no.

He sighed, squeezed her hands. 'Look, it's nobody's fault. But what matters is that there is nothing to point to us. Nothing at all.'

'Sure there is,' Ian said. 'The money. The cars. The guns.'

It was a fair point, and it froze him cold. Ian was right. He'd been so focused on thinking about what had already happened that he hadn't put any thought into what happened next. Still, he was the one holding it together, while the two of them seemed about to come apart, Jenn retreating into herself, Ian's swaggering a thin veneer over panic. If someone had to be strong, to make the hard decisions, it looked like it was going to be him.

He was surprised at how good that idea felt.

'You're right. We'll need to take care of all of

155

that. But first things first. We need to talk to Alex, see what happened on his end. With the shooting, the police will be involved. We hadn't counted on that. We need to know what they think.'

'I'll call him,' Jenn said, rising.

'Wait. He's probably on the way to the hospital.'

'The *hospital*? How hard did you hit him?' She glared at Ian, who sighed and dropped onto the couch.

'Harder than I should have, OK? I was nervous.'

She shook her head. Straightened her back and ran her hands through her hair. 'Which hospital would they take him to?'

Mitch realized she was asking him, him directly. 'I don't know,' he said. 'And we can't start calling around, or dial his cellphone a hundred times. We can't do anything that would raise suspicion.' His mind still churning steady and strong, focusing on the task at hand. *Maybe if you do that hard enough, you won't have to remember what you — stop.*

He took a deep breath. 'The idea from the beginning was that there was no reason why anyone would look at us. Far as we know, that hasn't changed. We need to talk to Alex and find out what happened on his end. He won't be in the hospital long. Overnight, probably.'

'So what do we do?'

'Leave one message on his cell, something perfectly normal. Tell him that we're getting together tomorrow morning. Here.'

'And until then?'

'Wait.'

14

The CT scan hadn't been a lot of fun. It wasn't claustrophobia so much as the noise — loud, rhythmic clunking and banging while his head throbbed like an apocalyptic hangover. But worse was just lying there, not knowing what had happened.

Maybe the gun went off accidentally? But there had been two shots.

Were one or two of his best friends dead in an alley right now?

'Mr Kern.'

'Yeah.' He opened his eyes. An Indian guy in a white coat stood in front of him. Weird. The guy looked younger than him. Alex pushed away his thoughts, struggled to focus. 'Doc.'

'How are you feeling?'

'My head hurts.'

'Any nausea?'

'No.'

'Numbness?'

'I wish.'

'Pain in your teeth? Double vision?'

'Huh-uh.'

The man nodded, made a note on a clipboard. 'Good. Well, the results are fine. No evidence of fracture or permanent damage. The blow hit just above the zygomatic arch, which protects some important nerves. Sort of like hitting your funny bone, how it shoots through your whole arm?'

He took out a pad and began to write. 'I'm going to give you some Tylenol-3 for the pain. Don't take any more than you really need.'

'What about the cut?'

'We stitched that when you arrived. You might have a little scar, nothing too dramatic.'

'You did?' He blinked. 'I don't remember.'

'You have a mild concussion. That can affect your memory.'

'Will it — '

'Be permanent? You shouldn't have trouble remembering things that happen from now on. If you do, come back immediately. Same with vision problems or severe pain.'

'Come back? You're saying I should go?'

'You have insurance?'

'I have child support instead.'

The man laughed. 'Look, if you want, you can stay. But my advice? You'll rest better at home, and it's a lot cheaper.'

'Rest? Am I allowed to sleep? I thought with a concussion . . . '

'Depends on the level. You'll be fine. In a couple of days or a week, follow up with your family practitioner.' The man handed him a slip of paper. 'Your prescription.'

After the doctor left, a nurse came in, helped him stand up, gave him his clothes, wallet, and cellphone. After he changed in the bathroom, she had him sit back down in a wheelchair. 'I can walk,' he said.

'Policy,' she said. 'You have someone here?'

'Someone?'

'To take you home. You shouldn't drive, sugar.'

'I can call a cab, I guess.'

'I got a better idea.' The voice came from behind. Very gently, Alex turned his head to look.

The man in the chair wore a suit and tie. He was tall and broad-shouldered, with short hair trimmed to razor edge. Something about him made Alex immediately nervous. 'My name is Peter Bradley. I'm a detective with the Chicago Police Department.' His hand held out.

'A detective?' Alex shook the guy's hand on reflex while his brain conjured images of the tip of the scissors an inch from his eye. For a moment, he thought about calling for the doctor, saying he sure felt some nausea now.

'Do you remember what happened?'

'Umm.' His mouth was dry, his thoughts sticky. *We robbed Johnny Love. Ian hit me too hard. Someone got shot, and I don't know who.* 'There were men with guns.'

'That's right. I'd like to ask you a couple of questions. I can give you a ride at the same time.'

'Do we have to do this now?'

'Not if you're not up to it. But the sooner we talk, the more likely we are to catch these guys,' the detective said. He gave an apologetic shrug. 'Since you need a lift anyway . . . '

You have nothing to hide. 'OK, yeah, I guess. Sure.'

'Good.' Bradley stepped behind the chair, took the handles. 'Don't you hate this crap?'

'What?'

'This. Everybody so worried you're going to sue. Cut your finger, leave in a wheelchair.' The automatic doors whooshed open. The night was

159

sticky after the hospital's air conditioning. 'Here you go.'

Alex put his hands on the armrests, stood up slowly. The motion sent a bolt of pain through his head. He wobbled for a moment, kept one hand on the arm of the chair.

'You all right?'

'Feel like I spent the night slamming tequila.'

The cop laughed. 'Doctors say you'll be fine. At least you probably got some good pills out of it, right?' He gestured. 'I'm over here. Where do you live?'

'Rogers Park.'

Bradley reached the car first, a pale blue Crown Vic. He unlocked the passenger-side door and held it open. Alex got in, his eyes scanning the radio mounted to the dash, the switches that controlled the sirens, the handle that moved the spotlight. Bradley climbed in the other side, fired up the engine. 'Ever been in a police car before?'

'Nope. Well, once. When I was a kid.' He realized how that sounded, continued in a rush. 'Got caught drinking a twelve-pack in an alley. The cop — the officer — put me in the back, drove me home.'

'Ouch. He talk to your parents?'

'No, he was cool. Just put the fear of God into me.' He reached up and gingerly touched the side of his face, his fingers tracing cotton and tape. There was something about the cop that he liked, an easy manner. Under other circumstances, he seemed like a guy it would be fun to have a drink with.

Bradley signaled, then nosed into traffic,

heading for Lake Shore Drive. 'So. Tell me what happened.' The headlights of other cars flared into stars.

Keep it simple. 'I was in the back room with Johnny Lo — with Mr Loverin.'

A smile danced quick across Bradley's lips. Alex continued. 'Two men came in. They had guns and masks. They told us not to move. One of them was close to me, and I, I guess I took a swing at him. He hit me with the gun. After that, everything is fuzzy.'

'You tried to punch one of them?'

'I wasn't really thinking.'

'Did better than most. People usually just freeze up.'

'Kind of wish I had.'

'Did you recognize the men?'

'No. Like I said, they had masks on.'

'Anything distinctive about them?'

'Guns.'

Bradley snorted. 'Anything else? Scars, tattoos, heavy, tall? Anything about the clothing?'

A memory came, a time two years ago when he'd been mugged. How afterward he couldn't remember a thing about what the man had looked like. It had been a strangely helpless feeling: all those hours lifting weights, all the standard male fantasies about what he would do, and in the moment, he'd done nothing at all — not even remember what the man looked like. 'No. It's weird, but I guess I didn't really see them.'

'What about their eyes? Anything unusual about them?'

'Not that I remember.'

'You didn't notice if one had a black eye?'

Something in Alex went cold. 'I'm not sure.'

'What were you doing in the office?'

'Mr Loverin asked me to come back.'

'Why?'

'I don't know.'

Bradley merged onto the Drive, pressed the gas. There was a party going on in a Gold Coast penthouse, men and women crowding the windows, smoking on the balcony. 'Tell me about Johnny Love.'

'What about him?'

'How long have you worked for him?'

'About ten years. Well, at the bar that long. He bought it, I don't know, six years ago?'

'Did you work with him before?'

'No.'

'You never did anything for him, any side jobs?'

'What kind of jobs?'

'Anything at all.'

'I never knew him until then.' These questions were hitting closer to home than he wanted. He faked a grimace. 'Look, Detective, I'm really hurting. Do you mind — '

'Sure. Lean back, relax.' Bradley moved a lane over, sped up. 'I don't want to wear you out.'

Alex felt an absurd surge of gratitude. 'Thanks.'

They rolled through the night, high rises glowing on the left, their windows too bright and plentiful. Out Alex's window, sailboats swayed in the harbor. 'I've never been through anything like this before.'

162

'You're lucky. Things could have gone a lot worse.'

'Is everybody OK?'

'A bad guy got killed, but none of your co-workers were hurt.' The cop stared forward as they rounded the curve, Lake Shore Drive merging into Hollywood. 'Do you know how Johnny Love made his money?'

A bad guy. Mitch? Ian?

'I heard rumors.'

'Bad ones?'

'I guess.'

'So you don't mind my asking, why stay?'

'I needed the money. I'm divorced, got a daughter.'

'You couldn't find another job?'

'Johnny was an OK boss. I figured maybe they were just rumors.'

The cop looked over, cocked an eyebrow.

Alex sighed. 'Look, I hear you. You and my ex-wife think alike. I probably should have quit years ago. I just . . . never got around to it. I mean, I never saw anything that made me uncomfortable, so I ignored the rumors.'

'Went along to get along.'

'I guess. I kind of get through life by not thinking too hard about it.'

'I hear you.' Bradley nodded. 'What's your address?'

'There's a Walgreen's at Western and Howard. Mind dropping me there? I need to get this prescription filled.'

'Sure. I can wait.'

'You don't need to. I'm just a couple blocks.'

163

He tried to sound casual as he spoke, to hide the part of himself that was desperate to get out of the car, ASA-freaking-P. At least they were moving fast. Traffic was light. He had a weird memory, how when he'd first moved to Rogers Park he'd been surprised to hear sirens most every night. At first he'd thought it was cops — the neighborhood was rough around the edges — but before long he'd worked it out. It was the old folks' homes that lined Ridge. Somebody was always dying.

'What about the shots? Tell me what you remember.'

A bad guy got killed . . . 'There were two. One a few minutes after they left. Then a pause, maybe thirty seconds or so — it's hard to say, my time sense was screwed — and then another.'

'Nothing after that?'

'Sirens.'

The cop clicked his tongue against his lip. 'Anything else?'

Alex paused. Tried to remember the scene, to envision it as if he had no greater knowledge. 'I don't think so. They were in jeans, work pants. Ski masks. The masks were black.' Shook his head. 'One minute I'm standing there, then the door bangs open, these guys come in yelling — '

'What did they yell?'

'Something like 'Shut the fuck up, don't move.' They were swinging guns around, and I just sort of reacted, went for one of them, and then . . . ' He shrugged.

Bradley pulled the car into the drugstore parking lot. He stopped outside the front door.

164

'Could I see your driver's license?'

'My license?' His back tensed. 'Sure.' He fumbled into his pants, pulled out his wallet, the chain rattling. Passed the ID to the cop.

'This your current address?'

'Yeah.'

Bradley scribbled it down in a pad he pulled from the dash. 'How about a phone number?'

Alex gave it to him. 'Do you think you'll catch these guys?'

'Sure.'

Ice slid down his sides. 'Really?'

'Why wouldn't we?' The cop looked at him curiously.

'I don't know. I just — well, I guess I'm just glad.'

Bradley nodded. 'Positive you don't want me to wait around for you? It's no trouble.'

'Really, it's fine. You know how it is, these things can take a long time.' The excuse sounding preposterous.

'OK. I'll be in touch if we need anything else. Meanwhile.' Bradley pulled out a business card, passed it to Alex along with his license. 'Just like on TV. Anything else occurs to you, don't hesitate. Even if it seems small.'

'OK.' He reached for the door handle.

'And, Mr Kern, a piece of advice?'

He hesitated, turned back. 'Sure.'

'Your ex-wife is right about this one. Might be time to start thinking about getting a new job.'

★ ★ ★

165

'I'm going home.'

Jenn looked up, blinking away the alley. Funny thing, it wasn't the violence she'd been replaying, the yelling and the fire. It was the part before, when the man pulled up behind their rental car. Those long moments, probably only two or three, when they'd been alone.

As the car headlights had splashed across her, she'd known what was coming. Not specifically, of course, but she'd been able to feel the weight of potential. And with it a chance, a slim and slippery chance to make things right. To change the future that was barreling toward them. A chance that depended on her being clever enough, quickly enough.

If only she had thought faster. All of this would be different.

'Hello?' Ian pulled keys from his front pocket. 'I'm going home.'

From the couch, Mitch said, 'Why?'

'There's nothing more we can do now, right? We just have to wait until tomorrow, talk with Alex. So I'm going to go take a shower and try to sleep.'

'Is that smart?' Jenn looked at Mitch.

'What are you asking him for?' Ian tossed his keys from hand to hand.

'It's fine,' Mitch said. 'It doesn't matter if he waits here or there.' He looked at Ian. 'Just don't do anything stupid.'

'Like what?'

'You know what.' The way Mitch said it, that carefully measured tone, made her think he was talking about some specific thing.

166

Ian made a sound that was part sigh, part frustration. 'I told you I was sorry.'

Mitch nodded. 'OK.'

Jenn rubbed at her eyes, ran her hands through her hair, pulling it into an unbound ponytail and then dropping it to fall on her back. 'All right.' She pushed off the counter she'd been leaning against. 'So we get together tomorrow morning.'

'You hear from Alex, you'll let me know?'

'Of course.'

The three of them walked to the front door. Though there was comfort in hiding here, it was still strange having them in her apartment. Ten years of unsuccessful dating had made her want a sanctuary that was all hers. It was just an apartment, but she'd painted every wall and picked out every piece of furniture, from the thin-legged hall table to the plush rug beneath the bed.

'You need a lift?' Ian asked.

'I'm going to stay in case Alex calls,' Mitch said. 'If that's OK, I mean.' He looked at her questioningly.

'Sure,' she said, realizing she was glad of it.

'All right. See you tomorrow.' Ian started down the steps. Jenn watched him go, Mitch beside her, the two of them standing like the hosts of a dinner party waving farewell to the last guests. When Ian was out of sight, she said, 'What was all that about?'

'What?'

'You telling him not to do anything stupid.'

'Oh.' Mitch looked pained for a moment, then

167

shrugged. 'I guess you should know. He was high.'

'High? When? *Tonight?*'

'Yeah. Cocaine. That's why he was so twitchy.'

'You've got to be kidding me.'

He shook his head. 'He told me he did it sometimes. I think that's what his bathroom breaks are about. But I never thought he'd do it tonight. I about killed him.'

'High. Jesus.' She closed the door. They looked at each other for an awkward moment. 'We aren't very good at this, are we?'

'At being criminals? No. But cut us some slack. It's our first time.'

Their eyes met and held for a second, and then she started laughing, and he joined in. He had a good laugh, one of those that came deep and unself-conscious. His fed hers, and they kept at it longer than the joke deserved. It felt good. Pushed away the weight of what they had done, reminded her that no matter what, she was alive. That, in fact, she felt more than she could remember feeling in the last ten years. Like her father always said, any day above-ground counted as a good one. She said, 'Vodka?'

'Oh *God* yes.'

She led the way to the kitchen, flipped on the overheads, then pulled Smirnoff from the freezer, the bottle frosted white. Took down two glasses, dropped an ice cube in each, and poured generous doubles. 'Cheers.' The first swallow was sharp and cold and real, a pure physical sensation.

The air conditioning was on, and she was

chilly in the dress, her flesh tight with goosebumps. Shopping for it had been fun. Playing the part in advance, life coming into focus, seeming to matter. Earlier in the afternoon, when she'd gotten dolled up, she'd stood in front of the mirror in her bedroom and liked what she saw. Not a woman in her thirties with a shit job and no plans. A heartbreaker femme fatale in a dress cut too low for a bra, gearing up for a robbery. She'd stood and stared, and then hiked the edge of the skirt up, hooked her thumbs in the waist of her panties and pulled them off. The feeling of air at the hinge of her thighs had been electric. Hundred-proof life.

'I like your place,' Mitch said.

'Thanks.' She took another sip of vodka. 'Me too.'

He nodded, looked around. She could see him struggling for something to say. 'Been here long?'

'About five years. Before I moved here I'd been living with Brian — you never met him, did you? — and before that with some girlfriends. When things fell apart with Bry, I decided, enough; time to have my own space. Do things my way. You know?'

'I guess.'

'You don't like living alone?'

'It's OK.' He paused, shrugged. 'Lonely sometimes.'

'I know. But there's a good kind of loneliness too. Where you realize that maybe you are alone, but that it's better than being someone you're not.' Thinking back to Brian's old apartment, the smell of cigarettes, him on the couch on

169

weekend afternoons, goofy-haired, watching football. Something sweet in it at first. But somewhere along the line she'd realized that their present was their future, that Brian, nice as he was, would never change, never be anything else. That he didn't want to. If he had his choice, it would be fifty more years of football Saturdays and Sunday-morning sex, of workday weeks and frozen pizza. Dropping dead within days of each other, shortly after a visit from the grandkids. It wasn't long after that she started picking fights.

For no reason but to have something to say, she said, 'You know one of my favorite things? Some days I'll come home, pour a drink, and climb into bed with a couple of magazines. Not real magazines, *Newsweek* or anything. I mean junk. Celebrity baby magazines. And I'll lay there in bed and drink and catch up on what crazy thing Britney Spears has done lately.'

He laughed. 'Really?'

'Yeah. I don't take it seriously. I mean, I like to check out the clothes and stuff, but that's sort of an excuse. I know it's silly, looking at the lives of these people I'll never meet, don't even want to. I just kind of get a kick out of being a voyeur.'

'Nothing wrong with that.' He took a swallow. 'I actually know what you mean. Sometimes when I'm on break at the hotel, I'll go up to the second floor of the lobby, where there's this big balcony. Lean over and watch people.'

'Watch them what?'

'Just . . . watch them. Twice-divorced sales executives hitting on each other in the lounge. Tourists with cameras asking directions to Navy

170

Pier. Couples that have been together so long they don't talk, don't seem to need to. If you watch long enough, you start to see that everybody looks like they're missing something. Like we all lost something and we're all looking for it.'

'True love?'

He laughed. 'I read a poem once, had a line that went something like, 'the heart asks more than life can give.' I think it's that, really. We all want everything. But we'd settle for a sense that things matter. That there's more to it than just getting up in the morning and making it through a day.'

'Do you see anybody who has that?'

'Not very many.'

'But some.'

'Yeah. Some.'

Their eyes met and then slid apart. Without warning, an image hit, the blast of light spitting from Mitch's hand, the way it seemed like it was the light that hit the man on the ground, that punched him in the heart and brought a dark circle to blossom on his shirt.

She set her drink down, covered her face with her hands. Her heart ached like something was trying to push it through her ribs. She pressed her palms against her cheeks, dug her nails into her forehead.

'Hey,' he said, his voice soft. She heard the click of his glass against the counter, and then he had his hands on her shoulders. The warmth felt good.

'Oh God.' She opened her hands, was

surprised to see him close, ducking his head down to look up at her, concern on his face. Her voice came out tremulous. 'What did we do?'

'What we had to.'

'How are you able to stand there and say that? I mean, you . . . you . . . '

Something happened in his eyes, a withdrawal and then a return, like a sea creature nearly surfacing before vanishing into the dark. He breathed through his nostrils. 'I did it for you.'

'We can't take this back. We did this, and we can't take it back.'

'It's what we wanted.'

'Not this.' Even as she said it, she heard a voice inside her, asking, *Are you sure? If you could go back a week, to the life before, the one where nothing really mattered, where you kept everything at a distance — would you?*

Yes, she thought. *I would. I think.*

'Come here,' he said. He stepped forward and wrapped his arms around her. She stood stiff at first, but it felt really good to have someone holding her. There was a comfort that drove away part of the horror. Jenn slid her arms under his, around his back, and buried her face in his chest. Her eyes were closed, and she could smell him, a faint hint of sweat. Her nose was running and her eyes were wet.

'It's OK.' His voice was soft. 'We'll make it OK. I promise.'

She gave a hollow half laugh, then sniffed, stepped back. Wiped her nose with the back of her hand. 'God, I feel like such an idiot. Some adventuress I turned out to be.'

'Don't.'

'I just' — she picked her drink up, took a long pull — 'I didn't tell you this before, but when I was in the alley, that guy, he and I talked for a couple of minutes.'

'You talked? What did you say?' The fluorescent lights heightened the contrast between his pale skin and dark hair.

'I was trying to get rid of him. At first I just figured he was a normal person, and asked him to move his car. But when I realized who he was . . . My mind was just . . . I was trying to figure out what to do, how to get rid of him. Finally I threatened to scream rape, and that started to work, but you guys came out.' She shook her head. 'I screwed up.'

'It sounds like you did fine. It was us that screwed things up.'

'No, but see, I had the chance. If I'd thought faster, he wouldn't have been there. I mean, my part in this whole thing was small, and I should have been able to handle — I should have been able to *help*. But when it came down to it, I didn't do anything.'

'Wait a second. You stood there and talked to this guy, right?'

'Yeah.'

'Knowing that he was a drug dealer with a gun. You managed to stand straight, talk to him, and cover our backs. Try to get rid of him. In an alley. Looking' — he gestured up and down her body — 'like that.'

'Yeah, but — '

'Sounds to me like you were pretty brave.'

173

The words caught her by surprise. She raised her head to look at him, expecting a teasing smile, the kind of look Alex might wear, playful from a distance. Instead Mitch looked back with perfect sincerity, his eyes wide and steady.

Without thinking, she went up on tiptoes to kiss his cheek. His skin was rough with blue-black stubble, and she could smell the remnants of his aftershave. She felt him tense, even though she was barely touching him, like every muscle in his body clenched at once. She froze, then started to lean back. 'I'm sorry.'

'No.' He put a hand on her arm, his touch gentle. His face was inches from hers, close enough that it was hard to focus. She could see him wrestling with something. In a bare whisper, he said, 'Jenn . . . '

No one had ever put so much weight into her name. Coming from his lips the single syllable seemed like sweet sad music, something lonely and haunting that she wanted to have, to be, and then he put his other hand on the side of her head, the palm against her cheek, fingers in her hair, and he kissed her lips.

For a moment she stood too stunned to react. A thousand thoughts flickered and danced across her mind, a collection of do's and don'ts, worry and excitement and fear and the lingering adrenaline of what they had done, that pounding sense of living on the ragged edge of now. And with it the pain of that existence, the fear of it, and the thought that distraction was fine, was what she needed. Then the simplest thought in the world hit, an old and familiar one that said

174

simply, a boy you care about is kissing you. Kiss back.

So she did.

It was awkward for a moment, that first-kiss sensation stronger than usual, but then their tongues touched, gently, tentative, his fingers moving in her hair, and it felt good, so good, to be in the moment, to not feel anything but this. She slid her arms to his side, his back, feeling his body beneath, and suddenly they were locked hard, their bodies thrust together, his belt buckle jamming into her stomach, his hand moving from her hair to her neck. Trailing down her back, fingers touching lightly. Reaching the small of her back and then hesitating, like he was asking permission.

She broke the kiss, a little dizzy. Paused. Asked herself what she was doing, if this was wise. Then remembered the version of herself she'd seen in the mirror that afternoon, the woman who wasn't afraid of anything, the one who would take the world for all it could give her. How free that had felt. How much better than the standard, everyday Jennifer.

She slid her hand on top of his. Then, looking him in the eyes, slowly pushed his hand down to her ass.

He moaned, almost a whimper, and squeezed, fingers gripping her flesh, digging in, and then it was happening, the two of them tearing into each other, ravenous, electric. She had a faint flash of surprise as she realized that he was a good kisser, soft and firm at once. His beard stubble ground against her upper lip. He stepped into her and she moved with him like they were dancing, let him guide her back against the refrigerator, never breaking the kiss.

His hands found the straps of her dress and slid them down her shoulders. Her nipples hardened in the cold air as the fabric eased past her breasts, her stomach. Caught at the swell of her hips for a breathless moment, and then slipped to pool at her feet. It was intoxicating, the surprise and heat of it, standing naked in her kitchen with this friend, this stranger, pressing against her.

He broke the kiss slowly, letting her lip slide from his mouth, and stepped back. His eyes drank her, top to bottom to top. 'God, you're beautiful,' he said. 'You're so beautiful.'

She raised her lips as he leaned in to kiss her, only he moved lower, his breath hot against the skin of her neck, his tongue darting and quick. He kissed the hollow of her throat, and then the space between her breasts. Ran his tongue down the flat of her belly, lower and lower, until he knelt in front of her on the tile floor. Like an act of worship, she thought, and then his tongue moved lower still, and she stopped thinking.

15

'I'm telling you, the only language these people understand is force. I'm sorry if that's not polite, but it's true. Iran, Iraq, al-Qaeda, the Taliban, they're all the same. They still kill people by stoning them. They behead journalists and post the video on the Internet. When the going gets tough, they hide in *caves*. They're barbarians, and barbarians only understand one thing. The sword. Or these days, the airstrike.' That got a laugh, and the man played to it, pausing to finish his single malt. He had the gentle pudginess of the very wealthy, not a beer belly but a general swelling, like he was entitled to more space in the world. 'We did it right in Afghanistan. Daisy cutter bombs first, questions later. See fifty men carrying AKs and riding camels, assume they're the enemy. The media loves to make fun of Bush, to question his intelligence, but I've met the man, and I stand by him. His policy worked in Afghanistan, and it's working in Iraq, and I don't see why we shouldn't let Iran know that if they want to tangle, we're more than happy to oblige.'

'Darling.' The woman who slid her arm beneath his had a face that looked thirty and eyes that looked twice that. 'You know it's not polite to talk politics at a party.' She nodded at Victor, said, 'Especially when you don't know everyone's point of view.'

'Oh, it's all right,' Victor said. 'I find it very

informative.' *These are the elite? No wonder this country is such a mess.* He smiled, said, 'Given your position on Iran, and your clear knowledge of the region, you must have very strong feelings about Betingan Makdous?'

'Umm, well, yes,' the man said, straightening. He coughed, glanced at the small audience staring at him. 'Of course, I'm not an expert, but again, I think the situation defines itself. The only way democracy is going to survive is if we give it a safe haven. Liberals go on about schools and roads and hospitals, but if you give the people *freedom*, they can take care of the rest themselves. If that means showing the barbarians the pointy end of an M-16, well, so be it.'

'You feel that's the proper way to deal with makdous?'

'Absolutely,' he said, and started to take a drink before noticing his glass was empty. 'Show them who's boss.'

'Really.' Victor shrugged. 'Personally, I like to just wrap makdous in pita and eat it. But if you want to shoot your pickled eggplant first, go nuts.'

A woman tittered. The man's face hardened, but before he could respond, Victor felt his cellphone vibrate. He glanced at the display, saw the number. 'I'm sorry,' he said, 'rude of me, but I need to take this call. Some of my clients are on the other side of the world.'

'Financial markets?' the man said between clenched teeth.

'More like import-export. Excuse me.' Victor gave a bright, blank smile, then turned away.

Opened his cell, said, 'Hold on.'

The party was in a magnificent Gold Coast penthouse, the east wall scored with windows framing Navy Pier and the cake-frosting traces of Lake Michigan. A string quartet played in the corner, and Mexicans in uniform wandered the crowd, passing trays. Across the room, French doors opened onto a small balcony, but even through the black-tie-bleached-blonde fund-raiser crowd, Victor could see that it was packed with smokers. A disgusting habit that somehow always got the best real estate.

He noticed a closed door on the far side of the room, strolled over, and stepped inside. The bedroom beyond was dark. He shut and locked the door, then walked over to the window and raised the blinds. A dozen stories below, cars raced up and down Lake Shore Drive, silent behind double-paned glass. He raised the phone. 'Go ahead.'

'I think there's a problem.' A pause, then, 'Someone was killed in the alley behind Rossi's. You know the restaurant I mean?'

'Of course. So?'

'He was killed by men who had just finished robbing the place.'

Victor closed his eyes. Goddamn it. He hated dealing with amateurs. Only pimps and porn stars would willingly adopt the nickname 'Johnny Love,' and the man didn't have the equipment to be a porn star. The business they'd done in the past had been strictly small-scale and very carefully regimented.

So why did you agree to meet with him? Why

179

tell him to make this deal?

Why, for the love of Christ, advance him a portion of the purchase price?

The answer was simple. The deal had seemed worth the risk. Thing about risk was, it was only worthwhile when you won. 'Interesting that it happened tonight.'

'That's why I called.'

He took a deep breath, stared out into the night. Watched reflected light dance across the surface of the glass. Someone laughed in the other room, a loud donkey bray. These people. Some of them were useful, and all of them were rich, and he'd made some even richer in ventures they were careful not to know too much about. But that didn't mean he had to like them. 'What do the cops know?'

'Nothing yet. They're focusing on the body. Our man in the department says the corpse's name is David Crooch. Freelance tough guy. Did a bit for stealing cars, a couple of assault charges.'

'What about our friend the restaurateur?'

'No word.'

'No *word*?'

'No. His lawyer met him at the station, had him out in twenty minutes, and he disappeared.'

'I want to talk to him.'

'When?'

'As soon as you can throw his fat ass in a chair.' Victor rubbed the bridge of his nose between thumb and forefinger. 'And do something for me. Throw hard.'

★ ★ ★

Mitch woke in the dark. Not the usual fuzzy-headed drifting, but wide-awake, just boom: eyes open, mind in gear.

In Jenn's bed.

It had all been real, then. Warmth spilled through his chest, a sense of possibility. The room was coming into focus, and as he lay on his side with his arm tucked beneath the pillow, he could see the outline of her body through the thin sheet. The memories tumbled happy and disconnected. The softness of her lips. Her hungry sigh as he kissed down her body. The ropy tightening of the muscles in her thigh as he tasted her. The soft, quick moans that echoed from her throat as she came. Standing up, taking her in his arms. Dizzy and happy. The two of them stumbling to the bedroom, giggling at the sheer wildness of it, the improbability, the sense of being in another world. How the giggling turned to full-on laughter as they fumbled with a condom package, until he finally took the edge between his teeth and ripped it.

The perfect connection of sliding into her, eyes locked and inches apart.

Oh God, she'd said. *Is this real? Are we doing this?*

It's real.

Are you sure?

Do you want me to stop?

No. No.

And finally, best of all, the melted softness of her body as she fell asleep against him, the cocoa butter smell of her hair, the miraculous sense that against all odds, he'd gotten what he wanted. In the dark of her bedroom, he smiled. It felt like a luxury, smiling just for himself. Smiling for pure joy.

Of course, if that was real, then the rest was, too.

His smile wilted. For a moment he was back in the alley, the smell of garbage and exhaust, the tinny radio playing Spanish love songs. The man staring up at him.

Mitch pulled the sheet off. Slid his legs out and sat on the edge of the bed. Silver light filtering through the blinds painted his pale thighs. He rubbed at his eyes, skin sticky with sleep.

What did you do?

The thought came fast and hard as a shiver. Panic soaked him, cold then hot, a flush that started in his chest. The man on the ground, helpless, teeth ground together in pain.

When he'd been young, Mitch had a BB rifle, spent months plinking away at bottles. One blue day a friend — God, what was his name, blond hair and bright teeth, one of those who would grow up to be a football star — it had been his turn with the rifle, only instead of the Coke can, he'd pointed it at a squirrel, a mangy thing watching them from a branch, and before Mitch could speak, there had been the soft pop of air. The squirrel had fallen. The two of them had stared at each other, horrified not only at what they had done, but at the swiftness of the consequence. The way the world reacted. There had been a moment of silence, total silence, and then they ran to stand over the poor thing. It had squirmed and writhed, tiny legs skittering uselessly, and Mitch had felt this same hot-cold sensation, even though he hadn't been the one to pull the trigger. The desperate desire to take it back, to rewind —

Stop.

He closed his eyes, straightened his back. Took a long, slow breath in through his nose, held it. Released.

Use your brain.

He forced himself to look at things logically. It wasn't a cute, fluffy squirrel that had been shot, a helpless creature that meant no harm. It was a drug dealer, an armed killer. One who had seen them, who could — would — wreck their lives. End them. His life, and Jenn's, and the others', too. There hadn't really been a choice.

But what were you even doing there?

That was easy. He was taking a chance. Going after something he wanted. The money, sure. But also the respect, from both the others and himself. And he had done what he'd said he would, what he had been afraid he would need to. He'd protected Jenn. If Mitch had walked out of the dinner party the other night, she would have been out there with no one but Ian. As good as alone.

What you did is no different from what people do every day. Not always with a gun. But the people you hold the door for, the ones who tip a couple of bucks before going out to a three-hundred-dollar dinner? You think they aren't ruthless in going after what they want?

Which is maybe why they aren't the ones holding the door.

Fabric rustled slightly, and he turned. Jenn mouthed dream words as she rolled to one side. The sheets pulled tight around her, hugging the swell of her hips. Hair slid down her milk-white back, draped across the pillow. Awake she was strong and sexy and dynamic. But asleep, God, she was like a stolen candy or an exotic flower, something delicate and almost unbearably sweet.

What had happened in the alley wasn't his life. This was. This was real. It was what he wanted, what he needed, maybe even what he deserved. Wasn't he a good guy? He didn't hurt people, didn't break laws and hearts. His action in the alley was the culmination of something. Something that had started days ago, as he began to push back against the world. To not sit still and take shit. To own his space.

And by that simple act, look what he had accomplished. Look where he was.

Put it away. Pack it somewhere deep and don't dwell on it. What you did is done. What you have, what you are, that's up to you. And don't forget. If you hadn't done it, would you be here with her now?

With the clarity that dwells in the silent heart of night, he knew the answer.

Mitch took another breath, then slid gently back under the covers. Jenn lay on her side, and he eased over, curled to spoon her. Her skin was warm and soft as he wrapped an arm around her, and she murmured something incomprehensible, then pulled him closer.

He was asleep the moment he closed his eyes.

16

'You have . . . one . . . new message and . . . four . . . saved messages. Press one for new — '

It was after two in the morning, and Alex had finally made it home. He pressed the button, held his cell to his ear.

Jenn's voice, her tone upbeat, perkily forced, like someone was listening in. 'Hey, Alex, where are you? We were all hoping to hear from you tonight. I guess you're busy. Anyway, the three of us are getting together for breakfast at my place tomorrow. Hope you can make it. We've got lots to catch up on. Hope all's well with you, and see you soon!'

It was like something had been inside of his lungs and chest, some thick toxic fog that had been choking him. He sighed, breathed it all out, felt his body slumping in relief. She'd said the three of them. Whatever had happened in the alley, it hadn't happened to them. Thank God.

Maybe things would turn out all right after all.

He called her cell, let it ring to voice mail. Hung up, dialed it again. Voice mail. He left a message saying he would love to join them for breakfast, then crawled into bed and collapsed into a merciful, dreamless dark.

When he woke in the morning, the first thing he reached for were the pain pills, swallowing two with a mouthful of tepid water. Then, still in bed, he called Jenn.

'Hello?' She sounded drowsy, half aware.

'It's me.'

'Alex? Are you OK?'

'I had to go to the hospital, but I'm fine. A couple of stitches and a headache. How are you?'

'I'm — we're — good. Things went . . . can you come over?'

'When?'

'An hour? I'll call Ian.'

'Should I call Mitch?'

She hesitated. 'No, I can.'

'All right. See you soon.' He closed the phone, then sat up slowly, the world wobbling as the blood drained from his head.

While the water warmed up, he peeled off the bandage, wincing as the tape tugged the torn skin. He squinted into the mirror. The cut was an inch long, ragged and swollen purple. Black surgical stitches gave it that Frankenstein look. Still, it didn't seem too bad, considering how it had scared him last night.

He washed his hands, then, very gently, his face. Dried himself, then put on more gauze and taped it in place.

'God, you're handsome,' he said and laughed. It felt a little manic. He pulled on jeans and a black T-shirt, his boots, and went into the shocking light of day.

By the time he'd made it to her floor, the door was open, Jenn standing in it. Her hair was brushed but not done up, and she wore shorts and a thin tank top. There were dark circles under her eyes, but her cheeks glowed as she stepped forward to hug him. He wrapped his arms around her hard, tugging her to him, inhaling deep.

She hugged back warmly enough, though her body seemed a little stiff, the way she was when others were watching. Over her shoulder, he saw Mitch, wearing the same outfit he had yesterday afternoon.

'Jesus, am I glad to see you.' Mitch held out a hand.

Alex let Jenn go, stepped past her, grabbed Mitch's hand and pulled him into a hug. 'You too, buddy. You too.'

Mitch clapped him on the back, and they both laughed, all of the worry and fear dropping away.

'Oh my God, your face.' Jenn reached for his cheek, stopped short of touching it. 'Are you — '

'I'm fine. Just a couple of stitches. Speaking of, where is the scrawny bastard?'

'Right here.'

The voice came from behind. Alex turned, saw Ian climbing the stairs, impeccable in suit pants and a jacket, no tie. The man looked wary, like he might dart away if the floor creaked. 'I . . . ' He ran a hand through his hair, dropped it to hang at his side. 'Fuck, man, I'm sorry. I'm really sorry.'

Alex narrowed his eyes. He curled one hand into a fist, took three fast steps forward —

'Alex, no!'

And threw his arm around his friend's neck, yanked him into a hug. The guy weighed nothing, felt impossibly thin through his clothing. For a moment he seemed confused, reluctant, but then he wrapped his arms around

187

Alex. 'Shit, you scared me there.'

'You think I'm going to hit you?' He shook his head. 'I'm too glad you're OK.' He stepped back, looked at the others. 'All of you.'

'We're more than OK,' Mitch said with a crooked smile. He glanced around, then reached inside the door of Jenn's apartment and came out with a big freezer bag, the kind that could hold half a chicken. Inside was a thick stack of green bundles.

'Ho-ly shit.'

'There's three more that size.'

'My God.' Alex stared at it, just stared. There it was, all he needed. His whole life, his daughter, a new job, a new start, all packed into a Ziploc bag. Something pounded through him, hot and happy, exploding in a grin. 'We did it. We fucking did it!' He started laughing, and the others joined, the four of them hooting and back-slapping like they'd won the Olympics.

After a few minutes, Jenn said, 'We should go inside. We have a lot to talk about.'

At her words, the smiles fell away. The two gun blasts seemed to echo off the bare white drywall. He straightened. Took a deep breath. 'Right,' he said. 'Tell me everything.'

* * *

She could see the good humor draining from Alex. Everything was shifting, and Jenn found that she didn't know what to do with her hands, how to cross her legs.

'Are you fucking *kidding* me?'

188

The hallway reunion had been great, a moment outside of time, but things had started to go south already. Strange enough to have them all in her living room. But then add to that the thing with Mitch last night. She wasn't sure how she felt about that. It hadn't been a planned decision, but it wasn't nothing, either. Sure, adrenaline had played a part, and the memory of what he had done for her, how far he'd been willing to go. But there had been a connection, too. It wasn't like the sex she and Alex had shared, a friendly, lusty sort of thing predicated on an understanding of boundaries. Last night felt like maybe the start of something.

In a normal relationship, they would have slept late, made love again, sipped coffee in bed and giggled. Whereas this morning, she had awakened, stretched, and enjoyed five peaceful seconds as her consciousness booted up — then been slapped by the memory of the alley. Her throat had tightened and her belly had gone acid. She'd put a hand over her mouth to catch a whimper. Slipped out of bed and into the bathroom to look at herself in the mirror.

You wanted life to have meaning, to feel real? Here you go.

She had a desperate urge to cry, to hug her knees in the corner, at the same time she wanted to collapse in front of the toilet and retch. Her body was flame and ice and needles. Jenn had spun the cold water tap on, held her wrists underneath, forced herself to take deep breaths.

What did we do?

Jesus Christ.

189

What did we do?

Had she really thought that sleeping with Mitch would somehow erase what had happened? It had provided distraction and comfort, and she appreciated both. But the horror was still waiting for her on the other side.

Then the phone had rung, and it was game-on from that point. She forced herself out of the bathroom to talk to Alex in code. After hanging up, she'd found Mitch staring at her, his expression filled with emotions too varied and conflicting to bear a single name.

'Is Alex OK?' he'd asked.

'I think so, He's coming over.'

He'd been silent for a long moment. 'Guess I better get up.'

'Yeah.' She opened her lingerie drawer, saw she needed to do laundry. The absurdity of it almost set her to laughing. She picked up the panties she'd discarded yesterday and stepped into them. 'Listen . . . '

'Please don't say 'about last night,' OK? Please?'

'I wasn't going to.' She found a bra that was a close-enough match and slid the straps over her shoulders. His eyes traced her breasts as she hid them. 'But I think we should be quiet about this. Not tell the others.'

'Not tell them what, exactly?'

She gestured to the bed.

'This wasn't just sex for me.'

'For me either. It's just, right now, it will make things more complicated.' *Especially between you and Alex. Way to go, Jenn. Nice timing.*

'All right,' he'd said. 'I understand.' Then he'd pulled on his pants and, threading his belt, said, 'Coffee?' with forced cheer.

And now, an hour later, she sat on the comfortable couch that was supposed to be her refuge, a knit blanket over her knees, and watched the boys square off. Sometimes it sucked to be right.

'Are you fucking *kidding* me?' Alex repeated. 'You shot him on purpose?'

'You weren't there,' Ian said. 'Mitch did what he had to.'

'You're right, I wasn't there. I was on the floor, bleeding from the head. Wonder how that happened, genius? If I had been there — '

'What?' Mitch leaned back. His voice was calm, his manner easy. 'What would you have done, Alex? There's a drug dealer on the ground, shot once, and he can identify your best friend. So what would you have done? Asked him nicely not to hunt her down and murder her?'

'I . . .'

'Yeah.' Mitch glanced at his watch like an executive late for his next meeting. 'Exactly. So how about we knock off the posturing and focus on the situation.'

She had to admit to being impressed. It was hard to reconcile this self-assured man with the wallflower she was used to. Alex looked startled too, said, 'So what happened next?'

'Ian drove the rental car, and Jenn and I took the dealer's Eldorado, this big purple boat — '

'Where are they?'

'Parked separately, a couple of blocks from

here. I wiped the Caddy down. Then we came up here, called you, and started waiting. Now, your turn. What did the cops say?'

'They mostly asked questions.'

'What did you tell them?'

'A couple of men in masks came in yelling. I tried to take one of them and got socked for it. After they left, I heard shots.'

'Did they ask what you were doing there?'

'Yeah. I told them Johnny had asked me back, I didn't know why.'

'Did they buy it?'

'Why wouldn't they?'

Mitch nodded. He had one leg crossed at the knee of the other, the foot bobbing. 'Good. So it's like we thought. No reason to tie it to us. We probably won't hear anything more.'

Was it really that simple? Could it be? Jenn couldn't think of a reason why not, but somehow she just didn't believe it. Maybe it was all those Sunday School afternoons. Sunlight filtering dusty through high windows, coloring books with pictures of Jesus and the disciples. Father Mike talking to them about God. God who was always watching, saw everything they did. Every cruelty to a younger sibling, every stolen cookie.

'Not to change the subject,' Ian said, 'but how much was there?'

'More than we thought,' Mitch said. 'Two hundred and fifty grand.'

The words fell like a change in the weather, a soft snow that muffled sound. Ian broke into a wide grin. Alex gave a low whistle. 'That's ... wait ...'

'Sixty-two thousand, five hundred each,' Ian said. 'Not bad for a night's work.' He reached for one of the bags, split the top open. Stuck his face in and inhaled hard. 'Goddamn, that's good.'

'Yeah, well, you're going to have lots of time to smell it,' Mitch said. 'We can't spend it.'

'What do you mean?'

'We can't. Not yet.'

'Why?'

Mitch sighed. 'Would you think for half a second? This was supposed to be untraceable. Johnny wouldn't even have gone to the cops. He couldn't afford to. But now there's a body.'

'So?' Ian's eyes were wide. 'What does that matter?'

'It matters because everything is more complicated. We have to cut every tie between us and the robbery. Dump the clothes, the masks, especially the guns. Return the rental. Get rid of the Cadillac. And go on living our lives just exactly as before. Which means that we have to pretend that money doesn't exist. Take it home and hide it somewhere.'

They'd talked about that this morning, as they'd broken the stacks up. Mitch had wanted to get a safe-deposit box, something secure, and lock it all away. But she'd pointed out that there was no way the others would go for just one of them having a key. And if all four of them were on record at a bank for a safe-deposit box? Seemed like a big clue.

He'd yielded, but she could tell he wasn't happy about it. She couldn't blame him, watching Ian cradle the Ziploc like a favorite teddy bear. 'For how long?'

'Probably just a couple of months.'

'No.' Alex shook his head. 'No way. We did this because we needed the money. I can't wait — '

'You have to. Or else you can't take your share now.'

'Who says?'

Mitch stood up. 'I do.'

Oh shit. Jenn supposed on some primal level this should have gotten her excited, strong men fighting for dominance, but instead she just felt tired. Tired of the way they talked and interacted, the way everything was a contest. Tired of the whole idea of men. She was filled with a sudden regret for having slept with either of them.

'I need that money,' Ian said. 'I mean, I really need — '

'Mitch, listen, I understand what you're doing, but — '

'This was your stupid plan in the first place, and now look — '

'*Shut. Up.*' Jenn made her voice a whip. 'All of you.' It was the first time she'd spoken in the last minutes, and the harshness cut the air. The boys wore sheepish caught-by-Mom looks. 'Jesus *Christ.* What's wrong with you? In case you hadn't noticed, we're in serious trouble right now. Would you stop it with the alpha-male nonsense? Next step, one of you shits in his hand and throws it.'

Ian started to argue, but she bulldozed him. 'Here's what's going to happen. Alex, you're going to get rid of the guns. Wipe them off and

194

throw them in the river or a storm drain or something. Ian, return the rental car. Along the way, take all of the clothes to a Dumpster across town. Mitch and I will take care of the spare car.'

'But — '

'No buts. We'll get it washed and cleaned, and then take it somewhere to get stolen.'

'Why the two of you?'

'Because one of us will need to follow in another car. In the meantime, *do not spend a dime* of your share. Mitch is right. We don't know the situation yet. If the cops get on us, or Johnny, or friends of whoever got shot last night, we're going to need it.'

'For what?' Ian asked.

'Maybe just to stay alive.' Mitch put one hand on Alex's shoulder, the other on Ian's. 'Guys, listen. I know this isn't what we planned. But neither was last night. This isn't a game. If we get caught, we're going to jail. And that's only if the *police* catch us. If it's Johnny, or someone else?' He blew a breath.

'We're in this together,' Jenn said. 'We get through it together or we go down together. That's the only way. OK?'

There was a long silence. Ian rubbed his nostrils between thumb and forefinger, and shuffled his feet on her rug. Alex looked like he was thinking of bolting out the door with one of the bags.

'*OK?*' she asked again.

'Fine,' Ian said, heaving a sigh. Alex only nodded. Neither of them would look at her.

And all of a sudden she had the strongest feeling they were fucked.

17

'You dipshits know who I am? You're in a world of hurt for this.'

Victor heard the voice through the doorway and paused to listen.

'You think I'm just some restaurant owner you can jack off the street and shake down? Not gonna happen, kid. I'm connected all the way up. I'm done, you're going to regret waking up this morning.'

The words were right, but the tone rang false to Victor. One of the things that made him good at his work was a nose for fear, and through the bluster, Mr Loverin was scared.

Good.

The ten-flight climb had Victor winded, and he took a moment to calm his breathing. Then he fastened the top button of his jacket, shot his cuffs, and walked through the open doorway.

The space would one day be suites, another anonymous gray Chicago office building. But now it was an empty room half a city block in length, sitting vacant while the owner wrestled the city council over permits. Coils of wiring hung from exposed girders. The wind whipped through open walls. Dawn was just breaking in the east, painting the sky with a blood-red brush.

Johnny Love sat in a chair at the far end, ten feet from the edge. His hands were cuffed behind him, and a black hood covered his face.

Victor smiled. Nice touch.

Slowly, conscious of the theatre of the thing, Victor began to walk over, his dress shoes ringing loud on the cement. The two men standing near Johnny straightened, nodded at him. Ex-Army guys. Real money bred an efficiency that love of the flag sometimes didn't. Especially after getting stop-lossed once or twice.

'Who's there? What the fuck is this?'

Victor stood for a moment, let the guy imagine the worst. Then he nodded, and one of his soldiers snapped the hood off.

'What the fu — ' Johnny's mouth froze open, and his eyes went wide. 'You.'

'Me.'

'I was going to call you.'

'Oh? When?'

'I was on my way when these geniuses grabbed me.'

'But you were robbed last night.'

His eyes darted. 'How did you — yeah, I was. But I was taking care of it. I have calls in, people out . . . '

'Calls.' Victor nodded. 'People.'

'What is this, anyway? We're partners, for Christ's sake.' Trying to recover his bluster.

'Stand up, Johnny.'

'What?'

'Stand up.'

Moving like he was afraid he was going to be knocked down again, Johnny rose. Victor gestured, and one of his men moved the chair. 'Now. Here are the rules.'

'Rules?'

'Don't worry, they're simple. I'm going to ask you questions. Every time I don't like your answer, I'm going to take a step forward. And you' — Victor gestured — 'you're going to take a step back.'

'What are you . . . ?' Johnny spun, saw the open air and the hundred-foot plummet to broken ground behind him. His skin visibly paled as he measured the distance. 'No, hey, listen — '

'Where's my merchandise?'

'I — I don't know, really, I don't know.'

Victor took a step forward. Johnny stared at him. 'I'm not going to — are you crazy?'

Victor sighed, glanced at one of the men. The soldier started forward, and Johnny took a hurried step back. 'OK, OK.'

'Good. Now. I'm curious. When was the last time you were robbed?'

'I've never — never.'

'But you were last night.'

'Yes. They came in wearing masks, waving guns, they — '

'Don't you find it a little unusual that you were robbed for the very first time on the one occasion we're doing serious business?'

'It wasn't me. I wouldn't do that. You know I wouldn't.'

Victor took a step forward, his eyes locked on Johnny's. After a moment's hesitation, the fat man took a step back. A gust of wind cut through the floor with a reek of garbage and exhaust.

'Where is what I want?'

'They must have taken it.'

'By 'they' you mean the men who robbed you, for the first time you've ever been robbed, on the exact night that you were getting my merchandise? Merchandise for which I graciously, and in violation of my general principles, supplied part of the purchase price?' He cocked his head. 'Do you see my concern?'

'Yeah, totally, but — '

Victor took a step forward.

'Hey, no, listen.' Johnny glanced behind him, his eyes measuring the half-dozen feet between him and the edge. 'I'll get you your money back. Right away. I know how this looks, but it's not that. I would never do that. Do you think I'm stupid?'

'I think you owe me a step. If you make me take it from you, it might be more than one.'

Trembling, the man moved back a scant six inches.

'Johnny.'

He winced and went another foot.

'That's better. Now. I'm afraid that the money isn't my only concern right now. I want the materials you promised. I have some gentlemen very eager to take delivery. And I have a reputation to protect. When I say that I have something for sale, I need to deliver. Otherwise, people don't trust me anymore. And it's important that people believe every word I say.' Victor curled his fingernails in to look at them. 'You, for instance. Do you believe me?'

'Yes.'

'Good. That's good. Because you have three

199

steps left, and that last one's a doozy.'

'I swear, I didn't say anything about you to the police.'

'I know you didn't, Johnny. I've read the report.' He let the words sink in. 'I want to know what you think happened.'

'I — ' He paused. 'Maybe it was an inside job.'

'Did you tell someone?'

'No, of course not. I had a bartender working as security, but no way it's him. He's a civilian, kind of a pussy. And he didn't know what was going on.'

'Then how could it have been an inside job?'

'Maybe someone on your end found out about it. No disrespect,' Johnny added quickly. 'Just that the guys who came in, they were pros. And that would explain the timing.'

Victor smiled. 'Do you think so?'

'I . . . maybe.' The man put his hand to his forehead, his eyes widening. 'Wait a second. Bennett.'

'Who?'

'Bennett! The guy who scored this stuff in the first place. What if he's burning us?'

'Go on.'

'He said he wasn't going to come himself, right? Told me in advance that he was going to send someone to bring me the stuff and take the money. A kid named David Crooch.'

'The body in the alley.'

'Right, right. What if Bennett also sent the guys to rob me, and told them to kill Crooch? That way it looks like he got burned too. Motherfucker!' Johnny straightened. 'He ripped us both off, partner.'

'So Bennett set up the meet as a con. He never intended to give us the merchandise. It might not even exist.'

'Exactly. Exactly.' The man hopeful now, his eyes wide. 'Sneaky *fuck*.'

'Of course, you could be doing the same thing.'

'Huh?'

'For all I know, this Bennett doesn't exist. Maybe you made him up, staged the robbery, and had Crooch killed in the alley.'

'No, I would never — ' He shook his head violently.

'Or maybe Bennett does exist, and you decided to burn us both. Keep the money, keep the goods.'

'No, I swear — '

'See, here's the thing, Johnny. I don't care. I really don't. I just want what I paid for, because I made deals based on your word. And I'm holding you responsible.'

'Wait — '

'So you need to understand something.' Victor took a step, and Johnny followed suit, trembling. 'Two more steps, that's all you've got. I will walk you right off the edge of this building. And you will do it, staring me in the eyes the whole time. You will walk yourself right out of life. Because you can imagine what will happen to you if you don't. Because you believe every word I say.' He took another step, and Johnny did too. 'Right?'

'Yes!' The man stood six inches from the edge, hands still cuffed, bent slightly forward as though afraid his balance would betray him. 'But I swear to God, I didn't have anything to do with this. I would have come to you right away — I should have come to you right away. I was just trying to handle it on my own. I'll get you the stuff, somehow, oh Jesus, I don't want to, please don't make me.' There was a sharp tang to the air, and the front of Johnny's track pants darkened. 'I'll get it for you!'

'How?'

'I'll find Bennett. If he didn't fuck me, I'll find the people that did. I swear, I swear I will. I swear on my mother.'

'Your mother, who lives in that lovely converted bungalow in Jefferson Park?'

The man's head snapped straight up. His face was nothing but eyes and panic.

'You wanted to be big-league, Johnny. Welcome. We play a rougher game.'

'I will get it for you. I promise.' His voice coming from a ragged place people liked to pretend didn't exist.

Victor stared him in the face. Lifted his foot, watched Johnny flinch. Then he set it back down and broke into a smile. 'OK.' He gestured to his men. They flanked Johnny, one standing ready while the other uncuffed him. The man made a sobbing sound, took a quick stride away from oblivion.

'First,' Victor said, 'I want to talk to Bennett. *Today*. Second. You put the word out to everyone that you were robbed. I don't care what it does to your reputation. Every pimp, every drug dealer, every bookie. Put money on it. Your

202

own, of course. Someone out there knows something. I want to know it too.'

'Yes. Yes. No problem.' His hands shook as he rubbed at his wrists.

'You can go.'

The man sprinted for the exit. Victor let him almost make it before he said, 'Oh, and, Johnny?'

He froze. Victor could see the animal part of the man wanting to continue. Slowly, slowly he turned around. 'Yes?'

'From now on, let's keep the lines of communication open, OK? I find business transactions run much more smoothly that way.'

'Uhh . . . yeah. Sure. I'll tell you the moment I hear anything.'

'Good. That's all.' Victor turned away, walked to the edge of the building. He stood with his toes hanging off, hands clasped behind his back. Chicago spread out in front of him, a wave of tall buildings breaking into a dark froth of two-flats and trees that extended all the way to the rising sun. Clean morning wind teased at his suit jacket. He took a deep breath, tasted the air.

From behind, one of his men said, 'You really think he had anything to do with it?'

Victor glanced back, surprised. 'Thought never entered my mind.'

18

What was it with women and their showers?

She had ten kinds of shampoo and conditioner, body lotion in tropical flavors, a couple of things of exfoliant, whatever that was, a washcloth, a loofah, two bright pink razors, and a scrub thing. But bar soap? No.

Mitch settled on coconut-lime body gel. You were probably supposed to put it on the scrub thing first, but that seemed like too presumptuous an intimacy. He grinned at that, considering he'd touched and licked every inch of her last night. Still. He squirted the stuff on his hands, rubbed his armpits, his shoulders, his crotch.

He felt better than good, filled with a sense that everything was going to work out OK. He'd always envied that in other people. Happier, better-looking, richer people. They had a basic belief that the world would line up the way they wanted, and it usually did.

Well, now it was his turn.

Don't get cocky. You're not out of trouble yet. Standing under the showerhead, hot water plastering his hair, running down his back, he thought through it again. Checking and rechecking, for the hundredth time.

Best he could tell, once they finished what they had to do today, they'd be clear. As long as they stayed cool and everyone did what they were supposed to, nothing should tie them to last night.

Once things had quieted down, they could tell the others about them. Jenn was nervous, he could understand that; hell, so was he. But now that she had finally seen him, he was going to do his damnedest to make sure it worked out.

Starting with them not getting caught. Best get moving. He reluctantly shut off the water, slid open the shower door, and reached for the towel Jenn had left, a big puffy thing. Where was the best place to abandon a car? A parking lot? Or maybe a rough neighborhood would be better. That made sense. He'd do a little Googling, find out where the most cars were stolen. Then run the Caddy through a detail shop to be sure there weren't any traces, leave it with the windows open and the keys in the ignition. Even if the police found it first, it wouldn't be a disaster. They'd just trace it back to the drug dealer —

Holy shit.

How had he missed that?

★   ★   ★

She was leaning on the counter, drinking a Diet Coke and thinking about that feeling of impending disaster, wondering what it meant. Were they being stupid even now? Should they go straight to the police and tell them everything? A big part of her wanted to, wanted to confess and get absolution, a detective standing in for a priest.

Absolution? You killed someone last night.

The liquid in her mouth went bitter, and she set the soda down, listened to the hum of the hot-water pipes. Mitch had asked if she minded if he showered, and while yeah, she kind of did, she didn't know how to say that. It wasn't that she wanted him gone for good or anything. She just wanted a little time to herself. Time to lay on the couch and stare at the ceiling and think about everything, the money and the alley and the dead man and Mitch and Alex. It was a lot for a girl to process.

'Jenn!'

Even muffled by the walls, she could hear his excitement. She started for the bedroom fast and had no sooner opened the door than they almost collided, him naked and dripping, the towel on his shoulders.

'Whoa.' She glanced down, then back up. Smiled at him. 'Hello there.'

He actually blushed as he wrapped the towel around his slim waist. For a second, she had a flash memory of Alex. It was hard not to compare their bodies, muscles and tattoos against pale and somewhat awkward flesh. *Not that it was awkward last night.*

'What's up?'

'We forgot, we totally forgot about it. How could we miss it?'

'What?'

'The car. We were so caught up in everything — '

'Slow down. What are you talking about?'

'He was there to sell drugs, right? But he wasn't carrying anything.' He cocked his head.

'So where would they be?'

She felt a moment of panic, then a cool revelation. 'In his — '

'Car. Exactly.' He ran his hands up through his hair, slicked it back. 'I think maybe we better take a look before we get it stolen, eh?'

★ ★ ★

'All right. Just look normal, like this is our car.'

'It is our car.'

Her morbid joke surprised him, and he laughed through his nose, then opened the door of the Eldorado.

The seats were leather, and the interior spotless. How did people do that? He never meant for his Honda to look like a rolling junk heap, filled with printed directions and crushed soda cans and a tattered map. It just sort of happened.

'Anything in the glovebox?'

She opened it, dug around. 'Owner's manual, sunglasses. Registration.'

'Let me see.'

The name on the form was David Crooch. As he stared at it, the letters machine-printed, he had a weird sensation, guilt and fear mixed together. David Crooch. That was the name of the man he had —

Push it down.

He folded the paper, stuck it in his pocket. It was getting easier and easier to ignore the things that tried to claim him. Mitch spun, looked in the backseat. An umbrella on the floor. Other than that, nothing. 'Let's try the trunk.'

A milk crate with emergency supplies: a bottle of tire-repair spray, a coil of rope, and a blanket. A lug wrench. And a black duffel bag, about the size to take to the gym. He'd gone his whole life without giving two thoughts to duffel bags, and now they were popping up everywhere. He started to unzip it.

'Maybe we should do this subtly?' She nodded to a mother pushing a stroller past them.

'Right.' He hoisted it to his shoulder. It was neither heavy nor light, and something plastic clanked inside it. Mitch shut the trunk, and the two of them climbed back into the Cadillac. The silence that fell seemed to radiate from the bag.

'Let's see what a quarter-million dollars in drugs looks like.' He unzipped the bag and split it open.

Inside were four bottles. He reached in, pulled one out. It was rigid plastic and felt like it might crack if dropped. It was filled with a thick, dark liquid. He passed it to her, took out another. The same. Mitch fumbled around in the bag, but that was it, just the four bottles. 'Huh.'

'What is it?' She leaned toward the window, holding it toward the sunlight. 'Looks like motor oil.'

'Liquid heroin? Some kind of designer drug?'

'What was that club drug that was really big a couple of years ago? One of the alphabet drugs, not E or K.'

'K is ketamine. Horse tranquilizer. I don't think it's a liquid.'

'G, that was it. GHB? Something like that. I

remember reading an article that said it was the new roofie.' She rolled the bottle, and the liquid inside moved sluggishly, leaving a trail around the side. 'But it doesn't seem like there's enough here to be worth that much.'

'Maybe it's something they use to process drugs?' He unscrewed the top of one bottle. Cautiously, he leaned forward and took an experimental sniff. It had a sharp chemical odor, nothing he recognized. He held it out to her, and she took a tentative whiff. 'Any idea — '

Something exploded behind his eyeballs. The pain was sudden and fierce, a slamming migraine that made him clench the armrest. He fought to keep the bottle from slipping from shaking hands. The pain spread, sending tendrils down his neck, his shoulders. His muscles seemed to be tensing, fighting against themselves.

'Shit!' Jenn had her hand to her face, covering her eyes, fingers white. 'Shit, oh *shit*.'

Whatever it was, it was bad. He reached for the top he'd tossed on the dashboard, the sunlight painting his arm in a glowing haze. Scraps of rusty metal tore through the tender meat of his brain. Jenn moaned, the sounds muffled by her fingers.

He concentrated on fumbling for the lid, trying not to breathe. His fingers trembled as Mitch forced himself to take hold of the plastic. He wanted to rush, to jam it down and run away, but whatever this shit was, he didn't dare spill it. He slotted the lid on carefully and turned until it stopped, then gripped the bottle and gave it a last crank hard enough his forearms jumped.

'Got it. Get out!' Without waiting for her, he opened the driver's-side door. The fresh air seemed to cut his nostrils. 'Come on.'

'What?'

'Come on.' He hurried around the side of the car, slid an arm under her shoulders, began to half support, half drag her along. The block seemed endless, the sunlight sparkling in shards, the world gone watery. They passed a woman who said something concerned, but he ignored her, just hurried along.

'Where — '

'Hurry.'

They stumbled across the intersection, a horn shrieking as a cab passed. He couldn't tell how much of what he was experiencing was from the drug and how much from the pain, whether his vision was blurry because his pupils had dilated or because he was squinting so hard. It didn't matter. All that mattered now was getting back.

When they reached her porch, it took more effort than he would have expected to haul his legs up the stairs, the muscles strangely tight and unresponsive. His lungs felt like something was squeezing them. She fumbled with her keys, finally popped the dead bolt.

'We need to wash.' He started for the sink, thought better of it. Pulling her with him, he headed through the bedroom and into her bath. He twisted the water to hot and started to strip off his clothing.

'I can't.' She clenched her teeth, her hands fumbling behind her back. 'My fingers.'

Mitch spun her around and undid the clasp of

her bra, yanked her skirt and panties down. Then he opened the shower door and stepped in, held out a hand to help her. They got under the water, the two of them huddling close. A week ago he'd have cut off a finger for this kind of situation, but now he had no thought at all for her nudity. 'Soap.' He cursed, fumbling through her stuff. Grabbed the same bottle of coconut crap he'd found before, squirted it into her hands and then his. He lathered hard and scrubbed his hands and face, alternating turns under the water with her.

It might have been the water or the soap or just time, but slowly, very slowly, the muscles in his back and shoulders began to relax. The headache didn't go away, but at least it stopped getting worse. He let out a long breath. 'Are you OK?'

She looked up at him. 'Is that a trick question?'

★　★　★

'We should get rid of it.'

'How?' They sat at opposite ends of her couch, him back in his robbery clothes, her in a soft bathrobe, knees tucked to her chin. 'I don't think we should just throw it in the garbage.'

'Why not? I mean, whatever it is, it will end up at the dump. Kill some seagulls. Big deal.'

'Maybe someone will get into it first. Maybe a kid.'

She bit her thumbnail. With her hair damp and the robe, the gesture made her look like a little girl, and he had the strongest urge to move to her, wrap his arms around her shoulders.

'Besides,' he said, 'this is what Johnny was buying. If something does go wrong — '

'You said it wouldn't.'

'I don't think it will. But if it does, this could be valuable. It must be some sort of concentrated chemical. Something for processing serious quantities of drugs.'

'It looked so *normal*.'

She was right. He could still see them in his mind's eye, the bottles ordinary, the liquid like thick, strong coffee.

Very damn strong. 'We need to hang on to it, at least for a while. If everything goes as planned, we can figure out a safe way to get rid of it then. Maybe, I don't know, put it in a box, pour concrete around it.'

'Concrete?'

'Whatever. You get my point.' Mitch leaned into the couch. His headache was fading, but the memory was enough to make him wince. 'I don't think we should tell the others about this.'

She looked at him over tented knees. 'Why?'

'You know I love them both.'

'But?'

'I'm not sure they need to know. I'm not sure . . . ' He hesitated. It was a big statement, especially considering what they were in the middle of. 'I'm not sure we can really trust them right now.'

He expected her to get mad, to call him a hypocrite or worse. But she just nodded slowly. 'I know what you mean.'

212

'You do?'

'Ian with the coke. And Alex . . . I don't know.'

The words spread like a warm balm through his chest. It had kept him up at night more than once, the thought of the two of them together, big strong Alex, the sensitive weightlifter with the daughter, the guy who never had trouble talking to women.

Focus. 'OK. So we keep it, and we don't tell them about it. That way we're covered if something comes up. If nothing does, they never need to know.'

'They'll think of it eventually. The same way you did.'

'We'll tell them we got rid of the car.'

'What do you mean? Aren't we going to?'

He shook his head.

'Why not?'

'Because that's where we're going to keep this stuff. At a safe distance. Besides, that way if somehow the cops do get involved, search our places — '

'We don't have to explain it.' She smiled. 'You think of everything, don't you?'

'I'm trying.'

She leaned forward to take his hand. 'I'm glad.'

That warmth spread farther.

19

The man reflected in the window was standard-issue Lincoln Park: designer jeans, faded Cubs hat, and a baby carriage. Somewhere between youth and middle age, in vaguely good shape. He stopped at the north corner of a restaurant called Rossi's and propped one foot up on the brick base of the storefront to tie his shoe. As he did, the dark shadow of a limousine slid wavering past in the glass.

It stopped in front of the restaurant. The blinkers came on. The side windows were opaque, but the windshield framed the driver, square-jawed with restless eyes. For a moment the car idled, and then a door winged open and Johnny Love climbed out. Two broad-shouldered men followed, glancing up and down the street. The three walked to the front door of the restaurant and went inside.

The man with the baby carriage exchanged one foot for the other, carefully untying and re-knotting the laces. Then he straightened and headed south, whistling as he pushed the stroller. He smiled down into it, and said, 'Beautiful day, huh? How's my favorite baby boy?'

When the carriage was parallel to the limo, Bennett leaned forward, lifted the fuzzy blanket and picked up the Smith he'd concealed beneath. Then he turned with a fluid motion, opened the side door and flowed in, pointing the gun at the man on the seat opposite, a stylish dude in a beautiful suit.

'Tell your driver it's OK.'

Victor's eyes narrowed.

'Sir?' The voice came over the intercom. 'Do you — '

Victor thumbed the microphone. 'Everything's copacetic, Andrews. Thank you.' His voice calm.

Bennett nodded and closed the door without looking. 'You know who I am?'

'I've got an idea.'

'Good. Now I know that Johnny told you he'd brokered a meeting. But instead of having it in his restaurant with your security watching, I thought maybe we'd have it right here. I hope you don't mind me changing the plans.'

'Depends what you've changed them to.'

'Fair enough.' Bennett leaned forward. 'I'll get to the point. I didn't burn you. We've never met, but I'm coming here with respect.' He spun the gun sideways, then set it in his lap and removed his hand. 'This was just a precaution to make sure we had a chance to talk.'

Victor watched him move. His eyes were difficult to read. A poker player. Abruptly he scratched at his chin, and Bennett forced himself not to react to the sudden motion. Victor said, 'You're a careful man.'

'The people who think consequences don't apply to them end up on the floor. Yeah, I'm careful. You're Johnny's buyer, I presume.' Bennett raised his hand. 'It's OK, you don't have to answer. I know you're careful too. What did he tell you about me?'

'That you had a specialized product. He also said that you may have been doing the whole thing as a con. That both the people who robbed him and the corpse in the alley might have worked for you.'

Bennett nodded. 'I figured it was something like that. You don't mind my asking, did he volunteer that, or did you have to press him?'

'Why?'

'I want to know how annoyed to be.'

Victor considered for a moment, then shrugged. 'I pressed him. But he's silly putty, not steel.'

'There's an understatement, brother.'

'My turn for a question.'

'Shoot.'

'Why are you here, Mr Bennett?'

'Just Bennett. Like Prince, only taller. Two reasons. First, to tell you that I didn't rip you off. Second, it wasn't just you that got robbed. Someone made off with my money.'

'So you don't believe Mr Loverin was in on it?'

'Johnny?' Bennett shook his head. 'Risk screwing me and you both? He's stupid, not dumb.'

'I agree.' The man paused. 'That does put the suspicion back on you.'

Bennett fired a grin. 'If I'd stolen from you, we wouldn't be having this lovely chat. I'd have blown your brains across the back window.' He said it lightly, theatrically.

Victor returned the smile. 'Andrews, show Mr Benn — sorry, just Bennett — what 'copacetic' means.'

There was a buzz, and the partition rolled

216

down. The driver was perched on his knees in the front seat, a Colt 1911 zeroed in perfectly steady hands. For a moment, Bennett's grin faltered. He snatched for it, got it back. 'Very nice. The partition isn't bulletproof, I take it?'

'Just the exterior glass.' Victor turned. 'Thank you, Andrews. That's fine. And you can relax now. I think we understand each other.'

Bennett picked up his pistol, snapped the safety on, and leaned forward to tuck it behind his belt. 'So. You know I didn't steal from you, I know you didn't steal from me, and neither of us believes Johnny is suicidal. Where does that leave us?'

'Seems unlikely the robbery was random. Someone knew something.'

'No kidding. How are you working it?'

'To start, Johnny is spreading his name and money around, asking for tips.'

'Risky.'

'Only to him.'

'Still.' Bennett cocked his head. 'Even if he gets something, Johnny is about as subtle as a strap-on cock.'

'You're right.' Victor leaned forward. 'What I need is someone on the ground who has a brain. Who can operate with a little grace.'

'Uh-huh. And what's in this for me?'

'I get my goods. You get your money.'

'No deal. The product they won't know what to do with. But money goes easy. I could find these assholes for you, discover they've spent what's mine.'

'How much did Johnny promise you?'

'I should say three hundred. But two-fifty.'

Victor nodded. 'All right. I'll stake you. Whatever we don't recover, I'll make up.'

'Your margin that good, huh?'

'My margin is my business. Deal?'

'Sure. Understand, though, I'm not working for you. We're cooperating. I work alone.'

'Fine. And I only stake you if I get my goods and they're intact. Half the product, half the money.'

'Fair enough. I'll be in touch.' Bennett reached for the door handle. 'By the way. You don't mind my asking, what was someone like you doing slumming with Johnny Love?'

'I could ask the same.' Victor leaned back, crossed his legs. 'And, Bennett, you find these people, then this — '

'Could be the start of a beautiful friendship?'

'Maybe 'profitable' is a better word.'

'I hear you, brother. Consider them found.'

20

'I'm sorry,' the teller said. 'I don't understand.'

'I want to make three deposits,' Alex said. 'Separately.'

'To the same account.'

'Yes.'

'So why not . . . '

'Look, I just want to deposit this money, and then I want a cashier's check cut for the total amount to Tricia Kern — I mean, Tricia Stevens.'

'I'm sorry, I don't understand.'

'Why do you need to understand?' He hated this dynamic: Give an imbecile a vest and a counter to stand behind, and suddenly they had some say in your life. Banks weren't nearly as bad as the post office, but still. And it wasn't like he could explain he was trying to cover up the cash deposit from his robbery. 'Why can't you just do your job?'

'Sir, I don't have to listen to that kind of talk.'

He started to snap at her, caught himself. 'I'm sorry. I'm just having a bad day.' He gestured at the bandage on his face. 'My head hurts.' Her face softened some, and he continued. 'I know it seems strange. But could you humor me?'

The teller glanced past him at the growing line, all of them checking their watches or glaring. 'Who was that check to again?'

Alex understood what Jenn and Mitch were

thinking, not spending the money. It made sense if you thought of this as a game. But that was bullshit. This wasn't about generational ennui for him. Everything he'd done, he'd done for Cassie. If not for her, he'd never have taken the risk. Wouldn't have gotten clocked in the head with a pistol or had scissors held to his eyeball or had to lie to the police. Wouldn't have had to lay there on the floor while his nice, simple plan went to shit out in the alley. *He* hadn't killed anyone. The Four Musketeers thing went only so far.

'Here you are.' The teller slid the check across the counter. 'In the future, I'd appreciate if you didn't take that tone with me.'

And I'd appreciate it if you'd fucking do what I asked. He folded the slip into his pocket, shouldered past the line, and stepped out the double doors.

The bad mood faded as he left the toxic quiet of the bank. He had a couple of hours to kill before heading out to Trish's, decided to grab dinner. One of his favorite bars was nearby, a place called Sheffield's, barbeque and a terrific beer selection. He got the same warmth he always got in a corner bar, that sense of coming home. Once this had all blown over, he'd need a new job. Maybe with his remaining fifty grand he'd see about buying in somewhere.

Or maybe not. He had time to figure it out. Regardless, everything would change now.

He ordered a pulled pork platter and a Jolly Pumpkin bomber. Someone had left the *New York Times* on the bar, and he skimmed through. The headlines were depressing, full of news of the mortgage crisis, the stock market bottoming, the recession.

Alex was conscious of a certain split in himself. Part of him was feeling good, excited, the other part wondering what they had done, and if they would get away with it. Processing the fact that one of his friends had committed murder.

The thought hit hard, as it had all day long. He'd forget for a while, and then it would hammer him again. What had Mitch been *thinking*? Aiming a pistol at someone and pulling the trigger?

Maybe that Four Musketeers thing had reached the end. Time to move on. To leave the three of them behind, start fresh. Hell, maybe even move out to the suburbs, be closer to Cassie. Start catching her soccer games more often, picking her up from school. Leave behind late-night drunks and casual gropes with Jenn. He cared about them, he did. But sometimes you got too comfortable in your old life, too built-in, and only an earthquake could shake things loose, show you that you weren't where you wanted to be.

It might be time to start standing alone.

★　★　★

Ian made it to Wednesday evening.

After leaving Jenn's apartment, he went to the office and threw himself into work, trying to use it as a drug to distract himself. He hadn't taken a blast of coke since Mitch had yanked his vial

221

away, and while he was proud of that, he was also ragged and sick. The burn on his balls fired raw, electric jolts every time he shifted position. And worst of all, he could hear Katz's measured voice in his head:

My money. All of it. By Wednesday. Or . . .

For you and your friends.

He knew what he had promised the others. If he wanted to keep that promise, he should go home, make dinner, turn on reality TV, and work his way through a couple bottles of wine. Not do any coke, not call Katz, not do a good goddamn.

But if he did, then he was on the line for the debt. They all were. And he had the money, could pay what he owed. Keep all four of them safe.

Besides. They would never need to know.

★ ★ ★

Trish had been hesitant at first, but eventually had told Alex to come out this evening, after dinner. It was typical that she hadn't invited him to join. Not cruel, just oh-so-practical. Ex and husband do not at the same table eat.

Her doorbell made a civilized *ding-dong*, nothing at all like the shrieking buzz of his city apartment. He heard the clicking of shoes against marble, and then the door opened. Trish wore a white blouse and a serious expression, hair pulled into a simple ponytail but nails done. She hesitated a moment, then surprised him with a hug. They hadn't done the hugging-hello thing for years. 'Thanks for coming out,' she said, like it had been her idea.

'I needed to talk to you.'

'I know. Come in.' She closed the door behind him.

'Where's Cass?'

'She's staying at a friend's.'

'What? Are you — ' He spread his hands. 'I wanted to see her.'

'I thought it was better we talk without her for now. Come on. We're in here.'

We? We who? He followed her, noticing the stack of moving boxes in the corner, the half-empty bookshelf. 'Trish — '

'Hello, Alex.' Scott stood beside the kitchen table. His ex-wife's new husband was the kind of guy who, no matter what he was wearing, always looked like he had a sweater tied around his shoulders. 'You remember Douglas, our attorney?' He gestured to a pale, suited man with watery eyes, who nodded, said, 'Thanks for coming.'

'Everybody keeps saying that,' Alex said, thinking, *attorney?* He fought the urge to bounce on the balls of his feet. The kitchen was bright and expensive-looking, with granite countertops and a stove that would have made Ian jealous. 'But I asked to see Trish, not the other way around.'

'Sure. Of course.' Scott made brief eye contact with his wife and their lawyer. 'Do you want a drink? Some coffee, or a beer?'

'I'm fine. What's he doing here?'

The lawyer smiled blandly. 'Mr and Mrs Stevens asked if I could join just in case there

223

were any, ah, legal questions.'

'There won't be. You can go.'

'Alex.' Trish came up beside him. He'd forgotten how petite she was, a little elfin thing. 'Don't be like that.'

He narrowed his eyes, looked around the room. 'I came to talk and to see Cassie. I didn't expect to get ambushed.'

'Nobody's ambushing anybody,' Scott said. 'We just thought the four of us should chat.'

'The four of us. My ex-wife, her new husband, and the vampire lawyer.'

'Come on. Let's be adult about this, OK?' Trish pronounced it ad-ult. 'Come on, sit down.'

He thought about storming out, couldn't see what it would accomplish. Reluctantly, he pulled up a chair.

'Now,' Scott said. 'I can imagine how you feel about our decision to move.'

'I doubt that.'

He looked pained. 'OK. My point is that none of us want this to get ugly. It wouldn't be good for Cassie.'

'That your big priority, Scott? What's good for my daughter? Because I would think that living near her father would be good for her. Staying in school with her friends would be good for her.' He leaned into the butcher-block table. 'Not moving halfway across the fucking country would be good for her.'

'Cassie will miss you,' Trish said. 'And she'll miss her friends. But you're welcome to come visit anytime. You can have the same privileges you do now. In fact, if you wanted to move — '

'If I wanted to move? To Arizona?' He shook his head. 'I'm supposed to uproot my life because Scottie got a job offer?'

'I'm just saying, we're still going to be flexible, like always.'

'*Flexible?* You're moving to another state.' He fought to keep his voice under control. 'You have no right to do this, to take my daughter — '

'Actually, Mr Kern,' the lawyer spoke for the first time, 'they do.' He paused, picked up a sheaf of stapled papers, and leaned forward to set them in front of Alex. 'In case you haven't read the divorce settlement recently, there are clear provisions — '

'For what? For taking a daughter from her father?'

'Clear provisions,' the man said as if he hadn't been interrupted, 'regarding the rights and privileges accorded all parties. Now, it's my understanding that you have missed a number of child support payments?' He glanced at Trish, who nodded. 'Which, I'm afraid, severely limits your rights in this matter. Especially as Mr and Mrs Stevens have been providing a stable household for . . . ' He paused, looked at his notes.

'Cassie,' Alex said. 'Her name is Cassie.'

'For Cassie. Under circumstances like these, I'm afraid that the situation is quite clear.' He steepled his fingers.

'What Douglas means,' Scott said, 'is that while we all want what's best for her, there are some rules . . . '

Alex leaned over, grabbed Scott by the hair,

and slammed his face into the table.

'That need to be acknowledged. Now, we all know that you love . . . '

He stood, took the chair by the back, and swung it in a home run arc that caught all three of them in their respective heads.

'Cassie, but the truth is, we are the ones that are raising her day-to-day . . . '

He snatched the cleaver off the cutting board and spun it in a glimmering arc. Both Scott and the lawyer's heads tumbled in the air.

'And this opportunity means the best for her. Patricia and I can pay for private schools, soccer camp, her clothes, and her books. We can guarantee she has a family dinner every night. Basically' — Scott shrugged apologetically — 'we can do the things you can't.'

'Motherfucker.' Alex whispered. 'You motherfucker.'

Trish sighed. 'I knew this wasn't a good idea.'

'Mr Kern,' the lawyer said. 'Please. Be civil. No matter how you feel, the fact is that you have not maintained your end of the agreement.'

Alex laid his hands on the table, palm down, to keep from clenching them into fists. 'Is that right? Well, this should make things simpler.' He reached into his pocket, pulled out the cashier's check, unfolded it, and set it in front of Trish.

She looked at it, and then at him. 'What is this?'

'That, *Patricia*, is a check. For more than I owe, I believe.' He grinned. 'Which I guess changes the circumstances some, eh?'

'May I see that?' Douglas held out a hand, and

Trish passed him the check. He looked at it carefully.

'It's real, you dick.' The table had fallen silent, and Alex smiled, feeling suddenly strong again. 'That's the money I owe. So I'm not in violation of the agreement. So you can't take her from me.'

The three of them looked back and forth like they were trying to communicate telepathically. He had them worried, he could see it.

Then Trish said, 'Oh, Alex.' She sighed.

'What?'

Scott shook his head.

'What?'

'I'm afraid,' Douglas said, 'it doesn't work that way.'

'Why not?'

'May I ask where you got this money?'

'No.'

'All right. In that case, it's a reasonable assumption that your previous failure to pay has not been inability, as you've claimed. You've simply been holding out.'

'No, that's not true.' Shit, shit, shit. He spoke quickly. 'It's a bonus. From my job.'

'A twelve-thousand-dollar bonus for a bartender?'

'Well, not all of it. Some of it is money I borrowed.'

'From a bank?'

'From friends.'

'I see. That, I'm afraid, only further proves that you are not capable of supporting, um, Cassie, on your own.'

'No, that's — ' It was all getting turned around. 'Look, what does it matter where it came from? It covers what I owe.'

'It matters a great deal, Mr Kern. But even setting that aside for a moment, I'm afraid that child support isn't like paying off a football bet. You can't just come in with the money when you have it. The purpose is to provide a solid household for the child.'

'Listen, you slick — '

'Alex.' Trish spoke softly. 'I should have known you'd try something like this. You couldn't just let things be.' She turned to him, hit him with steady brown eyes. 'You always did things the hard way. Always denied what was right in front of you. Ignored the facts that didn't fit AlexVision.'

'What's that supposed to mean?'

'Please. Can't you accept reality? Can't we do this without ruining everything?'

He stared at her, his mouth open. 'What are you talking about?'

'I know you think you're doing this for Cassie. But you're not. You're doing it for yourself. And I'm begging you. Please don't. Please?'

Alex looked around the table. 'Do you honestly think I'm going to just sit back and let you walk out with my daughter?'

Trish lowered her head to one hand, closed her eyes. It was a gesture he remembered well, a pose she held while she was gearing herself up for something. The recognition brought a surprising stab of sentiment.

Finally, she raised her head, looked at the

lawyer, and nodded.

Douglas said, 'Mr Kern, I'm sorry to have to do this, but in light of your pattern of missed payments, and at the request of my clients, I'm going to recommend to the judge that this settlement be reexamined, and specifically that visitation rights be limited, if not removed altogether.'

'What?' He felt his stomach fall away.

'In addition to which, while this case is being considered, I would ask that you make no attempt to see the child without seventy-two hours' notice, and only in the presence of one of the parents.'

'I'm one of the parents.'

Douglas sighed. 'I'm sorry, Mr Kern. I know this must hurt. Please understand that all of this is for the good of the child.'

'*Her name is Cassie.*'

There was a long silence, and then Scott said, 'It's time for you to leave, Alex.'

He stared at each of them. The lawyer, bland and lethal, a fountain pen in his hand. Scott marking his territory. Trish seemed like she was about to cry, but she wouldn't meet his eyes. His hands shook, and the pulse in his head seemed loud. 'What are you saying? Are you — '

'I'm sorry, Alex,' Trish said to the cabinets. 'I tried to warn you.'

★   ★   ★

He was drunk. That much he knew. That much made sense.

229

It had felt good to key the lawyer's Lexus on his way out, leaving a wicked scratch across the driver's side. But that hadn't erased the memory of what had happened, and the idea of staring at the walls of his shithole apartment was intolerable. So after driving back to the city, he'd gone to the shithole bar at the end of the block instead. It was one of those places no one knew the name of, a too-bright space decorated with neon signs for cheap beer. He'd taken a stool and asked the bartender for three shots of Wild Turkey, done them in quick succession, and gestured at them again.

'Bad day?'

'Fuck you.'

The man had snorted, shrugged, then poured the shots again. 'Hope you choke on them.'

'Me too.' He picked one up, knocked it down, then put his elbows on the bar and his head in his hands.

How had it come to this?

Alex was the first to admit that nothing in his life made much sense. Hadn't since he hit adulthood, really. There was a myth that everybody's life proceeded according to a larger plan. Where he'd gotten that idea, he wasn't sure, one of those things picked up in childhood, along with the idea that love lasted forever and that the good guys won and that it was never too late to change everything. It was a lie, all of it. Your buddies didn't come in at the last second to save you. Things didn't work out. People weren't happy. Or if they were, that was just so that when unhappiness hit, it stung worse.

And yet the fabric of the lies was so dramatic, so interwoven into every facet of his life, that he didn't know where to begin to untangle it. Every story his parents had read at his bedside, every teacher in every school, every sermon he'd ever heard, they all taught that life made sense. That if you tried to live well, and if you looked hard enough, there was a pattern and a plan.

But here he was. Here they all were, he and Jenn and Mitch and Ian. Four people of good health and no major handicap. They should have been happy. Content. Hell, just satisfied. He'd have settled for satisfied.

But was Ian, with his flashy suits and expensive apartment? Mitch, with his won't-harm-a-fly mentality and quiet daydreams? Jenn, hoping purpose would just land in her lap? They had everything going for them and nowhere to go.

It was close to one in the morning by the time he hailed a cab, drunk, tired, and desperate for comfort.

★ ★ ★

She'd been after the maintenance crew to fix the lock on the foyer of her apartment building for months, but Alex was glad to see they hadn't yet. He pushed through, climbed the stairs, hesitated in front of Jenn's door, then rapped three times, hard. He was wobbly on his feet and in his heart, and he just wanted to burrow deep into soft sheets warm from her body, breathe in the smell of her, and let himself fall into the abyss. He banged again. Waited a few moments, and was about to knock a third time when he heard footsteps.

The door swung open. Mitch stood inside, wearing jeans and no shirt.

Alex stared. Spun, glanced around the hallway. Had he somehow given the cabbie the wrong address? What was — this was the right place. He turned back to the door. Mitch said nothing, just crossed his arms. There was a hint of swagger in his pose, bare-chested and with messed-up hair, the guy clearly wanting him to do the math.

The corner of Mitch's lips curled into a slight smile. 'What's up, Alex? What do you want?'

Comfort. Safety. A fresh start.

The life I imagined.

'Nothing,' he said and turned away.

21

She wasn't much use at work, but she went. Didn't really see a choice. So while Mitch was in the shower, she'd gone through her closet, looking for an outfit that didn't take any effort. Settled on a calf-length black skirt and a fitted tee, thrown lipstick on, skipped the mascara, and told Mitch, over the hum of the water, that she had to run.

Last night had been unexpected. She hadn't planned to spend it with him, not again, not so soon. But after they had found the chemicals, something had snapped in her. She hadn't wanted to be alone. If she was alone, she might think about what they had done, and she didn't want that. It wasn't a rational thought, but then, the last few days hadn't been rational.

Again their lovemaking had been intense, the two of them moving well together. In the middle of it, when she'd been on her knees on the bed, she'd cocked her head and looked back at him, a patented move that always drove guys crazy. But when their eyes locked, for a second they'd both stopped. It had been a bad moment, as if all the fear and shame had poured into the room like fog. By unspoken accord they'd both started up again, more furiously than ever, knowing what the alternative to action was. Together they had blotted out the world, screwed it away until they collapsed in exhaustion and sleep seemed possible.

And half an hour later, Alex had come to her door.

'Who is that?' Mitch went bolt upright, his eyes darting.

She knew, from the first knock, but couldn't think of a way to tell him without explaining more than she wanted to. So she'd shaken her head, said she didn't know. He'd gotten out of bed, pulled on his jeans, and gone to answer.

When he came back a few minutes later, he said, 'Alex.'

'What did he want?'

'He didn't say. I think he was drunk.' His tone giving her an opportunity to add something. But she had just said, 'Huh. Hope he's OK,' and turned over, wrapping the sheets around her. After a moment, Mitch had lain back down, and they'd drifted into the awkward fugue of bodies not used to sleeping next to each other.

Her workday morning was a blur. She answered emails and checked airfares and talked on the phone in a daze. Twice her boss asked if she was OK.

Around noon, she finally made a decision. Yes, her life had gone crazy. Yes, the sky was falling. They had killed someone, and the police were looking for them, and they had a gallon of liquid heroin stashed in a stolen Cadillac. But there were two options. She could either curl up under her desk like some useless soap-opera chick. Or she could deal with it.

So she'd headed home, retrieved her share of the money, and gone to the bank. A politely bored assistant manager had walked her through

234

some forms, then led her into a back room. He handed her one key, and then took one from his own ring, and they turned them together to unlock a safe-deposit box the size of a shoebox.

'You can take it over there,' he said, gesturing to a small alcove screened off by a curtain. 'When you're done, put it back and lock it, and you're good to go.'

She'd thanked him, then waited for him to leave. She set the box on a small desk, opened her bag, and took out the money in its Ziploc. Hiding it felt right, gave her a sense of moving forward. One item checked off a list. That good feeling lasted until midafternoon, when Mitch called to remind her they had to go to Johnny's bar tonight.

Ready or not, the Thursday Night Club had to ride again.

★   ★   ★

When his cellphone rang, Bennett was sprawled on his back across the bed with his head hanging off the edge, the world upside down. His hands were laced over his chest. His phone pinged quietly, a sound like a depth charge. He glanced at the caller ID, then answered the call. 'Johnny Love, Johnny Love.'

'Yeah, hi, Benn — '

'Don't say my name.'

'Why?'

'This is a cellular phone.'

'But you said my — '

'So I had a chat with our mutual friend yesterday.'

235

'Yeah, I . . . ' The man sounded winded. Nervous, maybe. 'I heard about that. I don't know what he told you, but, kid, you gotta understand, I didn't give you up.'

'Why, Johnny, I never said you did.'

'Good. I'm glad to hear it.'

'But now that you mention it, you fat fuck, I think I might tear your spleen out.'

'No, hey, wait — '

'Just kidding. He told me he asked you pretty hard.'

'Well, you know, I hope you know that I would never sell you out. I told him you were involved, that's all.'

'You didn't mention anything about me running a burn on you both?'

'Well.' A pause. 'I mean, what do you want me to say? He was going to throw me off a ten-story building.'

'The more I get to know this guy, the more I like him. So what's on your mind, Johnny?'

'You know I been putting a lot of money out on the street. Letting people know I got robbed, that I'll pay for a lead on the fuckers that did it. Vic — our friend told me I get anything, I'm supposed to give it to you.'

'So what've you got?'

'A Jew bookie. Well, more than. Runs a private casino, some girls. Guy name of Katz.'

'Heard of him.'

'Apparently some dude, some yuppie dude, owed him about thirty. Katz was gonna whack him, the dude said that he had a mark he and his friends were going to rob, he needed a couple

236

more days. Anyway, short story shorter, the yuppie came in yesterday with thirty large. Cash money.'

Bennett sat up straight. The blood rushed from his head, and he closed his eyes to fight the world's wobble. 'Katz have a name for you?'

'Yeah. You got a pen? Guy's name is Ian Verdon, that's V-E-R-D-O-N. No address, but — '

'I can find him.'

'Right. So should I meet up with you?'

'No. Don't do a thing. Don't tell anyone his name, don't send guys looking, don't tell anyone about him, don't do a goddamn thing. Get me?'

'Yeah, sure, kid. Whatever you say.' He paused. 'You just tell the big man that I'm doing my part, OK?'

'Sure. By the way, Johnny, when this is over, I think I might shoot you.'

'*What?*'

'Just kidding.'

★ ★ ★

Mitch had a queer déjà vu feeling as he folded his jacket over one arm and climbed on the bus. No, not even that, exactly; déjà vu was more ephemeral, a sort of untraceable feeling that you had done something before, stood in the same spot, seen the same beam of sun. This was different.

It was more like a video game. That was it. Like this was just a level called 'The Ride to Johnny's,' and he'd played through it before. It had that same patent unreality, the way the bus growled and shook, the packed crowd, body odor and averted glances, glazed eyes and headphones. One week ago today he'd hopped on this same bus up from the Loop. Only in that round of play, things hadn't turned out how he'd liked. He'd been ignored, ridiculed, left hanging by his friends. He'd gone home drunk and alone to dream about a woman who seemed destined never to notice him.

Then, somewhere between then and now, he'd hit the Reset button. Decided to reload the level and play through again. To do it differently.

And would you believe it? The same bored-looking black kid in the same Looney Tunes jacket, his leg aggressively thrown into the empty seat beside him while standing passengers crammed the aisle.

Mitch smiled to himself, fought through the crowd to stand next to the guy. 'Excuse me,' he said, the same as last time, and the same as last time, the guy took a look and then turned away, ignoring him. Figuring him for just another scared white man.

Not anymore. Mitch didn't say anything else. He just leaned down, gripped the guy's shoe, and pushed it off the seat.

The man sat up fast, his eyes narrowing. Mitch stared back, no smile, no apology. Just a level gaze. His heart was going a bit — not like the guy would do much on a crowded bus, but still — but he didn't blink. Just stared.

And after a moment the kid sneered, said, 'A'ight,' and turned back to the window. Mitch slid into the open seat.

The rest of the ride, he replayed that moment, how simple it had been. How simple it was all turning out to be. You just decided what you wanted, and you acted like it belonged to you. Why the fuck hadn't he learned that years ago? Although, it occurred to him, the cooler move would have been to, after brushing the guy's foot off the seat, turn to someone in the aisle, a woman, and offer it to her. Like, *Jack Reacher, at your service.* That would have been suave.

Rossi's looked the same, and he had a claustrophobic moment as he remembered the last time he'd seen it, in the car with Ian, the guy playing weird music and drumming his fingers against the wheel, that manic intensity under skies saddening to dusk. He forced the thought away, replaced it with a memory of Jenn giving him a hug, wearing her Bond-girl dress. The dress he'd later slid off her long, sweet body. That was the world he lived in now.

Yeah? So why was Alex showing up at her place in the middle of the night?

Shut it down.

Thursday night, and the place was busy. The usual suspects, junior-corporate-whatevers, holding martini glasses and pints and longneck bottles, loosening ties and laughing too loud and leaning in to touch one another's arms. He slid through them to the end of the bar, and was surprised to see everybody already there, Ian slumped on his elbows, Jenn chewing on her plastic toothpick. Alex was in conversation with another bartender, and Mitch nodded in his

239

direction, got nothing in response.

'Happy Thursday,' he said. He stepped toward Jenn, but she pinned him with her eyes, gave the tiniest shake of her head. Fine, OK. He settled for squeezing her shoulder, the skin humming under his fingertips. Ian turned his head without moving his shoulders. Though his suit was as impeccable as always, the man himself looked like he'd been wadded up and slept in. 'Hey.'

Mitch glanced back and forth, said, 'Somebody die?'

Jenn snorted at that, a quick little sound that he wasn't sure was amusement, and Ian said, 'Funny.'

'Next round's on me.' Mitch raised his hand, gestured to Alex, but the guy still didn't seem to see him. 'So.' He smiled. 'Victory, huh?'

Ian nodded, not looking at him. Jenn said, 'Victory?'

'Sure. That was the plan, wasn't it? That when things were done, we'd celebrate?' He didn't want to talk too openly, but figured he could risk that much in the noise of the bar. After all, this was the cherry on top, ripping Johnny off and then drinking on his dime. Even if things hadn't gone quite as planned, it was still a good feeling.

But the others didn't seem to see it that way. He looked around for another chair, but the place was full, and so he rocked from foot to aching foot, trying to think of something to say, wishing he had a drink. Finally, Alex came over, drying his hands on a rag. He had fresh butterfly bandages on his face and a dark bruise. 'Mitch.'

'Alex.' There was a long moment, then Mitch

said, 'Can I get a beer and a shot?'

Alex reached for a martini shaker. 'I heard from Chip over there,' pointing with an elbow, 'that Johnny has been going crazy about the robbery.'

Mitch shot him a *shut-the-fuck-up* look.

'I guess whoever it was' — Alex bounced back a *you're-not-the-only-smart-one* look — 'they must have gotten a lot of money from the safe. Chip says Johnny came in yesterday afternoon looking like somebody was threatening his mother. That's a quote.' He shook his head. 'He's been in and out all day, making calls, yelling. Trying to find out who did it.'

'Did you talk to him?' Jenn pushed her glass forward, and Alex poured to the rim, the amount he'd mixed in the shaker precise to the drop. 'I hope he's paying for your trip to the hospital.'

'He said he would. Right now he's a little distracted.'

'The people that did it are probably in another state by now,' Mitch said, getting into the spirit of it. 'Besides, the police are after them. What's a bar owner going to do?'

'You never know.' Alex grabbed a bottle of single malt from the back bar, poured Ian a generous double. 'He seems pretty motivated. I tell you' — setting down the bottle and staring at Mitch — 'I wouldn't want to be the guy who robbed him. If Johnny ever finds out who it was' — he clicked his tongue — 'no telling what he'll do.'

A bloom of frost flowered in Mitch's belly. He was suddenly conscious of his breathing. Was

241

Alex threatening him? Was that what this was?

Jenn caught the stare and leaned forward, her face anxious. 'Let's not talk about that.' She glanced from one to the other, her bottom lip curled between her teeth. 'How about a game? Ian?'

'Huh?' His skin was pallid and sick, and he'd finished half the scotch in a gulp. 'Umm. I don't know.'

'*You* don't have a game?' Her tone light as May. 'What's the world coming to?'

'Fuck if I know,' Alex said.

'You have a bad day too?' Mitch put his jacket over the back of Jenn's chair, unbuttoned his cuffs and started to roll them up. 'You guys are about as much fun as a Smiths reunion.'

'I guess I just got up on the side of the wrong bed,' Alex said. 'You ever do that, Mitch? Get up on the side of the wrong bed?'

'You mean the wrong side of the bed.'

'Yeah. Right.' Something in his eyes an accusation. What was that? Did the guy actually think he'd be ashamed for being with Jenn?

Question: Who shows up at a woman's house at two in the morning?

It came in a flash. All the looks between Alex and Jenn that had stretched a half second too long. All those shared cab rides north. The man's moodiness, the way he still hadn't gotten Mitch a drink, the way he seemed to be trying to pick a fight.

Answer: Someone who's sleeping with her.

Something twisted in him. Alex with his broad shoulders and muscles and sensitive stories

242

about his daughter. All this time, even while he knew, he *knew*, that Mitch was carrying a torch. All that time he'd been fucking Jenn.

He felt dizzy, hot. The air in the bar was close and thick. He had a panicky feeling, like the world was slipping, or like he was. Like he was a little kid again, gawky and shy and falling down in gym class. In just a moment the laughter would start.

That's not you anymore. It's not.

'Come on, guys. Let's not be like this. This is a celebration, remember?' Jenn looked back and forth, brushed hair behind her ear.

'What are we celebrating?' Alex had the look of a man vibrating inside. 'Everything is falling to shit.'

'Hey, man.' Ian looked up from his empty glass. 'Keep it cool, OK?'

'Cool? Why?' Alex shook his head. 'I'm a thirty-two-year-old bartender. I live in a one-bedroom in a crap neighborhood. My ex-wife is taking my daughter away. *This is not the way my life was supposed to be.*'

'Everybody feels that way sometimes.' Jenn's voice was pitched low and consoling. 'It's natural.'

'Yeah, well, not everybody has detectives calling to talk to them about a robbery, do they?'

'You saying that's somebody's fault?' Mitch asked.

'It's the Jolly Green Fucking Giant's fault. It's whoever robbed this place and shot someone out in the alley's fault.'

It was like the guy wanted them to get caught, the way he was pushing the envelope, hinting too

243

broadly. If anyone heard this, told Johnny, they'd be in trouble. What was Alex doing? Didn't he realize he was putting them all in danger? Did he just not care?

'Get back up on the sumbitch,' Ian said in a startlingly realistic Tennessee drawl.

'Huh?'

'Something my dad used to say. He was a big one for clichés, my pop. Cleanliness and godliness, early birds and worms. 'Son, it ain't about falling off the horse. It's how fast you get back up on that sumbitch.''

'That's what I need. Platitudes.' Alex shook his head. 'All due respect, but fuck your dad right now, OK?'

Ian gave a thin smile. 'Sure, buddy. It's your world. We're just furniture.'

'Guys.' Her tone pleading.

Things were falling apart, but Mitch couldn't find it in himself to care. A week ago these had been his closest friends, his urban tribe. Only it was all built on bullshit. One of them was a secret cokehead, another had been screwing the woman he loved; and her, she'd lied to him about it. Not to mention that he was the one in the most danger for a risk he hadn't wanted to take in the first place.

Nothing was what it seemed, nothing was true. So fuck it.

He leaned forward. 'We were talking about games. Here's one. Answer this for me. What's the worst you've ever screwed over someone you said you cared about?' He fixed Alex with a glare. 'Ready, go.'

The toxic silence tasted of copper.

Ian stood. 'I'm taking off.'

'No, look,' Jenn's eyes wide, imploring. 'This is stupid. We're just — '

'We're just done with each other,' Alex said. He straightened, picked up a rag and wiped his hands. 'Right?'

There was a stab in Mitch's chest, and a child's urge to take it all back. But he said, 'Yeah,' then jerked his jacket from the back of the chair, turned to Jenn. 'I'm leaving. Are you coming?'

'I . . . ' She looked back and forth. 'No. I'm going home.'

'I can take you.'

'Not tonight.' She stood, picked up her purse. Pulled a couple of twenties from her wallet and dropped them on the bar. 'It doesn't have to be like this. But you guys with your egos. You'd rather all crash and burn than get over each other.'

'Yeah, well, you're certainly the expert on guys, aren't you, Tasty.' The look on Alex's face was pure meanness. 'All that experience.'

Her face paled and eyes widened. Then she just shook her head. 'Well, it was good while it lasted.'

'What was?' Ian asked.

'The Thursday Night Drinking Club.' She gestured with a sad smile. 'Us.'

22

The view was spectacular, Bennett had to admit. Outside Ian Verdon's floor-to-ceilings, the city was glowing geometries, the river tinged pink with that shadowless five o'clock light. Magic hour, photographers called it.

He stared for another moment, then turned away, spun in a slow circle. The condo was tastefully modern, with clean lines and low-slung furniture. He walked over to a set of bookshelves, more pictures and knickknacks than books: a shot of a dude against a split-rail fence, face lined as ten-year-old boots; a box of Montecristos with a broken seal declaring them Cubans; a sleek hourglass with pale blue sand. Idly, he opened the cigar box. Inside was a mirror, a razor blade, and a glassine bag filled with white powder. Lookie lookie. He poured a small bump on the back of his hand and snorted.

Damn.

He packed it back away, careful to put everything in the exact same spot. Addicts were clueless about a lot of things, but never their supply.

There was a cheap phone on the bookcase and a cordless in the kitchen. He chose the cordless. Shit was so easy these days. You could order any damn thing from the Internet. It took two minutes to crack open the phone, do what he needed to, and close it back up. He glanced at his watch: 5:30. On a Friday night, that might be pushing it a little. Best to head out.

Bennett replaced the phone, took one last look around the apartment, then stepped out, locking the door behind him. He strolled down the hallway, the indirect-lighting-and-muted-carpet combo that yuppies couldn't get enough of, then punched the button for the elevator. As he waited he whistled, badly, savoring that chill ease of quality cocaine.

The doors parted and a gaunt dude in a nice suit stepped out. His hair was gelled and mussed just so, but his eyes were sunken, and the greenish remains of a shiner marked one. 'Excuse me.'

Bennett smiled, stepped aside, then climbed into the elevator and rode it to the garage. He stood in the shadows near the gate, and when a black Wrangler pulled up to it, he waited till the Jeep was through, then ducked out.

His Benz was at a pay lot two blocks away. He climbed in, reached in the back and pulled out his laptop. As it booted, he opened his cellphone, dialed *67 to block caller ID, and then Verdon's phone number.

The man answered on the third ring. 'M'ello?'

Bennett said nothing, drew the pause out. Theatre.

'Hello?'

'I know what you did. And I'm coming.' He closed the phone, then turned to the laptop.

The trace program was silent for thirty seconds. Then the transmitter he'd put in Ian's phone sent the number the guy was dialing.

There was a pause as it ran the number against a reverse directory, and a name appeared. *McDonnell, Mitchell.* Twenty seconds, then the line disconnected. No one home. Ten seconds later, another number appeared, and another name. *Kern, Alex.*

Bennett smiled.

God, he loved predictable people.

23

Jenn was painting her toenails and trying not to think.

She wasn't a high-maintenance girl, one of those shiny chicks perpetually ready for a fashion shoot, blushed and mascaraed and highlighted, tanned and toned and bubble-butted. She'd had a girlfriend once who, when a boy would stay over, would set the alarm so that she could get up, put on her makeup, and come back to bed dolled up. Even did it with steady boyfriends, guys she saw for months. Everything about that sounded exhausting to Jenn.

But she liked to paint her toes. It was a summer indulgence, a celebration of sundresses and strappy sandals. She did it with the TV on something low-calorie, *Inside the Actors Studio* today, Matt Damon up onstage being charming. And she needed indulgence, needed something pleasant and routine to distract her from the steady rhythm of fear and guilt that beat through her. Ever since the robbery, her dreams had been nightmares, bright flashes and dark red liquid, shadows looming and reaching. Then the scene in the bar. And finally last night's conversation with Ian, the man panicking about a crank call. He'd been breathless and sputtering as he told her, and all she could think of was his coke habit. She'd reassured him it was nothing, but as always, the fear hit in the middle of the night, telling her that it could be more.

Which was why it felt important, justified, to sit calmly on her couch and paint her toes. A way of holding back panic. When the phone rang, she finished the nail she was on before setting the brush in the bottle and reaching for the cordless.

'Ms Lacie?'

'Yes,' she said, fanning her toes with a magazine and readying herself to hang up on the salesman.

'You're a friend of Mitch McDonnell?'

Something in the tone made her wary. She uncurled herself, put her feet on the floor. 'Yes. Who is — '

'He's been hurt.'

'*What?*'

'I'm sorry, my name is Paul, I work at the Continental with Mitch. He's been hurt and he's asking for you.'

'What do you mean, hurt?'

'My manager just gave me your number and asked me to call.'

'But . . . hurt how? Like he fell or something?'

'I really don't know. I just know that he's asking you to come down here right away.'

'OK.' She stood, looked at the clock on the cable box. A few minutes after one. Saturday traffic wouldn't help any. 'I'm leaving now. I should be there by about one thirty.'

'I'll tell him. He's in a conference room on the second floor. The Atlantic.'

'Is there a doctor — '

'I really don't know, ma'am.'

'All right. Thanks.' She hung up the phone and

threw it on the couch. In her bedroom she shucked off cotton pajama bottoms and hopped into jeans, jammed her feet into flip-flops, grabbed her purse off the dresser, and bolted for the door.

Outside, it was a perfect summer day, the kind where nothing could go wrong. She tagged a passing cab, gave him the address, and asked him to step on it. To her surprise, he did, running yellows and weaving through traffic.

What could that mean, Mitch was hurt? It couldn't be too bad, or they would have taken him to a hospital. It was kind of odd, him asking for her. They'd only just started, and it seemed like already she was getting the girlfriend treatment.

Unless . . . Did it have something to do with the robbery? Or with the call from last night?

The thought hit cold, and she bit her lip. If Johnny had found out, he might have come after Mitch. God, he might have —

It was a long ride.

Finally, the cab pulled up in front of the hotel. A man wearing the uniform she'd come to associate with Mitch hurried over to get her door. She paid the cabbie, tipping him an extra ten bucks, and hurried out of the car. 'The Atlantic conference room?'

'On the second floor, ma'am. The elevator is — '

She didn't hear the rest. The hotel was gorgeous, the kind of place people had honeymoons and affairs in. She saw a staircase and hurried up it. There was a sign with room

251

names etched in it and arrows in either direction. Atlantic was to the left. Something about the place made the idea of running seem impossible, so she settled for a sort of awkward power-walk. Two heavy wooden doors led into the conference room, and she threw one open and shouldered through —

To see Mitch and Ian beside a long mahogany table, Ian with his hands up like he was describing the size of a fish he'd once caught. They both turned. Ian's mouth fell open, and Mitch's eyebrows scrunched in.

'Jenn?'

'Are you OK?'

'What are you doing here?'

They had all spoken at the same time, and froze, then started again in unison, and stopped again. She jumped into the silence. 'Are you OK?'

Mitch looked at her, then at Ian. 'What? Why wouldn't I be?'

'I.' She stopped. 'I got a call from your friend. He said you'd been hurt.'

'Hurt? What? Who said?'

'Someone named . . . Paul?'

Mitch shook his head. 'I don't know any Pauls.'

'So — what . . . ' The adrenaline was fading, leaving Jenn's shoulders tense. She looked at Ian. 'What are you doing here?'

'I'm meeting someone.'

'Who?'

'A guy I know.' Ian looked at them, saw that they weren't going to let it go. Sighed. 'Katz. The man I got the you-know-whats from. He called and told me to get over here right away.'

There was a knock on the door, and then it pushed open enough for Alex to stick his head in. 'Detective Bradley — ' He froze when he saw them. His eyes darted from one to the other, and his face underwent a weird series of emotions, finally settling on a stony mask. 'What are you all doing here?'

'We're trying to figure that out,' she said. 'I got a call saying Mitch was hurt. Ian was supposed to meet some guy named Katz. What about you, Mitch?'

'One of the bellmen told me a manager wanted to see me.' He looked at Alex, jerked his chin. The tension crackled between them like electric current. 'You?'

Alex stepped into the room, let the door whisper closed behind him. 'What the fuck is going on?'

'You didn't answer the question.'

'What does it matter? The point is that someone brought us all here.'

'It matters, *Alex*, because we need to figure out who.'

'Guys.' Jenn put all her exhaustion into it.

Alex said, 'A cop called and asked me to meet that detective here.'

'The one from the other night.'

'No, the one who was gonna mow my lawn. What do you think?'

'I *think* you're an asshole.' Mitch paused. 'No, I'm pretty sure of it.'

She shook her head. 'Enough. We did this the other night.'

'Gentlemen.' The voice came from behind,

and she spun to look. A stranger stood in the doorway. He wore a charcoal suit and an open-collared shirt of subtly textured white cotton, and had the breezy good looks of a cologne model. He nodded to Jenn. 'And of course Ms Lacie.'

'Who the fuck are you?' Alex said in his best bouncer voice.

The man smiled, strolled into the room. Behind him, face hard and red, walked Johnny Love. Two men in suits followed, taking up positions on either side of the door.

Spiders crawled through her chest. Nobody spoke, and she could hear the faint honking of a car horn outside, the hum of the air conditioner. The smiling man strode to the head of the table. Johnny hit Alex with a baleful look.

'My name is Victor. And I believe you all know Mr Loverin?'

'Motherfucking right they do.' The fat man glared from one to the other. 'Kern, you ungrateful prick. After all I've done for you, you pull this on me? And you,' his eyes narrowing at Ian. 'Still got the shiner, huh? Wait till I get done with you. That's going to seem like a day at Wrigley.'

'Be quiet, Johnny.' Victor's voice was calm, but Loverin immediately shut up. He crossed his arms and leaned against the wall, the tough-guy demeanor not gone, but certainly throttled back.

Which made her throat go dry. Who *was* this guy?

'Alex, Ian, Mitch, Jenn,' Victor said, looking at each of them in turn. 'Let's not waste time, OK?

254

I know what you did.' He paused, raised an eyebrow. 'Can you guess who I am?'

Mitch said, 'You're the guy Johnny was buying for the night we robbed him.'

Victor practically beamed. 'Got it in one. Good. I'm glad that you aren't going to play around. That will make this easier.'

Ian said, 'How did you — '

'How did I find you?' Victor stood behind a leather conference chair, his hands resting lightly on the back. 'A piece of advice. When you rob someone, you should be careful who you tell about it in advance.'

Ian's jaw fell, and his face went pale.

'Wait.' Alex turned to him. 'What is he — who did you tell?'

Mitch said, 'He told his bookie. The man who got him the guns in the first place.'

'Oh, you stupid — '

'Also, showing up to pay your thirty-thousand-dollar debt the day after you steal a quarter-million is something of a dead giveaway.'

'Katz.' Ian had a hand to his forehead. He turned to look at them. 'I had to, you understand? I didn't have a choice.'

'So,' Victor continued. 'Mitch, you seem to be on a roll. Why don't you guess what I want?'

'The money back?'

'As a matter of fact,' Victor said, 'no. The money you stole from Johnny. Not from me. Part of it was mine, it's true. But it was money that was already earmarked for a purchase. Do you understand? I spent my money. But I didn't get what I paid for.'

255

'What' — Alex paused, looked around — 'I'm sorry, I don't understand. What do you want us to do about that?'

'I want you to get it for me.'

'How? I don't even know what we're talking about.'

'How old is your daughter, Alex?'

Alex's shoulders clenched into iron ripples under his T-shirt. 'My daughter is none of your business.'

'Cassandra? Sure she is.' He jerked his head toward Mitch. 'As is Mitch's brother, Michael, and Ian's dad in Tennessee. I haven't had the chance to check in on Ms Lacie's parents yet. But I will.'

This couldn't be happening. None of it. Her *parents*? This total stranger, a guy she'd never seen before, was threatening her parents?

She looked at the others, saw them thinking the same thing. Her leg started to shake, and she leaned on it.

Alex stepped forward. 'I don't know who you think you are — '

Moving with uncanny speed, both the men by the door brushed back suit jackets and drew pistols. One lined up on Alex. The other moved from target to target.

Jenn felt the floor shift beneath her, reached for the chair, barely got it.

'Be careful, Mr Kern.' Victor's voice was level. 'You should all be very careful. Last week you may have been normal people, but now you're in my day planner. Believe me when I say that's worth your attention. Right, Mr Loverin?'

256

Leaning against the wall, Johnny had the pinched expression of a child facing a bully he knew would make good. He cleared his throat, then nodded.

Alex took a deep breath. Paused. 'Listen, I'm sorry about my language,' he said. 'I didn't mean any disrespect. It's just that this is none of my affair.'

Something in his tone caught Jenn's attention. His shoulders were down, his hands up and open in a placating gesture. She knew what he was about to say before he opened his lips. It hit her with a sick shame and disappointment.

'I was in on robbing Johnny,' Alex said. 'But I was tied up inside the office when your friend came. I didn't shoot him. I didn't have anything to do with that part.'

'Are you kidding me?' Mitch looked back and forth. 'You're seriously putting this on us?'

'It is on you. I *wasn't there*.'

Mitch shook his head. 'You coward.'

'Gentlemen.' Victor's voice was cold. 'A couple of things you need to understand. The man you shot wasn't my friend. And I don't care which of you pulled the trigger. All I want is what's mine. Now. Where is it?'

Jenn's pulse was pounding. She looked at Mitch, could read his thoughts. He was going to tell Victor that they had found what he was after, that it was in the back of a purple Eldorado parked down the block from her apartment. And maybe that was best. Give it up to him and get on with their lives.

Only, what if that's not what he has in mind?

This is a man who has Johnny clearly terrified. What happens when you no longer have what he wants?

It was all happening too fast, event piling on event. She needed time to think, to figure this out. It was like being back in the alley, that sense that everything hung by a thread, but that she had a chance, a slim, delicate ribbon of a chance, to make things work out. Even just to buy them time to talk and make a plan. Only how? What could she possibly say?

Mitch said, 'Victor, sir — '

Suddenly she knew. Jenn cut in. 'Before we dumped the car, we went through it. And we found a bag in the trunk.'

Ian and Alex both whirled to look at her. Mitch was staring, and she could see him thinking, God bless him, see him trying to figure out what she was doing. She hesitated a moment, then said, 'It had four one-quart bottles in it.'

Victor said nothing, gave no outward sign of menace. Nonetheless, the air seemed to coalesce around him, a subtle hardening and cooling.

'We didn't know what they were. But we figured that if someone was willing to pay that much for them' — she shrugged her shoulders — 'we kept them.'

'Where are they?'

Her palms were moist, her armpits soaked. An old line flitted through her head, something to the effect of women didn't sweat, they dewed. She almost laughed, fought off the hysteria. She looked at Mitch, tried to beam the thoughts over

258

to him, praying that he would somehow telepathically understand.

'Ms Lacie?'

'They're in a safe-deposit box. At my bank.' She managed to say it without her voice cracking.

'A safe-deposit box? Why?'

Mitch said, 'We didn't know what they were. And they were worth so much.'

The urge to smile rose like champagne bubbles, but she fought it away.

'I see. Let's go get them.'

This was the risky part. She opened her mouth, closed it. Tried to think coolly, to let the panic show but not the calculation. 'It's Saturday.'

'So?'

'The bank is closed.'

'Convenient.'

She shrugged helplessly. 'Not to us.'

'Funny, though, isn't it? What I want is somewhere you can't get it?'

'Hey,' she said, 'you picked the time to bring us here. Not me.'

Victor made a sound that was a cross between a laugh and a *hmm*.

'Listen, cunt.' Johnny came off the wall. 'Stop fucking lying and get the man what he wants, and you do it right fucking now. Or so help me — '

'I have the key,' she said.

'What?'

'The key. It's in my purse. Can I get it?'

Victor made a *why-not* gesture. Hands

259

shaking, she dug into the change compartment of her bag. The key was a simple brass thing, unmarked, about the size of the one she used to get her mail. She held it up. 'See?'

The room was air-conditioned to January temperatures. She stood with the key out in front of her like a magic totem, like it was something that could protect them from harm. It felt flimsy and small.

'Let me have that.'

'No,' she said, her voice coming out raspy.

'No?'

'None of us meant to steal from you. I wish we hadn't done this at all. It was stupid. But if we give this to you now, how do we know you won't . . . '

'All I'm interested in is my product.'

'We'll give it to you. Monday morning. At the bank.'

'Because you'll feel safe there.'

'Yes.'

'You understand I could take it from you now.'

'I could scream.'

'And my people could shoot you.' He gave a small smile. 'But I'd rather not do it that way.' He rubbed at his chin, and in the pin-drop quiet of the room she could hear the grating of his fingers against stubble. 'You really never have done anything like this before, have you? You're honest-to-Christ amateurs.'

'That's for sure,' Johnny said.

'Look, Victor' — she leaned forward — 'you're right. We've never done anything like this, and we wouldn't have done it if we knew what would happen. We don't want to be any trouble. But we can't get them today. If we could, believe me, we would. But — '

Victor glanced at his heavy gold watch. 'OK. It doesn't really matter if we get it alone or with you, today or Monday morning.'

Fear's fingers unclenched a notch on her heart.

'What does matter is that you believe every word I say. For example, when I say that if you go to the police or try to leave town or try to in any way play me, it's not just your own lives in the balance.' He paused. 'I don't enjoy it, but believe me, I can make some very unpleasant things happen.'

'I believe you. I swear to Christ I do.' Part of her wanted to just give in, tell him where the bottles were, but it was too late now. She forced herself to stare back at him, and let the fear into her eyes.

'What about the money?' Ian had been quiet, and his voice came as a surprise.

Victor shrugged. 'The money was allocated for the purchase. It's not my concern.'

'Wait a second,' Johnny Love said. 'You're going to let them take my money?'

'You let them take it. Not me.'

'We can keep it?' Ian's voice was level, like he was negotiating a corporate deal.

'You've got my word.'

'No fucking — '

'*Johnny*.' Victor's eyes flashed like razor wire. He turned back to Ian. 'Yes. You can keep the money.'

'What about him?'

'I'll personally guarantee that Mr Loverin won't come after you.'

'How do we know we can trust you?'

'I hate repeating myself. I already told you to believe every word I say. So when I guarantee your safety, believe it. But also believe that if you play around, I *will* have men visit your father with a ball-gag and a belt sander.'

Ian paled. 'He doesn't have anything to do with this.'

'He does. Because what I can do to him will make you do what I say. Understand?'

Silence.

'Look, it's simple. The four of you are clueless. You found yourself in possession of something that belongs to me. I want it back. If you oblige, there's no reason for me to hurt you. I mean, what are the four of *you* going to do?' Victor smiled. 'Killing you would be a waste of resources. So yeah, it really is that simple. Give me what I want, and you can not only get on with your lives, you can keep the money. Or don't, and force me to start doing terrible things to you and yours until you cave and end up doing what I want anyway.'

The silence that fell had weight and texture. Victor held the pause, then brought his palms together like he was praying, and inclined them toward Jenn. 'Monday morning?'

She didn't trust herself to speak, just nodded.

'OK.' He smiled, showing bright, straight teeth. 'Have a good weekend.'

24

When he'd been a freshman at the University of Michigan with his whole life ahead of him, Alex had an intense friendship with two girls on his hall. It had started out the way college friendships did: easy. He'd met Tara doing laundry, Stacy in the TV lounge at the end of the hall. Throughout the halcyon days of a Midwestern autumn they'd chatted and laughed and shared bottles of tequila in his cramped dorm room. It hadn't been a sexual thing. They'd been so young, and free for the first time, and their friendship had revolved around conversation and mutually murdered hours. Back then it had seemed like the whole world was made up of time; hours and hours spent bullshitting in the glow of Christmas lights, playing euchre for cigarettes, sneaking into Scorekeepers with fake IDs. And for a while, it had been great. His first experience with a constructed family.

Around March it started getting weird.

The first thing was Stacy beginning to crush on him a little. It wasn't a big deal, flattering actually, but he didn't want to blow their friendship. Of course, after too much to drink one night, he and Tara had ended up in bed instead. They both enjoyed it, but also decided that it wasn't something they could continue. They agreed not to tell Stacy, but she found out, said she was fine with it. These things happened.

Then money went missing from Tara's purse. When Tara asked Stacy about it, she got offended, which led to a screaming fight on the Diag. Things got tense on the hall. Someone drew a picture on Tara's door that showed her doing inappropriate things to a horse. Stacy's colored laundry ended up bleached. Tara opened Alex's always-unlocked dorm room door late one night and crawled in with him, and when he refused her — he'd just started seeing Trish — she left in a self-righteous huff that woke the whole hall.

By April it had become a three-front war, and Alex, young and newly in love, opted out. He started spending most nights in Trish's room, avoiding both girls. Summer came, and then the following year he and Trish moved into an apartment together, and that was that.

But he'd never forgotten the way things had gotten out of hand, that claustrophobic feeling as each turned on the others. The way their erstwhile intimacy had become the fuel for rage. He'd never before realized that the best friends could turn out to be the worst enemies. And now, standing in an overcooled conference room in a hotel where he couldn't have afforded breakfast, he had a stab of that old feeling.

For a moment after Victor left, the four of them stared at one another in silence. His muscles had the shaky tension of near violence. Like things hadn't been bad enough before, when his little girl was being stolen from him and his ex-wife was hiring lawyers and the

264

closest thing he had to a girlfriend had taken up with a friend of his.

'Why didn't you tell us you found something in the car?' He looked from Mitch to Jenn. 'And don't say there wasn't time.'

Silence.

'Goddamn it.' He gripped the back of the nearest chair and rocked it hard on its casters. 'We're supposed to be in this together.'

'That's rich,' Mitch said.

'Hey, fuck you. He was after my daughter.'

'And my brother, and Ian's dad, and Jenn's parents.'

'I don't give a shit about them.' The words came before he could think.

Mitch made a sound of disgust. 'Yeah. You don't give a shit about anybody, do you?'

'Like you're better.' He turned to Jenn. 'What exactly did you find?'

'What I said. Four plastic bottles. Some kind of dark liquid. We opened one and smelled it.' She shuddered. 'Got a headache you wouldn't believe, and it made my muscles ache like I'd worked out way too hard.'

'You didn't think that made it worth discussing with us?'

'Things have gotten complicated. So we just hid them — '

'At the bank,' Mitch cut in. Jenn cocked her head, the two of them staring. Alex couldn't tell what it was about, didn't much care at that moment, their lovers' quarrels not his problem.

'What do you think it is?' Ian asked.

Alex turned savagely. 'Who cares? The man

wants it back. That's all that matters.'

'I was just asking.' Like a whipped dog.

'Yeah, well, I'm not too interested in you asking anything right now.' The anger in him turned like a hurricane, a spinning buzz saw that cut everything in its path. 'What were you *thinking*?'

Ian pulled out a chair, slumped in it. 'Will you let me explain?'

There was a long moment, and then Mitch sat down across the table, and Jenn followed suit. Finally Alex took out a chair. The four of them sat around the polished conference table like junior executives. Under any other circumstances the thought would have made him laugh.

'I . . . I might have a wee bit of a gambling problem.' Ian tried a wry smile that withered as the faces of the others told him charm wasn't going to cut it. 'Long and short, I owed this guy Katz some money. About thirty grand.'

'Jesus,' Jenn said. 'How? Aren't you rich?'

He laughed through his nose. 'Two years ago, maybe. I made a killing on this one deal, a biotech company. That's when I bought the condo, the suits, the car.' He shrugged. 'And around then I discovered high-stakes poker.'

'So, the eye,' Mitch said, tapping at his own.

'Yeah. I fell behind, and that was Katz letting me know that the bill was due. So when the plan of taking down Johnny came around . . . ' He shrugged.

'Gee, Ian,' Alex said. 'That's a real hard-luck story, what with you blowing a fortune while the rest of us were working hourly. But I'm still missing the part where you *told your bookie what we were doing.*'

'I know. And I'm sorry, believe me. I didn't plan to. But after I talked to him about needing guns, he had his bodyguard hold me while he' — Ian looked down — 'It doesn't matter. Point is, he thought I was working for the police, and I had to convince him otherwise. But I didn't say anything about who we were robbing, nothing. I swear.'

Mitch said, 'There's more, isn't there?'

Ian nodded. 'He said that since you were helping me, you were all responsible too.'

'Oh, *fuck* you.'

'That's why I paid him. If it was just me, I would have risked it.' The man's face was scrunched like a baby's, his voice coming fast and earnest. 'Don't you see? I did it for you.'

Alex snorted. 'You haven't done any of this for us.'

'Look, I had a cigar held to my nuts, OK? Besides,' anger coming into his voice, 'what about you? You just tried to dump everything on us.'

'That's because *I wasn't fucking there.*'

'No,' Mitch said. 'You were just the one who pushed us into it.'

'Bullshit. Everybody was in equally.'

'Yeah? That how you remember it?' Mitch met his gaze unblinking. Something had shifted between them. A week ago, he could have stared Mitch down in a second. Now, he found himself wanting to look away. His friend had become a dangerous man.

'Enough.' Jenn's voice broke the moment. 'We're missing the point. What are we going to do about Victor?'

'What we promised,' Mitch said.

'You believe he won't kill us?'

'We're white taxpayers. If he kills us, the police, they're going to start digging. There's no reason he would want the hassle.' Mitch reached out, laid his hand on top of Jenn's. Her eyes narrowed, but she didn't pull away. 'Monday morning, we give him what he wants.'

It was too much. The robbery, the dead man, Trish, Jenn, Victor, all of it. Alex felt that narrowing tension he'd had back in college, the sense that everything that had seemed safe and fun had become sour and hurtful. Only now there were men with guns involved.

No. No way. He had one responsibility, and that was to Cassie. 'Not me. I told Victor, and I meant it. I had nothing to do with this. You guys did the killing. You found this stuff. You hid it. You're on your own, the three of you.'

Jenn wrinkled her lips like she'd bitten something foul. Mitch only nodded. 'Fine.' He turned to Ian. 'But it's not the three of us.'

'Huh?' Stick-thin and hunched, the man looked like a bird as his glance darted around the table. 'What do you mean?'

'You're a fuck-up, Ian.' Mitch spoke calmly. 'I know it's not your fault. But you are. We can't trust you.'

'Look at the boss man,' Alex said. He didn't know why he bothered, what it mattered whether Ian was included or not. It was more the change

268

in Mitch that he was reacting to. 'Telling everybody how it is.'

'He's right,' Jenn said, her voice emotionless. 'I'm sorry, Ian.'

'But — ' The trader looked around the table, his expression so pathetic Alex had an urge to hug him. 'This is stupid. The four of us are best friends. We need each other.'

Mitch shook his head. 'Not anymore.'

PART III

Game Theory

'We might say the universe is so constituted as to maximize play. The best games are not those in which all goes smoothly and steadily toward a certain conclusion, but those in which the outcome is always in doubt.'

— George B. Leonard

25

In the cab on the way home, shaky and alternately scalding and freezing, Ian played a game with himself. Even now, he liked games. The thought made him sick.

This one was called Have You Ever Felt Worse in Your Life.

Round One, eighth grade. All summer he'd bugged his father for a trip to Six Flags, and finally the old man piled him and his best friend, Billy Martin, in the F-150. Dad paid the entrance fee, shaking his head at the price, and Ian had led them straight to the biggest ride in the park, a monster of plunging hills and loops. They'd waited for an hour, listening to the screams, watching people stagger off. At first he'd been giddy. But as they inched forward, a dark, flapping fear had grown in him. It was in the irrevocability, the way the car got higher and higher with no last chance. The terrible pause before it went over, and the screams started.

Then the bored teenager manning the gate had opened it, and they'd walked onto the platform, where the empty car was waiting. People were laughing and jostling, the air sweet with cotton candy and hamburgers, gulls shrieking above.

Just as they reached their seats, he said, 'I don't want to.'

His father had looked at him then with an

expression he'd never forgotten, one he saw sometimes late at night. A twisted-lip sort of contempt, and behind it, a thought Ian could read clear as day.

What kind of a pussy am I raising?

'Fine,' his dad had said. 'Wait here.' Then he'd turned to Billy, and said, 'What about you? You want to?'

And the two of them had climbed into the front seat of the front car like father and son, leaving Ian to stand and watch.

That had been bad. But not as bad as now.

OK, Round Two. Junior year at the University of Tennessee. Madly in love with Gina Scoppetti, a fierce Italian girl with sharp brown eyes and a body that reminded him of his favorite picture in the stolen *Penthouse* that had held him through his teenage years, the shot of a girl stretched and spread and glistening beside a perfect California pool, a world a million miles from pork rinds and Friday night football. Gina said she loved him too, and they made silly plans and drew on each other with marker and dry-humped till he bled.

Then someone told him that she'd gotten drunk at a fraternity party and ended up blowing three brothers in a back room. He'd confronted her, and she'd cried, said that she didn't remember, she didn't think it was true, that she loved him, that she'd been drunk. And he'd wanted to believe her, but thought about the frat boys with their expensive clothes and bright white baseball caps trading high fives as they used her, and he'd started to cry, and called her a whore, and said they were through. It was a

274

month before he found out it hadn't been Gina, it had been a friend of hers, that Gina had just passed out on a downstairs couch, and he'd begged her to forgive him, said she was the best thing that had ever happened to a kid from Shitsville, Tennessee, and that he would never doubt her again, and she hadn't even let him in, just shook her head through the crack in the chained door and called him a coward.

That one came close, all the more because then, like now, he was to blame. But as terrible as he'd felt — the racking crying that left him hollowed out, the sense that the world was empty — it didn't add up to the combination of cocaine shakes and paralyzing horror that he had let down and endangered everyone he loved.

How about the time he'd slipped on the icy steps of the Michigan Avenue staircase down to the Billy Goat Tavern, tumbling half a flight to hit the cement with a sickening crack, the pain vicious as broken glass, his leg broken in two places, cars sliding by, exhaust and the queasy yellow light of the underpass and the sense that he was all alone in a city that wanted to break him?

Nope.

Katz holding a cigar to his nuts?

Nope.

He felt an urge to giggle and retch at the same time. It had been almost four days since he'd had so much as a bump of coke, and he was shocked at the desperate way his every cell seemed to be screaming for it. The sky was a spotlight, white and hot and hard.

Hell with them, he thought. Jenn and Alex and Mitch, Katz and Johnny Love and Victor, his father, his co-workers. Hell with them all.

The cab pulled up to his building, and he paid without counting, just handing over bills and climbing out as the driver said, 'Hey, man, you OK?' Slammed the door and went in the lobby and hit the elevator button again and again.

His hands were shaking as he fumbled with the keys, and he dropped them and cursed and kicked the front door hard enough to hurt his toe, then bent and snagged them and jammed them in the lock and twisted and walked into his home.

The air smelled sour, and he remembered vomiting that morning, on his knees in front of the toilet, desperate for a line, not doing one. Lying on his side on the couch, the TV on mute, until the phone had rung, Katz on the end of the line, saying he needed to see him right now. Telling him to come to the Continental.

That Katz had betrayed him didn't surprise or sting. But his friends? The people he had tried to protect? That they couldn't even try to understand why he had done what he had, that there had been reasons —

Fuck it.

He strode to the bookshelves, snatched the Montecristo box, opened the lid, and shook out the contents to clatter on the glass table. Habit taking over as he unrolled the baggie of white powder, unzipping it to pour a too-large pile. The razor had bounced to the Oriental carpet, and he stooped for it, then dropped to his knees and began to chop the pile furiously. It was good stuff, already fine, and in half a minute he had broken the few clumps and then divided the pile into four thick rails, each long as the span between thumb and forefinger. Ian transferred the razor to his left hand and took the pre-rolled twenty and leaned forward, one end in his nostril, his body calmer already, the shakes easing as they sensed what was coming, the bitter winter snort of relief. The air conditioning was on, and he could smell his own sweat as he bent over. The motion reflected off the polished surface, the sunlight glaring oblique through the windows, turning the table into a mirror so that he could see his features ghosted over the powder. Pale and hard-angled, with dark pits instead of eyes. A cadaver with a rolled-up bill jammed up his nose.

It was the most haunting thing he had ever seen. Ian froze, staring down at his own face eight inches away. His fingers palsied on the twenty, and his breath scattered the edges of the cocaine like dust. Every part of him wanting to just take a quick blast, just one, something to ease this feeling, to let him think clearly, to banish the memory of the friends who had betrayed him and the job he had blown and the father who never knew what to do with a son who liked games and the man in the suit saying he would visit that same father and do terrible things to him. If he just did a little his mind would clear, and he wanted it, God, he wanted it, more than he'd ever wanted anything, more than Gina or his father's love or the thrilling uncertainty of the unturned card, and he hated it, more than he hated even himself, and the two feelings yanked at him, tore into him, made him clench and shake and want to scream, and then he felt a slick burning in his left hand.

The pain was sharp and immediate, and it broke the trance. He straightened and blinked. Blood was dripping onto the glass, big fat drops that spattered in perfect patterns, softening red to pink where they hit the powder on the table. Slowly, like a man waking from a dream, he unclenched his fingers. The razor blade. He'd forgotten he was holding it, and his tightening fist had jammed a good third of it into the meat of his palm. Gingerly, he tugged it out, the sliding sensation vaguely nauseating. He dropped it on the glass, where it hit with a *ting*.

Shit.

Ian closed his hand. Heat and the throb of his pulse. His fingers were red.

Is this all you are?

Is this what you want to be?

He heard Katz's voice from last week. Laughing, calling him a degenerate. A drug addict in a suit.

A wave of disgust pounded him. He yanked the bill from his nose. Grabbed the cigar box from the floor and upended the Ziploc into it, then leaned forward and used a forearm to shovel all the blow from the table into the box as well. He stood up fast, and walked hard to the bathroom. The toilet seat was still up from the morning's puking. He held the box over it.

He hesitated before dumping it. But only for a minute. Then he kicked the handle with the tip of his dress shoe and watched it all swirl away.

278

OK. He'd made some mistakes. And even the things that he had done with good intentions, like paying off Katz, had made things worse. But he wasn't going down like this. Not Ian Verdon, no way. He'd worked too hard, come too far. Cocaine wasn't going to beat him, and neither was Johnny Love or Victor, that sick fuck. And if his friends didn't want his help, well, fine. He'd do it on his own.

Do what, exactly?

The thought took the wind from him. What was there to do? Monday morning, Jenn and Mitch would go to the bank, get the mystery bottles, and give them to Victor. That would be that.

Or would it? Only as long as the guy held true to his promise. Ian had heard too many pitches to buy that 'believe every word I say' schtick on credit.

Ian's left hand was wet with blood. He spun the faucet, held his hand under it. The pain was steady but distant. Hell of a week. A black eye, a sliced palm, a second-degree burn on his balls, dope sickness, and the rejection by his only real friends. Hell of a week.

Somehow he had to make this better. Make up for all the ways he'd blown it.

How long have you got, kid?

All right. Maybe not *all* the ways. But as many as he could. Help his friends. Get back to being the man he once had been. The guy on the go, the Tennessee Refugee who had come to the Windy City and made a killing.

How, though? Beyond where to score premium flake or play in a private poker game, he didn't know anything about the criminal world. His cellphone didn't have numbers for ex-cops with friends on the force or gangbangers working as muscle.

Well, OK. What do you have, then? What are you capable of?

He could always go to the police. But while he wasn't sure of Victor's magnanimity in victory, he was damn sure of the man's willingness to carry out his threats if crossed. His father, Alex's kid, the others . . . Ian shivered in the cold tile bathroom. He couldn't risk it. Especially not knowing what he was dealing with.

Wait. There. He had a flash of the movie *Wall Street*, Michael Douglas as Gordon Gekko, preaching that information was power. God, how many times had he seen that flick? Fifty? A hundred? Lying on the couch of his shitty efficiency apartment, eating ravioli straight from the can, reciting the lines to get rid of his Southern drawl.

Information was power. And right now they didn't have enough.

So what? You don't know how to learn about a man like Victor. Not as if you can look him up in Well-Dressed Psychopaths Weekly.

OK. So he couldn't get much on Victor. So what could he —

Whoa.

He straightened. Left the bathroom, picked up his phone from the counter. Scrolled through until he found the number he was looking for.

'Davis. It's Ian Verdon. Listen, can I buy you a beer? I need to pick your brain.'

280

26

He was supposed to be on shift until six, but Mitch just couldn't find it in himself to give a good goddamn. When he thought about the sum total of hours he'd occupied the same patch of sidewalk, sun or rain or snow, in a monkey suit, smiling on cue, jockeying to open the doors of cabs and limousines, hauling luggage and giving directions, it made him not so much tired as physically sick. Eight hours a day, 250 days a year, times, what, ten *years*? Staring at the patterns of blackened gum driven into the sidewalk, at the building opposite, watching people walk to better jobs, talking into cell-phones, women in stockings and long soft hair not even looking as they strode home. His life. What a colossal waste.

Alex and Ian had both already left, the first storming out, the second slumping, leaving him and Jenn sitting in the conference room alone. He had a quick flash of hoisting her up onto the polished wood table, laying her back with one hand behind her head, whispering to her as he kissed down her body, but a glance told him that wasn't going to happen. She sat rigid, staring at her hands, elegant fingers splayed across the tabletop.

'Are you OK?'

She nodded but didn't look up.

'Let's get out of here.'

'What about your job?'

'I quit.'

She'd looked at him then, an appraising kind of stare. He met her gaze and put on what he hoped was a rakish grin. Maybe it was silly, but he felt good. Alive, and strong, and with the woman he wanted. They could stand shoulder to shoulder against the world. Forget the others.

It was a gorgeous day, the sunlight bright and pure, the colors fresh-scrubbed. He put his arm around her and steered east, no real destination in mind. They got lucky with the light at Michigan and crossed over to Millennial Park. The air smelled of fried foods and the lake. It felt good to walk with her, and he didn't break the silence, just wandered up the steps toward the massive chrome sculpture. The thing was shaped like a bean, maybe forty feet across and mirror-polished, the curves reflecting the whole world. Tourists and their children wandered staring, watching the surface warp and distort them. He liked that about it, the sense of disappearing in plain sight, of turning into something else.

'Aren't you scared?'

He turned to look at her, surprised. 'No.'

'Why not?'

'Because this is a good thing. It solves everything at once. We get to keep the money, don't have to worry about Johnny, and all we have to do is give up something we don't want anyway.' He watched a small boy, seven or eight, walk steadily toward the sculpture with his hands in front of him. 'That was smart of you, telling

282

him you'd put it in the bank, so we do it in public.'

'Is that why you think I said it?'

'Isn't it?'

She didn't reply. Whatever was spinning in her mind, he had a feeling he wouldn't like it, and so instead of asking again, he said, 'Can you believe Alex? I know we've had our differences, but I never thought he'd just abandon us like that. Prick.'

'He has his daughter to think about.'

'Like we don't have people to protect?'

'It's different for him.'

'Why?'

'He's a father. He's worried.'

'He's a coward, is what he is.'

'Come on.'

'What? Why are you defending him?'

'I'm not.'

'You are.' His forehead felt overlarge, the blood vessels in it pounding. 'Again. What's going on between you two?'

'Nothing.'

'Sure. He showed up at your place the other night for nothing.' The words were barely out of his mouth and he already regretted them.

'Excuse me?'

He sighed. 'I didn't mean that.'

'What did you mean?'

'I just' — a cab blared its horn, and another answered — 'I like you, Jenn. A lot. I have for a long time.' *Jesus, what are you, twelve?* 'I mean, I know this is new, and I don't want to rush.'

She didn't answer him, just brushed a lock of

283

hair behind her ear.

'Anyway, the thing with Victor, this is good. We can bring the stuff with us to the bank, then give it to him there. It won't matter that it wasn't in the safe-deposit box. He won't pull anything.'

'Maybe.'

'Nah. You have to understand, a guy like Victor, we're not on his radar. He'll just take what he wants and go.'

' 'A guy like Victor'? What do you know about guys like Victor?'

'He's a businessman, that's all I mean.' Nothing seemed to be coming out right, like they were having separate conversations. 'We'll take care of him, and he'll take care of Johnny, and then we're clear to use the money. We can start a new life.' He caught himself, flushed. 'I mean, you know, we all can.'

She turned and looked up at him. It seemed like she was searching for something, and he felt his face get hotter still. Finally, she said, 'You have the wrong idea.' He opened his mouth to speak, but she cut him off. 'You're a doorman. I work in a travel agency. I didn't lie to Victor to get us to a public place. I lied to buy us time to go to the police.'

For a second he felt like he was falling, that weird gut sense of imbalance. He stared, waiting for her to say it was a joke, that she had been kidding.

'Hey, buddy, got any change?' The man had that same look of a lot of Chicago's homeless, indeterminate age, clothes nicer than you'd expect, but eyes rheumy and worn.

'No,' Mitch said. Then turned back to her. 'Are you serious?'

'Come on, mister. Any change at all?'

'I said no.'

The man stood for another second, then grimaced and wandered away.

'You can't be — '

'I am.' She crossed her arms in front of her breasts. 'This is out of control. We need to get some help.'

'Think about what you're saying. We're going to walk into the police station and tell them what, we robbed a guy at gunpoint?'

'Whoever Victor is, he's bad news. I'm sure they'll take that into account — '

'Jenn, we killed someone.' He said the words under his breath, glancing around to make sure no one overheard.

'It was self-defense. We'll all swear to that.'

This couldn't be happening. He put a hand on her elbow. 'Do you understand what you're saying?'

She looked the other way.

'Oh, that's great. Fantastic.' He could feel the throb of blood through his body, hot and cold at once. 'So you and Alex and Ian get off for free, and I go to jail.'

'No, I'm not saying that — '

'*That's what will happen.*' He squeezed her arm tightly, and she jumped, turned to face him. 'Why are the rest of you being so blind? This isn't one of Ian's goddamn games. We don't get to start over.'

'Let go. You're hurting me.'

285

'Hey, buddy, seriously, help me out, just a quarter, anything.'

Mitch let go of her arm, spun to face the homeless guy. 'I said, fuck off.'

'Come on, I'm trying to get something to eat — '

Something in him snapped. Mitch stepped forward, put his hands against the bum's chest and shoved. The man staggered, and Mitch followed, one fist bunched up, his hand shaking. The bum took another quick step back, then his heel caught on something, and he went over, his arms whirling. He hit the ground with a *whoomp* and a yell.

People froze, their eyes on him, that same old schoolyard feeling, everyone watching with vampire eyes. A woman had her hand to her mouth like she had stuffed a doughnut in whole. A burly guy twenty feet away started forward. On the ground, the bum writhed, saying, 'Shit, man, all I wanted was a quarter.'

He was at once bulletproof and bleeding, that shaking intensity of being the center of attention. He grabbed Jenn by the arm and started away. He had to tug to get her moving. 'Come *on*.'

'Lady, you OK?' It was Burly Guy, one of those Chicago big men, not exactly fat, but no *GQ* cover.

'I'm fine.' She shook off Mitch's hand and started walking. Two teenagers were helping the homeless guy to his feet. The crowd turned as one to stare them out.

'Listen, that was — '

'What's happening to you? You're not the same.'

'What are you talking about?'

'It's like you've become someone else. I know this has all been crazy, but — '

'Jenn, fuck that, OK? I'm the only one doing what needs to be done. And if you go to the police, I go to jail. It's just that simple.'

'You don't know that.'

'Yeah, I do. And so do you.'

'So we won't tell them the whole story. We can lie, tell them that we found the bottles.'

'What, we stumbled on them in the alley? Don't be stupid.'

She stopped, whirled to face him. Her feet were planted shoulder width, and her eyes flashed. 'Don't you ever. Just because we fucked doesn't mean you get to do that.'

He raised his hands. 'I'm sorry.'

She stared for another moment, then turned and started walking fast. He was taller than she was, but had to hustle to keep up. 'Look, I understand. You're scared.'

'Of course I'm scared. So are you. The difference is that I'll admit it.'

'Jenn, please, listen to me, would you?' They reached the north end of Millennial Park, and she started across Randolph without looking. Horns shrieked and brakes squealed as she strode through traffic, parting it like the Red Sea. Even now, as everything fell apart, it was a thrill to watch her. 'Would you listen?'

'I'm going home, Mitch.'

'I'll go with you.'

'No.'

'Fine, but would you just listen for a second?'

She stepped up onto the sidewalk. 'What?'

'You're right. I'm scared too, OK?' He held his hands out in front of him, fingers almost touching, like he was squeezing an invisible ball. 'I have been since we started this.' It was only as he spoke that he realized it was true. What was he doing? What had he done?

Push. It. Down.

He made himself speak gently. 'We have to be realistic. We can't go to the cops. If we do, maybe, maybe you and the others will be OK. But I won't. You know that.'

Something flickered across her face like a cloud shadow. She turned to look at the half-finished high-rise to the west, her eyes tracing the girders. 'You did it for me, didn't you? Not . . . what happened in the alley. Before that. You agreed to rob Johnny because I was.'

'No.'

'Yes, you did.' She rubbed at her eyes. 'I told myself that I wasn't manipulating you, but I knew how you felt, and I took advantage. Because I wanted to do this. I wanted an adventure.'

'I — ' He felt he should say something but didn't know what.

'I was wrong to do that. I'm sorry.'

'Don't be. Maybe you're right, maybe I did do it for you. But you know what?' He shrugged. 'That's as good a reason as any I can think of.'

'But now everything is bad.'

'We have to keep it together. Just a little longer.'

'You're wrong.' Her smile a broken flower. She

288

threaded her arm through his. 'I think things are going to get a lot worse.'

★ ★ ★

Victor stared out the limo window at Jenn and Mitch walking arm in arm. Beside him, Bennett said, 'You think she's playing straight?'

'She *is* straight. All of them are. They're in over their collective heads, and I'm tossing them a line.'

'What about the cops? If they turn over the stuff, they'd have some heavy negotiating power.'

'They aren't thinking that way. They're civilians. Their idea of prison is Oz.'

'So you're trusting in their fear of anal invasion to keep them in line?'

'If they knew what they had, maybe it would be different.' Victor shrugged. 'Or maybe not. You know how little it can take to convince people to do the wrong thing. The money is a big temptation.'

'About that. You're letting them keep it?'

'Our deal stands. I'll still stake you the two hundred fifty thousand.'

'Why?'

'I'm being careful. That money is two hundred and fifty thousand reasons not to go to the police.'

'Why not just take them somewhere, lock them down?'

'Too risky. Who knows if someone is expecting them, will report them missing? This is safer. They don't know what they have, and they don't

289

know anything about us. So we watch, and we wait.' Victor leaned forward, tapped the mic. 'Let's go, Andrews.' The car began to move almost immediately. 'You'll watch her.'

'I don't work for you, remember? No orders.'

Victor sighed. 'If anything happens, it will go through her. She's the one who set up the safe deposit. No one will be able access it without her, that's why I didn't insist on the key. I've got plenty of men, but you're better than they are. So pretty please, in the interest of our partnership, will you keep an eye on her?'

'Fair enough.' Bennett paused, rubbed at his chin. 'You're right. If they do make a play, they won't leave her dangling. Three men, one woman, they're going to protect her.'

'They're going to try.'

27

They had spent another hour wandering the city before Jenn told Mitch she was going home. He'd said he would come with her, and she had been forced to say no. It wasn't that she didn't care about him, or that her apology had been less than sincere. But everything was moving too fast. Maybe, maybe, they had a chance to make something happen. Of the original foursome, he was certainly the only one she still trusted. But they'd only slept together a couple of times, and he seemed ready to propose, and she just couldn't take it.

'You'll be OK?'

'I'll be fine. I just need a little space.'

'Space from me?'

'Space from everybody.' She had taken his hand. 'What you said before — '

'I know, it was too fast — '

'It was sweet. And I like you, too, Mitch. But I need some time to think. Let's just get through all of this and let things settle down, OK?'

'Yeah,' he'd said. 'Sure.'

'And once it has, why don't you give me a call. Ask me out on an actual date.'

His face lit up like Christmas. 'Yeah?'

'I'd like that.'

'Me too.' He laughed. 'We'll do it right. Go somewhere nice. On Johnny.'

That had made her laugh too, and as she'd

gotten in a cab and closed the door behind her, she'd felt a quick pang of regret to leave him standing on the sidewalk, hands tucked in his pockets.

But it had also felt great to step into her apartment alone. To dodge out of the weight and meaning of everything. Habit, maybe, and one that she was looking to break. It was time to quit playing games, pretending that nothing meant anything. But it wasn't going to happen all at once. Right now, all she wanted was to put life on hold. To forget about the dissolution of her friendships, the transformation of her world, the monsters tracking them. To have a vodka and read a silly magazine and forget everything. Maybe it was weak, maybe it was regressive, but she deserved it.

So the knock on the door had been anything but a happy surprise. She strode across the hardwood fast, reached for the door. 'Damn it, I said I need a little space — '

Alex stood in the hallway.

'Oh.' She crossed her arms over her chest, feeling trapped and a little silly. 'You.'

'Listen, I can't stay. Cassie's got a soccer game, I promised I'd be there. But I wanted to — I couldn't say it in front of the others. First Victor, then Mitch, they got me so riled up.' He let out a breath. 'It doesn't matter. I wanted to say I'm sorry.'

'OK.'

He gave her a rueful smile. 'I really pissed you off, didn't I?'

'You bailed on us.'

'That's not what I'm apologizing for.'

'No?'

'I had to do that. I have my daughter to think of.'

'We all have people to think of.'

'I know. But you don't know what it's like to have a child. It . . . it takes over everything. When I heard Victor threaten her, I could have . . . Jesus. If it wasn't for his guards, I might have put his face through that table.'

There was something in the way he held himself, the tension in his shoulders, that touched her. In the genes, she supposed — hard not to be attracted to a man who would do anything for his family. 'I'm glad you didn't try.'

'I know.' He paused. 'I'm going to lose her, Jenn.'

'Mitch thinks that if we give the stuff to Victor — '

'I don't mean that. They're taking her away. To Arizona.' He looked down, rubbed at the back of his neck. 'I brought Trish the money. I know, I shouldn't have, just like Ian shouldn't have paid his bookie, but I had to. And they had this lawyer there, this slick as shit corporate killer, and he — '

'Unbelievable.' She shook her head. 'You're a piece of work, you know that?'

'Huh?'

'First, you come down on Ian for doing the same thing you did.'

'That was different — '

'But beyond that, it's always the same for you, isn't it? You never look at the things you don't

293

want to. You convince yourself of something and screen out the rest of the world. *Of course* you can't just waltz in, give her some money, and make everything OK. Did you really believe that was going to work? For a bright guy, you sure miss the obvious. You did it with your marriage, your job, the child support, even — ' She stopped herself.

'Even you,' he said. 'That's what you were going to say, isn't it? Well, maybe you're right. That's why I'm here. To apologize.'

She waited, gave him nothing.

'I've been stupid in so many ways. Everything you said, and more.' His gaze was level, challenging. 'The other night, when I came over . . . it was . . . I'd just come from Trish's — well, from a bar — and I was hurting, and I needed someone to help me, to make it better. And the only person I could think of was you.'

Jenn stared at him, the hard line of his jaw, the muscles his shirt didn't conceal, the haunted look in his eyes. There had been a time when hearing that would have made her happy. They'd told each other that they were just passing time and taking pleasure. But though she'd been willing to go along, it wasn't the way she was wired. The way women were wired. Not really. No matter the promises, the words spoken, the secrets, she couldn't sleep with someone for a year and not care about him. Not wonder about a future. Once upon a time, hearing him say that would have made her very happy indeed.

Now, though, it just annoyed her. 'I don't really know what to do with that.'

'I know.' He shifted. 'I know.'

'Mitch and I . . . '

'I'm not trying to get in the middle of that.'

'Yes, you are.'

'How are things with the two of you?'

'I like him. It's nice to have someone want you, want to be with you, want to let everyone know it.' She saw Alex wince, but didn't feel like making it easier on him. 'And he's smart, and strong. Stronger than any of us thought.'

'But?'

'Why do you think there's a 'but'?'

'Isn't there?'

'It's just, it's all so fast. He thinks it's true love, that this is a musical and all the excitement is part of the fun.'

'And you don't.'

'I don't know. Everything is complicated.' She sighed. 'You know how I told Victor that the stuff was in the bank? I lied.'

'What? But the key — '

'I got a safe-deposit box, but it was for the money. The bottles are still in the drug dealer's car. I lied to buy some time so we could go to the police. But Mitch said that if we do, he'll go to jail.'

'He's right. He killed someone. He would go to jail. He should go to jail.' Alex paused, then something came into his eyes. 'But you can't live with that. Because he did it for you.'

'It wasn't that simple, like he — '

'Come on.' Alex shrugged. 'You know the truth. He did it for you. All of it.'

'Screw you.'

'You know I'm right.' His voice, in its calm certainty, was too much.

'You know what? I don't think I know a thing when it comes to you.' The anger came quick and hot. 'You spend a year alternately sleeping with me and telling me that what we're doing doesn't matter. Then the moment someone else is willing to step up, suddenly I'm all you can think of.'

'How's this for stepping up?' He moved toward her, put his hands on her shoulders and pulled her to him, his lips pressing hers, his body hard against her, muscular and sure. It felt at once familiar and exhilarating, that old heat rising between them —

She turned her head away. 'No.'

'Jenn — '

'I said *no*.' She pushed him, and he stepped back, looking wounded.

He said, 'You lied to me too, you know. And I told you, my daughter — '

'Yeah. You told me.' She snorted, the anger making her hands shake. It felt good, better than being scared and confused. 'Fine. Thanks for telling me.'

'I didn't come here to fight.'

'No. You came to apologize.' She stepped back, put her hand on the door. 'Well, mission accomplished.'

'Jenn, wait.'

'Go watch your daughter play soccer.' She closed the door.

* * *

Everything had turned to shit.

Alex stood outside her door for a long moment, wondering if he should knock again, wondering if she would open it if he did. Finally, he slunk down the stairs, got in his car, and started counting the things he didn't have.

No job. No family. No friends. No girlfriend. And all of it, every problem, every pain, was his fault. He'd methodically deconstructed his own life.

Jenn was right. He did only look one step ahead, did ignore the things that didn't work for what he wanted. And that had cost him everything.

Worse still, he'd put the lives of others in danger. That sick fuck Victor was out there somewhere, right now, planning ways to hurt his child. He cocked his fist back and punched the steering wheel. *Dammit.* He'd brought the boogeyman into his own daughter's world. The reasons didn't matter. All that mattered was that now Cassie was in danger. If something happened to her . . .

Cassie. He glanced at the clock. He'd be late, but there was still time to make her soccer game. He fired up the car and headed for the highway.

What now? Go cheer on the sidelines with the other divorced dads and hope everything worked out? That Trish and her new hubby could protect his daughter if a psycho came calling?

What if Jenn and Mitch blew it on Monday? What if they decided to go to the police? What if they didn't, but Victor thought they had?

'Fuck, fuck, *fuck*.' He jammed on the gas and

blew by a CTA bus pulling to the corner.

Everything was so tenuous. Cassie should be safe *if* Mitch didn't screw anything up. *If* Victor didn't decide they were playing him, or that he needed some extra insurance. Hell, Alex had been so distracted in her hallway, trying to talk sense to Jenn, it hadn't hit him until just now what a risk they were running. Lying to a guy who had managed to find them effortlessly, a guy who had Johnny Love terrified, that was beyond dumb. It was reckless. Mitch and Jenn were throwing dice with his life. A horn blared as he passed a sedan on the right.

He remembered the conversation at brunch the other day, Ian explaining another one of his games. What had it been called? Prisoner's something. How the point of the exercise wasn't trust. How in the logic of game theory, abstracts like trust and love and goodness didn't come into play. In a world where everything had consequences, where it was always a choice between the lesser of two evils, the best strategy was to betray before you were betrayed.

That was a lesson Mitch and Jenn, the happy couple, sure seemed to have learned.

The helplessness was the worst. Back when it had just been the four of them in danger, he was OK with the risk. But this? His daughter?

He had to protect her. He had to make sure that no matter what happened, she was safe.

That she was somewhere no one could get to her.

★ ★ ★

298

After flushing the coke and making a plan, all Ian wanted was to get moving, to make something happen. But while Davis was more than happy to hear from him — damn near ecstatic, actually — he'd explained that it was his little girl's birthday, and that they were having a party. 'She's turning six. Twenty friends, a clown, the works.'

'Jesus. What happened to a cake from the store and those candles that relight when you blow them out?'

'Tell me about it. My wife, you know. It's what they do these days. Anyway, what's up?'

'You remember Hudson-Pollum Biolabs, right?'

'Remember it? You kidding? It's financing the party. And Janie's college education.' A pause. 'Why? You have something else like that, something hot?' The hunger in his voice was unmistakable.

'Maybe. Can we get together?'

'How about lunch on Monday? My treat.'

'Can't wait till then.'

'Something I can help you with over the phone?'

'No.' It was one thing to buy drinks, ease him into it. Another to chat while Davis stood in his family room. Ian had to sell the guy. 'Listen, don't take this the wrong way, but it's something I don't want to talk about over the phone.'

'Why, is it . . . umm . . . '

'No, nothing like that. It's just, I need to be careful. It's complicated . . . ' He let his voice trail off, imagining Davis leaning forward. The guy might be a brilliant scientist, but a poker player he was not. 'There are confidentiality issues, regulations.'

'I hear you.' There was a pause. 'You think it might have a payout like last time?'

'Hard to say. But if you help me, and it does turn into something . . .'

Davis sighed. 'All right. My wife'll be pissed, but I could sneak away tonight. Say about nine?'

'No earlier?'

'It's my little girl's birthday, Ian.'

'Right. Right. Nine.'

Which left him with nothing to do but pace and stare at the carpet and try not to lick his coffee table for leftover powder.

It was one thing to realize he'd been a fuck-up — to have his only real friends tell him — and decide to do something about it. It was another to actually have to suffer through the hours. That was the thing about decisions. The act of deciding was easy.

The living with it, that was the trick.

28

The girl had hairless legs that flashed white as she drove downfield, the soccer ball racing ahead like a puppy. Her hair was bound in a ponytail, and her look of grim determination was visible from the stands. The first defender fell for a fake, had to turn and come back, out of the running with one bad move. The second put everything into a wicked slide-tackle, right foot out, back arched, other leg curled beneath, but was half a second late. Then the only thing between the girl and glory was one dirty-kneed ten-year-old. The attacker set up with a soft left tap, wound up her right, and the ball was a black-and-white streak rocketing for the goal.

Even knowing what he planned to do, panting under the terrifying enormity of it, Alex was caught up in the moment. The smell of grass and dirt. Team jerseys bright as candy. A coach's yell from the sidelines. Late afternoon sun basting his shoulders.

And especially Cassie, in the goal, making a flying leap, her arms stretched out, braids whipping behind, coming not just off the ground but near horizontal, suspended for a moment of grace as her fingers stretched, stretched, and then tagged the ball, knocking it down to bounce harmlessly in front of the line.

The crowd exploded. It was a play-off game on a beautiful day in an expensive suburban neighborhood, and packed with parents and grandparents and siblings and friends. Even so, Alex had thought it a little too risky to sit on the home-team side. Which meant that as his heart filled with joy for Cassie, as he looked across the field and saw Trish and her new husband leap to their feet and scream, all he could do was sit among the parents of the other team as they groaned at his daughter's perfection.

A few minutes earlier, he'd sensed Trish's eyes rove across him. He'd made a point of staring downfield and clapping, his baseball cap pulled low to screen his face. He'd tasted bile at the back of his throat, sure that even at that distance she not only recognized him but saw into his heart, saw what he planned to do. He imagined flyers in post offices, digital billboards on the highway flashing the Amber Alert. That weird disconnect of the pictures that would be included, snaps taken at happy times, a birthday or a vacation.

Was he really about to do this?

His stomach was sour, and he couldn't stop tapping his toe. A woman muttered something as she passed, and he snarled, 'What?'

She turned, spooked. 'I said excuse me.'

'Oh.' He exhaled, forcing a smile. 'Sure.'

This was the only option. On the surface it looked foolish, but to anyone who knew the whole picture, what he was planning made perfect sense. His daughter was in danger. He was going to take her somewhere no one could hurt her. Simple as that. When it came down to it, what more important role did a parent have than keeping his child safe?

Besides, maybe Mitch and Jenn could pull it off, and if they did, Victor would leave them alone. At that point, he could bring Cassie back, no harm done. Trish would be furious, but she might learn something along the way. Like what it felt like to be helpless while someone took your child.

Whoa. Jesus. What kind of thinking is that?

When Alex had arrived, he'd pulled past the neat lanes of approved parking spaces onto the grass at the edge of the lot, then did a three-point turn to leave the car facing out. It was a walk of maybe fifty yards. As soon as the ref blew the whistle for halftime . . .

On the field, Cassie's team had regrouped and were steadily moving the ball forward, maintaining a good passing game. Her coach was big on not cultivating stars, said that soccer was a metaphor for life; you had to work together for victory. In the opposite bleachers, Trish nuzzled into the crook of her new husband's arm. He leaned down to whisper something in her ear, and she laughed and punched his shoulder.

How had he ended up here? How had he ended up . . . this?

Stop. You screwed up. And you'll pay for it. But are you going to let your daughter be a chip in that game? Or are you willing to risk everything to make sure she stays safe?

An easy choice in a hard world. When it came to priorities, he'd only ever had one.

One of Cassie's teammates dribbled ahead at an angle, then turned and banked it to the other forward, who fired off a straight blast, plenty of power but no artifice. The opposing goalie caught it easily, then spun and discus-hurled it down the field. As it landed, the referee blew the whistle. The first half was over.

The world seemed to be phasing in and out. Not quite wobbling, more a wet sort of zoomy feeling tied to his heartbeat. Alex wiped his palms on his jeans, suddenly aware of the texture of the fabric. All around him happy fathers talked to happy mothers. Little boys with action figures turned the bleachers into war zones. Girls Cassie's age had cellphones out and were texting one another. The sun beat down, hotter somehow at this hour than at noon. Hundreds of voices, the sounds of scraping shoes and clicking cameras, it all blended into a whirlpool of noise, spinning and scraping past his ears, a maelstrom he couldn't separate into individual elements.

It was time.

He closed his eyes. Took a deep breath. Then opened them, stood up, and started down the bleachers. He pictured it all in his head — going over to the sidelines and calling to Cassie. Her delight at seeing him, the puzzled trust in her eyes when he told her that they had to go, right now, yes, right now. He wondered how long it would be before Trish would notice. Five minutes? In the confusion, he might be able to count on five minutes before the questions started. The panic. The announcement over the loudspeaker, the calls to police, the appeals on the local news.

This is for her.

He hit the bottom step, dropped to the faded grass. Behind him, he heard someone say, 'Did you see that goalie? What a talented girl.'

Goddamn right, he thought, and took another step before something made him freeze, literally freeze in place, one shoe arrested an inch over the ground. Something about that voice —

'She's truly something,' the voice continued. 'A child like that, you sure hope her parents are taking care of her.'

Alex put his foot down. He felt his hands start to shake, clenched them, but it only made his whole arm tremble. Slowly he turned.

Victor was splayed out across the second row, feet propped below, elbows behind. With his open suit jacket and white shirt and casual posture, he looked like a Ralph Lauren ad. He smiled. 'Your daughter has a lot of talent.'

'What are you — ' Alex started forward, his fists coming up. 'I'm going to fucking kill you.'

Victor's smile widened. 'Be careful.' He nodded his head ever so slightly to the left. Dreading what he was going to see, knowing what he was going to see, Alex followed his gaze. One of the bodyguards from earlier was on the other side of the field. His gaze was fixed on them as he stood with his hands in his pockets.

Ten feet from the bench where Cassie and her teammates sat.

'I'm not a father myself,' Victor said. 'In my line of work, kids are at best an encumbrance. And at worst' — he sucked air through his teeth — 'a man with a child, he's at the mercy of the world. Know what I mean?'

Alex stared, his teeth clenched so hard they ached.

'Man with a child, he loses his head. Gets irrational. He thinks that the fact that he would give anything to protect her is actually enough to keep her safe. But it's not. If he really wants her to be safe, well' — Victor shrugged, looked down the field — 'he remembers that he's just a man. He sets aside his ego, and he does what's best for her.'

'What are you talking — '

'There's nowhere you can go that I can't find you.'

'I wasn't — I mean, I — '

'Yes, you were.' The voice calm and certain. 'You were going to run. Which makes me wonder if I should wait till Monday. Where does this leave our arrangement? Should I just start making good on my promises to you? Can you get me what I want, or is your little girl going to be doing some very fast growing up?'

'You sick fuck, you touch her, I'll — '

'Daddy!'

The voice came from thirty yards away, maybe more, but rang like a bell in his soul. Alex whirled, saw Cassie sprinting across the field toward him. Her hair fell in unruly braids, there was a smudge of dirt on her chin, and her jersey was grass-stained. She was the most beautiful thing he'd ever seen.

He opened his mouth to yell at her to stay away, to get back, and then caught himself. Victor was right. A man with a child was at the mercy of the world. He had to play cool.

306

She didn't slow as she drew near, and hit him like a wave. 'You came!' Her hair smelled of sweat and sunlight. 'Did you see my save?'

'I did, baby. It was amazing.' He kissed the top of her head.

'It was something,' Victor said. 'You're an absolute peach.'

Cassie looked at him, then at her shoes, gone suddenly shy. 'Thank you.'

'It's Cassie, right?'

Alex glared, shook his head. 'Don't you — '

'I'm Victor. I'm a friend of your dad's.' The man leaned off the bleachers, held out one hand. Still looking the other way, Cassie shook it formally. 'I came to talk to him, but when I saw you playing I had to stay and watch.'

'Daddy, why are you shaking?'

'Huh?' Alex tore his eyes from Victor, made himself smile for his daughter. 'I'm — I'm just so excited for you.'

'Well.' Victor stood, brushed the knees of his suit. 'I'll let you two be.' He winked, started away, then snapped his fingers and turned. 'I almost forgot. You never answered my question. About whether we could work together?'

Alex stared at him, his lips turning up in a snarl. He thought about launching himself at Victor, tearing the guy's throat out with his bare hands, and knew that if a lifetime in prison would be the only cost, he would have paid it gladly.

Man with a child, he loses his head. Gets irrational. He thinks that the fact that he would give anything to protect her is actually enough to keep her safe. But it's not. If he really wants her to be safe, he remembers that he's just a man. He sets aside his ego, and he does what's best for her.

Victor's words in his head. But that didn't make them wrong. He couldn't keep Cassie safe by wishing it so. He couldn't keep her safe by taking her away, or by wrapping her in his arms and making promises.

But there was a way. A way to be sure. To go not around, but through. *What you're thinking, you can't take it back.*

Alex took a deep breath, then said, 'We can work together.'

'Glad to hear it.'

'I'll call Johnny soon. In the meantime,' he said, gesturing at Cassie with his eyes, 'you keep your end.' *Because so help me, if you so much as touch her hand again, this earth isn't big enough for you to hide, motherfucker.*

'Fair enough.' Victor smiled. 'Nice to meet you, Cassie.'

'Nice to meet you, too,' she said, very properly.

Alex stared until the monster had walked away.

'Who was that, Daddy?'

'He's . . . my boss's boss.'

'He was handsome.' She turned to Alex, beamed up at him. 'So I was good, huh?'

Something was eating him from the inside out. Alex smiled through it, said, 'Not good, baby girl. The best.'

29

It had been a long day.

Ian made it through by relentlessly cleaning his already spotless place. A bit after seven he took a long, long shower, hot enough to slough the skin from his shoulders. Dried off, then spent an hour getting dressed. His best suit, tie crisply Windsored, hair gelled into submission. A little cover-up for the yellowing bruise under his eye, a little cologne. When he looked in the mirror, he almost recognized his old self. Thinner and older, but filled with restless purpose. He still felt awful, but at least he had a plan.

He met Davis at a martini place in River North. Pale amber light splashing on polished wood, soft trip-hop in the background. The woman tending bar wore boots that came halfway up her thighs. The chemist looked just the way Ian remembered: a short-sleeved oxford tucked into his slacks, a haircut his wife had obviously had a say in. Add a pocket protector and a pair of Coke-bottle glasses, and he could have worked for NASA.

'There's the man! Look at you, Ian. Still conquering Wall Street, huh?'

'Doing my best.' He ordered a Glenlivet, neat. 'How was the party?'

'Expensive. The clown smelled like marijuana. But Janie loved it.'

'She's six, huh? Crazy how time flies. When we

did Hudson-Pollum, I think she was four.'

'I want to thank you again for that.' Davis glanced around, then said, in a low voice, 'I made a killing. You really helped me out.'

'Glad to hear it. Couldn't have done it without you.' Which was true. The Hudson-Pollum Biolabs buy had made Ian. On the surface, HPB had looked like a loser; a small company with a long-delayed patent and serious cash-flow problems. But something about it had caught Ian's eye, and he'd worked it hard. The breakthrough had come when he stopped talking to analysts and traders and started talking to chemists. It had been Davis who had explained how revolutionary their pending patent could be. It didn't seem sexy — a complex process for manipulating volatile organic compounds — but Davis lit up as they'd talked. With proper financing, the thing had potential to become industry standard for certain segments of the pharmaceutical industry. Most of what the man had told him had flown several miles over Ian's head, but the essence had hit him square, and over the next weeks he'd quietly put together a major buy. When the patent cleared review, he'd gone from a junior trader to a respected wunderkind with a private office.

And in the time since, you've gone from a wunderkind to a fuck-up. Ain't life a card.

Ian took it cool at first, keeping the conversation on innocuous subjects so Davis had time to get a martini down and order another. Felt good to be maneuvering again, going after what he needed. It was only once the chemist

310

was halfway through his second drink that Ian began to broach the subject.

Davis's cheeks were reddened by booze. 'I'm not sure I understand.'

'Which part?'

'You want me to figure out what something is by description? It's just, I don't see how this fits any sort of investment. Is this one of your games?'

'No,' Ian said. 'No, it definitely is not.'

'What are you, doing research for a screenplay or something?'

'Can you just trust me for now?'

'There are a million possibilities.'

'You know what? Pretend it is a game. You're not writing an article for *Nature*.'

'Yeah, but — '

'It's a thick fluid. Dark-colored.'

Davis shrugged. 'Crude oil.'

'It looks like that, yeah. But even smelling it causes massive headaches. Trouble breathing. Clenched muscles.'

'Some kind of industrial solvent.'

'But extremely valuable. Four quarts are worth, say, a quarter of a million dollars on the black market.'

'The black market? What the hell?'

'Assume it's illegal. For the sake of discussion.'

'Tell me again how this will help my portfolio?'

'Davis . . . '

The man sighed. 'OK. A dark, viscous, illegal liquid. You said four quarts?'

'Yes.'

'Not a gallon.'

'Aren't they the same?'

'Yeah. But you said four quarts. Why?'

'Oh. Separate containers. Four one-quart containers.'

Davis nodded, and Ian could see him starting to get engaged in the problem, enjoying the intellectual exercise. 'What kind of container?

'Plastic.'

'Any seal?'

Ian wasn't sure, but figured Jenn and Mitch would have mentioned that. 'Let's say no.'

'Chemicals are most commonly stored in glass or metal. Since it's in plastic, it's probably something that reacts with them. That narrows it down some.'

'Drugs? Or something for cooking up drugs?'

The man shook his head. 'Doesn't make sense.'

'Why?'

'Do the math. Four quarts of the stuff are worth $250,000? It would have to work out to a huge pile of drugs. Or else a drug that was worth an unbelievable amount. Unless a gallon of this stuff makes, you know, pounds and pounds and pounds of cocaine, it doesn't make sense. Plus, most drugs aren't that hard to synthesize. You hear stories every now and then of chemists who wash out, it turns up they'd been cooking their own heroin. The ingredients are easy enough to come by if you work in a lab. So the math doesn't make sense.'

The simple logic smacked Ian hard. This whole time, they'd been assuming that this was a drug deal. They'd taken it as a base assumption — Johnny used to sell drugs, and what else was worth that kind of money? But now that seemed silly.

'I guess it could be some sort of superdrug we haven't heard of,' Davis said, 'but Occam's razor. The simplest explanation is the right one.'

'So what is the simplest explanation?'

'It's not drugs. It's illegal and moving on the black market, so it's not likely for industrial uses. It's not radioactive, or it wouldn't be in plastic. It reacts to glass and metal, and just smelling it results in a headache and clenched muscles. My best guess?'

'Jesus, Davis, what have I been asking for?'

The man paused for a moment, and Ian felt irritation like an itch, fought the urge to reach across the table, grab the chemist by his lapels, and shake the answer out of him. Finally, after a long moment, Davis began to speak.

And as the bottom fell out of his stomach and the room began to spin, Ian realized why Davis had hesitated.

And why Victor wouldn't.

★ ★ ★

In the dream, she was on a beach. A beach unlike any she'd ever actually seen, the likes of which she booked trips to for other people. Soft white sand, rustling palms, and no one for miles and miles.

She was in a hammock, in a bikini, and her belly was enormous. Ripe as tropical fruit.

313

Swollen and heavy with child. She was eating a mango. The juice ran slick down her chin. The sound of the waves was steady and constant, each paving the way for the one to follow.

When she woke on the couch in her apartment, sweating and awkward, twisted into the cushions, the first thing that hit was joy. Then she realized that it had just been a dream. And for reasons she couldn't quite explain, she began to cry.

She wasn't much of a crier, and it took her by surprise. Was she crying because of the dream? Because she wanted a child? Or was it deeper than that?

Maybe she just wanted life to matter. To mean something. Maybe that was all she'd ever really wanted. A life engaged. No more games, no more calculated distance and ironic detachment. Everything else was a smoke screen, crap sold to her by Hollywood. After all, now that she was living her adventure, what she really wanted was to take it all back. Not just the robbery — the years. All that time wasted, the hours and months pissed away instead of seized with both hands. She'd watched life flow by like it would never end, like there was always more.

But there wasn't. What she had squandered was gone, and where she had ended up wasn't where she wanted to be.

After a while, the tears slowed. She felt vaguely self-conscious as she wiped her face. Lying in a dark room, crying existential tears, it was sort of pathetic. She stood and washed her face in the bathroom. The cold water brought color to her cheeks, snapped her mind back to her body. Her head hurt, and she realized she was hungry. No food since breakfast, and it was after nine.

It was as she was walking back from the Thai place at the end of the block that the police arrived.

30

The cop was a good-looking guy, broad-shouldered and tall, his face ruddy and hair neat. 'Ms Lacie? I'm Detective Peter Bradley. Do you have a few minutes to answer some questions?'

Her heart went fluttery. She forced herself to stay calm. So this was it. This was how it would end. 'About what?'

'Why don't we talk inside?'

She nodded, stepped past him, led the way up the stairs to her apartment.

'Thanks for your time. This won't take too long.'

'Uh, sure,' she said. Wondering what the hell he was talking about, how he thought it wouldn't take long. Wouldn't take the rest of her life. 'Coffee?'

'I'm OK.' He followed her into the kitchen, watched as she set down the carryout bag. 'Go ahead and eat if you like.'

'What's this about?'

'It's about a robbery. And a homicide.'

She was reaching in her cabinet as he spoke, and her hand fumbled. The glass she almost had slipped, hung for a long fraction of a second, and then fell. It burst against her countertop, glittering pieces flying in all directions. '*Shit.*'

'Are you OK?'

'I'm fine,' she said, feeling anything but. 'Just clumsy.'

'There's no reason to be nervous,' he said. Then he cocked one corner of his mouth up in a little smile. 'Unless you have a lot of parking tickets I don't know about.'

She shook her head, forced a smile over her shoulder as she began to collect the broken shards. Her mind felt like the one time she'd tried acid, like it was on a relentless slalom, racing in all directions with reckless, slippery speed. Mitch had begged her not to tell the police anything. But was he right?

'Why don't we sit down?' The detective's eyes roamed her kitchen with easy habit.

'I'd rather stand.'

He shrugged. 'Well, what I wanted to talk to you about. You know a restaurant named Rossi's?'

Here it comes. 'Sure.'

'This Tuesday, there was a robbery there. Several men broke in, tied up the owner and a bartender, and made off with some money from the safe.'

She started to say, *I know.* Then knew that she would have to follow that with *I was one of them*, and froze up. Simply couldn't make her tongue work.

The detective continued. 'On the way out the back door, they shot and killed a man.' His voice was matter-of-fact, almost bored.

And it occurred to her, finally, that he wasn't here for her. That he didn't know. The surge of relief was an almost physical thing.

Hard on its heels was confusion. If that wasn't the reason he was here, then what was? And

317

regardless, wouldn't now be the time to make things right?

'Do you remember the last time you went to the restaurant?'

'Umm.' A lie? The truth? The guy had to know something. Better not to lie without knowing what. 'I think it was Tuesday, actually.'

He nodded, and something in him seemed to relax.

She said, 'I often meet a couple of friends there.'

'Were you meeting them that night?'

'No.' Technically true. Jenn had finished piling the glass on the counter, and to have something to do with her hands, she opened the cabinet again, took out a plate. 'Why?'

'Well, I'm investigating the incident. We're trying to get as complete a picture as possible. We pulled the credit card records for the evening, and saw that you paid your bill a few minutes before everything happened.'

She had an urge to laugh. What rotten criminals they made. That the police might look at something like that had never occurred to her.

'Do you remember anything about that evening?'

'I had a martini, I think.'

He smiled. 'I meant more like, do you remember anything unusual. Anyone acting strange, or seeming to pay a lot of attention to the staff? Any sort of fight or altercation?'

You mean besides the one where we killed someone in the back alley? She stared at him, realized that if she was going to speak, now was

318

the time. Maybe there would be consequences to pay, maybe Mitch would end up in trouble. But at least it would all be over. The police could step in and protect their families, catch Victor tomorrow. All she had to do was tell the truth. Just own up, take responsibility, and be done with everything.

'No,' she said. 'I'm sorry, I don't.'

★ ★ ★

She had sold him out.

Mitch stood at the end of her block, shaking. The anger flowed from some hard hot center, radiating in fiery waves. His fists were clenched and his arms were trembling as he watched a cop walk out of Jenn's apartment.

At first he hadn't been sure. It was after ten, and raining, and the cop just looked like a guy in a suit. But when he'd stopped on the porch to look at the sky, his jacket had pulled open to reveal a gun and star. A detective. As Mitch watched, the man hurried out into the rain, heading for a pale sedan parked in front of the fire hydrant.

She had called the police. After everything he had done for her. After everything they had shared. After promising not to.

She had called the police, and she had doomed him.

Mitch dropped to a squat, pretended to tie his shoelace as the cop drove past. A lucky break that Jenn didn't know he would be here. After they had parted, he'd walked and walked, let his

319

mind run. Thinking about Johnny and Victor and the money and the four of them. And especially about her. About whatever had been going on between her and Alex. Because something certainly had.

And it had hit him, as he walked, that if it had, it had probably been going on for a while. So many shared looks he'd sort of registered, so many conversational dodges and changed subjects. They had probably been sleeping together for a while. And that whole time, they had kept it a secret.

Which meant that Alex had been unwilling to commit, that he'd been using her. It also meant that what she needed might be a romantic gesture. Something to let her know he was different.

So he'd bought a dozen roses and taken the train up to her neighborhood. Roses for the woman who had sold him out. The woman for whom he had raised a pistol, had —

Push it down. The thought came swift with force of habit.

He stood up and started down the block. Tossed the roses aside, still wrapped in plastic. There was a man sitting on a stoop, talking on a cellphone, but Mitch didn't even look at him. Took the stairs to her apartment two at a time, the echo thundering off the hallway. He was composed of energy, toes to fingertips. He banged on her door, the sharp impact feeling right and good.

When she opened it, he watched her face. Saw it change. It looked like she was folding into herself. 'Mitch.'

'You called the cops.'

'No, I — '

'Don't *lie* to me!' He pushed past her, down the short hall to her living room. He heard her following, saying, 'Listen, I swear — '

Mitch whirled, and she blanched.

'Do you understand what I have fucking done for you?' He stepped forward, and she retreated. Her eyes were wide, her hair loose, and she still looked beautiful to him, even now, and that stoked the rage. He had been faithful. He had waited. When she needed protecting, he had been there to do it. Not Alex. Him. And in return, she'd mouthed lines about needing space, about wanting time, strung him along with lies. Given him up to the cops, to prison.

'Mitch — '

He slapped her beautiful mouth.

Her head snapped sideways. The fleshy sound hung in the air. His palm tingled. Slowly, like she couldn't believe it, she turned to face him. Raised her hand to her cheek. Touched it with delicate fingertips. He could see the flesh beginning to redden.

Her lip trembled like a little girl's.

And just like that, the anger was gone. It didn't drain away; it evaporated. And it left a terrible void. 'Oh God.'

She stared. 'You hit me.'

'Oh. God.' He staggered back, wanting to get away. Hit the wall by the fireplace, and felt his legs going weak. Let himself slide down it. The drywall cool through his shirt. He had that same disconnected feeling he'd had in the alley, that

321

sense of standing outside of himself and outside of time.

The way he had raised the gun. Stared down the barrel at the man on the ground. Realized, a half second before he did it, that he was going to pull the trigger.

Half a second before he had swung at her, he had known that he would. Known it that same way. The same way . . .

The same way he had killed someone.

Push it down.

Jenn said again, 'You hit me.'

Push it

He saw the look in the man's eyes, the way he, too, had known what was coming. The moment fear had hit, as all that he was and all that he had was taken away.

Push

The kick of the gun in his hand. The same right hand that stung from hitting the woman he loved.

What had he become?

A dangerous man. A killer.

A monster.

Jenn said, 'Get out,' but Mitch could barely hear her. His mind was filled with a static roar and a video of what had happened after he pulled the trigger. The way the man's body had jumped as the bullet slammed into his chest. The spreading circle of red, moving slower than he would have guessed. The faint and final exhale, barely audible over the ringing in his ears.

He had killed someone.

Jesus Christ. He had *killed* someone.

All the waves of emotion he had been walling away crashed with tidal force. Horror and shame and guilt and especially fear. For days he had been telling himself to push it down, to lock it away. Hiding from what he had done. Bargaining with the devil, but never looking him in the eye.

But now it was right in front of him. He wasn't the strong man he had tried to pretend he was. The cold calculator, the one who had acted like this was a game and he could play a role.

He was just Mitch. That's all he had ever been. All he ever would be.

He buried his face in his hands and wept.

★   ★   ★

The shock had come first. No one had hit her, ever. This didn't happen to her. Her cheek burned, and her brain felt scrambled. She touched her fingers to her face to check it was all still there.

When she looked at Mitch again, she saw something happening in his eyes. Something terrible. For a moment she was afraid he would hit her again, but then he staggered back as though he was the one who had been struck. Hit the wall and slid down it. His hands were shaking and his face was pale. He looked like he might vomit.

'You hit me,' she said, incredulous. The words making it real. 'You hit me.'

He said something, but she didn't hear it. 'Get out.' Anger replacing fear. Ready to scream at him, to kick and slap and claw. To beat him out of her house if she had to. To fight him if he dared.

But instead of moving toward her, he collapsed. His head fell to his palms, and he made a terrible choked sound, and his chest began to heave.

He was crying.

She was surprised to feel her rage ebb. The last days had been a constant swing from one primal emotion to another — exhilaration to terror, lust to loneliness, rage to sympathy. She was wrung out, weak on her feet. Standing over the lover she hadn't planned on taking, the man who had killed to protect her and then mistrusted and hit her, she didn't know what to think. Where to stand.

'I didn't call the police,' she said softly.

He didn't respond. His tears were slowing, but he looked like a glass vase hurtling toward a marble floor.

'The detective had run the credit cards for that night. That's why he came here.'

'What did I do?' His voice thin and aimed at his lap.

'I'll live.'

'Not that. I mean, yes, that too.' He looked up at her. A little boy's face tracked with tears. 'I'm so sorry. I can't believe I did that. But I meant — '

'In the alley.'

He nodded.

She sighed. Lowered herself to sit cross-legged on the floor a few feet away. 'I've been wondering how you were so calm.'

'I haven't let myself think about it. Not once. I just decided that I would pretend it was something that had happened to someone else. The old Mitch. And that the new Mitch would break free from that. Rise from the ashes. And not just from that. From everything.' He wiped at his cheek with the back of his hand. 'I wanted to be, I don't know . . . strong. Decisive. Able to take care of you. More like' — he turned away, barely whispered the words — 'more like Alex.'

She didn't respond. Wasn't sure how much she wanted to comfort him. Or even who he was, exactly. The new Mitch, the old Mitch, the Mitch on her living-room floor. It was too much to deal with.

Finally, he said, 'What did you tell the cop?'

'I told him I didn't know anything about it.'

The words brought his head up, and he looked her in the eye. 'You did that for me?'

'Yes. No. I don't know.' Her cheek hurt, and she tasted copper from where her teeth had cut the inside of her mouth. 'I was scared, I guess.'

He nodded. 'Scared I understand.'

They sat on the floor, not touching, not looking at each other. She could hear the faint sounds of life going on around them, but she felt apart from it. In a bubble.

Then she heard a voice from the door.

★　★　★

Ian had broken every traffic law racing from the martini bar to Jenn's apartment. It was Saturday night, and after eleven, but even so, he made it in

325

fifteen minutes, Davis's calm voice ringing in his mind as the chemist explained what it was they had stolen.

When he found her front door standing open, he imagined the worst. Forced himself to keep moving anyway. 'Hello?'

There was a long silence, and then he heard Jenn's voice. 'Come in, Ian.'

He stepped inside, closed the door behind him. Until last week he'd never seen the inside of her apartment. Now, as he rounded the corner into her living room, he felt almost at home. Until he saw her and Mitch sitting on the floor.

At first he thought maybe they had been attacked. But by the weary way they both looked up at him, he realized it was something more complicated than that. Her cheek was bright red. 'Are you OK?'

'I'm fine,' she said, looking not at him but at Mitch. 'We have bigger problems.'

'You don't have any idea how true that is. You know how we assumed this was a drug deal? It wasn't.' Ian took a deep breath. 'It was something much, much worse.'

31

God, he loved predictable people.

Bennett was used to watching, to spending long hours staring at someone's window. Waiting for the five minutes that justified days or even weeks of patience. It wasn't his favorite part, but he'd developed a kind of Zen about it.

But watching the chick's place hadn't required much patience thus far. Victor's hunch had been right. She was at the center of everything. Each member of this little drama had stopped by. Even a cop: Around ten, Bennett had gone to piss in the alley, and was just walking back when he saw the sedan pull by. Municipal plates going the wrong way on a one-way street. Police, gotta love them. Enforce the rules for everybody else.

He'd taken a seat on someone's stoop, dialed Victor on his cell. 'There's a cop going into her apartment.'

'Uniform?'

'Detective. Alone.'

There had been a pause. 'OK. There've been some developments on this end too. I applied a little more pressure. We may be moving ahead faster than anticipated. Maybe even tonight.'

'Great news. Any specifics I need to know?'

'Not on a cellular line. What's your read on the detective?'

'Not sure. If he stays more than twenty minutes, or any others show up, I'll call.

327

Otherwise it's likely nothing.'

They hung up, and Bennett leaned back on the porch. Something was happening. He could feel it, almost taste it.

This thing would end tonight.

★ ★ ★

Jenn wondered how much worse it could get. Wasn't there a limit to how messed up life could become?

First things first. Get off the floor.

As she wobbled to her feet, Mitch said, 'What do you mean? Johnny is a drug dealer — '

'Yeah, well, he seems to have moved up in the world.'

'But — '

'Would you *shut up*?' Ian's voice had none of the comic distance he usually tried for. The tone was iron, and it caught them both. He continued, 'I talked to a chemist friend of mine. No way that stuff was drugs. When I described it to him, do you know what he said? He said' — Ian paused, rubbed at his eyes — 'he said that it sounded to him like it was . . . '

'What?'

'A chemical weapon. Nerve gas.'

She was suddenly conscious of the little sounds, of the slow, regular draw of her own breath. The continuing pace of the world, the way it just kept going, like it or not.

Then she started laughing.

It wasn't a giggle. It was high and came from somewhere deep and flavored with hysteria. 'A

328

what?' She choked the words out.

'Chemical weapon. Probably sarin gas.'

'Sarin?' Mitch's tone was strangely dead. 'The stuff from those subway attacks in Tokyo?'

'Yeah.' Ian raised his hands. 'I know.'

'But. We opened it.'

'You didn't touch it, though, right?'

'No.'

'That was one of the things that told him what it was. If that had been sarin, you might have died. This is what's called a precursor. Apparently, if you're the kind of evil fuck who makes chemical weapons, you make them in two parts. The part you guys found is called the precursor. Based on your description, the headaches, the clenched muscles, the rest of it, my friend said it sounded like something called' — he dug in a pocket, came out with a bar napkin, squinted — 'methylphosphonyl difluoride. DF for short. That's the part that's hard to make, and that's worth a lot of money. The other part is just alcohol.'

Her laughter got harder. *Drug dealers and terrorists and chemical weapons, oh my!* Her breath came in short gasps between gales that hurt her stomach.

'I'm serious,' Ian said. 'The dangerous half of sarin gas. That was what Johnny was buying. What he planned to sell to Victor. That's what the money was for.'

'That doesn't make any sense. How would Johnny — '

'I don't know. Maybe the guy you killed put him up to it. Maybe he was just a middleman. It

329

doesn't matter. The stuff was moving through the black market, and we intercepted it. That's why Victor is coming after us this hard. Drugs are easy to get. But can you imagine how much something like that would be worth to the wrong people in Iraq or Afghanistan?'

Jenn's vision was getting spotty from lack of air. The boys were talking around her, talking sheer madness, and neither of them could see how *funny* it was.

'We cannot give this stuff to Victor,' Ian said.

Mitch stood up, walked over to her. 'Jenn?'

She gasped, fought for breath. 'Don't you see — '

'Pull it together.'

'I'm . . . I'm . . . I'm a fucking travel agent.' She doubled over again. Mitch caught her shoulders gently.

'Shhh. Come on.'

'This is bad. This is so bad.' Ian had his hands to both cheeks like the kid in those movies, and it didn't make breathing any easier.

'Jenn. Stop.'

She closed her eyes, clenched her fingernails into her palm. The sharpness helped. Just as the laughter was dying, another thought occurred to her. 'You,' she said, fighting back more, 'your timing was lousy, Mitch.'

'Huh?'

'You slapped me too early.'

It was meant as a joke, but no one else laughed. She felt them looking at her and saw herself from their eyes. Slowly, she stopped, the sounds dying like a baby's cry, strangled and

330

kind of embarrassing. She straightened, wiped tears from her eyes.

'This is serious.' Ian's voice was somber.

'I know,' she said. 'I know.' She took a deep breath. 'It's just, you can't be right.'

'Why not?'

'Because . . . just because.'

'I'm sorry,' he said. 'I am. And if you two will listen to me for a second, you'll see.'

The laughter was gone, but the hysteria was still inside her, twisting and coiling and looking for release. She took a moment to calm herself. 'Tell us.'

Ian started, his words like freezing water. How he had called a friend who had helped him before, and described what it was that they had found. How the man had gone through it logically, the possibilities; the material the bottles were made of, the value, the reaction they had both suffered. The logic cool and hard and diabolical. On some level, she realized, it wasn't really a surprise. Some part of her had known all along that whatever was in those bottles was more important, and more dangerous, than mere drugs. She just hadn't wanted to admit it.

And still didn't. 'What if he's wrong?'

There was a moment of silence, and then Mitch said, 'What if he's not?'

'This stuff, you know how it kills people?' Ian somehow looked even worse than he had that morning. 'It causes all of the muscles in your body to contract to their maximum amount. People break their arms, their spines. They eventually die of suffocation because their lungs

331

won't move. But first they feel their body tearing itself apart. He said that a drop of it was enough. One drop on bare skin.'

One drop. Jesus. There had been a gallon of the stuff.

The silence was unlike any she had known. Within it, her thoughts and fears curdled and spun, foul twisting things. She felt a childish panic at the enormity of what they were dealing with. It made her want to crawl under the table. 'If we hadn't robbed Johnny, this would still be out there.'

'So?'

'So, it's not our fault. We didn't make it. We wouldn't sell it. It's not our fault.'

'Not our fault?'

'Like you said. We just intercepted it. We weren't even supposed to be there, but we were, and we ended up with it. But that doesn't make it our fault.'

'Did you understand what I told you? This stuff, it could kill — '

'Ian, *Victor will kill my parents.* And your dad, Mitch's brother, Alex's daughter.' She knew what she was saying was selfish, but she wasn't sure that made it wrong. Who didn't look after their own first?

'That doesn't make it right to ignore — '

'I didn't say it does. But that's the situation. If we don't give him what he wants, he'll kill our families. And regardless, it's not my *fault*.'

There was a pause. Then Mitch said, 'It's like one of your games, Ian. An impossible situation, no way to win, just ways to lose less. Is it better to lose a few people you love or a lot of people you'll never meet?'

Ian looked from one to the other of them. 'Those are just games. This is real.'

'Yeah. But it's also true. He'll kill them.'

'That nerve gas could kill *hundreds* of people. Maybe thousands. And maybe it won't be in Iraq or Afghanistan. Maybe it will be in Chicago or New York. Maybe it will be in a subway station at rush hour.'

'I didn't ask for this,' she said. 'I didn't agree to it.'

'None of us did.' Mitch stood, walked to the window.

The whole thing was surreal. It reminded her of the kind of talk they used to have on Thursday nights, back when life made sense and everything was casual. When it could all be viewed with ironic detachment, when their problems were jobs and rent and their love interests. Back when everything had been play.

Even their lives.

They had all been treading water. Playing the game of life, but unwilling to actually make a move, put their chips on the table. Staying in dead-end jobs and bull-shitting themselves about what mattered. Pretending nothing did.

'Do you remember,' Mitch said, staring out the darkened window, 'how we used to talk about the rich guys, the CEOs and politicians? How we used to hate them for acting in their own interests instead of for the good of everyone else?

'We went into this thinking we were going to

333

stick it to guys like that. Like Johnny. People who broke the rules for their own good. And now here we are. Thinking the same way.'

'So what do we do?'

He took a breath. 'All I know is what I won't do.'

'What's that?'

'Settle for the lesser of two evils.' Mitch spoke with a quiet calm. His back was straight and his voice steady.

'But — '

'There has to be a third way,' he said. 'There has to be something better.'

Again, the silence fell.

Then Mitch said, 'You know what?' He turned to face them. 'There is.'

'What?'

'I take the stuff to the police. I turn it over and tell them everything.'

'But — you — the alley. You . . . ' Even now, she found it hard to say the words.

'I killed someone,' he said. His voice was steady, but she heard the stress beneath it. 'I shot someone. And I'll admit that.'

'They'll arrest you,' Ian said.

'Yeah.' He shrugged. 'But it's the only way. Take responsibility for what I did.'

'That's crazy. They'll send you to jail.'

'Maybe that's where I belong.' His voice cracked a little, but he kept going. 'Look, I've been hiding from this since it happened. Pretending I can be something else, that I can just go on with life. Maybe there are people who could forget it, but that's not the way it works for me. I did it to protect you, and I'll tell them that. Maybe it will help. Maybe not. But I can't go on pretending, and we cannot let Victor have this.'

'But it's not our fault,' she repeated, hating that they were making her play this role. 'I know that sounds weak, but if we hadn't come along, Victor would have bought and sold it, and we wouldn't have known a thing.'

'Sure. But if we give this to him, chances are, one morning we'll turn on the news and see a story about a terrorist attack with sarin gas. Maybe here, maybe somewhere else, and we won't even know for sure it was the same stuff. But there will be hundreds of people dead. And we'll have to stand and watch, and wonder if we could have done something. Can you live with that?'

She looked at him. The street light outside cast raindrop shadows across his face. His back was straight, but his hands trembled. She imagined herself making breakfast in her kitchen. The radio on, a bagel in the toaster, hummus on the counter, coffeepot gurgling. Alone in her little world. And on the TV, images of innocent people twisted and broken, their faces locked in eternal screams.

'No,' she said. 'No, I can't.'

'Me either,' Ian said. 'But there's a snag in this plan, right? The DF is in a safe-deposit box. How do we — ' He stopped, caught the expression on their faces. 'What?'

'It's not in the bank,' she said. 'It's here.'

'*Here* here?'

'Down the block, in the trunk of the drug

dealer's car.' She paused. 'Are you sure you want to do this, Mitch? You understand — '

'I understand.' He raised his hands above his head in a stretch, then let them drop. 'I'm not happy about it. But that choice between the lives of people we love and the lives of a lot of people we don't know? I won't make it.'

It was a simple enough statement. But she didn't know if she would have been strong enough to say it.

'What are you going to tell them?' Ian asked.

'What happened, more or less. I don't need to mention you guys.'

'Yeah, you do,' Ian said. 'Johnny saw me, too, remember?'

'I can just say that I won't tell them who my partners were.'

'That will make them go harder on you. As it stands, you're a civilian without a criminal record. The man we robbed is a former drug dealer, and the one you killed was selling chemical weapons. Weapons you brought to them.'

'Yeah, but — '

'Besides. Screw the Prisoner's Dilemma.' Ian gave that lopsided grin. 'I'm not letting you take this on alone.'

Mitch smiled. 'If you're looking for me to convince you otherwise . . . '

'We're not,' she said. She stood up. 'I'm going too.' Some part of her wanted to do this, she realized. Wanted to admit the wrong and take the punishment, to stand with her friends. 'Guess the Thursday Night Club isn't done yet.' She

336

took a deep breath, the air rasping cool into her lungs. 'OK. So when do we go?'

'Now.' Mitch stood. 'Right now.'

The rain had been going steady and soft for the last few hours, and the air had that smell that told her it might go all night. It had put a damper on the usual Saturday revelry, and the sidewalks were nearly clear. They walked in silence, all of them lost in their own thoughts.

Abruptly, Mitch spoke. 'I'm sorry.' He turned to Jenn. 'I can't believe I — that wasn't me.'

She turned responses over in her mind, looking for the right one. Finally, she said, 'I know.'

'You too.' Mitch turned to Ian. 'If you hadn't figured out what this stuff was, we would have gone through with it. I was wrong to call you a fuck-up, man.'

'No, you weren't. I am a fuck-up. But I'm working on it.'

'We all are,' she said and meant it. Still, there was a calm replacing the panic of earlier. They had come up against an impossible decision, and they had made the right choice. Whatever sins they'd committed, that had to count for something. And if nothing else, at least this would all be over soon.

They crossed the intersection, passing two women holding hands. Weird to think that just days ago she and Mitch had run this course in reverse, in pain just from smelling the chemicals. How much worse must the actual thing be?

She thought about the police, wondered what the three of them would say. The truth, obviously. But what exactly? Maybe it didn't matter, she thought. Fast or slow, elegant or graceless, the facts spoke for themselves. Maybe it was just a matter of telling them —

'No.' Mitch stared straight ahead. 'No.'

She followed his gaze. In the dark, the Eldorado had a richer hue, the purple almost looking good. The car radiated a certain cool, that big grill, a hood that could sleep three. The sharp, almost dangerous lines of the body, leading back to where —

The trunk was open.

★ ★ ★

In the city proper, Saturday night made for lousy, slow driving. But at this hour the freeways weren't too bad, and even with the rain, Alex made good time. The dashboard clock read 11:32 when he pulled up outside his ex-wife's.

He sat in the car for a moment. He could hear the ticking of the engine and the soft, steady spatter of the rain. Through the windshield he could see her house: porch lights on, the quiet domestic comfort of aluminum siding, squares of warm yellow hidden behind curtains. It looked comfortable, cozy. Everything he had ever wanted.

The rain made him want to hurry up the walk, but the thought of what he would say — or rather, the total lack of any idea what to say — made him keep his pace steady. With shaking fingers, he rang the doorbell. Listened to the soft tones, wondered what it felt like to hear them from inside.

Footsteps, and then Scott opened the door. Trish's new husband looked surprised, but quickly wiped it away. He stood in the doorway, his body blocking the light. 'Alex.'

'Scott. I'm sorry to come out here like this. But I need to talk to Cassie. Just for a few minutes.'

'I can't do that.'

'She's my daughter.'

'I know. And you can see her. But we went through this. It's almost midnight. You can't just drop by. We need you to let us know in advance, so that we can — '

'For God's sake.'

Scott pursed his lips. 'Why were you at the game today?'

'I wanted to see her play. Jesus, man. I'm not going to do anything to her.'

'I know you would never intentionally hurt her.'

'What does that mean?'

The man shrugged. 'Take it how you like.'

Alex had two inches and twenty pounds on Scott. Shoving him out of the doorway would be the easiest thing in the world. Push past him, head straight for the stairs, find Cassie up in her bedroom. Close the door, sweep her into his arms, hold her close. Whisper in her ear. Tell her . . .

What?

That he loved her?

That everything would be OK?

That she might never understand what he was doing, what it was likely to cost him, how many

339

people he was betraying, but that he was doing it for her?

Instead, he said, 'Please?'

Scott wavered. Alex could see him considering it. See that he didn't want to be the bad guy. That, in fact, he wasn't. A voice came from down the hall, female, maybe Cassie, maybe Trish, he couldn't be sure. Whoever it was, it made up Scott's mind. He straightened. 'I'm sorry. Not tonight.'

'Listen. I know this doesn't make sense. But I might not have another chance. Please?'

'You're right, that doesn't make sense. We're not leaving for a couple of weeks. Why don't you come back tomorrow afternoon?'

He sighed. 'Yeah.' He turned and started back down the walk.

'Alex.'

He spun on his heel, stood with the rain running down his shaved head.

'Are you OK?'

He almost laughed. Instead, he said, 'Sure,' and started for the car. He had almost made it when he heard sounds behind him, Scott's voice saying, 'Cassie, wait — '

'Daddy!'

He turned in time to see her sprinting down the walk, bent to scoop her up into his arms and hoist her off the ground. His little girl. He could smell her hair, feel the warmth of her body.

In that instant was every other. The way he used to sit in his beat-up chair, legs going numb, unwilling to move as she napped on his chest, her baby's breath and milk smell. A Fourth of

July, Cassie maybe six, spelling her name in the air with a sparkler. The frozen perfection of her guarding the soccer goal this afternoon, captured mid-lunge by his mental camera. 'My girl,' he said. 'My girl.'

She wrapped her arms tighter around his neck. 'I don't want to go to Arizona. I want to stay here with you.'

I want it too, baby girl. I want only that forever.

Over her shoulder, he saw Scott hurrying toward them, his gaze wary. The front door was wide open, and Trish stepped into it, squinting to see what was going on.

Alex allowed himself one more thought of hopping in the car with her, forgetting all about drug deals and police and dead men, just hitting the road together. Best friends and partners in crime. It was so beautiful it hurt to look at.

He said, 'It's OK, Cass. It will be OK.'

Scott had reached them, stood with his hands out, like he was thinking of tackling them both. Alex looked at him, saw the fear in his eyes. Realized that he was scared of exactly what Alex had been thinking.

Alex lowered her to the ground, knelt in front of her. 'You know I love you, right?'

She nodded, eyes wide.

'Promise me that no matter what happens, you'll always remember that.'

'I promise. But don't make me go!'

His knees felt weak. For a moment, he closed his eyes. Reached deep inside himself, not sure he had the strength to say what he knew he had to. 'It's for the best, Cass. Scott and Mom, they both love you. You can have a normal life with them.'

'But I want to be with you.'

'I know, baby girl. I want that too. But this is better.' He clenched his fist. 'This is better.'

Scott said, 'Alex.'

He nodded. Glanced up at the man, imploring, not sure what he was asking for. Everything, maybe. Their eyes locked, and for a moment, he forgot all his anger toward the guy, forgot all the ways he'd been wronged. Just saw a man who also loved his daughter. 'You take care of her, all right?'

'I will.' The words solemn and the gaze steady. 'On my life.'

Alex turned back to his daughter. 'I have to go, sweetie. I just wanted to tell you how much I love you.'

'Where are you going?'

'I have some things I need to take care of. They're important.'

'More important than me?'

'Nothing is more important than you.' He put a hand on her shoulder. 'Nothing.'

Then, before his will broke along with his heart, he stood and turned around. The ten steps to the car were the hardest of his life. Behind him, he heard her voice, saying, 'Don't go,' and then he opened the car door and got in. Fired it up and slammed it into reverse and spun out of the driveway fast.

This is for you, Cass. It's all for you.

When he reached the end of the block, he

stopped. In his rearview, he could see the three of them. Cassie staring, Trish behind, her hands on his daughter's shoulders. Scott stood alongside, his back straight. They looked like a family. Like they would be happy.

Time to make sure they stayed that way. He turned the corner and reached for his cellphone.

32

The three of them stared into the Cadillac's empty trunk. Mitch kept fighting the urge to close and open it again, as if the stuff would magically reappear. The rain soaked him.

'Victor?' Ian asked at last.

'No,' Jenn said. 'He didn't know about this.'

'No one knew about it,' Mitch said, his voice hollow. 'No one but us.'

Think, think, think. What does this mean?

Part of him felt an enormous relief. If the stuff was gone, then there was nothing they could do about it. There was also no point in turning themselves in. They had decided to do the right thing, been willing to, but circumstance had made it impossible. A lucky break.

Except that one drop could kill, and they had hidden a gallon of the stuff. Not taken it to the police, or called the FBI. And now it was gone. How many would die because of that?

'Oh my God.' Jenn put a hand to her face. 'Oh shit.'

'Yeah.'

'No, it's' — she looked up at them, her face pale — 'it just slipped out.'

'Huh?'

'I didn't tell him on purpose. He came to see me this afternoon. To apologize, and we were talking, and I just said it without thinking. That it was in the trunk of the car.'

Mitch stared. 'Who? Who did you say that to?'
But in his heart, he knew the answer already.
'Alex.'

* * *

It was all falling apart.

Not, Ian reflected, back in Jenn's kitchen, wet suit plastered to wet skin, that it had ever exactly been *together*. Everything about their situation had been screwed pretty much from the jump.

OK. So things are bad. What do you do?

Only one answer. The same one he'd always fallen back on. Think about it like a game.

Not gambling or one of the political modeling games. Strategy, then. Like the battlefield sims he'd played in college. Balance strengths and weaknesses, figure the goal, and then move toward it. *Meanwhile, try to forget that you have a phone number memorized, that relief from sickness and doubt is one call and a stop at an ATM away.* It was only midnight. He could be the proud owner of an eight ball by 12:30 —

A game.

Right. OK, then. Strengths.

'I can't believe he took it.' Jenn was twisting a lock of hair like a phone cord.

'I can,' Mitch said.

'I know, you hate him — '

'No, I don't.' Mitch sighed. 'I don't. I was trying to become him, I think. But you had it right from the beginning. His daughter. He wouldn't be thinking about anything else.'

'But to give Victor chemical weapons — '

345

'He didn't know what they are, remember? Maybe on some subconscious level, he suspects. But he'll be ignoring that, same way we did. Telling himself that it's just chemicals to cook up drugs. Set against Cassie, that won't mean much.'

Strengths. Well, they knew what the bottles held. Neither Johnny nor Victor would expect that. What else?

Nothing leapt to mind.

Against that, the weaknesses. Victor and his bodyguards and their guns and easy violence. Alex's head start. Nothing to take to the police now, no bargaining chips. The fact that the four of them couldn't manage to have each others' backs for half an hour.

Who was he kidding? They were fucked.

'You know how I said this wasn't our fault?' Jenn's voice pitched like she was talking to someone who wasn't there. 'That's not true, is it?'

'Well, you were right, we didn't make it — '

'Mitch.'

He sighed. 'Yeah. It's our fault.'

'And a thousand people could die because of it.'

Her words hit Ian hard, took him back to September. No matter how many years passed, he would always think of it simply as September. How he had watched TV for hours, the towers falling over and over. That terrible video of the second plane, the way every time it ran you prayed that somehow this time it would happen differently, that it would slide sideways, miss by inches. That there would be a Hollywood ending.

The sick feeling when it didn't. Over and over again.

He'd just been starting out then, working from a half cube under fluorescent lights. But trading was a virtual gig. He spent all day on the phone, on the computer, talking to people all over the world, but especially in New York. He'd had friends in those towers. Every time he'd watched people jumping, that agonizing footage, too grainy to tell anything, he'd wondered if the body plummeting through the air was someone he knew.

Now they would have to live with the fact that the next time they turned on the TV, it might have another ungraspable story of broken bodies and mass panic and that sudden awareness that they were not invulnerable, that there were people in the world who wanted to hurt them, and that those people could.

Only this time, he had helped them.

★ ★ ★

Mitch felt a scream building inside. All that time they could have done right. Not just when they had the chemicals. Before then. When they sat around and bullshitted each other about what mattered, when all the time in the world lay splayed at their feet.

And worse, this final irony. By giving Victor the bottles, Alex had made them safe. It was over for them. No one would come after them. The police would never know. They could go on with their lives. With a lot more money.

All they had to do was nothing.

'Goddamn it.' He hit the counter with the flat of his palm. The sting was sharp and clean, and reminded him, for a half second, of what it had felt like to hit Jenn. He pushed the thought away. One more sin. 'I'm not going to let this happen.' He rubbed his hands together. 'Jenn, call your detective. The two of you go meet him. Tell him everything. The robbery, the guy in the alley, the DF, everything. Tell him that I'll turn myself in soon.'

'What are you going to do?'

'I'm going after Alex. I've got a guess where he'll be.'

'Where's that?'

'Where this all started.'

'Johnny's restaurant?'

'Victor isn't going to invite Alex over to his house. But they need a place where they can be alone. It's after midnight. Johnny's is closed. It's safe ground. No risk of being seen, and no chance Alex can have cops with him.'

'If he's there, then so is Victor,' Jenn said. 'You'll just get yourself killed.'

'Maybe not. If I can get to him first, I can tell him what he's carrying. Alex is stubborn, but once he knows, he'll come with me to the police, and we can end this thing.'

'And what if you can't get to him before Victor does?'

'Then I'll just have to try anyway.'

'That's suicide.'

'I don't care.' He stepped closer to her, took

348

her hands in his. Looked her in the eye. 'Jenn, I have to do this.'

'Why?'

For my sins. For a body in an alley and the lie that was my life and the lie I tried to turn it into. But what he said was, 'You know why.' He thought about trying to kiss her. Instead he turned to Ian. 'Can I borrow your car?'

The man dug in his pocket, pulled out a slender ring of keys. Mitch took them. It felt good to be moving, to finally be acting instead of letting life happen.

'This is stupid,' Jenn said. 'You're feeling guilty, so you're just walking into this?'

'If there's even a chance to stop him, I have to take it. Besides,' he said and forced a smile, 'I have insurance. You two.'

'Why don't we just call the cops and tell them to go there right now?'

He shook his head. 'They wouldn't believe us. You'll get transferred around, have to tell your story over and over. Eventually maybe they would send someone. But it will be too late.'

'I could call Detective Bradley and tell him — '

'You'd just be a voice on the phone. No, you have to go and turn yourselves in and tell him enough details, in person and in his custody, to convince him. It's too big a risk otherwise. You have to convince him. And do it fast, all right? I'm depending on you.' He took a deep breath, held it for a moment. It took all his strength to make himself look calm, like fear wasn't scrabbling inside of him, a living thing. 'OK.' He started down the hall.

'Mitch.' It was Ian's voice.

He turned. Ian opened his mouth, closed it. Finally he said, 'We won't let you down.'

Mitch looked at them. Two of the three friends he'd once considered the only people who knew him. Torn apart by stupidity and selfishness, and now responsible for something more horrible than they could imagine. Average people, each weak in their own way, all afraid and lost and lonely.

'I know,' Mitch said. 'I trust you.'

Then he turned and headed for the door.

★ ★ ★

The detective answered on the fourth ring. It was after midnight, but she supposed Saturday night was prime time for a homicide detective.

'This is Jennifer Lacie. You came by my house — '

'Yes, Ms Lacie. What can I do for you?'

She took a deep breath. Once she said what she had to say, there was no going back. No return to safety.

You have to convince him. And do it fast, all right? I'm depending on you. Mitch's voice in her head.

'Remember how you said that if I remembered anything else, I should call you? Turns out I have a lot to say.'

There was a pause. 'Go ahead.'

'I lied to you. About, well, everything.'

'What does that mean?'

'It means that I know exactly who did the robbery. And everything that happened after it.'

'And who's that?' His voice curious, but not excited.

'I did. Me and three of my friends.'

He laughed.

'Detective, I'm not kidding, I — '

'Ms Lacie, I'm flattered, I am, but I'm also very busy — '

'The men who went into Johnny's office used duct tape to tie him and the bartender up. The bartender, Alex — who's in on it, by the way — threw a punch and got hit in the head. We did that to keep him above suspicion. The man in the alley was shot twice, once around the shoulder, once in the chest, with the same gun.'

There was a long pause. 'Maybe we better talk.'

'Good.'

'I'll have some officers come by your place in the next few minutes to make sure you're safe.'

'Wait, what? I need to talk to *you*.'

'You will. I'm on a scene right now. I'll get there as soon as I can.'

'When?'

'When I'm done.'

'No. It has to be now. Right now. It's a matter of, well, life and death.'

'Ms Lacie, you need to understand, you're in very serious trouble — '

'Detective, you need to understand that if you don't meet me right now, I won't be here when the officers arrive. And I'll deny everything I've just said.'

When Bradley spoke again, his voice was steel. 'All right. If you're in that kind of a hurry, why don't you come into the station? I'll head there now. I'm in Rogers Park, so we'll be meeting halfway.'

Damn it. She could hardly refuse, and at the same time, once she was in the station, it would be easy for them to detain her. Still. What choice did she have?

'All right. I'm leaving now. But, Detective?' She took a breath, let her emotions show in her voice. 'Please hurry. I'm begging you. There are a lot of lives at stake.'

'This had better not be some sort of a joke.'

'I've never been this serious in my life.'

She hung up the phone. Ian said, 'I guess blowing this off and heading to Disneyland is out of the question, huh?'

'Kinda.'

'OK. Let's grab a cab and go to jail instead.' He held out a hand, and she took it. His palm was sweaty, but it was comforting.

Walking out the front door felt surreal, a routine she'd done a hundred times rendered strange. There was a habitual urge to check that she had everything, pick a coat, take a last look in the mirror. But none of that mattered. She just grabbed her purse and opened the door, and they headed down the stairs.

'I wasn't sure you were going to tell them about Alex.'

'We have to,' she said. 'Mitch is depending on us. We can't risk any lies at this point.' They stepped onto the porch.

'Yikes,' Ian said. 'The whole truth? Not my specialty.'

'Yeah, well — '

'Ms Lacie?'

The stranger had the kind of face that always seemed familiar, a bland average of decent looks. He wasn't wearing a uniform, but her first thought was that somehow Bradley had managed to get an officer over to her house in that short a time.

Then she saw the gun pointing at her.

★ ★ ★

Twelve thirty on a Saturday night. Plenty of places would just be getting started. In Wicker Park, the bands would have wrapped up, and Estelle's and the Violet Hour would be mobbed. Down on Rush Street, the Viagra Triangle, wannabe sugar-daddies would be putting moves on administrative assistants. Even here on Lincoln, a mile in either direction the bars would be full, music pounding out open windows.

But the stretch where Rossi's was located was quiet. Not dead; a few revelers strolled the sidewalks, cabs cruised, and in an apartment up the block, a party was winding down. Mitch had driven as fast as he dared and had made good time. As he passed the restaurant, he felt a weird shiver at the sight of the place. So many events, good and bad, all clustered into one small space.

Focus.

Though they thought of it as a bar, Rossi's was primarily a restaurant, and the cursive neon sign was turned off, the building radiating that closed energy. There was just enough light for him to see chairs up on tables as he passed. No sign of anyone inside. What if he'd been wrong? Mitch had dialed Alex's cellphone half a dozen times on the drive over, but the guy either didn't have it or wasn't answering. Mitch was betting on the latter.

He turned down the side street, then into the alley, pulling the car up to the same place they had parked the rental. Dread hit as darkness flooded into the car. Ten feet from where he sat, he had murdered a man.

The air was cool and smelled of rotten milk. A scrap of yellow crime-scene tape was still attached to the Dumpster, stirring in the breeze. He walked out of the alley, forcing himself not to glance at the place, not to look for a dark stain or a chip in the concrete.

Mitch hurried around the corner, under the awning, and up to the front door. He paused to listen. No sounds from within, no shouting voices or screams. He gripped the handle, the metal cool beneath his fingers. Once he walked in, there was no going back. If Victor was inside . . .

He froze, his legs trembling. Every muscle was screaming to turn around, to walk away. His mind ran wild and slippery, imagining killers on the other side of the door.

If Alex is there alone, you can reason with him, get out fast. If Victor is there, then you'll just need to stall until the police arrive. Jenn and Ian are talking to the detective right now. He'll

354

have cops here in ten minutes, maybe fifteen. You can do this.

You have to.

Mitch pulled the door handle. It opened.

He felt like his intestines were being unspooled. The entry was lit only by the Exit sign. The hostess stand loomed empty. He could hear his footsteps and the beat of his heart. Mitch rounded the corner, saw the empty dining room, set for tomorrow's meal, white tablecloths and neat silverware arrayed like a banquet for ghosts.

There was a light in the bar, and he headed for it.

The first thing that hit him was the familiarity. Chairs up on tables, ammonia smell from the damp floors, the muted buzz of the beer fridge. How many nights had they sat there after closing, the four of them at the end of the bar? Drinking and talking, trading theories on the world, laughing at everyone from their towers of irony and distance. Killing time.

He took another step, his eyes adjusting.

A voice said, 'Hello, Mitch.'

★ ★ ★

The figure in front of her moved with brutal grace, rocking forward to drive a fist into Ian's belly. Her friend made a gasping whoop, then dropped to hands and knees, leaned forward, and retched. Thin ropes of spit and vomit trailed from the corner of his lips.

'Hi,' the man said, raising the pistol in his other hand. 'Don't scream.'

355

The world narrowed to a long hallway, like the gun had black-hole gravity that warped space.

'Pick him up.'

She stared at the gun, and at the man beyond.

'*Jennifer.*' His voice sharp. 'Pick Ian up, and help him up the stairs. Now.'

Without thinking, she bent down, put her arms under Ian's shoulders, and helped him slowly rise. His body felt thin and hollow, and he smelled of bile.

'Up the stairs.'

'Who — '

'Now.'

She wanted to scream, to run, but instead she turned around, started back to her apartment. Her vision was wet and smeary, the carpet blurring into the walls. From a great distance, she felt her mind racing, telling her that she should fight, or else bolt up the stairs and into her apartment and lock the door. But fear and her grip on Ian, all that was holding him up, stopped her from doing either. She prayed for a neighbor to come home, for someone to save her.

When they reached her door, the man said, 'Open it.'

'It's locked. The keys are in my purse.'

'Get them. Slowly.'

Jenn glanced over, fear spiking hard through her veins. The man stood half a dozen feet back, just far enough that she couldn't reach him, not far enough that she could make it in and close the door. Not unless she abandoned Ian. 'Can you stand?'

Her friend coughed, nodded. She leaned him against the wall, then unslung her purse. Keys, keys, keys, where the fuck were they? Her hands shook as she fumbled, and the purse slipped from her grasp, landing upside down. 'Shit.' She bent to pick it up, a clatter of everyday things falling free: sunglasses and Chapstick and a pill bottle and her wallet and mascara and a leaf she had liked the shape of and her cell and her keys. Jenn retrieved them, fit them in the lock, and turned.

The moment the door creaked open, the man lunged forward, shoving her. Suddenly flying, she struggled to get her feet beneath her, barking her shin on the edge of the coffee table, the impact ringing straight up her legs. She staggered, managed to catch herself with a hand on the table. The bottle of nail polish from that morning tipped and fell.

Nail polish. Beside that, several files, and her pair of shiny manicure scissors.

'Join us, Ian.'

Moving before she chickened out, Jenn palmed the scissors, then turned. And found herself staring at the barrel of a pistol. The gun was maybe four inches from her face, so close she couldn't focus on it.

Her blood felt like ice chips.

Doubled over, Ian lurched into the room. His face was a sallow, yellowish green, and he was gasping. His suit was spotted with vomit. He collapsed on the couch.

'Ian?' She looked at the man with the gun, then slowly moved away from him, keeping her fingers closed around the reassuring steel of the scissors. They were tiny, but they were sharp, and that was something. She knelt beside Ian. 'Are you OK?'

He forced a brief nod, his eyes wild. She glanced over her shoulder, saw the man with the gun grimace, then walk over to the door to kick the pile of belongings inside. As her Chapstick rolled across the floor, Jenn put her left hand on Ian's knee, and flashed her right open, just long enough for him to see what was inside. His eyes widened.

Then she heard the sound of the door closing and found that it took all she had to draw a shuddering breath.

'Now,' the man said. 'Have a seat, sweetheart.'

'My name is Jenn.'

'I know.' The man gestured. 'Next to your friend.'

Jenn straightened, stood perfectly still.

'Lady, I like your spirit, I do. But you ought to know that I'm a feminist. When it comes to hitting people, I don't draw gender lines.'

She hesitated. The suddenness of everything had made the last minute a blur, but she was coming back to herself, and anger was infusing the panic. This was *her* apartment, her private sanctuary. And now this man, this stranger with a gun, had invaded it, hit her friend and dragged them back into her own world as prisoners. The last thing she wanted to do was curl up like some useless woman on TV. The scissors weren't much, but maybe now was the time, while she was standing up.

Then the man raised the gun. Her knees went watery. As slowly as she dared, she eased herself onto the couch.

'Good. Now. Hands under your thighs, palms down. Both of you.'

Ian looked at her, a question in his eyes she didn't know how to answer. Then he did as the man said, and she did the same.

'Excellent.' He slid the gun behind his back. 'Thank you.'

'What are you going to do with us?'

'We're just going to sit here for a little while.'

'Why?' *Keep him talking. Maybe he'll relax. Maybe he'll give you a chance to . . .*

What? Launch into a flying spin kick, knock the gun free, do a Jet Li roll for it, and blast him? Kickboxing classes at the gym were as far as her experience with fighting went. Sure, she could do some work on a heavy bag. But heavy bags didn't hit back.

Who was he? What did he want?

One of those questions was easy to answer. He worked for Victor. The way he carried himself, his easy menace and complete calm. The way he hadn't hesitated to hit Ian. He was . . . professional.

Professional what, exactly?

Something chilly slid down her spine. Another easy question to answer. But it raised a much harder one.

What chance did a stockbroker and a travel agent armed with manicure scissors have against a professional killer?

Mitch stepped forward. There was a figure at the end of the bar, but he couldn't make out any features. 'Alex?'

'He shoots, he scores.' The figure reached for a highball. Took a long sip. In the quiet of the closed bar, Mitch could hear ice clink in the glass. 'You want a drink?'

Mitch started forward. On the drive here, he'd imagined all sorts of last-second scenarios, catching Alex just as Victor pulled up, the two of them jumping out a back window. But now that he had made it, he realized he didn't know what to say. It was partly the situation and partly a strange note in Alex's voice. Something sad and final and yet oddly menacing. 'No, I — '

'Where's the rest of the crew?'

'On their way to the police station.'

Alex gave a brief and bitter laugh. 'If you can't win, you may as well piss all over everyone else, huh? Drag them down with you.'

'What are you talking about?' He walked closer.

'How many nights do you think we spent here?' Alex leaned back against the bar, thick arms braced on either side. 'A hundred? More? The four of us, sitting right here,' he patted the end of the bar. 'Our private table.'

Mitch froze. On the bar, the four plastic bottles sat clustered right next to an open fifth of vodka. Jesus *Christ*.

'So what's the deal? You here to talk me out of my diabolical plot?'

'Something like that.'

'Have a drink first.'

'Listen, Alex, that stuff — '

'I said, have a fucking drink.' His tone suddenly hard. 'If you don't want vodka, we've got everything.' Alex gestured at the wall behind the bar, the mirrored shelves holding row on row of liquor. 'What'll it be?'

Something was wrong. He'd imagined that Alex might be surprised to see him, angry even. But this was different. He didn't sound quite together. Not raving, but not exactly centered, either.

'Alex, the bottles — '

'Alex, Alex.' The man mocking him, his voice high. 'The bottles, the bottles.'

Mitch paused. Could he just grab the chemicals and run? Skip reasoning with the man? Not likely. Four bottles, and his friend had fifty pounds on him, all of it muscle.

'I'll have a beer. And a shot.' He strolled over as casually as he could. Whatever was going on, he needed to roll with it. He couldn't take the bottles from Alex. So he had to convince him, and if that meant playing along, then that's what he had to do. Even as time ticked agonizingly away.

'Help yourself.' Alex reached for a pack of cigarettes, lit one. 'It's self-service night at Johnny Love's fabulous dining emporium.'

Mitch nodded, walked around the edge of the bar. His nerves were barbed wire in the wind, singing jangled and raw. He took a pint glass, held it under a tap. 'So, about those — '

'I saw Cassie tonight.'

'Yeah?'

'Yep. Her and her mother and her new dad. One big happy.'

'I'm sorry.' He skipped the shot, walked back around to sit. 'That must have been hard.'

'You think?' Alex's smile a little loose. He lifted his glass. 'What are we drinking to?'

'Listen — '

'I've got it. To the Thursday Night Club. May we all get just *exactly* what we deserve.'

Mitch forced himself to lean forward, clink glasses. 'Cheers.' He brought the beer to his lips, took a sip —

And found himself falling, the glass knocked sideways, beer slopping everywhere, the side of his head ringing from the back of Alex's hand. He flailed wildly, got hold of the edge of the bar, kept himself from going down. Had time to say, 'What the fuck?' before Alex was off the stool, his hands shooting down to grab the front of Mitch's shirt. The big man hoisted him in the air with a grunt, spun, took two steps, and slammed him down on a table. Pain exploded up his spine, and the air blew out of his lungs.

'Here to tell me how it is again?' His friend raised him, then slammed him down against the table again. 'Big boss man?'

Mitch brought his pint glass up in a whistling arc against Alex's head. It shattered, and he felt a burning in his fingers. Alex gasped, let go of him, his hands at his head. Mitch pulled himself off the table. A chair was on the floor at his feet, and he grabbed it as he stepped away.

Alex had regained his footing and braced himself like a boxer, one hand in front of his face, the other by his ear. He was breathing hard, and blood ran down the side of his face. The two of them faced each other. Frozen. Part of Mitch screamed to move now, to step forward and swing the chair and try to knock Alex down, to hit him again while he fell, and then take what he wanted and go. To leave his onetime friend bleeding on the bar floor.

Instead, he straightened. 'I'm not going to fight you. I came here to talk.'

'We don't have anything to say.'

'You're wrong.' He kept the chair cocked back. 'Ian figured out what's in those bottles. It's not drugs, man. It's poison. Nerve gas. Those things have the chemicals that make sarin gas.'

Alex snorted, shook his head. 'You'll say anything, won't you?'

'I swear to God — '

'You've been wanting this for a long time. You think I don't know? I know how you feel about Jenn. About me. All that time you were the quiet one, the smart one, too shy to live, you think I didn't see the way you looked at me?'

'What are you talking about?'

'I think it's time we dropped the bullshit, don't you?' Alex circled sideways, rocking gracefully from foot to foot, and Mitch moved in response. 'We don't really like each other much. Haven't for a long time, have we?'

'That's not true.' But even as he said the words, he thought back to Alex's regular condescension, the way he had spoken the night they'd met Johnny. Or his own quickly suppressed joy at the big man's humiliation and helplessness. The thought of him and Jenn in bed together, muscular, tattooed Alex, the golden boy who always had it easy.

'Bullshit. We've been coming to this for a long time. Years. So let's do it.' He nodded at the chair. 'If you've got the balls.'

Juvenile, maybe, but the barb hit. Mitch narrowed his eyes. Why not? What did he owe this guy? The supposed friend who had betrayed him over and over. Mitch wasn't the shy weakling Alex thought. This was the new Mitch, the man who decided who he wanted to be and just did it. Who moved through life with force and purpose.

Who hit the woman he loved.

Who killed a man and tried to hide from it.

He took a deep breath and a step back. 'You know what? Maybe you're right. But that's not what I'm here for. Whether you want to believe it or not, those bottles have the stuff to make chemical weapons. That's why I'm here.' Slowly, he lowered the chair. Set it down and stepped away. 'So you want to hit me, man? Go ahead.'

Without even a pause, Alex stepped forward and slammed a right hook into his side. There was a crack and an explosion of pain and Mitch collapsed, legs folding beneath him. Hit the floor hard, the impact ringing through his whole body. He tried to get up, found he could barely move. It was all he could do to curl himself into a fetal ball and wait for the kicks to start.

Nothing happened.

After a long moment, he opened his eyes. The floor was inches away, old tile with grime beaten into every crack and crevice. He turned his head, saw Alex standing above him. For a moment they just looked at each other.

Then Mitch managed to croak, 'Feel better?'

'Yeah.' Alex lowered a hand. Mitch took it. Standing up sent razors spinning through his chest. He paused a moment, drew a shallow breath. 'I can't believe you hit me, you fucker.'

Alex snorted, then rubbed at his face with one hand. 'Let me get you another drink.'

Mitch let his friend help him to a stool, sat down stiffly. Took the glass Alex offered, three fingers of Jameson, neat. The burn felt good.

Alex said, 'Chemical weapons?'

'Yeah.'

'You're serious.'

'Yeah.' He straightened, finished the rest of the glass. Set it down. It was stained with blood, and he looked at his hand. Looking at it was enough to make it start throbbing.

It didn't matter. 'Ian and Jenn are talking to the police.'

'So why did you come here?'

'In case they couldn't make it in time. Victor is on his way?'

Alex nodded.

'We have to get out of here. We'll be safe with the police.' He started to stand up.

'No.'

'Did you hear me? We can't let — '

'I called him, Mitch. I called him and I told him that you guys had lied, that I had the stuff,

365

and that I would meet him here with it.'

'Yeah, but we can still —— '

'Where do you think his first stop will be when he shows up and I'm not here?'

'We can go there right now. Get Cassie, take her with us.'

'What if he's already got someone there? What if they're watching? If it was just me, that'd be one thing. But it's not. It's my daughter.'

'Alex, do you understand what I'm saying? This is the main ingredient in sarin gas. A gallon of it. All someone needs to do is mix it with alcohol and it could kill hundreds, thousands of people.'

Abruptly, the big man chuckled.

Mitch stared. 'I'm not kidding.'

'No, I just . . . Alcohol.' Alex shook his head. 'No wonder you freaked when you saw me drinking.'

Despite himself, Mitch felt his lip twitching upward. The two of them looked at each other across the bar, and then they both started laughing. It didn't last long — the motion sent shivers of pain through his chest — but for just a second, Mitch felt like he was home.

'Come on. We have to go.'

He could see his friend wrestling with it, doing the same thing they had done earlier. Trying to decide whether he could live with either set of consequences. Struggling to find a way out. And for a moment, Mitch wondered what would happen if Alex refused.

Then he heard a voice behind him.

'What's the hurry? We just got here.'

The seconds hurt.

Jenn had never realized it could work that way, that time could have physical weight and sharp edges. That each slow tick of the clock could cut. While she and Ian sat on the couch, helpless, Mitch would be pitting himself against Victor. And she'd seen the light of too much self-sacrificial joy in Mitch's eyes. He had finally torn down the walls he'd erected to hide from the things he had done, and it was killing him. He wouldn't act cautiously, wouldn't hang back. No, he'd go forward in typical male fashion.

Which meant they were his only chance. And every second they sat here, prisoners in her living room, was one closer to too late.

The scissors had gone warm in her hands, the metal slick. Though they were a lousy weapon, they were what she had, and some comfort.

The man pulled a cellphone from his pocket, dialed, said, 'I've got them.' A pause. 'Yes.' His eyes were cold and steady as some deep-sea creature. 'OK.'

Beside her, Ian whispered, 'Are you all right?'

'I think so.' She saw the man watching them, didn't bother to hide her words. 'You?'

He shook his head. 'Not really.'

'Hold on. You have to hold on.'

'You remember the game I told you about?'

'Jesus Christ, are you kidding?'

'Prisoner's Dilemma. Remember it?'

She sighed. 'Yeah.'

'Remember what I said? It's about iteration. The point is that you play over and over.' For a moment, she thought she saw the faintest crinkle of skin around his eyes, like he was trying to tell her something. 'But if you know you're only going to play once — '

'I know, I know. Then you betray.'

'Right.' He coughed long and hard. When he could breathe again, he said, 'Especially if it's the last game. Or if there's something truly important at stake. Something larger. Then *you* betray. You make sure you get out.' His gaze locked on her.

'Jennifer, Ian, do me a favor?' The man smiled. 'Say cheese.' He pointed his phone in their direction, and she heard a faint click. He'd taken a photo. A trophy, and another violation. They were toys for him, a way to amuse himself.

'If all you wanted was a picture, you could have asked,' she said. 'I might have posed.'

He smiled. 'That's a generous offer. But this way is better, I think.'

'What do you want?'

'Little late to play innocent, don't you think, sister?'

'Yeah, but what do you *want*? Why are you here?' It was part anger, part hope that he would tell her. 'Did Victor change his mind? Because you can't get into that safe-deposit box without me. Even if you have the key.'

'But we're not trying to get into the bank, are we?' His eyes hardened. 'Are we, Jennifer?'

'Oh God,' Ian said. 'You're here to kill us.'

Jenn looked over at him. He was wax and

sweat, all pale and runny. How hard had he been hit?

'Alex has the stuff you want, and you know that. So once you get it from him, you're going to kill us. Right?' Ian leaned forward. 'Please. Tell me that much. I need to know.'

'Why?'

Ian's arms were trembling. 'Listen. I'm a trader. I make deals. Let's make one.'

'Like what?' The man sounded genuinely amused.

'You know that we got the chemicals when we robbed Johnny Love.'

'So?'

'So we took money, too. That's the reason we did it.' Ian's eyes darted. 'Promise to let me live, and you can have it.'

What the hell was Ian doing? He couldn't possibly believe that a promise meant anything. Could it be some sort of play? Was he making a move, trying to distract him?

Then the words hit more clearly: *Promise to let me live*.

Was he selling her out? Was that what he had been saying, with his reference to the game? Explaining in advance what he was going to do, assuaging his conscience for betraying her?

Jenn stared at him: expensive suit spotted with vomit, skin pale and shiny, arms shaking. He didn't look much like the cocky player she knew, the one who hid behind a mask of wit and sarcasm. The man she considered a friend.

She thought back to brunch, Ian talking about the game, its results. How if both people betrayed, they both got medium prison time; if neither did, they both got just a little. And the worst result of all, if one was faithful and the other betrayed. One walked free and the other suffered for a decade.

Is that what he was setting her up for? If so, then according to the rules of the game, the best thing she could do was betray him right back.

Only, what would that mean? How could she betray him?

More important, did she want to?

She'd no sooner thought of the question than she had the answer. It was like the dream she'd had earlier, the one where she was pregnant. When she'd woken, she'd been genuinely sad that it was just a dream. Not because she wanted a kid. Because she wanted things to matter. She wanted to live as though they did.

So screw the rules of the game. Whoever this guy was, he likely intended to kill them. Maybe they could get out, find a way to help Mitch. Maybe not. But either way, she'd rather go out being faithful.

Ian said, 'I mean it. There's a lot of money at stake. More than two hundred thousand dollars. You let me live, you can have it.'

'I know all about the money, Ian. You think you stole it from Johnny Love, but really, you stole it from me.'

'Well, this is your chance to get it back.' Ian paused, let the words sink in. 'Look, I understand you don't trust me.'

'Not too much, no.'

'Let me prove I'm serious.'

370

'What do you have in mind?'

Ian took a deep breath, then glanced at her. 'If you look in Jenn's right hand, you'll find a pair of scissors. She picked them up when you weren't watching.'

33

Victor wore the same outfit he'd had on earlier, a charcoal suit and a white shirt, the top button open. His hair was neat and his smile broad. Leaning by the entrance of the bar, he looked like a man who had already won.

And there was a reason for that, Mitch realized, looking at the four bottles on the bar top. Looking at himself, a busted rib and cut hand and screaming headache; at Alex, blood drying on the side of his face from the broken glass, the wound on his eye bound in butterfly bandages. Both of them unarmed and worn down and out of their depth. And, Mitch realized, not done with the discussion they'd been having. He wasn't sure which way Alex would have gone. Which meant that, again, each stood alone.

Johnny Love was behind Victor. He had on a mauve silk shirt. The pistol in his hand was bright chrome.

Game over.

'Where are you off to, Mitch?' Victor slid his hands in his pockets.

'Just . . . away from here.'

'Away from me, you mean.' The man shook his head. 'That's not playing by the rules.'

'You're selling chemical weapons, and you're talking about *rules*?'

Victor's eyes hardened. 'I see you've been busy.'

'Let me ask you.' He knew he should be frightened, and was, but there was more than that. Maybe he was in shock. Maybe it was just exhaustion, and the fact that he couldn't think of any other way to behave. 'How do you live with yourself?'

'How do I live with myself? You mean, as a nasty evil arms dealer?'

'Yeah.'

Victor smiled, then strolled across the room. For a second, Mitch considered tackling him, taking a shot, but Johnny had the pistol up and aimed. He'd be dead before he started moving. *Think, goddamn it. You have to find a way.* Victor walked behind the bar like he owned the place. Took a highball glass, set it on the back bar, then eyed the scotch. Chose a dusty bottle of Johnny Walker Blue. 'Is this the part,' he said, his back to them, 'where I'm supposed to tell you that I'm just a businessman, that people will find ways to kill each other whether or not I'm involved?'

'Is that true?'

Victor shrugged, then turned. 'Sure. But you know what else?'

'What?'

'I don't really care.' He sipped his scotch. 'All that moral relativism crap, it's for people who feel bad about what they do. It's for little people.' He pointed with the glass. 'Like you two.'

'We may be little people. But at least we don't sell chemical weapons. Who are they going to? Al-Qaeda? The Taliban?'

'The Michigan Militia? The KKK? MS-13?

373

The next Timothy McVeigh or Ted Kaczynski?'
Victor smiled, shrugged. 'You know who they're
going to? You really want to know?' He leaned
forward. 'Whoever pays me.'

Though Mitch could hardly have expected
different, the words still floored him. The simple
ease of the man, his comfort playing such a
monstrous role, it was unlike anything Mitch had
imagined. If the man had been a true believer
out for a cause, that would at least have made
sense. But this?

And that wasn't the really terrible part, he
realized. The terrible part was that it was his
fault. Their fault. Whatever happened, whoever
this plain-looking poison went to, whichever
poor crowd of innocents suffered and died, the
weight of it was on them.

How many people had they murdered?

★   ★   ★

For a moment, nothing happened. The room was
silent. Then Ian felt the couch shift as Jenn threw
herself at him.

He yanked his hands out from under his
thighs, barely got them up in time to catch her
wrists. The wicked curve of the manicure scissors
gleamed inches from his cheek.

'You fucker, you *motherfucker* — ' Jenn
screamed at him. 'What's *wrong* with you?!'

He struggled backward, surprised at how
strong she was, or how weak he was. It must have
looked comic, him in a business suit, bent
halfway backward over the arm of the couch

374

while a hundred-and-fifteen-pound woman came at him with nail scissors. The man with the gun laughed. 'Sister, you really are something.'

'Get her off me!'

The guy continued to laugh as he took the gun from behind his back. 'That's enough.'

Jenn continued to thrash against Ian's arms, her face furious red, the shining edge of the scissors coming closer.

There was a loud click as the man cocked the gun. Jenn froze, then slowly looked up. She narrowed her eyes, then slowly eased back to her side of the couch.

'Drop those bad boys.'

Jenn tossed the scissors to skitter across the table. She turned back to him, glared, then reared her head back and spit a gob of wet phlegm on what used to be his favorite suit.

That set the man off again. 'I hadn't figured you for a fighter. I love a girl with spunk.'

'Fuck you,' she said, her voice gone sullen.

'Even if she isn't too creative.' The man turned to Ian. 'You, though, I've had pegged since I spoke to your bookie. A weasel.'

Ian held his hands up in surrender. 'I just want to live.'

'And you'll sell out your friends to do it. Hell, you've screwed them from the beginning, haven't you?'

He felt the flush in his face, the sickness in his belly. 'More than two hundred thousand dollars, cash. All but the money I gave Katz. That's not bad for letting me go.'

'Where is it?'

'Here.'

'Where?'

'Do we have a deal or not?'

The man shrugged. 'Sure.'

'You promise?'

'You've got my word.' He gestured with the pistol. 'Let's go.'

It was like he could feel the blood racing through all the miles of veins in his body. Dread and adrenaline and hope. That same rush that he got gambling, before the last card fell. Success or defeat just a turn away. Only this time, he was playing for stakes unlike any he had ever played before, and on a thinner hand. Sweat soaked the armpits of his designer shirt.

Hey, kid, don't quit on me now. This is the game. Play it.

Slowly, he stood. His body hurt in a hundred places, and breathing took conscious effort.

'Remember,' he said. 'More than two hundred thousand dollars. All of it right here.'

'So?'

'So please be careful where you're pointing that thing.'

The man smiled. 'Oh, I'll be careful. But you should be too. If you're wasting my time, I can promise you, the next hours of your life are going to be bad enough to erase every good thing you ever had.'

Ian shivered. No control over it, a feeling like an ice cube sliding down his spine. *You have to do this. It's the only chance.*

He looked at Jenn, wanted to wink, to give her some sign, but didn't dare. He could only hope that she had been listening, that she had heard him promise all of the money. The biggest bluff of his life, and he wasn't sure if his partner was paying attention — or if she trusted him enough to follow his lead.

It didn't matter. He'd made his play. No backing out now.

'You too, sister. On your feet.'

Shit. In his best-case scenario, he'd figured that the man might leave her here, figuring that he would be enough leverage to keep Jenn from trying anything. More likely, she'd be tied up, but that would still be better odds. It was a flimsy plan, but it wasn't like he'd had a lot of time. He'd been winging it, hoping that if he could distract the guy, Jenn would have her chance. A better chance than a pair of three-inch scissors would have offered.

Now, though. What had he set them up for?

'Let's go.'

Ian nodded, started across the room. He could feel every inch of his skin, every bruise and cut and blow and burn. A turn of the card. It all came down to a turn of the card. He moved as slowly as he dared, limping a little bit. His mind in overdrive, examining possibilities, looking for every option, coming up with nothing. The man kept a careful distance. No chance Ian could jump him.

Shit, shit, shit. What had he done? When the man realized he was bluffing, he would —

He had just started down the hallway when an idea hit.

More than a long shot. A Hail Mary.

And just like the game, it all came down to trust. Whether Jenn would trust him enough to see what he was doing. Whether he could trust her to recognize what was important.

Whether they had gone too far to ever make it back.

★ ★ ★

Alex's brain was static. Raw and unfocused and going nowhere.

Desperate to move, he sat still. He heard Mitch talking to Victor as the man poured himself a fifty-dollar drink. Trying to reason with him, or maybe just stalling for time, but not getting anywhere. Johnny had moved to the center of the bar, the gun held at arm's length. Aimed with the loose ease of someone who had used a pistol before, who had looked down the barrel at another human being and pulled the trigger.

Alex's head throbbed in time with his pulse, the pain back in full force, and yet the least of the pain he was dealing with. Thinking that all their discussion, all their debate, it came down to this. Four plastic bottles filled with death, and a man who had just admitted he'd sell them wherever someone was buying. That this might be used not in some faraway desert. That it might be used at an El station or a museum. A church, or a shopping mall, or a school.

That it might be used in the kinds of places Cassie went.

Victor said, 'Now, if we're done with the philosophy lesson, I'd like my merchandise, please. Put it in the bag.'

Mitch felt hollowed out. Pulled too hard in too many directions. He was standing in front of the devil, and there was nothing he could do about it.

Well, one thing. Small and pointless, but something. 'No.'

'I'm sorry?'

'You want it, it's right there. I won't be part of this.'

Victor laughed. 'Won't be part of it? You are part of it. All four of you. Don't you see? You had it for days. You knew it was dangerous. I'm betting that you had to know in your heart more or less what it was. Right?'

Mitch shook his head, but Victor only smiled, said, 'Sure you did. You knew. You just didn't want to admit it. Because if you did, you'd have to do something about it. And doing something, well, that's not what the four of you specialize in.'

'What do you know about the four of us?'

'I know that if you really wanted to stop me, if you truly wanted to keep this from hurting anyone, all you had to do was go to the police. And I know that you didn't.'

Words like ball-peen hammer blows. Part of him wanted to argue, to say that it was more complicated than that. And it was. But it was also that simple. They had not only failed one another. They had failed hundreds, maybe thousands, of innocent people. They had become everything they used to despise.

'You see? If you had never gotten involved, then you'd be innocent. But you had a chance to stop me. And you didn't take it. Which makes you guilty, Mitch. When my clients use it — and they will — it will be your fault.' Victor paused, took a sip of his liquor. 'Now. Put those bottles in the bag and bring them to me.'

'Why?'

'Because I want you to know that you're beaten. That you lost completely.' Victor's smile was broad and bright.

Mitch knew it didn't make a difference, but he didn't care. 'I won't do it.'

'Remember when I told you to believe every word I say? Believe this.' The man's voice hard, pure alpha dog. 'You will put those bottles in the bag, and you will bring it to me, and you'll thank me for the privilege.'

'I won't. And meanwhile, the police are on their way. We told them about you. They'll be here any minute.'

'I don't think so.' Victor reached into his pocket, pulled out his cellphone. 'Amazing gadgets, these things. Used to be, a phone was for making calls. Now they can give you directions, play music' — he turned the screen to Mitch — 'even take pictures.'

No. Oh, no.

The image was small but clear. Ian and Jenn sitting on the couch in her living room.

'So you see, no police. And I think at long last you may be starting to take my word.' His voice

380

hardened. 'Put the fucking bottles in the bag and hand it to me. Or I'll have my people start cutting pieces off your girlfriend.'

★ ★ ★

She couldn't believe it.

OK, Ian had had his problems. The drugs, paying off the bookie. But those things had made sense in their way. They had been mistakes, but they hadn't been malevolent.

But to actively sell her out? Not just to promise the money in trade for his own life — not theirs, *his* — but then to tell them about the scissors she'd palmed? He'd killed her. And for what? He couldn't possibly believe this guy would let them live.

'Let's go,' the man said. Ian stood and limped slowly toward the hallway, not looking at her. Coward. He started toward the kitchen, where an hour ago the three of them had planned to try to redeem their failures.

'Sister, you follow right behind him.'

Grimacing, she did as she was told. What was the point of this, anyway? Ian had promised all that was left of the money, more than two hundred thousand dollars. Which was impossible, because they had split —

Wait.

She looked up, clues snapping together with an almost audible click. At that same moment, she saw Ian stagger, fall against the wall with a hollow sound. For a moment he hung there, then he collapsed, hit the floor hard, not putting his hands out to catch himself. His limbs shook and twitched, arms and legs beating a pattern on the hardwood floor. He looked like he was having some sort of a fit, like demons had taken control of his body.

'What is this happy horseshit,' the man said. 'Get up.'

For a bare half second, as Ian flopped to his back, his eyes opened and locked on hers, and in that moment, she knew what he was doing.

'Get the fuck up.' The gun swiveling.

'I think he's having a seizure,' she said.

'So what do we do?'

'Let him choke,' she said.

'You're all heart.' The man hesitated, then took a wary step forward. 'Hey.' He nudged at Ian with his shoe. 'Hey.'

The second time his foot touched Ian, the trader grabbed it with both hands, tucked it against his chest, and rolled. Caught off guard, the man's knee buckled, and he came down hard onto Ian, who gasped at the weight. There was an explosion, loud and brilliant in the dim light of the hall, and drywall dust rained from a hole punched in her ceiling.

The guy may have been taken off guard, but he reacted quickly, spinning his other knee onto solid ground and then bringing the pistol down. Ian saw it, grabbed for the gun with both hands. The man lashed out with a fast jab that cracked Ian's jaw. On his back on the ground, her friend looked like a child, thin and waxy-skinned and bleeding from his mouth. No chance he could win.

Not alone, anyway.

She was starting forward when Ian rolled his head sideways and stared at her. The look couldn't have lasted more than a fraction of a breath, but it burned into her retinas. He saw her step forward and gave a tiny shake of his head. His eyes were locked on hers. Pleading with her.

His words on the couch came back to her, the ones she'd wondered about.

If you know you're only going to play once, or if there's something truly important at stake, something larger. Then you betray. You make sure you get out.

The emphasis on 'you.' He had known what he was going to do then. He'd been telling her.

And he'd been telling her that he had already made a choice. That he had weighed the factors and decided what was truly important. He wasn't trying to win. He was trying to keep them from losing entirely. It wasn't chivalry or some misguided attempt to protect her. He had simply treated it like a game. He had set the cost of his life against the pay-off of her getting to the police and decided that it was a good move.

She stared at him. Thought about running to his aid, trying her kickboxing moves. An amateur against a professional; cardio classes against a lethal, armed criminal. As she watched, Ian took a vicious punch that snapped his face sideways, breaking their stare — and freeing the killer's gun hand.

And she realized what would happen if she tried and failed.

Last game. If it's the last game, and the stakes

are high enough, there is only one thing to do.

Jenn turned and sprinted for the door.

★ ★ ★

Alex looked over Mitch's shoulder, to where Victor held the cellphone, a smug expression on his face. Even from there, he could make out the picture. Jenn and Ian. Victor had them.

They had failed. Completely. He'd even failed to protect Cassie. It wasn't that he believed that the gas would actually be used on her. He wasn't stupid, could run the odds. But Victor had as good as said it would end up used on someone like her. Some innocent child who chose the wrong day to go to the mall. Someone else's daughter.

'One more time, Mitch.' Victor's voice was cold, but Alex could hear the anger beneath it. 'Pick up the bag. Put the bottles in it. Now.'

Mitch. His friend, his doppelganger, the flip side of his coin. His partner in defeat. Alex could see in his eyes that the man was beaten. Mitch, who always had a plan. Beaten. Slowly, like his body was a wooden puppet under someone else's control, his friend bent down to retrieve the black duffel bag from the floor.

Alex looked over at Johnny Love. His former boss's hair was slicked back, but a clump had come loose and stood at odd attention. His smile was as slippery and self-satisfied as a television commercial lawyer's. 'I told you, kid. You don't fuck with me.'

Mitch reached a shaking hand forward. Picked

384

up one of the bottles. Slid it into the bag.

It was happening. It was really happening.

They were going to let these two assholes walk out with chemical weapons. They were going to put them in the bag politely, hand it over, and wait for Johnny to shoot them.

Or, maybe worse, wait for him not to. For him to walk away, and let them wonder when they would hear about sarin gas in a high school.

No.

Maybe they would be safe if they did nothing. But they would never be OK. They had to fight. Maybe it would cost them everything. Their lives. But it would be a cause worth dying for.

Mitch put the second bottle in the bag.

Alex gently slid one foot to the floor, shifted his weight, counting on Victor and Johnny to be watching Mitch.

If only they had a weapon. He remembered throwing the guns in the river, the heft of each and the plunk as they splashed into dark water. He would have given his arm to have one of them now. For a weapon of any sort: a knife, the baseball bat Jenn kept under her bed. A weapon, one little weapon. That was the only thing that was holding them back, keeping the odds from being even. A weapon —

Mitch put the third bottle into the bag.

Holy shit.

Alex would have laughed if it wouldn't have slowed him down. Instead he slid off the stool, turned to grab it by the back, spun hard, and hurled the thing at Johnny.

It was a clumsy throw, awkward and overfast,

and Johnny sidestepped easily, raising the pistol. But dodging had distracted him, and Alex put everything into a lunge, his shoulder down, feet scrabbling on the tile floor, the clean and perfect rush of motion, his insides piano-wire taut. He was going to tear Johnny apart, rip the smarmy fucker into pieces with his bare hands. Payback for a thousand minor indignities and one unforgivable sin. For Cassie.

The pistol in Johnny's hand spat flame twice.

There was a sticky feeling like a thin finger poking through his belly, like a yellowed nail scraping through his intestines, and where it touched was agony beyond fire, and his feet were still moving, his momentum carrying him forward as he realized that he had been shot, that Johnny had hit him at least once, maybe twice, and that the gun was steadying again, centering on him, and everything disappeared but the gap, the horrifying gap between him and Johnny, six feet, five, the man so close he could almost see the pores on his nose —

Another explosion.

Alex staggered, his feet starting to tangle. His belly burned and his fingers were numb and his shoulder felt weak and he realized he had his tongue stuck between his lips and was biting it, and then he reached Johnny, the fat fuck's face gone shiny. The pain was unreal, whirling and sharp, a spinning saw blade in his chest, ripping and tearing, and it took all his strength to lift his arms and clamp them on Johnny's shoulders, then slide them around his back, to squeeze the man to him like they were dancing, Johnny's aftershave sharp and chemical, mingling with the boxing-glove stench of his own sweat and a coppery smell from his chest, Johnny pinned with the gun between them, and then there was another explosion, this one muffled, and Alex felt part of his chest rip out his back and fly free and wet, and knew he was going to die.

It was OK. It was for Cassie.

He just had to do one thing first. One more thing.

He had to trust Mitch.

★ ★ ★

Ian saw the fist coming, couldn't do anything about it, tried to close his mouth but only managed to get his tongue caught between his teeth as the blow hit. His head yanked sideways, white and black bursting. His fingers started to slip, and he made himself hold on, hold on, and he prayed that Jenn understood.

And then he heard the sound of the front door opening and knew that he had won.

'Fuck!' The man rose fast as a snake. With the last of his strength, Ian grabbed his calf. The man spun back, wound up, and unleashed a vicious kick. The foot exploded into his ribs with a crunching sound, and Ian's grip broke. He flopped back on the floor, strength gone. His eyes were closed, but he heard the man stand up, his fast footfalls down the hall. But he had bought her something. Maybe enough.

For a moment, he just breathed, every inhale agony. Then he heard steady footsteps. He opened his eyes, saw the man standing above him, shaking his head, a smile on his lips. 'That was your big escape plan?'

Ian tried to speak, coughed, blood and bile mingling in his mouth. He turned sideways and spit it on the floor. Looked back. 'Yep.'

'The money isn't here?'

'Nope.'

'Well, I give you credit for heart, brother. But you really are a fuck-up, you know that?'

Ian coughed again. Stared at the barrel of the gun. 'Yeah.' He smiled through broken lips. 'But I'm working on it.'

A finger moved on the trigger. There was a loud sound.

And then there was nothing.

★　★　★

Mitch's hands were sweaty on the plastic. His brain felt like a prisoner, walled away and forgotten as it screamed and threw itself against the bars of its cage. Every breath felt stolen.

He put the third bottle in the bag, aware of every sensation, the way the zipper grated against his wrist, the cool of the plastic leaving his hand, the pressure of the edge of the bar against his stomach. Victor was smiling, a wolfish, ugly grin. The look of a man winking at you as he fucked your girlfriend.

Then there was a squeak and a scrambling beside him, and his head whipped around to see Alex in motion, a bar stool hanging in the air like it was on wires, the big man surging forward at

Johnny and his big chrome pistol. It lasted forever. The chair didn't fly, it drifted, no kin to gravity, turning slowly, a play of light gleaming off the polished wood back. Alex was a freight train in slow motion, power and energy moving through jelly, shoulder down. The gun drifting lazily as Johnny took a step sideways to avoid the stool.

The sound was incredibly loud and terribly familiar. It jolted him, shook that secret center of him that was all he really was. The part that wore the rest of him like clothing.

A gunshot, just like the one he had heard in the alley, when he sighted down the barrel at the man on the ground and pulled the trigger.

A second blast followed, and a third. They sounded crass, unnecessary. Alex took the shots like a charging boxer tagged by jabs, slowed but not stopped, his body rippling where he was hit. And then he was on Johnny, had the man pinned in a bear hug, and Mitch wanted to howl, to scream his friend's name.

The fourth shot was muffled, and a piece of Alex's body blew out the back of him to spatter on the bar.

The moment broke like a mirror.

Mitch had the last bottle, felt the heft of it, light for so much death, but heavy enough in his hand. He turned to Victor, saw his mask crumbling. The man stood directly opposite him, a dark shape against the rows of glowing bottles, whiskey and tequila and vodka and gin standing side by side like soldiers. He thought about jumping the bar but saw Victor's hands moving, realized he must be going for a gun. Thought of dropping to the floor, into the safety of a child hiding beneath a bed. Thought about rushing to help Alex, and turned to do it, only to see a twisting mass of bodies, Alex and Johnny, spinning and sliding and falling. Tumbling toward him. Somehow Alex, shot more than once, had kept hold of Johnny and yanked him toward the bar, the two of them embracing like lovers.

They slammed into the bar beside him, still scrabbling, Johnny red-faced and furious, spit flying from his lips as he yelled, a grunt of effort and pain, struggling to get his arms free. A moan wrenched from Alex at the impact. His skin skim milk. Mitch couldn't believe the man was still standing, that his reserves of strength and fury and shock had given him the power to hold on, to drag Johnny here. Some part of him wondered why, what the point of the gesture was, whether it was a plan or just a reaction.

Victor's hand behind his back.

Alex slumped, Johnny starting to push away from him. His friend's head lolled, eyes wild. Staring. Staring at Mitch, and then lower. His lips moved, nothing coming out at first. Then a sound. A plea. The words more gasped than spoken.

'Do it.'

His eyes staring at Mitch but not. The will draining from his friend's body like oil from a punctured drum. Johnny started to push himself free.

Do what?

He looked where Alex was staring. To the bottle in his hand.

Words in his mind.

Ian: *Apparently, if you're the kind of evil fuck who makes chemical weapons, you make them in two parts.*

Alex: *No wonder you freaked when you saw me drinking.*

Jenn: *Guess the Thursday Night Club isn't done yet.*

Victor's hand swinging around, a blur of something black in his grip.

And for a moment, it all made sense. Every step of the confused dance that had brought them here. Every wrong move. A pattern that he had never suspected, like something had been conducting them toward this moment, playing each of them like an instrument, point and counterpoint, building to this crescendo.

Mitch turned at the waist, the bottle in his hand held parallel to the bar. His mind split, part of it cool and focused, the rest of the world gone away, nothing but this motion. The other part screening moments from his life. His father teaching him to ride a bike down leaf-shaded streets. Sunlight and Jimi Hendrix and the spray of water as he leaned back in a friend's speedboat smashing the waves of Lake Michigan. The first snow of a forgotten winter, walking past the bookshop on Broadway as soft faint white fell around him. The cello curve of Jenn's sleeping body in the moonlight.

He spun and hurled the bottle at the bar back with everything he had. It wasn't just his arm that threw. It was his whole life. Everything he was, everything he had ever hoped to be, put into one perfect motion.

It could have flown a mile. Could have sailed into the limitless night and blown by the moon.

Until it hit the wall of shimmering bottles above Victor's head and exploded, plastic and glass cracking and shattering, the force of the motion driving everything against the mirrored wall an inch back and then rebounding, the geometric precision of liquid spattering in perfect globes, a slow-motion film of a bottle hit by a bullet, the invisible immutable rules of the world taking over, a shower of spray rebounding, an arc like a dying sprinkler.

And through it all, his mind still showing the things that had made up his life. His mother fussing over his prom tuxedo. His $86 LeBaron with the crooked-smile bumper. The kick of the pistol in his hand and the primal joy he had been afraid to acknowledge.

The night the four of them met.

Right here, at this same spot in this same bar. The recognition each had felt in the other, that strange glow of assumed camaraderie that came from nothing but some inner certainty that here were friends, that whatever was to come, however they might fail one another, they shared this sense of newfound completion, of being made whole.

Mitch was laughing as the liquid rained down on them all.

34

Later, Jenn Lacie would spend a lot of time trying to pinpoint the exact moment.

There was a time before, she was sure of that. When she was free and young and, on a good day, maybe even breezy. Looking back was like looking at the cover of a travel brochure for a tropical getaway, some island destination featuring a smiling girl in a sundress and a straw hat, standing calf-deep in azure water. The kind of place she used to peddle but had never been.

And of course, there was the time after. And all the days yet to come.

There was never just one picture, one clear moment. Everything came in juttering fits and starts, all of it snarled, one circumstance leading into another. Untangling it would be no simple feat. But it seemed important to try. That was her work now. Her tribute.

Tonight, though, the moment she kept coming back to was the flash of a second when Ian was on the ground and their eyes met. When she had realized what he was doing. When they committed to the right thing, even if it was hard. Yanking open her front door, sprinting down the steps, abandoning him there, that had been hard.

There had been crazy adrenaline, an energy unlike anything she had ever known. She had run with everything in her. She'd wanted to look back but hadn't dared, just leaned into it, legs flying long and free as she sprinted toward Clark. There would be people on the street, and cars. Even if the man followed her, she knew she could make it.

It was when she heard the muffled crack from behind her that she almost screwed up. She'd known what it was. What it meant. Ian had gone all-in.

The feeling that climbed from her belly to her lungs to her mouth was raw and horrible, a recognition that life had stakes, consequences, and that they were playing for them. And with it, a furious anger at the forces that had come into her life, into her house, that had killed her friend. The rage made her fingers tremble, and for a moment, she wanted more than anything to stop. To hide behind a parked car and wait for the man to chase her. To turn from prey to predator, snapping a hard kick into his belly that dropped him to the ground. Then kick him again and again and again, kick until her toes were broken and there was nothing left to kill.

But there was the look in Ian's eye. He hadn't given his life for her to attempt an action-hero ending. He had played by the rules of the game, accepting the ultimate penalty to give her a shot to secure the most important outcome. And she had to play by them too, or she truly would betray him.

Besides. Ian was gone, but it might not be too late to save Mitch and Alex.

So she ran. Arms pumping, lungs burning, heart screaming, she ran. She might have run all the way to the police station if she hadn't almost tripped in front of a cab cruising for partygoers.

Detective Bradley told her it had been the right move. That she had saved lives, the innocent men and women, cops and EMTs, who might have gone into Rossi's without a warning.

She supposed he was right. But like most truths, it was comforting only to a point.

Bradley had been dubious, then interested, and finally incredulous as she told him everything. She spilled it all with a manic intensity, knowing that the faster she could get him to move, the more chance her friends had. Praying that even though she had been delayed, she might still be able to hold up her end of the plan and bring the police screaming down on Victor.

Because the alternative was too terrible to consider.

As Mitch had predicted, she had really had to sell Detective Bradley. It was the details that won him over. She told him everything, every step of the robbery, the murder in the alley, the discovery of chemical weapons, their response tonight. Inch by inch, she watched the screens behind his eyes lift as he began to believe.

The details worked. But they took a long time. And just as she was wrapping up, another cop came in the room. 'Detective — '

'I'm busy here — '

'I know, but it's about that restaurant. Rossi's.'

Jenn had been leaning forward, forearms on the table, eyes locked with Bradley's like a conspirator or a lover, but at the mention of the restaurant she jerked upright. She stared at him, knowing what he was going to say, dreading it. Until the moment she heard it, until a stranger spoke it, it wasn't true. Alex and Mitch were strong and clever and good. They might have found a way without her.

'Dispatch got reports of gunfire. Multiple shots. That's your restaurant, right? From the body the other night?' The cop continued, his lips moving, facts spilling out, but Jenn didn't hear it, not another word.

They were gone. Her friends were gone.

Something had almost swallowed her then, as she realized with utter certainty that she was the last surviving member of the Thursday Night Club. It was panic, but of a different sort than she'd been suffering. A black and consuming loneliness, and a suffocating sense of failure. Everything in her wanted to collapse at that moment, to put her head down on the table in the dingy interview room and sob.

Later, she would remember that moment as maybe the one that saved her, that gave her a chance. Because instead of giving up, she told Detective Peter Bradley he had to hurry. That there might still be men there, dangerous, armed men. Men with chemical weapons. In calm, clear tones she told him not to let anyone go inside, to clear the streets and guard the door. That if there were men inside, they were armed.

He may not have believed her, not really. But he'd at least seen there was no point in taking the risk.

The rest of the night blurred into a succession of interview rooms and men in suits. Snatches of news gleaned from the things they said, the gravity of their manner. The whole police station came to wild and whirling life around her: shouts she could hear through the walls, phones constantly ringing, men yelling, men pointing fingers. When she was alone, she stared at the wall and fought the urge to cry. When cops came with questions, she answered completely and without thought of self-preservation. At one point, someone she didn't know came into the room and cuffed her hands. When Bradley returned, he undid them, set down a cup of coffee. Touched her shoulder. 'Ms Lacie, I'm afraid — '

'I know,' she said. Two words that took all she had. 'They're dead, aren't they?'

'I'm sorry.'

She nodded, wanting to cry from the emptiness, the loss. First Ian, and now Alex and Mitch. Gone. She closed her eyes.

'We found four bodies at the restaurant. We're working the — '

Four?

It took a moment, and then she got it. She almost smiled. *Good for you. I hope you made it hurt.* 'What about the DF, did you find it?'

'It was hard to miss. One of the containers had been broken and mixed with alcohol from the bar. Apparently there are pools of sarin spattered all over. Which is actually good news, means that it's relatively easy to contain. If it had been strapped to an explosive device . . . ' He blew a breath. 'We've locked down the restaurant, kept everyone out. Hazmat teams are working it now.

Homeland Security is involved, and the FBI, and — ' He shook his head.

'And the man in my apartment, the one who shot Ian?'

'No sign of him. Not that we could really expect one. We'll dust for prints, look for DNA evidence. With chemical weapons involved, it'll get the full-court press.'

'Will you find him?'

The cop hesitated. 'I don't know.' They sat in silence. Then he said, 'Can I ask you something? Why did you do it?'

'We had to. We couldn't let that stuff get into the hands of — '

'No, I mean, why did you *do* it? How do four normal people decide to do something like this? Risk everything? I mean, from what you've said, your lives were OK, more or less. So why? Just money?'

Her head hurt, a dull throbbing ache. 'Have you always wanted to be a cop, Detective?'

'Pretty much.'

Jenn absently picked at a cuticle. 'You're lucky. I never knew what I wanted to be. Not really. When I was a kid, I used to have these fantasies. The typical stuff kids think. That they'll be pirates and astronauts and movie stars. That they'll save the world. That they'll . . . matter.' Jenn looked up. The detective was listening intently.

'But time just keeps passing, you know? And you don't end up astronauts. You don't save the world. And one day you wake up in your thirties and realize that this wasn't where you meant to be. Not that it's awful. It's just not what you meant.'

'I can understand that. Life, liberty, and the entitlement to happiness. But talking about it's one thing. Doing it . . . '

'It started as a game. Everything with us was a game. Even our lives. We sat back and watched the time pass and met for drinks on Thursdays.' She shrugged. 'I think we were just playing. Until the end, we were just playing.'

'When did you stop playing?'

'Tonight,' she said. 'We all stopped tonight.'

He grimaced, and she could see that he misunderstood her. That he thought she was talking about the fact that the others had died and that she was in a police station. He was missing the larger point — that there had been a moment when they had a chance to walk away, when all they would have had to do was pick the lesser of two evils. That, and live with their decision. And instead, they had decided that it was worth fighting for something. Even if it cost them. And while she never would have guessed how *much* it would cost, she also knew that even armed with that knowledge, they would have done the same thing.

In the end, game theory was one thing, and life another.

She thought about correcting him, figured it didn't matter. He wouldn't understand anyway. 'What's going to happen now?'

'I'm not sure,' he said. 'No one can decide if you're a criminal or a hero.'

'My friends were heroes,' she said quietly. 'I'm

399

not sure I'm either.'

'Maybe you're both.' He stood up. 'Come on. It's late.'

'Are you taking me to a cell?'

'Not yet,' he said. 'Until I hear otherwise, I'm focusing on the hero part.'

He put out a hand, and she took it, let him help her up. Bradley led her to a small room off the detectives' offices lined with thin cots. 'You can rest here. No one will bother you.'

'I can't sleep.'

'You should try.' He guided her to one of the beds, found a clean blanket. 'This is just getting started.'

'No,' she said. 'It's over now.'

He passed her the blanket and walked to the door. He hesitated for a moment, his hand on the light switch. 'You and your friends. The things you did. Robbery, homicide. Coming to us will help, but — '

'I know,' she said. 'I don't want a free pass.'

He looked at her strangely. For a moment, she thought he might say something else. Then he flipped off the lights and gently closed the door.

Jenn Lacie lay down on the cot. The springs sagged beneath her, and she could feel the outline of the people who had slept there before her. Detectives working cases, trying to save lives or avenge them.

As she lay there, the next months and years played out in front of her. The media would go into a frenzy. There would be questions upon questions. Days of explaining, over and over. A trial, and probably punishment. And why not?

They may have done right, but they'd done wrong, too.

Those things, they didn't matter. Not really.

What mattered was trying to unravel everything that had happened. Trying to find meaning in it. To give herself over to the long hours. The pain, the tears, the guilt. The time thinking of the things they had done. To honoring her friends by trying to untangle everything so that she could see it all plain. The good, the bad. The wasted years and the beautiful moments.

The others had paid their price. This was hers. Her burden.

And when it was all over, as it eventually would be, then her tribute to them would be simple. It would be about finding a way to make it all matter. To make her life matter.

For herself. And for them. The Thursday Night Drinking Club.

Her friends.

ACKNOWLEDGMENTS

My sincere gratitude to my uberagent, Scott Miller, and my extraordinary editor, Ben Sevier. It's an honor and a privilege, boys.

A big thanks to all the folks at Dutton, especially Brian Tart, Christine Ball, Kara Welsh, Amanda Walker, Rich Hasselberger, Melissa Miller, Carrie Swetonic, Aline Akelis, and Susan Schwartz. Also to the fabulous Sarah Self, my film agent.

Before there was a Thursday Night Crew, there was a Wednesday Night Crew. It involved as much drinking and talking, but significantly less sex, strife, and murder. Carnita, Molls, Bets, Reverend Waechter, and Dr Peebles, I love you all.

Prior to writing this novel, I knew nothing about chemical weapons; Dr Karl A. Scheidt of Northwestern University was incredibly generous with his time and energy, guiding my research and even inadvertently giving me the ending of the book. I had additional technical help from Regan Thomson, Steve Thornley, and Dr Jeffrey Anderson. My old buddy Mike Biller rather gleefully filled me in on head wounds and hospitals.

All my love and all my gratitude to Matt, Mom, and Dad.

And as always, my deepest thanks to my wife, g.g. You know all the reasons why.

We do hope that you have enjoyed reading this large print book.

Did you know that all of our titles are available for purchase?

We publish a wide range of high quality large print books including:
Romances, Mysteries, Classics
General Fiction
Non Fiction and Westerns

Special interest titles available in large print are:
The Little Oxford Dictionary
Music Book
Song Book
Hymn Book
Service Book

Also available from us courtesy of Oxford University Press:
Young Readers' Dictionary
(large print edition)
Young Readers' Thesaurus
(large print edition)

For further information or a free brochure, please contact us at:
Ulverscroft Large Print Books Ltd.,
The Green, Bradgate Road, Anstey,
Leicester, LE7 7FU, England.
Tel: (00 44) 0116 236 4325
Fax: (00 44) 0116 234 0205

THE BLADE ITSELF

Marcus Sakey

Evan and Danny were as close as brothers. But when the robbery of a pawnshop goes wrong, Evan is caught and gaoled. Shocked into clarity, Danny, his accomplice, flees the scene . . . Seven years later, Danny has turned his back on crime and is now the manager of a successful construction company. Then Evan is released, and he wants the debt for his silence repaid. He wants Danny to join him on one last job . . . Brutalised and desperate, Evan holds all the cards. At every turn, Danny tries to do the right thing, but with terrible inevitability, every decision seems to push him ever deeper into trouble. Until, with no one to turn to, Danny fears for all he holds dear. And his life itself . . .

SISTER

Rosamund Lupton

When Beatrice hears that her little sister, Tess, is missing, she returns home to London on the first flight available. But Bee is unprepared for the terrifying truths she must face about her younger sibling when Tess' broken body is discovered in the snow. The police, Bee's friends, her fiancé and even their mother accept the fact that Tess committed suicide. But Bee is convinced that something more sinister is responsible for Tess' untimely death. So she embarks on a dangerous journey to discover the truth, no matter the cost . . .

BREATHLESS

Dean Koontz

Alienated from the modern world, Grady Adams lives in the wilds of the Colorado mountains. And there, something miraculous comes into his life, and he knows that one of Nature's great mysteries has been revealed to him. He takes his friend, scientist Cammy Rivers, to bear witness to the phenomenal presence. She is stunned and awed, and emails photos to colleagues in far places to try and find a name for the wonderful beings. But soon Homeland Security has the wilderness around them quarantined, with scientists to track down and 'neutralize' the threat to the known world. Grady and Cammy, determined to prevent this atrocity, go on the run, and a pursuit of hair-raising suspense is under way, with no happy ending in prospect . . .

FEAR THE WORST

Linwood Barclay

It was the worst day of Tim Blake's life. His seventeen-year-old daughter, Sydney, was staying with him while she worked a summer job at the Just Inn Time hotel — father-daughter time to help with the after-effects of his divorce. Syd didn't arrive home at her usual time. Then, worryingly, she didn't answer her phone. And when the people at the Just Inn Time told him they'd no Sydney Blake working at the hotel, he was plunged into the abyss every parent dreads most. Where had she been every day, if not working at the Just Inn Time . . . ? To find his daughter Tim must discover who she really was, and what could have made her step out of her own life without leaving a trace.

THE MAGDALENA CURSE

F. G. Cottam

Two visits are enough to convince Dr Elizabeth Bancroft that Adam Hunter isn't just having bad dreams. He's a child possessed. His father is desperate: adamant that his son's affliction is the result of a curse he incurred in the depths of the Amazon, where a misguided military operation ended in a terrifying and macabre encounter. There he met two women — one more bad than good, who placed the curse — and the other more good than bad, with whom any hope of saving his son resides. Mark Hunter leaves the Scottish Highlands to beg help from the mysterious woman, leaving his son in the care of Elizabeth — who is about to discover there are equally dark secrets on their own doorstep. And in her blood . . .